First, they came for his sister's eye. Now they're coming for his—and what's even worse is he deserves it.

Henry has never had anything good happen to him, period. That's why, after school, he's going to put on his big-boy pants and confess his love to his best friend—because the universe owes him one, dammit, and he *needs* a win.

But maybe it wasn't the best idea to do it on Drill Day—the one day a month that healthcare conglomerate Axiom infiltrates schools across America to select a new candidate to give up one of their eyes, for... research? When the new candidate is selected, Henry's plans go awry, and he and his friends must figure out how to escape from Axiom. But when the past threatens to eat him alive, things aren't as easy as they seem.

THE CYCLOPES' EYE

The Cyclopes' Eye, Book One

Jeffrey Haskey-Valerius

A NineStar Press Publication
www.ninestarpress.com

The Cyclopes' Eye

First Edition, April 2024

ISBN: 978-1-64890-752-4

Also available in eBook, ISBN: 978-1-64890-751-7

CONTENT WARNING:

This book contains depictions of alcoholism, self-harm, suicidal ideation, abuse of a child by a parent, death of a secondary character, and medical procedures.

To you, who could never be blinded, no matter how hard the world will try

Note From the Author

Some of the darker topics explored in this text include active alcoholism; verbal abuse from parent to child; physical violence, sometimes toward women and teens, and both active self-harm and fantasizing about self-harm, as well as suicidal ideation.

If you are on your own journey toward healing, please proceed with care.

Jeffrey Haskey-Valerius

I know the bottom, she says. I know it with my great tap root:

It is what you fear.

I do not fear it: I have been there.

Is it the sea you hear in me,

Its dissatisfactions?

Or the voice of nothing, that was your madness?

—from Elm, by Sylvia Plath

Chapter One

THIS ISN'T WHAT I signed up for, but that seems to be a common thread in my life these days. So, sure, universe, you do you. Pile something else on top of the mess.

I can't see straight, for starters. I'm on a bus from hell, and everything's a blur, and I don't know what's worse—keeping my eyes open to watch the world zip by, or squeezing them shut and letting my stupid, *stupid* imagination do the work. When I close them, every bump in the road feels like I'm being launched into space, so maybe for now I'll keep them open. But both options are awful. Both are making me sick.

I've been on the verge of puking all morning, and nothing seems to help. Especially not this driver. Some tragic car accident blocked the route we normally take, so we had to go on a long detour. And now that we're running behind, the driver's been speeding and turning corners like this is a rollercoaster and not a school bus.

Oh god, do not think about rollercoasters right now, Henry.

No, this is just a bus. A bus. Sure, we're going well above the speed limit, but at least not, like, a thousand miles an hour.

Okay, calm down. What are the facts? Think of what's around you. The bus is almost at full capacity today, with only one person missing: Judith, who's been home from school. So, if she's not here, that means there are eighty-eight people around you.

God, that's so many.

No, that's not so many. That's a *normal* amount, Henry!

Okay, eighty-eight people, plus me, is eighty-nine. Double that, and we get—take your time, Hen; use your fingers if you have to—a hundred seventy-eight. There should be a hundred and seventy-eight eyeballs on this bus…except we know there are five patched kids on our route this year—six if we count…well, no, she's not here. A hundred and seventy-eight, minus five stolen eyes, equals a hundred and seventy-three.

Wait, what about the driver? Is that why he's driving so crazy, because he's an eye short?

I glance up to the mirror above him to double check—only I can't tell because he's wearing sunglasses. Even at six thirty a.m., the California sun is blinding. But that's all right; I don't need to know.

A hundred and seventy-three. That's how many eyes are on this bus.

One.

Seven.

Three.

Slowly, the breaths come. My lungs expand, and the nausea begins to fade. It helps, knowing a simple statistic like that. But it's weird, and if people knew I counted eyeballs in my head, I would die. Actually curl up and die.

Or maybe everyone does that in secret. Maybe everyone is a secret freak like me.

A loud screech. My head plows into the seat in front of me. *Ow*!

The driver slammed on his brakes! As soon as I realize what's happened, anger builds in my chest. What in the actual *fuck* is this fucking driver doing? He's trying to kill us! I want to scream my head off, scream until the windows shatter. Until this guy's ears explode, because screw him!

But I won't. I never scream when I want to. Not anymore. Instead, I sit on my hands and start to count eyes again, while I let the world shift back into place.

All around me, people are moaning and groaning.

"Dude, what the hell?" someone shouts.

I look over, and the girl across the aisle is rubbing her neck, her eyes closed and mouth downturned in obvious pain. The girl next to her has her head between her legs. At first, I think she must be as sick as I was feeling, but she starts searching around for something on the floor and finally retrieves her phone. When the screen lights up, there's a giant spiderweb of cracks across it.

Slowly, the bus lurches forward, and I no longer feel like screaming. The anger is abating, and it morphs into something closer to pity as I remember for the hundredth time what today is: Drill Day. If the driver doesn't get us to school on time, he'll be accused of trying to help us escape. He'll get his eye taken out.

I can't be mad at him for saving his own ass, even if it means ushering me to what very well might be my own demise.

Oh god. I feel a gurgle deep in my stomach. And so it begins. Again.

I'd be lying if I said I didn't feel at least somewhat nauseated on most Drill Days. I definitely was last time. I could have puked when Judith's name was called. I'm surprised I didn't.

The memory of her walking up to that stage and standing up there, crying, is burned into my brain—only parts of it are fading. The most important parts, like what exactly her face used to look like with two eyes. I remember they were beautiful. I remember the color. But I can't picture *exactly* what she looked like. It's only been a week, and it's like she's been eyeless our entire lives. A better brother would remember. A better brother wouldn't have let it get taken out in the first place.

At the very least, a better brother would have listened to her this morning when she said she had something important to tell me. I was too preoccupied with other thoughts, already fighting the nausea well before I got on the bus.

"Yeah, I know," I yawned. "Drill Day."

"Obviously, I don't mean Drill Day," she sighed. "I mean, yes, it's Drill Day-*adjacent*, but—"

"Jude, I'm gonna be late. You can regale me later, okay?" And like the asshole I am, I opened the door and left.

My own twin sister, recovering from surgery, was trying to tell me something important. Yet I couldn't give her the time of day.

Classic Henry.

Ugh, I really do think I'm about to barf—and it's my own fault. My own stupidity. It's not Drill Day *or* the bad driving, really. Those are just exacerbating it. When it comes down to it, I'm the source of all my misery—and one of these days, I'll learn that lesson.

But not today. After school—assuming I don't get my eye taken out—I'll be reading a poem, *out loud,* in Ink Stain, the creative writing club at school. But it's not just the public speaking—which I do get nervous about. Mostly, it's because the poem I have planned isn't just any old poem. It's the single piece of work that will determine the trajectory of the rest of my life.

Judith would call that turn of phrase a little…dramatic. But she's not here right now, and I can confidently say that it *will* determine the rest of my life. That's why I couldn't listen to her this morning, I was too busy trying not to freak out—which is going *really* great for me currently.

It's not just any old poem. It's intended for one of my best friends, Sam, who's also in Ink Stain. Over the last few months, something has changed, and I started getting feelings for him. Awful, huge feelings I've literally never experienced before, that make me imagine a wedding and kids? Disgusting.

Maybe a rational person would tell him in private or even just keep it to themselves. Wait until those feelings go away. But not me! Apparently, I have a death wish. Either that, or I've convinced myself big romantic gestures, like reading somebody a poem in front of all your friends, works in the movies, and so it has got to work for me.

I've never done anything so brave or grand in my life. I have always, always taken the easy way out of things, like any cowardly lion. It's just more comfortable to sit quietly in the shadows.

But here's the thing: I don't want to be a coward my entire life, and I think if I do something big and grandiose like this, then maybe the universe will throw me a bone and give me something good for once. And I want my first something good to be really, *really* good.

And Sam would be amazing.

Could it backfire, and I'd lose one of my best friends in the world? Obviously. Which is why I'm currently fighting with my entire being to not puke on this bus right now as we take yet another turn at the speed of light. It's probably my imagination but we practically tip over and swipe into a car before we straighten out.

Someone nearby starts to laugh and shouts, "Sick, bro!"

The rest of us groan.

A few minutes later, we pull into the parking lot, and I realize I've managed not to spew this entire ride. I take a deep breath, proud of my small accomplishment. I could have puked, like, twenty times, but I haven't!

But wait, we're barely slowing down. Apparently, just because we've reached our destination doesn't mean this ride from hell is over.

We hit something—a speed bump, I realize—and boom, liquid sloshes the back of my mouth, the strong taste of bile percolating across my tongue. It burns as I swallow it back down. And this is just the first of three bumps.

I get that it's Drill Day, and I get that we need to be at school on time, but this is outrageous. Moronic, actually. There's no need to risk our lives anymore; we're literally on school property now.

Judith is the opposite of me—much braver, much more direct—and while I stew in shock and indignation again, she would have gone up to the driver by now and had a word with him. Shut this down the first time he took a fast turn.

But she's not here, and we're about to hit the next bump. I jump to my feet so the impact on my stomach is lessened, holding my breath and bracing for impact. It helps, I think. I don't feel as bad as I did the first time.

When we're over it, I'm suddenly very aware of myself and how I must look, having jumped up like this. I'm in one of the middle rows, and I can feel everyone's eyes on the back of my head. Since Judith isn't here, I have the seat to myself, which is a small blessing. But now I almost wish I had her here making fun of me because this is worse, feeling like the entire *bus* is pointing at me.

I hate attention. I hate causing a scene. I hate being *noticed*. And I'm very, very aware that, right now, that is exactly what's happening. I'm also noticing how sweaty I am. My face is either ghost white or bile green. Or beet red. All three?

A part of me knows they can't be looking at me any worse than they usually do, though. Poor Henry with his one-eyed sister. Poor Henry with his drunk of a dad. Poor Henry with his convict of a mother.

I think about reaching down to my thigh to catapult me out of this moment, the tangle of cuts and scars I could squeeze and knead like dough so the jolt of hurt would replace this ache of embarrassment. But I can't. Not here.

We take the third speed bump slower than the last two, but I still feel touch-and-go. At this point, the best option is to just get out of here as fast as I can. Since I'm already standing when we pull into the parking spot, I don't wait for all the people in front of me to get off first. I march right on up to the front like I own this bus. And you know what? For right now, I do, fuckers.

"You in a hurry or something?" asks the driver. He removes his shades to reveal two very intact and very brown eyes. His fist is wrapped around the lever to open the door, but he's not opening it.

I wasn't expecting this, and with each second, my blood feels thicker and thicker, like sludge. I mumble something about a test I have to study for.

"One day you'll realize life's about more than school," he says, believing, I'm sure, that he's being very profound at six-thirty.

I just nod and smile, hoping my face doesn't betray my anguish.

He smirks and finally pulls the lever, and the door squeaks and sighs as it opens. I jump down the stairs, and I must go a little too fast because there's no way I can hold it in anymore. I've got to puke, and I've got to puke *now*.

I race around to the front of the bus, shielded on all sides by other buses that I really hope are empty, and let it go.

It's so painful coming up, like someone is stabbing me. My eyes flutter open and closed as it comes pouring out, and it's like I'm watching myself in stop motion. It forms puddles around my feet. Some of it gets on my shoes.

It's hot and gross, and some of it sprays up into my nose, which might make me puke more. I try to be quiet so nobody will hear me, but the bus engine is so loud that it probably doesn't matter. Or maybe that's delirious thinking. Maybe the driver is watching from his window right now. But if anybody does come over to see, they don't wait around long enough to say anything.

A minute later, when I'm sure it's all out of me, I feel light, free. Empty. I think this might be the best I've ever felt in my life. Maybe I *can* read this poem today. Maybe Sam *will* respond the way I want. I should puke more often.

Everything in me goes still and quiet. It's almost like I'm floating through fog as I wind my way through the maze of buses all parked in a cluster. I'm so light, it feels like a dream. Like I'm not real. Is this what it's like to get high?

As soon as I round the last bus, I come down.

If getting sick was a dream, reality is not worth waking up for. The nightmare of my life is as bleak as it's ever been.

Ah, yes, here we are. Drill Day.

Across the parking lot, a few hundred feet away, is the entire student body—two thousand of my peers. They've been rounded up like cattle in front of school, their incessant chatter like primal, god-fearing cries for help before being led to slaughter. And just like real cattle, they know there's no escape.

But at least the cows get to die before *their* mutilation.

Chapter Two

I'M FROZEN. I don't think I could move even if I wanted to—which I definitely don't. But I don't want to stay here either. The nasty taste in my mouth gets worse the longer I stand still. The longer I watch. But how can I just…join them?

Everybody's lined up in rows—sort of. Toward the middle of what should be five distinct and orderly lines, they all do this zigzag thing and start trickling and bleeding into one another. There's not enough space for all two thousand people to form five perfect lines, so everybody in the back hangs around mingling in a huge blob.

They're all either talking with one another or staring down at their phones, mindlessly scrolling away as they wait for their turn to be scanned. I recognize some of them even from this distance. This will be the last time one of them looks like this: with two eyes. Standing tall and sure of themselves. Unbroken, untraumatized. In a matter of a week or two, they'll be walking into school with a pretty blue patch, their new disfigurement hidden with a decorative fashion statement.

Of course, this also might be the last time *I'll* be here with both eyes. I can't imagine they would pick Judith and me in back-to-back months, but I guess it's not impossible. It's enough to make me want to run away. Sneak back onto the bus and curl up under one of the seats. Wait until it takes me back home. I would too if it weren't for the fact that if I'm not accounted for today, I can absolutely kiss my eye goodbye.

That happened to one of the sophomores last September, at the first Drill Day of the year. He skipped school without a good enough reason, like being legitimately bedridden, then the next Drill Day, he was conveniently chosen as a donor.

But that's just speculation, technically, even though it's obviously true. It's not like you can ask anyone from Axiom if they did that on purpose. They would never admit to that sort of malice—they're the good guys, after all. They're trying to cure blindness and other afflictions…by making people half-blind.

A stone sinks in my stomach as I trudge toward the crowd. I dodge sideways glances as I make my way to the back, but I don't have to work too hard to avoid bumping into people. They practically jump out of my way when I near them. It's like I'm a bad-luck charm or something because of what happened to Judith. But I'm no victim. I've done the same thing to others in the past. I avoid talking to kids with patches whenever I can, and when I'm forced to interact with one, like when we have to do a project together or something, I try not to look at them. It's too sad. Too real.

"Yo, Henry, up here!"

Norah. I look around, but the crowd is so dense and I can't see her anywhere. Then there she is, jumping up and down, waving like a lunatic. I have to walk at a snail's pace, and I do so head down, muttering apologies as I pass. It's not like most people mind when you cut because it means their own scan gets delayed. But some people do. Some want to get theirs over with and move on with their day.

And there's even the choice few who *want* to be scanned. Want to be selected because Axiom always gives you something in return for your eye. That's how they get away with it. Judith's eye, for instance, rewarded my family with a brand-new house.

The back of Norah's head greets me. She's whispering with someone I can't see but who I'm pretty sure is Sam. My insides turn cold at the prospect of seeing him, knowing full well what I have planned after school. Don't fuck it up, Hen.

I clench my jaw and lightly kick the back of her leg with my shoe, which I just now remember has specks of vomit on it. Great. She turns and cocks her chin.

"Ah, the lord finally bestows his greatness upon us."

"How kind of him!" Sam calls, and appears beside her, smiling wide. "Took you long enough."

He looks incredible, because of course he does. Dimples so cute you could die? Check. Wild blue eyes with crinkles at the corners and long beautiful lashes? Check. Tight-but-not-too-tight cardigan accentuating his perfect arms? Check. Oh, and what's this? Looks like he got a new pair of corduroys, which do amazing things for his legs. God, kill me now.

In comparison, I'm a mess. Always. Most of my T-shirts either have stains I can't get out or holes I don't know how to fix. I'm wearing the only pair of jeans I own, the same ones I've had for at least three years. They're too short at the ankles now, so I recently started rolling them up to seem like a new pair of capris. People see right through me, though, because I think it's fairly common knowledge that the Youngwell family is too fucking poor to afford new clothes. And they're not wrong. We can't afford food either, some weeks. As people have pointed out before in a *concerned* way, Judith and I look undernourished. Gaunt. Those are some of the nice words they use. I've also heard cadaverous.

Yet somehow, I think this perfect, impeccable specimen would ever go for…me? God, I'm a dumbass.

"Hi, hello, good morning, how are you," I say all at once, trying my best at upbeat and chipper despite…well, everything. On Drill Day, upbeat and chipper is imperative, at least for me. Something about faking it till you make it. Or else I'd implode.

Norah narrows her smoky eyes. She can see through my bullshit a mile away. "What's wrong?"

Heat creeps up my neck. "What are you talking about?"

She gets closer and lowers her voice. "You look like you died and came back to life, no offense."

I grin, making sure it absolutely radiates, and use my hand to fan my face in a mock-scandalized sort of way. Really, it's to block my breath from wafting toward her.

"Oh my goodness, thank you, sweetie pie. Bless your heart!"

"Don't listen to her, Hen, you look dapper as always," Sam says, and I know he's just being nice, but my tongue ties into knots regardless. I stammer for a response, but nothing coherent comes, so I give up.

"Excuse me, how dare you," Norah scoffs. "I just meant in a concerned way, as in like, are you all right?"

I rack my brain. I can't exactly tell them I puked next to the bus a few minutes ago because then they would ask why. But maybe I *can* be vague and cryptic about it. Vague and cryptic is my specialty.

"It's my week to read in Ink Stain. I was up late working on it. I want it to be perfect or whatever, blah blah blah."

"Ooh, la-di-da." Sam beams, clapping with each syllable. "Can we say excited *already*? You have such a way with words, my friend."

Here is where I die. I've been friends with Sam since elementary, but lately, the way he says *my friend* makes my chest feel like it's dissolving. Like I'm fading away into the ephemera. It's awful and mortifying, and I just want to go home.

Norah smirks. I think she might have picked up on my crush, but she hasn't said anything to me, and I have definitely not breathed a word of it to her.

"You'll be amazing," she sighs, pulling her long, silky black hair over one shoulder. She dyes a streak of it a new color every month. Right now, it's emerald, which complements her warm brown eyes. "Your poems are always amazing. It's kind of obnoxious."

I make the stupidest face I can think of to deflect. If there's one thing I hate—and I hate lots of things—it's sincerity. Especially in the form of a compliment thrown my way.

"Don't embarrass the gentleman," says Sam, stepping over to me and placing an arm around my shoulders. "You can't just talk about a poet's craft right in front of him this early in the morning, you know."

The smell of blueberry muffin wafts into my nose. He's not eating one, but it's just part of his natural scent now. The very first day of freshman year, Sam declared he was going to become a blueberry muffin guy and eat one every day from then on. He said it was sophisticated. Classy. Norah and I both yawned, used to these kinds of declarations, but now, near the end of junior year, he truly has had one every single morning. It's way more commitment than I've ever had, to anything.

"You okay, dude?" I open my eyes to find Norah smirking at me. I got lost in a daydream, and even worse, she caught me. Did Sam? No, he's using his free hand to type some words into his phone. It looks like character notes for a short story I think he's writing, but I shouldn't pry. I envy the ease of whipping out a phone to write—or do anything, really. Text. Email. Look up shit online. But, again, the Youngwells are too poor to afford basic necessities. And what's more necessary than a cell phone?

I clear my throat. "Of course I'm okay. Are *you* okay, Norah?" I pride myself on being a master of deflection.

She yawns in response, a master of not taking my shit. "Other than waiting around to sell my soul to the devil, I'm fabulous," she says dryly, and nods toward the school entrance. Inch by inch, we're getting closer to the doors, closer to finding out if we're eligible this month for a *donation*, as Axiom calls it. The donation, of course, being our eyeball.

Sam puts his phone in his pocket and lets go of me to reach out and squeeze both of Norah's cheeks. "That's right, my precious little Norah-Worah. You'll sell that soul of yours, yes you will!"

It's hilarious, but Norah is nowhere near as amused as I am. When he lets go, her eyes are twice their size. "He did not just do that. Henry, tell me he did not just do that."

"I'm Switzerland," I whisper.

Sam smiles, batting our shoulders with his open palms. "Oh stop it, you two. You know what I've realized? We have *got* to stop framing this whole Drill-Day-Schmrill-Day in such a negative light. We are not selling our souls to the devil—we are doing just what Axiom and their pretty little Watchers say we're doing. We are *making a difference!* We're helping them find a cure, just like they've been telling us all this whole entire time, all these years."

The sarcasm is thicker than usual today, and it's making me aroused.

"Oh yeah," Norah sighs. "That's why students all across these United States gladly, and without question, donate their eyes, don't you know? Because the national health care conglomerate is definitely, one hundred percent, no question about it, trying to find a cure for diseases! By using our eyes!"

I double-check our placement in line, and we're far enough back from the entrance—about thirty people deep now—to where I don't think the Watchers can hear us. I feel safe enough to chime in.

"You know, I think you guys are right. That's why it's only high school and college kids who get the honor of making donations—because everybody knows that if you don't go to school, your eyes aren't worth jack shit!"

"Who knew eyeballs could contain life-saving answers in them anyway?" asks Sam with a thumb under his chin. "I sure didn't."

I grin like a game show host. "Well, you know what? Axiom did, and that's all that counts. Thank god for those bastards!"

Norah erupts in laughter and immediately smacks her hands to her mouth, but she winds up snorting, which makes her go pink in the face with embarrassment. This makes Sam and me laugh too, and I cover my mouth to try to stop my rancid puke breath from infecting the entire school. I laugh even though I feel uneasy. The laughter grows wilder, like when it's three in the morning and you're so tired you can't see straight but also so delirious that every single thing becomes hilarious.

Then something makes me come to a sputtering stop, like a car running out of gas. All the noise around us has died, and when I look around, everybody is staring at us. I'm normally so conscious of everybody's eyes on me, but I guess being caught up in the moment with my best friends in the world, somehow, I wasn't.

I don't know if people are staring because of our laughter on such a bleak day or if they were listening to us beforehand—to our sarcasm, our audacity.

But it's not as if they don't think those very things. Everybody talks like that on non-Drill Days when Watchers aren't around. It's just different when they're in plain sight.

Sam and Norah must notice the silence too because they stop just as suddenly as I have.

"Ew, whatever," Sam says, and dusts off his shoulders. "Don't you swine have anything else to look at?"

Something else I admire so much in this man is his candor. His nonchalance at living his truth, speaking his mind. Where I'm constantly worrying about everything, he couldn't give a single shit. I could pull out my poem and start reading it to him right now.

He looks at me and rolls his eyes, then pulls out his phone and begins typing again, unbothered.

For the next several minutes, the regular chatter of the school gets back to normal, and so does the mood. As our bodies inch closer and closer to the entrance, my chest tightens as I flash back to last Drill Day, when Judith's name was announced.

After an initial wave of nausea, I began trembling in my seat, every nerve in my body firing. She climbed the stairs onto the stage, and all I could think was, hey, we're twins. We're twins! I must be just as good a candidate as she is. *Take me, take my eye instead! Don't you fucking touch her, you bastards.*

Except I never said that. Of course I didn't. I was scared. It's something I'll carry with me for as long as I live. I take after my dad in that way; he always takes the easy way out too. And if I'm not careful, I'll end up a loser just like him.

I count five people ahead of Norah. Five.

Four.

I reach down to scratch my thigh, feeling the world of hurt that brings me so much relief. The knots in my chest begin to loosen. The gears in my brain begin to slow.

Norah turns to me, and I bring up my hand immediately. I don't think she caught me because I see something else in her face. Something distant and deep and almost tremulous in her eyes.

"How's Judith doing?" she asks, and it's barely a breath. Barely a whisper. It's like she read my mind. But then, how could she not? How have we survived all this normal-ish talk on a day like today? It's like rote. Sure, it's what we do every Drill Day—continue as normal, or else collapse into a ball and wither away—but this one, the first one afterwards, is different. So much bigger.

I don't mean to shrug at her, but my shoulders do it on their own. I'm embarrassed to admit that I have no idea how my sister's doing. Besides this morning, when she came out of her room with this serious look in her eye, trying to tell me something bad was about to happen, she's been holed up in her room all week. Whenever I've checked on her or brought her food to eat, she's been zonked out on painkillers. I scroll the days through my head—Saturday when she had surgery, then Sunday when we moved into the house, then Monday, all the way through today, Friday—and realize I haven't seen her outside of her room once, except this morning. Which, in retrospect, I should have taken as a sign not to ignore her when she was trying to warn me.

"Is she adjusting to…"

"How the world looks with one eye?" The bitterness is thick on my tongue. I don't like how it tastes. I can feel Sam's eyes on me as he puts his phone in his pocket.

Norah scratches her elbow. "Yeah, that."

"I think so," I say, and I realize I need to lighten the mood or else the world will stop and I'll have a panic attack. I let words spill out of my mouth, whether they make sense or not.

"She walks totally fine and everything. Mostly she's just anxious to come back here on Monday. You know how nerdy she is."

"Man, just one weekend left of her break, and then—" Sam stops when Norah glares at him. He did not consider the irony of calling it a *break*, I guess.

"Sorry," he says. "I'm really sorry, Henry."

"It's…" I'm about to say fine, but is it? "She's tougher than me," I reply instead.

"That's not hard to be, is it?" Norah smiles.

"I hate you," I say in bubbly baby-talk, hoping for the same. "I hate you, I hate you, I hate you."

"You love me, shut up."

From the corner of my eye, I see Sam hesitate. He opens his mouth but closes it. Then he almost lifts his arm as if to put it around me like before, but he's not sure if it's appropriate right now. I have no idea either, but it's all I want. Norah and I lock eyes, and she sees it too. She knows what I'm thinking. Of course she knows.

Sam does not put his arm around me, though. He crosses it over his chest, then puts his other arm across it, like he's cold. Is it awkward? Did *I* make it awkward? Did he catch me scratching my thigh?

Or maybe he just feels bad about what he said. Maybe he's lost in his own brain right now. It's possible, but Sam isn't the anxious overthinker I am.

Stop it, Henry. You're being paranoid.

Or maybe you're not. Maybe this is a sign that he doesn't like you, will never like you. If he did, he wouldn't shy away. Don't read your poem. You'll just ruin your already pathetic life.

There are now two people in front of Norah. I take a breath. Two breaths. Three. We just have to make it through the scanners, and maybe things will go back to normal.

"Well, how's the new digs then, my friend?" Sam asks. He bites his lip, hands now on his hips. I close my eyes and try to focus on the question, not on what just happened. What didn't happen.

"Huge and creepy," I say, a scratch in my throat. "It's fancy but also, like, eerily quiet because it's so big?"

He claps. "Ooh! Haunted mansion?" His smile is bright, as if nothing is happening for him right now, like his entire chest didn't just crush in these last few moments.

So, I laugh away the pain because what else is new?

"Mansion? Not quite." Though any upgrade from our old run-down apartment might be considered rich and luxurious. "But maybe haunted. Axiom built it just for us, so maybe the walls are made from the *eyes of little children*." I whisper the last part because we're pretty close to the Watchers now, and I don't want to find out what they would do if they heard me.

"Oh nooo!" Sam puts his hands up and pretends to melt.

Finally, with just one person in front of Norah, I see the Watcher stationed at the scanner we'll be using. I recognize him from previous Drill Days, and he looks extra stoic today in his shiny blue sunglasses. His jaw is clenched like he means serious business. I love the pretty gold pin fastened to his bulletproof vest. The letters A-X-I-O-M are designed in the shape of an eye. So designer. So chic.

He doesn't say a word to Norah as she steps up. Doesn't even nod. But silence isn't unusual for them; it would be weirder if he *did* talk.

She pulls the straps of her backpack to her chest as the scanner, a helmet-type device, adjusts to her height, whirring and whizzing as it lowers into position.

Norah clears her throat as if to say something. She doesn't. The helmet unfurls itself, then wraps around her, forming perfectly to her skull.

"They need to find a more efficient way to do this shit," Sam says in my ear. "This is seriously inconvenient."

"I know, right?"

"Do they not, like, care about our education?"

"I don't believe they do, my friend," I say. "I don't believe they do."

He scoffs. "Hey, way to steal my phrase, jerk."

"What? Are you saying you don't want to be my friend anymore?"

"Are you kidding, Henry Youngwell? There's nothing else that matters in the world."

Chapter Three

I BARELY REGISTER Norah finishing her scan, then it's as if I'm floating on a cloud, my feet soaring on the words from Sam's mouth. *There's nothing else that matters in the world.* Then suddenly, I'm here at the scanner, and I'm back on the ground as the weight of reality pushes me to my feet.

Oh, yeah. This is what I'm here to do. To find out if I'll be the second Youngwell getting their eye out.

I can hardly remember a time when people didn't have to scan. I think Axiom began implementing it in schools about ten years ago. Luckily you don't have to start doing it until high school, so for a few blissful years, I was ignorant of what it meant.

Before I was even born, Axiom began as a health insurance company, but soon they began merging with other insurance providers across the state. Then across the country. It became a monopoly. They held people's lives in their hands.

But they weren't satisfied with only offering insurance, so they crossed over to the front lines and opened clinics. Hospitals. They stole staff members from other hospitals by offering their employees huge amounts of money. These places had to shut down, and the ones that didn't, Axiom bought them out.

They influenced politics too. Bribed Congress members with cash prizes and lavish gifts, bent them to their will. Laws were passed—laws allowing them to take people's *donations* with no repercussions, as long as they offered payment. Laws implementing scanners into schools so that the bright young minds of students could be infiltrated too. Right now, scanners are only in high schools and colleges, but who knows how long before they go younger and younger. Before they start mutilating babies.

All for the sake of science. Axiom alleges our donations are used for medical research. They aim to cure all different types of ailments and diseases. Lupus. Cancer. Blindness. Because apparently, the eye contains the secret to life. It's the window to the soul, as the saying goes—and also, supposedly, everything else.

As for the cures Axiom promised? It's been all these years, and there's still no cure in sight, for anything. Yet here we are.

Here I am.

It's my turn again.

Since I'm taller than Norah, the helmet rises on its little platform. Before it unfurls to wrap around me, I read the pretty, swirly font across it: *Surgical Revolution*. I glance at the Watcher but only see myself in the reflection of his glasses. Bye, Henry. Take care, little one.

Soon, I'm encased. It's all too familiar, this void, as the darkest of dark swallows me. My stomach flips and my knees buckle, even after doing this every fucking month for three years. For a split second, I always think I'm falling to my death. I start to reach for my thigh as I drop, as if for one final joy ride.

But then the little yellow lights flash directly in line with my pupils, and I remember very painfully that I'm alive. I move my hand away before it can make contact with my leg. The lights swell as they recognize me, then they crackle like static and burn as bright as little suns. Independently of each other, the lasers rotate and spin around and around, morphing into circles, into figure-eights, into tiny diamonds. They turn green and blue and purple and red. They pirouette like ballerinas and burst like supernovas.

Once, I tried tricking them by clamping my eyes shut as soon as the lasers came on. It made this horrible clicking noise like a rattlesnake, and the Watcher cleared her throat to warn me she knew what I was doing. Another time I tried just squinting until my eyes were the thinnest little slits, like a quick flick of a razor through flesh, but the scanner kept on working as if my eyes were wide open.

The scan takes maybe thirty seconds to complete, then there's this satisfied sighing noise it makes, sort of like the sound my dad makes after the first sip of a drink. It releases my head, and the metal sides of the helmet retract into itself, folding itself back up all neat and presentable.

I try to stand tall, though I can't really make sense of anything because of the floaters—these little orange and blue demons in my line of vision that won't disappear no matter which way I look. There's like ten thousand of them in each eye, and the way they swirl around makes me dizzy. They only get worse the more I blink, so it's just another fun part of the whole Drill Day experience.

I vaguely register the Watcher lifting his chin as I turn to go. Part of me thinks they do this for fun, just to make fools of us. I mean, would it be wonderful if they invested in technology that wouldn't blind us? Sure, but that might be too much to ask. It's a marvel we all don't crash into each other.

That's what the escorts are for. Admin forces some of the already busy teachers to lead us by the arm into one of two alcoves right off the front hallway. Each alcove seats nine benches around its three walls, where we're supposed to wait patiently for the floaters to go away.

Through the blurriness, I recognize the teacher I had for history last year. He puts his huge hand on my shoulder and guides me until I'm sitting next to Norah.

"You good, Youngwell?" he asks before he leaves. I hate it when grown men address me by just my last name. It always seems to be the ex-jocks trying to hold on to their youth or something—which is fitting because he's also the basketball coach. I roll my eyes, knowing I can blame it on the floaters if he notices. He doesn't, so I nod and smile like a good little subject—whoops, I mean *student*—and listen as his shoes click on the tile as he walks away.

I wonder if Judith will have to go through this whole rigamarole when she comes back on Monday. Like maybe it won't even work if you only have one eye. If there's any plus at all to getting mutilated, maybe this is it.

"This is literally hell," Norah says through a sigh.

Sam's laughter rings in my ears as he sits next to me. "It would be seriously epic if we all walked around like zombies till first period. Everyone bumping into each other? We could make an apocalypse movie or something." I turn and furrow my brows at him, which he doesn't notice because he's rubbing his eyes. Or at least I think he is. I can't see very much.

I can never tell if closing my eyes makes the floaters better or worse, but today I decide to close them and wait it out. And if I happen to fall asleep in the meantime, that's not my fault.

After a couple minutes, I'm on the verge of dozing when a voice rouses me.

"'Sup, Youngwell?"

Ugh. I think for a second it's that teacher again, but when I look up, the floaters have mostly, well, floated away, and I see Kent Cross on the bench across from me. How could I mistake his nasally mouse squeak of a voice? We're about fifteen feet apart, and my eyes could burn just looking at him.

Kent addresses people by their last name as though he's one of the jocks, but he couldn't be further from it. When it's not me who gets picked on, it's Kent—which is a little sad because he genuinely thinks everybody loves him, whereas I knew my fate from day one. Maybe he'd be more liked if he weren't so whiny, so know-it-all, so…Kent. He's the quintessential teacher's pet, but even the teachers are sick of him. When they ask a question in class, Kent raises his hand as high as it'll go and *has* to be the one to answer it, but he rarely gets called on. He reeks of cheap cologne and keeps his hair spiked with thick globs of hair gel because he thinks it makes him cool—but I think it just brings out his desperation.

"How can I help you, Kent?" I ask, sounding as bored as I possibly can. There's over a dozen other students in the alcove waiting until they can see again, and I don't want any of them to know I'm giving him the time of day. Also, I kind of had a crush on him for like two weeks freshman year before I learned how terrible he was, and if I got found out, I'd die.

Kent stands and raises the handlebar of his suitcase-backpack, sweeping it behind him in one fluid motion. He's the only kid in school with this kind of backpack, and I always wonder if he's legit trying to save his back or if he's too weak to carry a regular one.

He stifles a laugh. "I just wanted to say how sorry I am."

I look up to him deadpan. "Spill it, Kent."

"You know. About your sister." He calms himself down, but he's still trying to contain his laughter. My chest begins to swell. "How does she like being a cyclops and all?"

The alcove goes silent. The whole *school* seems to go silent. Blood rushes into my ears.

He flashes his buck teeth with a grin. "Guess she didn't want you to be the only freak in the family. That was nice of her, don't you think?"

Not even the popular kids, the meanest of the mean, have said that word to me. To even the patched kids themselves. Even the biggest bullies of them all know it's off-limits. Why is Kent suddenly being so cruel?

For a few more seconds, no one breathes or utters a word, as though trying to figure out if they misheard him or not.

And I have to admit I did not wake up thinking that I would kill someone today. I guess there's always room for change.

In a breath, I leap off the bench and jolt across the alcove. I swing my fist into his ugly fucking face, and again, and again, three times for luck.

This isn't my first time hitting someone, but it's the first time this year, and god, I've missed it. It's the most exhilarating feeling in the world. Every bone in my body registers the weight of smashing into him. It's *crushing*, but I feel so light, like I'm fucking flying. Like we're not on the ground, we're upside-down on the ceiling. I'm laughing. Cackling.

Something hot lands on my cheek, and I don't know if it's sweat or spit or blood—or even if it's mine or Kent's. We fall to the ground, and the floor slamming into my back makes me groan. Everyone gathers round, laughing and hollering like they've been waiting for bloodshed.

I'm about to give Kent another blow when someone from behind holds back my arm. They pull me to my feet by the armpits. I almost fall but they catch me and raise me up again.

A Watcher? They've never spoken to me and definitely have never laid a hand on me. But now, under the weight of their strong grip, I liquefy. Instantly, I accept my fate of getting my eye out.

It should have always been me instead of Judith anyway.

Floaters swarm my vision, and I don't think they're from the retina scanner anymore. I'm breathing so hard. My chest is heavy and hot, like a simmering volcano. I'm sweating—my face, my hands. Even the back of my neck is getting wet.

"You're okay, you're okay," whispers the person behind me, someone with a cool, comforting voice. How have I never heard a Watcher's voice before? How are they consoling me right now?

I turn and see Sam, not a Watcher. He's got a halo around him or some kind of spotlight, his blue eyes bright and electrified. My knight in the kind of shining armor that looks like corduroys and a cardigan, rescuing me from this hell. Is this our moment? The moment where he leans down to kiss me, sweeps me off my feet, and carries me into the sunset—well, seven a.m. sunset?

"You're okay," he says again. Or maybe he's saying, "It's okay." Either way, I believe him.

A screech like I've never heard before in my life, like a fucking siren, wails and pulls me away. It's Norah and Kent both, shouting over one another.

"What in the actual hell, punk?" Norah yells.

"Get the frick off me!" Kent cries.

She's grabbing his ear and yanking as hard as she can. He screams, and it's probably the most satisfying thing I've ever heard. When she lets go, he recoils, wincing. His ear is purple, and it's amazing. If only she'd pulled a little bit harder and ripped it clean off.

"What is wrong with you?" he screams while scrambling to his feet, cupping his ear.

"Yeah, that's right," she hisses—like, actually hisses at him, like a cat. "And if I *ever* hear you say that fucking word again, I swear on my grandfather's *grave*, you asshole."

"I was kidding," he shouts at the top of his lungs. "Kid-ding! If you can't take a *joke*, that's your own fault."

"Some joke!" Sam yells. "Did you *want* to get beat up today?"

Kent scowls. "You have no idea who my mother is, do you? We're gonna sue your crazy ass." He locks eyes with me. "You too, Youngwell—not like we'd get a dime from your impoverished family, so maybe I'll just press charges since you started it."

I can't believe what I'm hearing. "Oh, *I* started it?"

Sam lets go of me, and I realize he was the only thing keeping me upright because my knees are wobbling, and the next thing I know, I'm on the ground.

"Dude, whoa!" Norah crouches down beside me, getting herself low to the ground so she can put my arm across her shoulders. Sam leaps over to Kent in one jump and whispers something in his ear.

Oh god, I'm just now remembering the last time I beat someone up. It was some asshole in my geometry class last year. Math is one of my worst subjects. I'd failed an exam, and the kid, some jock I had a secret crush on, told me I'd wind up just like my mother, a degenerate in prison. I didn't know that anyone besides Norah and Sam knew about her until then. Well, I couldn't see straight, and the next thing I knew, I was on top of him, a desk was toppled over, and I had blood all over me. The principal said if it happened again, I'd be expelled. As Sam whispers into Kent's ear, I know this is it for me. I'm done. Will I ever see Sam again?

When I'm on my feet, with the help of Norah, Kent scurries away, his luggage in tow, like a little rat on vacation, getting smaller and smaller until he turns a corner.

Sam turns back, his cheeks wet with what I think are tears.

"What'd you say to him?" I ask as he wipes them away, and suddenly I'm on the verge of crying myself. Like, I'm trying *really* hard, making sure to breathe through my mouth to get as much air as possible. It's a combination of appreciation for him and Norah, and absolute terror of getting expelled. Or arrested. And somehow, it's even worse knowing that I'm about to cry in front of all these people. I don't have to look around to *feel* the weight of their stares.

"I just let him know what would actually happen if he ran and told his mommy," Sam says, and he shrugs like it's no big deal, like it's every day he practically saves my life.

The warning bell rings for first period. Everyone around us scatters. I release Norah, but she doesn't release me. Her hand stays lightly squeezed around my forearm to make sure I'm okay.

I'm not. It turns out that no matter how hard I try, I cannot hold my tears in, and they are fighting their damnedest to break free. I cough, choking on these tears. My heart is beating so fast and so strong.

I've got to get to the bathroom before I start losing it. Only one trick works for me to stop the panic in its tracks, which is something simply *grabbing* or *scratching* my thigh won't do. I don't care how late it makes me. I can try to make it quick so that maybe I'll slip into my seat just as first period starts, but I've got to go *now*.

I shake free of Norah. Surprisingly, my feet stay flat on the ground.

"See you guys later," I mumble without looking at either of them, then I hightail it down the hall, through the giant sea of humans that seems to part for me.

I only know two things right now. First, the razor tucked away in my backpack is calling my name. Second, I won't be able to function the rest of the day if I ignore it.

Chapter Four

"WOULD YOU HURRY it along, Mr. Youngwell? Jeez Louise, you kids are slow today."

Third bell just rang for physics, and I'm almost to the door when Dr. Maas hurries me inside. Somehow, I've made it this far in the day without once getting called to the principal's office. I don't know if Sam's threat to Kent worked, or if I'll have to wait until Drill Day is over to be expelled, but here I am.

Once I'm in the room, Dr. Maas slams the door closed. I quickly roll my eyes at Norah on the way to my seat, and she rolls her own right back at me.

This is the class I dread coming to most, especially today. Not only because I suck at physics and I'm one bad grade away from flunking, but Drill Day means third period ends early. We get about twenty minutes of class before the entire school is called to flock en masse to the auditorium for Axiom's monthly presentation about how amazing they are and to see who is slated to become the next donor.

Dr. Maas leans against the door frame. She raises her cat's-eye glasses to the top of her head and squeezes the bridge of her nose. This is weird for her. She's normally in a great mood and starts the class with a smile and, like, celebrity gossip or something. But this?

I meet Sam's gaze from all the way across the room. He shrugs, just as confused as I am. Is our teacher having a breakdown? I look to Norah next—all three of us are luckily in the same class but spaced far enough apart to not make trouble, as was Dr. Maas's intention with the seating assignment—and her eyes are wide. My friend Mel, who's also in Ink Stain, has one eyebrow raised to her hairline and the other scrunched and furrowed. As I look around, it seems like everybody feels just as uncomfortable.

Without releasing her nose, Dr. Maas groans. "How are y'all today? I'm peachy. You all peachy?"

"Um, yeah, peachy keen," Mel says slowly. "…I guess."

When Dr. Maas does return to normal, she smiles sadly. "Super-duper. That's great to hear."

Sam clears his throat twice, loudly. "Everything all right, Doc?"

"Now that you mention it, not really," she says, beginning to do some stretches like she's about to exercise. "Just a little tired of having to schedule around…" She gestures all around her, I'm guessing to indicate Drill Day. Axiom. *Their* plans. But the thing is, Drill Day has been happening for years, and she's been teaching for years, which means she's used to having to schedule around them. But maybe the more you have to do it, the more you grow tired of it.

"Anyway," she sighs, "if we had the full day, we could do this amazing lab that I think would really help you guys grasp centrifugal force. But instead, here we are."

Okay, no lab in a science class is amazing, and she knows it. Physics is awful and should be abolished. But if I had to choose, I would much rather do a lab than Drill Day.

"Well, let's not go," Sam calls out. "Why don't we just say fuck it?"

The girl next to him gasps like she's never heard someone curse before. Granted, it is shocking to hear it in class, in front of a teacher, but I have a very different reaction. My eyes focus on him in a sort of tunnel vision. I'm in love with how he can so calmly and brazenly say fuck it, fuck Axiom, fuck Drill Day. I imagine it so clearly: reading my poem to him, the smile on his face, the tears in his eyes. My heart picks up. Our eyes meet now, and I swear he knows what I'm thinking. And I swear he feels the same way.

Dr. Maas lets out a single, guttural "Ha!" and I'm pulled from my trance. She swivels on her gym shoes to face the whiteboard. After a few moments of quiet deliberation, she walks up to it, uncaps a blue marker, and writes in all caps *FUCK IT*.

Then promptly erases it.

"Any other ideas?" she asks, turning around, and I don't know what she means. Does she want ideas for how we can do the lab? Girl, you're the teacher, just have us do it on Monday. What's the big hullabaloo?

"Ideas for what?" somebody asks.

Dr. Maas puts the back of the marker in her mouth and chews, gazing up at the ceiling in serious thought. As she does, I get into my backpack and pull out my notebook, where I have Sam's poem that I've rewritten almost fifty different times. I need to quickly add a line about how bold he is. How much I admire it. How, when he opens his mouth, even if it's just to say *fuck it*, he makes me want to be more courageous. But how can I add all that and not make it sound amateurish and trite, while also not ruining the flow?

As I scribble away, scratching out words and drawing arrows to where I should move things, Dr. Maas begins talking again, but I don't really listen. It's not until there's a noticeable silence that I look up.

She's staring at me. Everybody is. I close my notebook and wish my skin would melt off my bones. Wish my bones would crumble to dust. Wish, honestly, that I would die.

"Do as Mr. Youngwell is doing, class," Dr. Maas calls, smiling. "If we should all be so passionate, maybe we'll come up with something. Work on your own, or in groups. Whatever will serve you best, I don't really care. I can't wait to hear what you come up with. Be invigorated!"

The classroom erupts into conversations, chairs scrape this way and that on the tile, and I have no idea what is happening. She wants the class to do what I'm doing? She better not know what I've been doing.

Norah's sharp cackle cuts through the noise. I turn to see her pointing at me.

"Your face!" she whisper-shouts, her own face pink from laughter.

She's right. I don't know what I look like right now, but I try to compose myself the best I can and call for Dr. Maas. She smiles and trots over to my desk.

"Sorry, what's going on?"

"We're all taking a page from the Youngwell notebook, of course. So to speak."

"I don't know what that means."

Dr. Maas takes off her glasses. "My dear, don't look so constipated. You're not in trouble. You're *inspiring*. Just now, I mean. You were writing so intently on what I only could imagine was ways to, as Samwell put it so bluntly, fuck it. Were you not?" I look over at Sam, who's now joined desks with Norah and Mel. "Whatever that means to you, Mr. Youngwell. We're veering away from physics today, since we can't do much of it anyway. You don't have long now."

Norah is still chuckling when I make it across the room to sit with her, Sam, and Mel.

"What on god's green Earth is she talking about?" I ask.

"I don't know, but I'm pretty sure she done finally lost her mind," Mel whispers, side-eyeing Maas, who sits down and begins furiously typing away on her laptop.

Norah's phone vibrates on her desk, and as she checks it and types something in return, Sam leans back in his chair and yawns. He stretches his arms wide, and his shirt rides up, and I try my best not to stare at the band of his underwear poking out. "Apparently, she wants us to fuck it," he says. Air gets trapped in my throat, and I have to cough it away.

"You good?" Mel asks when I'm done. I nod, avoiding everyone's eyes—especially Norah's because I'm pretty sure she knows exactly what just happened.

"So," Sam says, "how exactly do we do that?"

Mel rubs the top of her shaved head, then scratches her pierced cheek. "Can someone please explain what that *means*, though? Fuck it? What exactly are we…you know…"

"Drill Day," says Norah. "I think she wants us to brainstorm how to feel empowered in spite of—" She pauses because her focus has been redirected to her phone again. But Sam finishes her thought for her.

"—empowered in spite of powers that are out of our control."

How to *feel* in control when you're not in control of anything? When your life is spiraling? I certainly don't know anything about that, as I cross my left ankle over my right thigh and dig in, quietly basking in the shock it sends through me. A fresh cut is the best cut.

"Makes sense, I guess," Mel says. "But we're all writers, you know. We just hole up in our rooms and scribble in our notebooks or laptops or whatever. Complete solitary confinement. I mean, maybe it's not empowerment exactly, but that's at least how I deal with this shit."

Sam smiles and gestures wildly. "But that *is* empowerment. For people like us—writers—writing is power. Right? That sounds cheesy or whatever but, like, it trains you to see the world in a different way." I watch in amazement as he talks, confounded by the way he composes beautiful words out of thin air. "You hand any one of us a pen and paper and give us a while, and we'll feel like we can solve all of life's problems."

"Speaking of, Henry—" I whip my head over to Norah, her plastered-on cherubic smile hiding what can only be described as chaos. "What were you writing over there that inspired Maas to get on this little empowerment kick?"

I smile just as sweetly. "Just about how you're the best friend in the world, my dear."

She yawns and stretches her arms out wide. "Obviously."

"Is that what you're reading today in group, an homage to Norah?" asks Mel. Her eyes go wide as she slams the desk in excitement. "Ooh! Or an homage to *all* of us?"

Sam laughs. "I love this. It is one of the last Ink Stains of the year, so it better be big, Hen."

I roll my eyes. "You guys are full of yourselves."

"That's what you love about us," says Mel.

"Who says I love any of you?" I ask.

Sam clutches his beautiful chest. "Hey, that hurts, my friend!"

I blush. I know I blush because it feels like fire in my entire face, like I'm boiling from the inside. I bend down and start rummaging through my backpack until it goes away. When it does, I take out an entirely different notebook.

The others have already started writing in their own notebooks or phones, and I have no idea what to do, so I just start doodling.

A while later, the bell rings. I've filled up the entire page with random swirls and barely realized it.

"Shoot, I lost track of time," Dr. Maas calls and goes over to open the door. "Well, I can't wait to hear your ideas on Monday. And good luck in there!"

*

IT'S A FAMILIAR stampede in the hall. A jungle. Chaos incarnate. Some kids rush to the bathroom. Some stop at their lockers to shove in their textbooks. And some hightail it straight to the auditorium, a pep in their step like they've been waiting all month for today.

"Gonna go find Sari, and we'll meet you guys in there," shouts Mel over the sound. When I turn to say bye, she's already gone, trampled by the stampede. Mel is almost never without her girlfriend Sari, class being the only time when they're forced to be apart. I've always been envious of that kind of commitment. That kind of love.

I look over to see if Sam is maybe thinking the same thing, but he's gone too. I'm left with Norah, who's so engrossed in her phone, it's basically like she's not here either. I poke her arm to get her attention. She barely rouses, but she does spare me a glance.

"Where'd Sam go?" I shout.

She shrugs one shoulder. "I think the bathroom or something. Told me to save him a seat." She puts her phone in her back pocket and puffs her cheeks. "Shall we?"

I hold her hand as I follow her, like a child afraid to lose his mother at the zoo, sidestepping to dodge bodies left and right. It *is* a zoo in here. The stairwell is clogged, and the minutes inch by just to get down half a flight. I watch each passing one every time Norah whips her phone out of her pocket to text whoever she's been texting.

Sometimes it's weird to be the only person on Earth without a phone, but other times it's kind of a blessing. I do miss out on things, but that's fine because I get anxious in most social situations anyway. I'm always the last to hear about gossip because I have to wait for Norah to tell me either at school or whenever we work the same shift at our job. So that sucks. But I also get out of a lot of things. I don't have to send in my homework electronically, which means I always get the morning to finish an assignment on paper when the rest of the class has to turn things in online the night before. With our new house, we did finally get a home computer, courtesy of Axiom, but I don't think my teachers know that. Besides, none of us have really gotten onto it yet—or at least I haven't.

I'm not sure if my teachers know all the reasons my family is so poor, but it's not hard to piece together that we are. The lack of phones. Judith and I both being so rail thin. The fact that we never buy school lunches and only bring food a few times a week. Our backpacks falling apart. Our clothes too small in some places but always stretched out in the neck from being worn too many times.

My mom's been gone for the last nine years, so they have to know we've been without at least one income for most of our childhood. They would probably assume our dad's job made up for the shortfall, but that would only be true if my dad could actually keep a job for longer than a week…which is hard to do when you spend every single day either extremely drunk or extremely hungover. And that leaves it up to me to be the sole income-earner.

Judith used to work, until very recently. Her surgery wasn't the official reason behind her getting fired, because that's technically covered under discrimination laws. It's a little shocking to think the government pretends to care enough about us to make such a law but still allow Axiom to get away with the thing in the first place. Even with the law, everybody knows people with only one eye don't find work very often—especially when they work in customer service, like Judith did as a barista. It reminds people of the inevitable: that they, or their children, could be next.

Norah pulls out her phone again. I want to ask who she's texting, but it's impossible to hold a conversation in the hallway. Sometimes when the noise gets this loud and digs into my eardrums, I start to panic. My nerves fray like wires. But there's no escaping this hell. People are literally running into each other.

When we get to the auditorium, it's quieter, but my brain is still rolling around. A Watcher perches here, his purpose not to oversee a scan this time, because there are no scanners, but to shut you up. To remind you why you're here. His gloved hand squeezes the handle of the long baton tucked into his belt, silently intimidating. His padded vest tells you he is invincible. His tree trunk of a neck, a thick vein threaded down one side, shows he could snap you like a twig. His shiny blue sunglasses make you feel small as you glance into them and see your cowering reflection creep by.

Other Watchers are stationed in here too, one at the entrance on the opposite side of the room, and one at the bottom of the staircase leading up to the stage, which is currently blocked off by red velvet curtains. She's there to prevent someone from storming the stage when one of their friends gets selected for a donation. When Judith was called last month, it crossed my mind. I wanted to. I fantasized about barreling through those smug pieces of shit, grabbing Judith, and hightailing it out of school with her. Go into hiding. Instead, I sat paralyzed, watching her tremble onstage.

She told me later that an Axiom representative drove her home after school to discuss it with our dad and tell him the news. My dad, who was already drunk at one p.m., was giddy, though he tried not to show it. He demanded a house before he would sign away his daughter. A respite from rent and bills, that's what Judith's eye was worth to him. Not that I was any better. When I got home a few hours later—because I still had to finish classes, as though I could be a functioning person after what had happened—the rep was still there, drawing up papers. My continued silence was just as much a corroboration as my dad's demands. For the next few weeks, Axiom built the house, all the while having a Watcher escort Judith everywhere she needed to go, to make sure she didn't run. Not once did I ask him to take my eye instead or say, "You know I'm her twin, right? Mine is just as good, take it instead."

It's bright in here, and barely half the seats are filled. I look around for Sam, or Mel and Sari, or anybody else in the group, but nobody seems to be here yet. Norah and I take one of the empty rows toward the middle and put our bags down to save some seats.

I close my eyes and take several deep breaths, telling myself I just have to make it through this. Twenty minutes, then it's lunch. And this is the last one of the year, so I won't have to go through this again all summer.

The lights burn my eyes for just a second when I open them. Norah's leg is shaking. Violently shaking. She's chewing on the emerald streak in her hair and staring at the empty seat in front of her. Is it about who she was texting? Is she seeing someone and she didn't tell me?

I put on my fakest grin and cross my legs toward her. Her own leg stops when she realizes I'm watching her.

"Care to tell me who you've been talking to, my sweet?"

She spits out her hair and returns the grin, happy to oblige my charade. "Holy potatoes, I was just about to tell you!" She opens her texts and points to the words "Boss Man" at the top of her screen. "See? Your fave person in the whole wide world."

"I guess that's one way to put it," I sigh, trying to ignore the flashbacks of our manager forcing me to clean up piss and shit from the bathroom tile of our convenience store last night. It had dried in the grout and in the corners, and it took me a full hour to remove.

Norah smiles in that chaotically cherubic way of hers. "Yeah, Hen, remember how I put in a good word and landed you a super amazing job after you were complaining about all your money issues last year, and I haven't asked you for a single favor since?"

I uncross my legs. "Sounds vaguely familiar. What do you want?"

She looks me square in the eye. "Okay, fine. I need you to trade shifts with me tomorrow. Please? If you take my afternoon hours, I'll go in for you in the evening." I narrow my eyes, waiting for an explanation. She knows I like to sleep till three on Saturdays. "I had some family stuff pop up last minute, so I was texting Boss Man to ask, and he said it's cool."

"Wow, shocking. He never thinks anything is cool. What kind of family stuff? Everything…okay?" I'm hesitant because I know she's had some drama at her house recently. Her parents are on the verge of a separation. They fight constantly, and even worse, both are trying separately to get Norah on their side, which puts her in a horrible situation.

"Actually, yeah, everything's cool this time. My dad had some work stuff pop up, so there's an extra ticket to my niece's ballet recital."

"Work stuff? Isn't he retired?" Norah's dad is a veteran, after having served for god knows how many years. He was some sort of officer in the National Guard or something like that. But as far as I know, he retired a few years ago, and I'm pretty sure Norah's mom makes enough money as an attorney for him to not have to work anymore—well, unless they divorce, then maybe he *would* get another job. Duh, Henry.

Norah deadpans. "Yes, he is retired, Henry, and I have told you literally three times this year that he got a new job."

"Oh," I say, vaguely remembering this. "He's a—" I panic, blanking on what his new job is. "I mean, yeah, of course I'll switch with you." My guilt about forgetting this, more than anything else, makes me agree.

As she rolls her dark-brown eyes, flecks of amber shine in the light. "Thanks, pal."

"Why do you need a ticket to your niece's recital, though?"

She groans. "Ugh, it's this ultra-prim, super prestigious, really small dance studio or whatever. I don't know, it's weird. Family members only get a set number of tickets."

"And they didn't want to give you one?" As soon as the words leave my mouth, I want to swallow them back up. Each of her parents is trying to pit her against the other. "Sorry."

"It's—" She looks toward the stage. Taps a finger on her knee. "—fine."

It's not, but what else can I say to her that I haven't already said a hundred times this past month? *I'm sorry all this is happening? I'm sorry your family is being shitty? I'm sorry, I'm sorry, I'm sorry?* There are only so many sorrys people can give you before they start to sound fake and hollow.

So, I tell her again I'll pick up her shift instead, knowing her six-year-old niece is really important to her. There's no way I'll let her pass this up. She smiles genuinely despite my assholery, and I stick out my tongue because I can't help myself when it comes to destroying tender moments.

After a couple minutes, her leg starts to shake again. She looks around and says, "Where in the hell are they?"

The auditorium is a lot fuller than it was when we got here, but still no sign of our friends. Somebody I don't know tries to take the two seats next to me, but it's clear my backpack is there to save them, so I give them a nasty look because how dare they?

Kent Cross is in the front row. I would recognize his tiny freckled ears anywhere. My rage from this morning has subsided to where all I feel when I see him is this wave of rancid bile in my stomach. But if I vomit, I would have to move, and I'm too comfortable where I am. He's sitting alone, which makes me happy. Kent is grating to everybody he meets, so it's not a surprise he's by himself.

A few seats down from him is a woman I don't recognize. She's probably from Axiom, but I don't know why she's in the audience. She would be backstage if she were presenting.

Norah's phone lights up. A text from Sam.

Here!

This is one of those cons of not having a phone. How would Sam and I communicate if we dated? I briefly wonder if Sam is who Norah was texting all that time, and she just made up a story about texting Boss Man on the spot. But that doesn't make sense, and I actually hate the way my brain works sometimes. Sometimes it tries so hard to see the worst in people, even my best friends.

I take another look around, and there he is, walking through one of the back doors. He sees me immediately and must sense my relief because he rolls his eyes and mouths, "I'm fine."

Our friend Greta is holding him by the elbow, her walking stick upright as she allows Sam to guide her to our row. Greta is in Ink Stain too. She's a foreign exchange student and has the prettiest Austrian accent. She mostly writes poems about her family and her *motherland*, as she calls it. Whenever it's her turn to read aloud in group, she starts off in German, then translates it for us. I don't know what it is about the way she speaks, but I swear, even though I don't know a word of German, I always know what the poem's about before she reads the English version.

"Nice of you guys to make it," I say, moving my backpack. Greta sits in the aisle seat, her long blonde hair draped like curtains in front of her shoulders, and Sam takes the one right next to me.

He clears his throat as if to say something, but instead, he only wipes his hands on his legs. I look over to Norah to see if she's noticed, but she's busy stopping people from sitting in the three seats she has blocked off for Mel, Sari, and Patrick, the last of Ink Stain.

"Sorry, it was my fault," Sam groans. "There was a huge line for the bathroom. It was a pain."

"We're just glad you're here, loser," whispers Norah while shooing someone else away. "You too, Greta, but you're obviously not a loser. Only Sam. Well, Sam *and* Henry. They're like a perfect match."

I grow warm and gnaw on the side of my tongue to keep cool. Greta only giggles at Norah's joke, and Sam winks. "Sweet as always, Nor," he says.

"I'm just saying it's good you made it. They would totally go psycho if even one person was missing. Do you remember back in September when that sophomore didn't show?"

I look around to see if I can find him, but then I remember he's backstage. During the presentation, Axiom always shows off the kids they've mutilated, as a way to *honor* and *thank* them.

But before I turn around, I see that no, he's not backstage. There he is, just a few rows behind us. Nobody's in the seat next to him. He's wearing a maroon hoodie, even though it's practically summer, and it's drawn up loosely around his head. Without being too obvious, I gesture for Sam and Norah to look. It takes a moment for them to register.

Norah sighs. "Poor guy. He knows he should be up on stage, right? He's been up there every other time this year."

"Maybe they're not doing that this time," Sam offers.

"Why would they abandon everything they've always done, on the last Drill Day of the year?"

"I don't know," Sam groans. "But what I want to know is, like…do they still even scan him?"

"Yeah, I've watched him and some of the others have to do it," says Norah. "But I don't know why. It's not like they're gonna take his second eye, right?"

I shrug. I wouldn't put it past Axiom, which is terrifying when I think of Judith. I've wondered before if we can be like refugees and move to another country, because as far as I know, this only happens in America. Some people here flee to Mexico or Canada to escape the possibility.

I think of something. "Greta, do they scan you on Drill Days?"

"Oh, no," she says, her deep-hazel eyes moving involuntarily up and down, back and forth, from a condition called nystagmus. "As an international student, I am protected, yes? I think there would be outright war if they did this to non-Americans. There is an agreement which diplomats from your country must swear to before we are permitted to enter your borders."

I wonder, but don't ask, why they don't wage war anyway. Isn't there some sort of international organization that could make this stop? Why do they just allow our government to let Axiom do this to us? Doesn't anybody care? Then I realize maybe they do care. Maybe they do want to help us, but don't know how. The American military is the best in the world, or so we're told, so maybe that's why nobody has waged war. They're afraid of losing, that it would be worthless. Or maybe Axiom hands out loads of money worldwide like they do to our government, to shut them up. But they can't be *that* rich, can they? I don't know. Maybe I should just stick to my own lane and worry about poetry or some shit.

"Greta, I can't believe they make you come to this if you're not even a part of it," Sam says.

"Oh, you know why." She closes her eyes, but still they move underneath their lids. "Because they are powerful. We are the almighty Axiom, see what we can do. It's as simple as that, I am afraid."

Silence for a while as we let her words sink in. She's right. This entire presentation is just a power move, there's no other reason for it. It would be a lot easier for them to just silently take aside the chosen donor and tell them they were picked.

Sam takes out his phone to jot down some lines—not that I'm snooping—and I see it's only two minutes till the presentation. Where in the hell are Mel, Sari, and Patrick? As I look around again, noticing that almost all the seats behind us are packed, Greta clears her throat.

"I am very excited to hear you read your work after school today, Henry," she says. "Your words always move me to tears. There is such sadness in them, but they're so beautiful."

I can't make a stupid face at her like I would Norah or Sam, so I just thank her. My eyes rake over Sam in this angle, from his gorgeous, messy hair to the tops of his knees, back up to his amazing mouth. His lips are wriggling, like he's biting the side of his cheek.

"Today will be a lot different than my usual stuff, though," I say. "Get ready because you have no idea."

"Some experimental shit," says Norah dryly. "I'm literally about to pee my pants, I'm so excited."

"Wait, why are you gonna pee your pants?" asks a voice behind her. I turn, and Patrick waves at the rest of us as he sits next to Norah. Mel and Sari are right behind him.

"Apparently, Henry's about to wow us in group today with some special poem."

My mouth goes dry now that I see everybody else and picture them sitting there while I read. I always knew they'd be there since I first came up with this stupid plan, but now it feels so real. What if they laugh me out of group? Am I making the worst decision of my life?

"Can't wait, my friend," says Sam.

My heart lurches. I turn to find him smiling at me, and for the longest two seconds of my life, I gawk at him. I think to smile back, but before my face can register what my brain is telling it to do—darkness. All the lights have shut off. I look up to the ceiling. There are these ultra-faint rings of electricity still lingering in the lightbulbs, and I watch as they slowly fade all the way to black.

This doesn't normally happen. Usually, the curtains part and someone from Axiom is standing on stage with a microphone. They go on about how wonderful Axiom is or whatever, then they bring out all the past donors from the school so we can clap for them, and the new donor is revealed. But the lights always stay on.

Seconds tick by. I hold my breath and feel, almost, like I'm underwater.

"What the hell is going on?" Norah whispers, and I'm glad I'm not the only one confused.

A loud screech splits the silence. I jump, thinking it's a gunshot or something. Lots of people around me gasp as well, but then immediately laugh at themselves. It was just microphone feedback over the loudspeaker. I catch my breath.

"And now, your final Drill Day of the school year," comes the low baritone of our principal.

Surrounded by blackness, a sliver of blue light appears on stage, bright enough to make me squint. It inches wider. Wider. The curtains must be parting. I look over and see the blue reflected in the whites of Sam's eyes.

Soft music plays, the sounds of wind chimes and trickling water. Then a slow, melodic piano. I think of Judith behind the keys. The prodigal daughter and her unparalleled mastery of music. The only time she's ever truly happy is when she plays that thing. You can see it in the way her juniper eyes shimmer with the rush of total rapture, the way her whole body moves with the art she's creating. Moving forward, it might be the one thing that gets her through the trauma of what happened to her.

The vast electric blue of the screen slowly fades and gives way to a giant eye. It's way zoomed in and takes up the entire screen, but it's obviously a human eye, still in someone's face. Open. The color is impossibly brilliant. It's this rich espresso color with flecks of peacock purple and bright lime green and smooth amber honey. The blood vessels on either side of the iris look like a roadmap, like the confusing highway system in Southern California. The eye blinks, and each individual eyelash is defined in amazing detail: thick, long, curved. The pupil expands as the lids open again, then constricts ever so slightly as it adjusts to the light.

The music fades out, and still the eye blinks. Over and over, it blinks. For an entire minute, nothing happens except the blinking and the dilation and contraction of the pupil. The colors seem to shift very faintly back and forth, as if there's a tiny tremor somewhere underneath, like the rumblings of an earthquake, but it's so slight that I could be making it up.

The silence is so thick in here, so palpable, I think I can hear Sam's heartbeat.

Finally, the screen cuts to black. A dull ache forms somewhere behind my eyes. I squeeze and massage them with my fingers, and when I open them, the lights in the auditorium are slowly fading up. There's nothing on stage. The curtains are open, but the TV is lifting higher and higher until it's out of sight.

My mind buzzes in the silence. Why were we forced to stare at an eye doing nothing but blinking? And *whose* eye was it? Someone we know? Someone from this school?

I turn to Norah, who's chewing on her hair again. When she notices me watching, she spits it out and whispers, "What the frick was that?"

Beyond Norah and Patrick's legs, I see Mel and Sari holding hands, resting atop Mel's lap. They're a couple who don't care about PDA, constantly cuddling each other in, say, a random corner of a hallway between classes, or even in Ink Stain, keeping their chairs as close together as possible, their legs wrapped around each other's.

But they're not just holding hands. There's something anxious about it. Some unfamiliar energy between them, their usual shared contentment replaced by the way Sari's long, burgundy nails dig into Mel's palms. Replaced by the way Mel taps her fingers on her other knee. I don't think they're normally like this on Drill Day.

A screech over the loudspeaker turns my attention to the stage. It's still empty. A giggle, as though whoever is about to speak is amused or embarrassed by the noise.

"Well, everyone, what do we think?" they say, with a thick and unmistakable French accent. "Was that the most beautiful work of art you have ever seen, or what?"

Heads turn, searching left and right for the source of the voice, but nothing. There are zero clues until the Watcher stationed at the stairs by the stage, standing still with her hands clasped at her waist, bows slightly and nods her head. But it wasn't her who spoke. It was whoever she's answering to.

Just a few seats down from Kent Cross, the woman at the end of the front row stands. Even from back here, I can see that the angle of her jaw is sharp enough to cut. Sharp enough to deflate the fluffy blonde bun nestled like a meringue at the crown of her skull. The bun is studded, polka-dotted, with small plastic eyes. She smiles at the Watcher, who steps aside to clear her path to the stairs.

As she slowly ascends, dramatically pausing on each step, I watch her hands. They're folded behind her, the wire-like fingers of one clutched around a metallic microphone. Her nails are studded with the same plastic eyes as her hair is.

When she's finally onstage, she struts across to the center of it in her shiny blue heels, her calves just as sharp as her jaw, below her pinstriped pencil skirt that perfectly matches her blazer.

She turns front and center, smiling wide with bright-white teeth, and I get this awful feeling in my chest. I feel as if I close my eyes, the ground is going to fall out from below me, or the ceiling is going to crack and the entire sky will cave in, and the Earth will fly into the sun. I look down to my lap to find my hand squeezing my thigh for dear life. But I barely register the jolts.

"That was such an inspiring movie, was it not?" the woman says. Her accent is thick but her voice is soft, even as it booms into the microphone. Norah quietly scoffs beside me, and I feel the same way. Inspiring? She must not have been watching the same thing we were. An eyeball blinking for an entire minute?

The woman straightens her back and adjusts her shoulders. As she scans the crowd, left to right, she smiles once more, but this time without showing her teeth. She lifts the microphone to her mouth and takes a deep breath.

"I see we are all a bit tired today. Let me not waste your time then. Some of you may know me already, if you have been generous enough to gift us a donation. I am Madame Berenice, Seer of your hospital's Donation Wing."

I wonder if Judith knows her, if this woman—who refers to herself as Madame, apparently—was there at the hospital on the day of her surgery. If she was, I didn't meet her, and I met so many people that day. Anesthesiologist. Surgeon. Nurse. Never this woman, though.

"I have the very distinct privilege of sharing a spectacular discovery with you all."

Movement from the corner of my eye. Patrick's knees dance up and down as he taps both of his feet. Norah is chewing her hair again. Mel and Sari's grips seem tighter than ever. I shift my gaze to the other side of me. Sam's eyes are closed, but he's clenching his jaw and slowly nodding his head as if counting something. Greta grasps the white walking cane folded on her lap like she's in battle and it's the only weapon she has.

They're all nervous that their names are going to be called. Except…this doesn't seem like typical nerves because I know without a doubt they would each just decline surgery. Refuse to sign their names, because you can still do that, even if they bribe you with millions of dollars. But by the looks of it, each one of them is freaking out, maybe experiencing the same sense of impending doom I was. About what, though? This announcement, whatever it is? Do they know something I don't?

All at once, movement on the stage. Madame Berenice saunters forward, high heels clicking. In seconds, she nears the edge of the stage, as if she plans to dive into the orchestra pit, and right before she does, she halts like she's slammed on her car brakes. I gasp as though I'd just seen her fall, as if I was really expecting her to. Patrick's knees stop bouncing. Mel and Sari's grips loosen. They were all thinking the same thing.

But Madame Berenice simply smiles. "Tell me something," she says. "If I were to tell you that Axiom has made the most wonderful discovery—something that would change *everything*—what would you say?"

I would tell her to stop ruining people's lives. To fuck off and go get hit by a bus. To go drown in the fucking ocean.

She smiles. Her teeth gleam in the lights. Well? Get on with it, lady.

"That video we showed to you, of the eye? Perhaps you will find it unbelievable when I tell you what the scientists at Axiom have done. That simply beautiful, vivid, and completely astounding eye you saw, which blinked exactly like normal and reacted to light in ways such that a natural eye would? I am excited to announce that we have discovered a way to build…to construct…to make from scratch…a human eye! An eye that takes in everything it sees and sends it to the brain to process information!"

She pauses with her arms outstretched beside her, a big grin plastered on her thin face. Nobody responds. What in the hell does she even mean?

After a few moments, she lowers her arms and rolls her shoulders back. Her eyes shift to Kent and linger for a moment. "I thought you might be a little more excited about this. Perhaps I am not explaining myself sufficiently."

She pivots on her heels and slowly walks away—*click, click, click*—and what a sense of relief, as if she's going away forever. I know she's not, but the temporary respite is tactile. I meet eyes with Sam and start to smile, but he puffs his cheeks, exhaling a steady stream of air.

I tilt my head. "What's wrong?"

"This is bad," he sighs.

"Very, very bad," says Norah.

Two years before I got my mother taken away from us, she screamed so loud I thought my ears would split. "This is *bad*, Alister. Very, very bad."

But my father ignored her like he was prone to doing and threw my six-year-old body up in the air for the fifth, tenth, twentieth time. I could barely breathe because I was laughing so hard—also because every time he caught me, his hands clutched my ribcage so hard I felt like I was about to break. But I didn't care. It was the most fun I'd ever had.

My mother shrieked and shrieked for him to stop, but at first, I thought she was laughing right along with me. It took me a while to realize she was scared of him. Scared he was going to hurt me. He'd started drinking in the afternoons by then. But he was fun, so I didn't really care too much.

"You're gonna kill him, you know that? You and your drunk ass are going to kill our baby."

I was screaming in my head at her, "I'm not a baby! I'm not a stupid crying baby!" But I couldn't make the words leave my mouth because I still couldn't breathe. It stopped being fun, and I wanted to make my dad stop, but I could not say a word. The pain in my ribs grew more with each catch, until I was sure he was killing me. Each time he threw me again, he made these stupid faces that were supposed to be funny but made him look like the devil instead.

Next thing I knew, I was throwing up all over him, midair. At the first sign of vomit, he recoiled, and so he didn't catch me, and I fell hard on the ground, banging up my knee real good. He tried to laugh it off, saying it was his own fault as he flung my puke off him, each one of his words slurring together like they were covered in glue. But it was the way my mother came to tend to me and not him that made me realize something had changed.

I don't have to puke now, but the consternation in Sam's face does turn my stomach a little.

"What's bad?" I whisper.

He looks over at Norah. So do I. She picks at a hangnail while silently staring at Sam. I repeat myself, but maybe one decibel louder.

"Jesus, Henry, don't scream at me," she whispers.

"Seriously, what is going on?"

Sam grips my shoulder, and as I shift my head toward him, my eyes rake over the stage. Madame Berenice is staring right at me. Or I think she is, she might not be. I could be imagining it. Oh, god. A tremor runs down my spine, down my legs, into my feet. I have to shake them out.

When she looks away, I feel cold. Hollow. As if with her gaze alone, she has scooped out all my insides. And what, if anything, is left of me?

Chapter Five

SAM SQUEEZES MY shoulder again. I swallow, though my mouth is dry—has it been dry?—and turn to him.

"Seriously, Axiom *made* an eye?" he says, defeated. "An artificial, lab-grown, like…fully-Axiom eyeball? Nah, I'm good, thanks anyway."

I search his face for more answers, but I can't find any. What I want to say is: yeah, Axiom is evil and wreaks havoc and destroys lives and all these things—I should know—but isn't this what they've been doing all this for? Medical breakthroughs? They finally found a major one. A cure for blindness. Maybe this means they'll stop taking our eyes.

But that would sound stupid—or worse, like I'm on their side. Like I'm betraying Judith for even thinking it. I imagine my web of scars and wish I could make a new strand, deeper and more beautiful than ever.

Madame Berenice's voice rings out. "We have revolutionized the Surgical Revolution!" Axiom's slogan. I saw it a lot in the hospital: on brochures and across the walls, even slapped on the headboard of Judith's bedframe. "Just when you think we couldn't become any more groundbreaking, we outdo ourselves yet again. We call it the Third Eye, and it's going to change the state of the world as we know it!"

As she goes on, I look again into Sam's eyes, dim like the night sky, and suddenly her words are so far away. They're across the globe. At the bottom of the sea. Buried underground. Maybe I should spend the rest of my life in these eyes so I never have to hear or see or feel anything else ever again.

A rattling noise pulls me away. Beside Sam, Greta fumbles around, reaches forward. She's dropped her cane. Sam goes to help, but she bats him away.

"I've got it, I've got it." She sits up again, cane in hand, and sighs quietly. "Did you hear what that lady said? Third Eye. What are we supposed to do, Sam?"

What does she mean, what are *we* supposed to do? Do about what? And "we" as in…her and Sam? Ink Stain? Me? I'm so confused. I want to ask, but Sam is staring intently at the stage, silent. I look too.

The spotlight exaggerates the sharp angles of Madame Berenice's face. "At last, your donations, as well as those we have received across this great land over the last several years, have culminated in this discovery. No longer will we be a sightless people, for we have cured the blind!"

In the front row, Kent Cross stands and claps. He raises his arms above his head, as though to ensure the entire auditorium sees him. My jaw stiffens. His clapping alone tells me this is bad. Some others join him from the first few rows until it's a scattered, disjointed applause.

Beside me, Norah rubs her eyes, squeezing tightly. "This cannot be happening."

For a moment, Madame Berenice nods as if to welcome the applause, but then she holds up her hands to make it stop.

"Time for business," she says with a conclusive nod. "While our Third Eye has proven effective in one hundred percent of subjects, we are still in need of our beloved donors to…test it out. We require the most comprehensive data possible."

I'm so confused. Do they plan to take our eyes like usual and put these new ones in, or "replace" the ones they already took out of people, like the sophomore? Like Judith?

"Furthermore, it is Axiom's hope to spread this amazing discovery to new lands, so as to help restore sight to the sightless. We wish for every soul on our precious Earth to really *see* each other—to see the world around them! Exciting, yes? Blindness shall be an affliction of the past. This is why we need your help."

I look over to Greta, hoping her face will tell me what she thinks about this—about the possibility of being able to see—but she is perfectly, perfectly still. Maybe it's because she's the most Zen person in the world. Whatever she's feeling, it's probably deep under the surface.

"In many ways, this is a typical Drill Day. Once I call their name, I will ask the candidate to join me on stage and to consider donating their eye for medical purposes. Then I will ask, for the first time ever, to be a part of history! To help your country like never before and receive the Third Eye!"

She claps for herself, and Kent and the other assholes join in. She must have been expecting the entire auditorium to erupt into applause because when she realizes the majority of us aren't clapping, her shoulders droop and she frowns. This is her first time doing Drill Day here. She may have done them at other schools, though, and I wonder if, elsewhere, people get more excited than we do here. I don't have any friends at other schools, so I have no way to know.

"Well then," she coughs, "time to find out who will be the lucky history maker."

Slowly, the giant TV screen lowers from the ceiling, still showing the same video of the blinking eye. Madame Berenice steps out of its way and turns to watch it, her hand preciously on her chest.

From either side of the stage, two Watchers appear, which is odd. Watchers don't come onstage. This Third Eye is changing everything. And these particular Watchers are *big*. Their legs. Arms. Necks. Big, big, big. They march, backs arched to make their huge chests even wider, batons bouncing against their tree-trunk thighs. Madame Berenice's nostrils flare as she looks between them, and when they frame her like giant stone gargoyles, her grin returns.

Movement stage left. Our principal walking out from backstage. A short, balding man with dark bags under his eyes, he gives a terse nod and sits in a small folding chair at the back corner. He is so small, so inconsequential in this moment. There's no reason for him to be here.

Now the familiar silence and anticipation. The quiet almost hums, like the buzz of a bright fluorescent light. It's so quiet, I hear the squelch of Patrick swallowing saliva. Sari is quietly sniffling, trying her best to hide it. Sam's nose whistles as he draws in a deep breath.

I want to tell each of them that their names aren't going to be called, so they don't need to be nervous. It'll be somebody who has already had their eye taken out so Axiom can "restore" them with the Third Eye and claim they did them a favor. It's so obvious, I don't know why they don't see it.

Or maybe I'm wrong. Didn't Madame Berenice just say they want to spread this thing globally? I look over to Greta, her eyes darting left, right, left, right.

And now I know what everyone is freaking out about.

Not Greta, sweet, sweet Greta, who doesn't take anyone's shit. Who sticks up for herself when assholes mock her walking stick in the hallway. Who writes such amazing poetry and offers the best feedback on my own. Who shares heartfelt and beautiful stories about her childhood in Austria with her grandmother.

But how can it be Greta when she just said that international students are exempt from all this? That there would be outright war if Axiom even tried? No, it can't be her. Which leads me back to my first thought. Somebody who's already had their name called once before. Maybe even Judith, if she were here.

Beside me, Norah squeezes the tops of her thighs. Something I would do. But I doubt she's doing it for the same reason; I think she's just nervous.

Oh my god. Fuck. I remember something. It's Norah's birthday. She's eighteen.

Sometimes, Axiom likes to choose seniors who are eighteen because they don't need parental consent. They offer extravagant bribes knowing a high school kid is more inclined to take it. They whisk them straight away to the hospital, and the parent doesn't get notified until it's too late.

I look up into her eyes, but she doesn't notice me.

I can't believe I forgot my best friend's birthday. She had to repeat the sixth grade, so while most of us turn seventeen our junior year, she already has. Why didn't she say anything? Why didn't anyone else? Worst of all, how in the fuck could I forget something like that?

But I can punish myself later. Right now, I close my eyes and try my best at telepathy. *Norah will be fine, Greta will be fine, Norah will be fine, Greta will be fine.* I scream it in my mind as my ears listen for Madame Berenice to utter a name. But a name never comes, so I keep on screaming, keep on hoping I'm right. Maybe I'm right. Maybe—

My eyes fling open. There's something warm in my hand. I look down to see…another hand. In mine. I follow the forearm up to his bicep, his shoulder, his neck, his face, because I don't believe it. Sam. Oh, this hand. It's the same size as mine, but more substantial. More *real.* Where my fingers are bony, ghastly, his are thick. Where mine are so cold—always so, so cold—his are warm, like fire.

He's staring at me with eyes so wide and misty they suck me in. He looks…scared? Maybe he really does care for me, more than I thought, more than just a friend. I have a quick flash of maybe, just maybe, my poem being a success, where he stands breathlessly and kisses me. Where we…

A few people in front of us turn around to look. Some of them I recognize. One gives me awkward glances, like she's caught me fangirling over Sam. I'm so embarrassed.

Then more and more turn. Some meet my eyes, some turn away. The ones who do meet my eyes look at me with pity, as if…

One second.

Two seconds.

Three.

Four.

It's not until Norah takes my other hand that I realize what's happening. Why they're staring.

I look up to the TV screen. No longer is there the blinking eye. It's a head-to-toe shot of whose eye it belongs to.

It's me.

My breath lodges in my throat. Time, it seems, is not a real thing anymore, because am I even alive? Am I dreaming? Everything is frozen. Everything is fading.

I'm confused. Me? I don't even wear glasses. I mean, as far as things being wrong with me, vision is not one of them. My eyesight is fucking perfect. If you're going to cure blindness, why not start with a blind or half-blind person *you made that way?* It doesn't make any sense.

Also, this video. This *fucking* video. When did they record me—during the scan today? I don't get it. On the screen, it's some depiction of me, maybe graphics or special effects. Something. I'm just standing there against a white backdrop, completely still.

But I can't deny that my right eye is…gorgeous. So much brighter and more intense than the left. That's how I know for sure it's some kind of simulation.

My throat is dry. I'm mouth breathing. About to choke on a sob if I don't control myself. Sari's sniffles turn into full-blown tears. Sam and Norah both squeeze my hands tighter and tighter, until my bones are on the verge of crumpling in on themselves. Patrick reaches across Norah to squeeze my knee.

"What has happened?" Greta whispers. Sam leans over to tell her. She gasps, and tears form curtains over her eyes. The nystagmus and her emotions marry in some awful amalgamation to make them dart and dance this way and that, in hysterics. She rocks back and forth, back and forth, muttering in German. Perhaps praying to whatever god she thinks can save me.

"Henry, look at me." Norah. Her eyes are desperate, clawing their way into mine. "You don't have to go. You sit right here. Don't you dare. Don't you dare, Henry Youngwell, do you hear me? That bitch did *not* call your name. It's nothing. It's just a stupid fucking video. It doesn't mean anything."

I forgot her birthday, and still she's worried about me? I've never deserved her. Besides, she's wrong, of course. I do have to go.

"Happy birthday," I mutter.

She shakes her head. "What are you—"

She's interrupted by Patrick, who groans as he leans forward with his head between his knees, like he's going to be sick or something. The dozens of twists on his head shake this way and that as his shoulders heave. He's the kind of guy who would volunteer for me if that were possible. I mean, I know I wanted to volunteer for Judith, but at least that argument would have made sense—we have the same DNA. But Patrick? That wouldn't even cross his mind. *Nothing* would cross his mind; he'd just do it. Oh, my friend's in trouble? Here, let me take his place.

There are no theatrics with Mel. Stoic, statuesque Mel. With her jaw clenched, she nods once, solemnly, as if paying her respects to a dead man. Sari, melted into Mel's shoulder, can't look at me. She's too busy wailing. Too swallowed by her grief. And this could break me, this alone. I love Sari, but I'm not *that* close with her. To see her reacting like this is maybe worse than the actual thought of having my eye out.

"Don't go, Henry. Please," Norah chokes, pulling me back to her. As if I have a choice, as if a Watcher wouldn't drag me up there. And I realize, *this* is the actual worst thing. My best friend's desperation. Her brokenness.

I can't help wondering what Judith would do if she were here. She might just sit there silently, like I did for her. Maybe she would think I deserve this because I didn't stand up for her. And she'd be right. That's what my friends don't get. That's why I have to do this. I'm going to sign the consent. *They* wouldn't if they'd been chosen—and I'm so fucking glad they have that resolve. But it's not them up on that screen, and this is what I have to do.

A part of me knows that makes no sense, that getting my eye taken out and this Third Eye put in isn't going to change what happened to Judith. But the truth remains the same. I deserve this. And my time is running out.

"Henry Youngwell, would you please come to the stage now."

Madame Berenice has her hand placed over her eyes like a visor, searching for me in a theatrical way. Apparently, when I thought she was looking at me earlier, she actually wasn't. Or maybe she was, but she didn't know who I was.

I glance over at the principal, who's looking straight at me. Is this why he didn't expel me this morning? Because Axiom told him I'd been chosen, and he didn't want to give me two blows in one day? His face doesn't betray a single emotion. He's so used to seeing new kids, month by month, get their lives turned upside-down that I wonder if he feels anything anymore. I'm glad he doesn't point me out to Madame Berenice, though. Maybe this is his little act of penance. His tiny way of rebelling against the powers above him.

Norah clutches me so tight, it's like she's trying to break my hand. I try to let go of her, but then she grabs my elbow with her other hand. I don't understand what she wants me to do. Stay? If I did, one of those Watchers would just drag me up there. Better to go with whatever dignity I can pretend to have left.

She pulls me into an embrace, hot tears scalding as they fall onto my neck. Patrick reaches around Norah's body to hug me too, his arms long enough to pull me in and sandwich Norah with him.

"You'll be all good, bro," he says. "Don't even sweat it." Maybe he's right.

"Be seeing you soon," Mel says, reaching out for my arm.

I realize they all know I'll agree to it. Where I have always known they wouldn't, because they've said so, they somehow know I will. They're acting like it, anyway. Norah being so emotional, clingy. Sari sobbing. Mel talking like I'm dying. But how do they know? Maybe they just figure I'll do it because I'm so poor—because even though we have a new house, that doesn't mean we have money now. I would almost be offended if the logic didn't add up so well. Or maybe they know the dark places my mind can go.

Reluctantly, I pull away. It's not that I want to go. It's not that I want to devastate my friends. It's that I have to do this so the universe—my karma or whatever—will be aligned again.

My other hand is still in Sam's. I've been holding it this whole time. I don't let go. This—this I want to hold on to. Remain here for. When he looks into both of my eyes now, for maybe the last time, I wonder if he can see the questions running through me. *Do you like me, the same way I like you? Will you still, even after my surgery, even after I've been mangled and maimed? Every time you look at me, will you only see the part of me that's fake? That's been branded? The part of me that isn't Henry?*

Tears spill from his eyes, and I cannot reach in for a hug. I just can't.

I'll lose it. I'll never let go. Watchers will have to pry me away from him.

Instead, I raise his fingers to my lips and kiss them. My poem, but in a single gesture. Please be here, after. Please.

Please.

Chapter Six

I STAND AND somehow don't fall over, even though my knees are shaking. As I sidestep my way to the aisle, Greta reaches out to touch my leg.

"Be strong, my Henry," she says. I reach down and give her hand a squeeze, but don't say anything because I'm very aware that even though my feet are on solid ground, I could melt away any second. And I'm more liable to do that if I speak.

I hold my breath as I stride toward the stage, my heartbeat thudding in my chest. My ears. It feels like I'm marching to my execution.

The Watcher standing guard by the steps juts out her chin and tightens her grip on her baton, prepared in case I try to lunge for her or something. Nobody would be that stupid, but I guess there's always a first. Just looking at it, I imagine her slamming it into me. My bones pulverize. Arteries burst. Sweet justice for all the things I've done. And haven't.

Almost every head in here is turned toward me like I'm the belle of the ball, and they're here to watch me find my prince. It happens every time, to every person called. Most of us gawk with no semblance of shame or decency, like the mouth breathers we are. We want to see how they react— if they'll cause a scene. We don't want to miss a second. I've been guilty of it too.

I count at least three kids who have patches, but that's just at a quick glance around. One of them nods at me, a girl I barely recognize. How can I not even tell who she is? I have the vague feeling she had her surgery last year. I wonder if she'll be getting the Third Eye too.

But wait, shouldn't she and the rest of those with patches be Axiom's priority, if their goal really is to cure blindness? Why was someone who doesn't even wear glasses chosen?

There's one person who isn't looking at me. Kent Cross. Good. I hope he feels like shit. I hope now that he knows I'm about to join my sister, he's filled with shame for what he called her this morning. There's no way he would ever have the balls to say that to someone who *did* get their eye out. If he never looks at me again, it'll be too soon.

As I ascend the stairs, the edges of my vision burn in and out. Madame Berenice watches me with lust in her eyes, practically salivating, like I'm a delicious meal being brought to her.

Behind her, on the TV screen, is me. I watch myself, and myself watches I. With my new bright eye, I'm almost handsome.

I look down at my feet and wonder if any of this is real. I'm watching my shoes make contact with the wood of the stage, but I can't feel them at all. It feels like I'm floating. Or rather, it doesn't feel like anything at all. It's like a dream or a hallucination. Like one huge cosmic delusion.

I realize I don't know where I'm supposed to stand, and this small detail, this little awkward moment, magnified by two thousand people watching, makes me remember that *all* of this is real.

Madame Berenice doesn't direct me. It's a Watcher who does. The one on the right steps away and indicates for me to take his place. When I do, he pulls a microphone out of his pocket, turns it on, and hands it to me. My hand shakes as I take it.

I refuse to turn toward the audience. Maybe it's because I'm embarrassed. Maybe I'm afraid of throwing up with all these eyes on me. Either way, I stand facing this woman in front of me instead, whose pale skin glows like a ghost.

Her face is more angular than it appeared from afar, her cheekbones high and pointed, her jaw sharp. She's thin-shouldered. The plastic eyes studding her blonde bun are cartoonish. She holds the microphone right up to her lips, like an ice cream cone.

"Hello, Henry. How are you?"

Of all the questions she could have asked me, why does this one throw me off guard?

"I—um—fine," I stammer into the microphone. Fine?

I look down at my shoes again and focus on the vomit splatter from this morning that I never cleaned off.

"Tell me something, Monsieur. How do you feel being the first in your school, and among the first in the nation, to be offered a chance to change the course of history?"

I don't lift my gaze while I think of what to say. I know the game she's playing. She works for Axiom; she has to pretend they're a benevolent company doing the most good for the most people. Look at what they've just invented. Look how they've proven that what they've been doing all these years *is* a good thing!

The rest of us are also players. The government plays along because they get money. Donors play along because we get rewards. And everybody else—the ones on the sidelines, the bystanders and spectators—they play along too, with their obedience. Their silence. If they don't, they could get their eyes taken out. They will end up like the sophomore. Because even if we delude ourselves into thinking we have a choice, even if Axiom claims we have free will…do we really? They'll find a way; they always do. Take the sophomore, who was conveniently chosen as a donor immediately following the Drill Day he skipped. Somehow, it would be even worse if someone were to speak out against them.

And while it's true that donors are legally allowed to decline the surgery, I've never heard of someone actually doing so. I imagine it's hard to refuse when you're offered things like riches or a new house for your eye.

I'm very glad my friends think they have a much stronger willpower than I seem to, though. I want to believe they actually *would* say no. I want to believe that so much for them. But I'm not sure anybody's that strong. Are they? Or am I so fucking weak that I think everyone else must be too?

But even if I am wrong, and someone would refuse…Axiom would find a way to get that eye. Of course they would.

That's why I wouldn't say no even if I wanted to. And right now, I'm more sure than I've ever been, of anything, that I want to do this.

But still, to admit it out loud—to play along in front of everybody and pretend that I'm fine with what they did to Judith, to so many of my classmates—feels like a betrayal. My chin quivers. What I wouldn't give to dig my nails into my thigh right now. I imagine what it would be like to scream in this woman's face. *See this, Madame? This is what the game makes me do to myself.* Like she would care. Like she wouldn't just laugh in my face.

"It's a lot to think about," I say, neither giving in nor straying away. Playing safe. Neutral.

She looks down to the microphone at my side and nods at it, urging me to repeat myself into it, so that everyone else can be witness to my strategy. I didn't even notice I'd dropped it. When I do, she giggles in a soft but measured way and sighs heavily into her own mic. She saw my tactic from a mile away.

"This is fair," she says, and pauses. Purses her lips as if to think, deep grooves forming in the skin around her mouth. "I would have perhaps thought you would be excited to be an integral part of rolling out the Third Eye."

She pauses again, as if waiting for me to ask why. I don't give her the satisfaction, but she doesn't seem to care. She tells me anyway.

"Have you considered, Monsieur, it might just help your sister to return to normal? To allow her both eyes once more?"

A long shiver runs up my body, but I try not to let it show. How can she just bring her up so casually?

"Ah, yes," she exclaims, her eyes so wide they're almost lidless. She knew I wouldn't be expecting her to bring up Judith—and why wouldn't I? Only an idiot wouldn't. She turns to face the audience and smiles. "For those who may not know Henry Youngwell personally, I shall inform you that his beautiful twin sister, Judith, was chosen as your school's most recent donor on this previous Drill Day. And I believe she is still at home recovering from her surgery, taking the recommended week off school, am I correct?"

I nod, but she isn't happy with it. She glances down at my microphone again.

"Yes," I say into it. I hate the way my voice sounds over this thing. It's normally high-pitched, but because my throat is so dry, it also comes out scratchy. Whiny.

Madame Berenice furrows her brows, as if pondering something. "But if she was chosen last month, and she is taking *this week* to recover, then this must mean she waited to gift us with her donation until—" She pauses to think, rolling her eyes to one side, as if she doesn't already know. "—last weekend?"

"Saturday," I say.

"Why so long?" she asks pointedly. I know where she's going, but I'm unsure how to veer the conversation elsewhere.

"We were waiting for our new house to be completed," I say slowly. My father specifically had it added to the contract that they could not touch Judith until after the house was built and the keys were handed over. The construction workers must have worked day and night under the threat of getting their eyes cut out if they so much as sat down to rest. I'm not sure how else they could have managed to construct an entire house in so little time.

It had been a long time since I'd seen him smile, my father. Months, maybe. But the moment we walked into the house, after Judith was discharged and Axiom sent a moving van to pack up our apartment because we couldn't afford to even buy boxes, the way his face lit up is burned into my brain. His unfettered joy unrecognizable while I helped Judith up the stairs and into her new bedroom. It was as if his only daughter hadn't just been mutilated. As if, now unbothered by rent or a light bill, he had no concerns in the world anymore.

"Ah, yes, that's right," says Madame Berenice. "A cautious man. I certainly can't fault him for that."

I would love to go into the many faults of my father, but this isn't the time. Instead, it's my turn to ask a question, because if she's going to interview me, why can't I do the same? I take a deep breath and lock my knees when they start to buckle.

I hold the mic too close to my mouth, my shaky breath booming like thunder. "How long have you had the Third Eye prototype?"

Madame Berenice doesn't blink, doesn't even dream of shying away, before she looks out into the audience and smiles. "How sweet of you to ask. I'm glad you are showing interest. While this has been several years in the making, the first fully functioning Third Eye was developed about six months ago now. And we are so delighted to move on to the next phase of our trials. That's where you come in, Henry—we hope."

Through my nerves, I crank my head to the side and look out into the audience. The sea of faces. I search for my friends while trying to ignore the rest of these eyes staring at me and stripping me down. I find them pretty quickly and lock eyes with Norah.

"What the—" she mouths, her face screwed into a knot. It gives me the strength I was looking for to ask the next question.

"And for the last six months," I say, avoiding Madame Berenice's eyes, "why have you been taking people's donations? I mean, why my sister, after you finally found the cure you were working so hard to find?"

She shrugs. "Simple. Blindness is one of *many* ailments which we hope to cure." She turns toward the video, which, at her gesture, zooms in again. "Inside the eyeball are the secrets to life, and we will not stop until we have found them all. This is why you are the perfect candidate,

Monsieur. Our scanners have found your eye to contain a gene which will aid our team of researchers to help fight disease."

Perhaps I don't look convinced. She looks me up and down and smiles weakly.

"On top of this, you will be helping us to refine the Third Eye so that we can restore normalcy to Judith. How exquisite does this sound?"

She doesn't look to me for an answer. Instead, she leans forward to peer over my shoulder at—who? The Watcher behind me? Before I can look for myself, whoever it is shouts across the stage. "Sounds good to me!"

It's not a Watcher. I would recognize the rough, gravelly voice anywhere. It slides down the back of my neck and makes me cringe.

Of course, my father is here.

Air falls out of my chest as the finality of this hits me. They brought him here so he can sign the consent form and they can take me into surgery as soon as possible.

He didn't appear last month when Judith was chosen, so it didn't even cross my mind that he'd be here. If the donor is under eighteen, what normally happens is Axiom escorts the donor home to obtain a signature from the parents. I guess with a new type of donation comes a new protocol.

In the audience, both Norah's and Sam's eyes are wide. So, so wide. As wide as the empty seat between them.

"Welcome, Alister Youngwell! We are so glad you are able to be here." Madame Berenice beams, her eyes alight, her smile wide.

My father claps me on the shoulder as he takes his place next to me. I don't look at him because maybe I'm imagining it, and if I look him in the face, then I'll know I'm not. So I burn my eyes into Madame Berenice, the woman who is so happy to see me suffer. Her smile is firm and blank as she resists the urge to look him up and down, to examine and judge him the way she would if she weren't on stage right now. The same way everybody does. His grayish skin and sallow eyes. His wispy eyebrows, blowing with every breath he takes. His carved-out temples and hollow cheeks. His skeleton limbs juxtaposed by the paunch of his swollen abdomen.

He takes the microphone from me, and I smell the sour breath he has tried to mask with toothpaste. He puts his arm around my shoulders, and I can't escape the odor oozing from his pits and every pore in his body as he recovers from another long night of getting wasted. When the stench finally hits Madame Berenice too, she cringes and takes a few steps backward, as if the giant Watcher on her other side will jump in and shield her from it.

My father's voice cracks when he starts to speak, so he clears his throat and goes again. "I'm thrilled my boy's been chosen! Thank you *so* much for inviting me. You know, when one of your men came to the house to tell me the good news—uh, you see, our phone's been broken—" Lie. None of us Youngwells, including him, have a phone. "—well, you couldn't keep me away. I did have some work to finish up, but I came right on over." Another lie. The only job my father has is manipulating me into giving him a cut of every paycheck I earn.

Yet, even through his lies, there's an unusual inflection in his voice. Similar to the night we moved in, it's one of genuine joy, of unfamiliar pleasure, like he truly is happy to be here. And I suppose he is. First a house, and now something else—whatever he wants. Two kids, back to back? It might be the first time in history. If I were him, I'd feel on top of the world. Maybe he'll get a small fortune this time. A new car. An endless supply of vodka—but the good stuff. None of that cheap, bottom-shelf junk.

"We certainly appreciate your making time," says Madame Berenice with a placating smile, folding her hands around her mic. She takes a moment to step away and walk across the stage, surveying the crowd as if to remind me that everybody is watching, that everybody knows who my father is. Where I come from.

I glance at my friends, at Sam leaning over my empty seat to whisper something to Norah. My skin prickles as it remembers the touch of his hand.

My father hugs me closer. Softly, I try to shrug him away, but he refuses. He whispers into my ear, his stench like a cloud around me.

"So proud of you, boy. Your mother would be too."

I picture myself elbowing him in the face. Stomping on his feet. Slamming him to the floor and making him say it again in front of everybody. It feels euphoric, to beat him within an inch of his miserable life. How many times I've dreamed of doing it. And if we weren't in public, I like to think I would.

The euphoria fades just as quickly as it came, though. I would never. I did punch Kent this morning, but that was different. He insulted Judith. And also, Kent is not my father. Kent is not the only parent I have left after I got my mother taken away from us.

Madame Berenice's voice rings out. "So, Henry, it would appear your father is ready to see his only son on the right side of history." She turns and squares her shoulders at me, her eyes narrowed, her jaw clenched. "How about you? Are you ready to join us?"

As if the decision to not go through with it——to keep both of your eyes——is to be on the *wrong* side of history.

Sam is upright in his seat now, and when I meet his eyes, he nods. A sense of dread grows in my stomach because I don't know what it means. Does he *want* me to agree to the Third Eye now? Maybe that's what he was talking to Norah about—it's inevitable now my dad's here. Or maybe the nod was his way of saying, *It's all right. I'll be here no matter what.*

I do not want to cry on stage, but the tears form behind my eyes. Maybe I should let them out. This might be the last time I'll get to cry with both of them anyway.

Movement. Madame Berenice is waving her hand, trying to get my attention. "Are you still with us?" she laughs. I catch her exchange a brief glance with one of the Watchers, a thousand words unspoken. I wonder what the Watcher behind my father and me is doing right now.

"Don't be rude, son," whispers my father, squeezing my shoulders tighter and tighter. I see bruises up and down his forearm, some black and purple, others old and yellow, from running into things over the weeks and months. He nudges me to turn toward him before he lets go and flashes a smile wide enough to show his missing premolar.

We're the exact same height, him and me. Not even an inch differ-ence. Judith too. It's creepy. Mom was the tall one, I think—taller than Dad. It's been nine years, so my memory could be playing tricks on me. I just remember her always seeming so big, so important.

I stare into my dad's dirty-dishwater eyes, hoping he can see the anger in mine. But his smile doesn't falter.

"Answer the nice lady, Hen-Hen," he says, and I cringe at the nick-name, one he hasn't used since I was ten. "You know what you need to say."

I gaze past Madame Berenice, standing there at the edge of the stage, with her eyeball-studded bun and her tight-lipped smile, and find the row with all my friends in the world. Greta all the way down to Sari. I can't look into their eyes or else I'll shatter into a million pieces, so I just stare at the row of their necks, the collars of their shirts.

All I can think as I watch some of their shoulders heave, some of their chins quiver, some of their hands ball up into fists, is that I'm the luckiest coward in the world to have found them. The luckiest fucking idiot. And I have to pry my eyes away.

Madame Berenice's eyes are so dark yet so ablaze, they remind me of a pitch-black room lit only by a match, most everything swallowed by shadow. She must sense that I'm about to give my answer because she points behind me to the microphone in my father's hand. He gives it to me, and I raise it to my lips with the steadiest hands I've maybe ever had.

"Yes," I say. "I'm ready."

Silence, then the sound of sobbing. I've heard Sari's wails enough today to know it's her. Then there's more, like someone else joining in, but I don't look. I can't.

Madame Berenice grins through it, as if she can't hear the grief. She grins like the rest of her life is just beginning, nods like she's just closed a deal. And she has. She struts over to the Watcher, who pulls out a tablet from the deep pocket of his pants and hands it to her. My contract.

She flicks the screen to life, its bright light reflecting in her eyes like morning sunlight on the ocean.

I close my eyes, and through no choice of my own, I'm on the beach. The waves roar in my ears. The salt fills my nose and lungs. Judith is here. She has two bright and gorgeous eyes the color of wild juniper. She's burying me in the sand, determined to cover every inch of me.

"Not your brother's head, sweetum," my mother calls from her beach chair, her voice as raspy as usual. "And careful of the wind, or you'll get sand in his eyes." Judith obeys, being very deliberate and careful.

We've just driven across the country after my dad got taken away by the ambulance. We're both restless but very careful to be on our best behavior.

Mom's eating the trail mix she brought for us. She knows I only like the M&M's. But those are Judith's favorite too, so we always have to split them, which is the most annoying thing in the world. Mom eats everything else—the salty, bitter parts we think are gross.

After a while, when Mom's not looking, Judith gets more careless with the sand, shoving it in piles across my chest, flinging it in a way that it flies into my eyes. It stings worse than even the eye drops when I had pink eye, but I can't let Judith know it hurts because she would do it more. It's in my mouth, gritty and nasty between my teeth. It's making my mouth taste bitter and throat feel so dry. I want to kill Judith, and it's not the first time I've thought this. She's so mean sometimes.

I see Mom's shadow move as she stands before I hear her voice. "Kids, look!" She's pointing out to the ocean. "Henry, sweetie, look out there!" I turn my head. "Henry!" Her voice carries, as though echoing off the waves. "Do you see them, Henry? Henry." My mother's voice trails away with the wind. "Henry. Henry. Henry."

No, not my mother.

"The hell is wrong with you, boy?"

The harsh lights of the auditorium fade back in. I squint through the brightness, aware again that there are two thousand sets of eyes on me. Two thousand people just watched me remember one of my most horrific memories. Was Sam watching? Norah? I've never told them the details of my mother's last day with us.

My father's brows are furrowed as he repeats himself in a hush. "What's *wrong* with you?"

Madame Berenice stands just a couple of feet from me now. She chuckles while my mind and vision focus, and I wonder if *she* knows what I did. Or maybe she's only laughing because she finds all of this amusing—finds pleasure in torturing me. Torturing all of us. It's not the first time I've thought that must be Axiom's end goal: grief. Despair. Although, if they truly have discovered this new cure for blindness, they must have the best intentions, even if their means to an end is horrible.

My father takes the tablet from her, and I see my name filled in on one of the lines, the words LEFT-SIDED ENUCLEATION WITH THIRD EYE TRANSPLANT on another. Not far below that, a dollar sign and more zeros than I've ever dreamed of. This is what I'm worth to him. I wonder how much negotiation there was backstage before he agreed to let them have their way.

And yet even though the contract needs my father's signature because I'm under eighteen, it also needs mine. That's why they can't just negotiate with the parents and drag the kid away. They need to appeal to both parties. It's a provision under the law, because when the government passed it, they needed to pretend to have *some* semblance of decency, I suppose.

"Look good to you?" Madame Berenice asks into the mic, then holds it up to my father's mouth.

"Indeed, it does," he says. Then, like it's no big deal at all, he signs his name with his finger, his signature crooked and sloppy.

Madame Berenice claps, and it's clear she expects uproarious applause—the contract of the century! But again, she must not realize that at this school, we don't tend to get excited about one of our own getting butchered. Even if they're getting a small fortune in return. One person might, and I look out to the front row to see his reaction, but Kent stares down at his phone, the light of his screen shining up on his face. He couldn't care one way or the other. Neither could the principal, who has his legs crossed now and impatiently taps his foot. I'm sorry this isn't going as fast as you'd like it to, sir.

My father, on the other hand, is all smiles. All grease. His oily face shines brilliantly under the lights, and his grubby fingers have left smears on the tablet. As he hands it to me, I wonder if it'll slip out of my hand. It doesn't. I wonder the same when he takes the microphone from me, which I've just realized as he does so that I've been holding on to this whole time. I could have used it to smash in Madame's face, the Watchers', and my father's.

My father's gravelly voice booms through the auditorium. "We are so excited to help you in this small way, and thank you so, so much for all that you do."

Small way? What *small way* is that?

"Why, of course!" Madame Berenice beams. "All we need now is your signature, Monsieur, and we will be on our way to healing the world!"

A loud sniffle from the crowd. Sari. A couple others. Without thinking, I look over, and each one of my friends is crying, or in some state of tears. Sari is no longer wailing, but through the dim light out there, I can see her cheeks are puffy. Even Mel and Patrick's eyes are shiny. Norah might have been crying, but right now she shakes her head slowly from side to side, as though to warn me not to sign the contract. Sam and Greta hold hands, and I watch painfully as Sam's shoulders heave, as Greta wipes her cheeks with the back of her wrist.

Madame Berenice notices them too. "Ah, so your friends are concerned, are they?" she says, and I seize with fear. I can't believe I'm stupid enough to be *staring* at them. I can't believe *they're* stupid enough to cry. Especially Sari with all her sobbing. With one glance to the Watcher, Madame Berenice could have them silenced. Removed.

But she doesn't. At least not right now. She walks toward the stage and waves to them. "Oh, friends! Please, you mustn't worry. We will take good care of your buddy, Henry. We have the very best surgeons in the world, and he will be back to school in no time. It will be okay!"

How fucking fake. If there weren't two thousand witnesses here, she wouldn't be as pleasant.

The stench of foul breath pulls me away as she keeps talking, keeps smiling, keeps trying to placate them.

"Hen-Hen. You will not embarrass me like this. Be a good boy and do the right thing."

I take a step back and size up my father. How dare he try and guilt me into doing this. I should refuse just to spite him. I should rob him of this money, burn down the house, and move away with Judith. I look down at the tablet in my hand and think about smashing it over his head.

He smirks. "Besides, you can't let Jude keep on being the ugly twin. How about you do it for her, huh?"

Something bigger than rage consumes me—this primordial instinct to attack him—and it's too strong, too present, too real, to ignore.

I yell. Open my jaw and scream. My stomach somersaults as I lunge for him, smash the tablet into his neck, and toss it aside. He recoils and ducks for cover, one hand over his throat, the other outstretched. I smack it away and lift my knee to thrust it into his side, but something barrels into me and pushes me to the floor instead.

It feels like an elephant is on top of me, and I become aware that it's a Watcher crouching over me. He has my trunk and each of my limbs pinned to the floor effortlessly, like I'm a piece of paper he's dropped and he has stopped me from blowing away in the wind. I look up into his face, and his sunglasses have flown off. Staring back at me are two very different eyes—one a dull brown and the other a rich espresso with flecks of amber and swirls of peacock purple. Just like the one in the video. He has a Third Eye.

I have this sudden realization that he's going to kill me. And I think I might be okay with it.

But he doesn't. He looks behind him for a few moments, then gets off me, standing up just as quickly as we fell. I stay where I am, as if I'm trying to make a snow angel and I've forgotten how to move.

Madame Berenice comes into view. She extends her hand for me to grab and says something I can't hear.

"Huh?" I ask as she pulls me up, my throat scratchy and dry, my leg aching from being pummeled down.

She enunciates. "I said, Monsieur, you have a spark within you. It is admirable indeed. And very, very dangerous."

Chapter Seven

"WHAT SORT OF music do you enjoy, Monsieur?"

Through the open roof of her convertible, I'm watching palm trees float by when she asks. She reaches for the touchscreen on her dashboard to select a song, but I shrug, unsure of how to answer. I'm still too confused. Madame Berenice is driving me home. Like, really?

Madame Berenice—the Seer of Axiom or whatever she's called—is driving me home. I, Henry Youngwell, was selected as the donor, and now Madame Berenice is driving me home. Usually, a Watcher does it. But I guess I'm special.

At first, I thought she was lying. She *said* she was taking me home, but I really thought she would fly me straight to the hospital. But this is the same route the bus takes, so at least there's a chance she'll stay true to her word. I just hate that she's the one doing it. I think I would prefer a wordless Watcher.

The contract was nullified because I destroyed the tablet. And after I attacked my father, he had to be examined by the school nurse, so Madame Berenice couldn't draw up a new one with a new tablet. I could tell she was getting antsy, and instead of waiting around for my father to be given the go-ahead, she decided she would just take me home. I suggested staying at school and finishing up my classes, but it was out of the question. No donor has ever stayed at school after they were chosen. I think Axiom is too afraid they'll either run or get talked out of surgery by their peers.

Judith's case was a little different. After last Drill Day, Watchers were stationed outside of our apartment for three weeks while Axiom built us the new house. They rotated on twelve-hour shifts to make sure Judith never left. She wasn't allowed to go to school or even work for the same reason; they didn't want the outside world to influence her decision. But they couldn't just keep her out of school for that long, so the Watchers let her use a tablet to attend livestreamed classes—but only while they watched her like a hawk from across the room. They wouldn't let her use it during breaks or after school.

As for her job, there was no way for her to go in, even though she begged. The Watchers provided her a phone to call in sick for each of her shifts, but she was forbidden from saying more than "I'm sick, I can't come in." Then a few days *before* her surgery, she received an official letter of termination in the mail, citing continued absenteeism. By that time, of course, word of Drill Day had spread, and we knew the real reason she was fired.

"How about this?" asks Madame Berenice, turning up the volume. The sound of trombones and a low guitar fills my ears, light jazz at its finest. I'm not a jazz person, but Norah's parents are. I used to go over to her house all the time when we were kids, and jazz was always playing instead of the sound of a TV.

I don't say anything. I'm going to try very hard on this entire ride to say as little as possible, so I stare out the window instead. I trace the tops of the distant mountains with my eyes as we sail by, palm trees in the foreground grazing the cloudless, pale-blue sky—fat palm trees with big, scruffy necks and the skinny minis, thin like straws waiting to suck up the rain whenever it finally decides to come to Southern California. It's such a beautiful day outside. Such a shame. I feel like this beauty is wasted in the kind of world we live in.

The music fades into a trumpet solo that lasts for several minutes as we cruise down the long stretches of road, the light traffic of an early afternoon not quite dense enough to be irritating yet.

I think about absolutely nothing as we drive. Whenever something pops into my head, I force it out. I deserve to be thoughtless for a while.

Eventually, the music fades into silence, and Madame Berenice switches off the radio entirely before it goes to a new song.

"I'm not going to ask you why you hit your father, Henry, if that's what you're worried about."

"I'm not." I don't mean to cross my arms, but I do.

"All right," she says, "then what *are* you worried about? I sense a little…trepidation."

There are a hundred things I want to ask. Why did I get chosen? Why did Judith? What's the Third Eye, and why were my friends freaking out about it? What happens now? Do I have to pay for a new tablet since I destroyed the other one? Did I really hurt my father, like seriously injure him?

"I have a physics exam next week," I lie. I don't know why; I think I'm just afraid to say the wrong thing. Afraid that if I bring up what I did to my father, she'll bring up the contract, and we'll have to do the whole thing over again. I don't regret what I did to him, but I definitely don't want to talk about it.

Madame Berenice looks over and smirks. "Well, hopefully, we can get you out of that one, yes?" A pause. "Is your father good in that area? He seems like a smart man."

I bite back a laugh and realize that no matter what I say, she'll find a way to bring it up. So maybe I should just ask.

"You said he's fine, right?" A part of me hopes he isn't, hopes I might have killed him, but realistically, I know that would not be cool. I don't want to go to prison, first of all, and second, even though he's completely awful, Judith and I would be literal, actual orphans left to the care of the state if he died. Or to the care of Axiom, maybe. I have a small feeling there might be fine print in the contracts that says "We own you now, so deal with it" or something. And unlike me, Judith actually signed that contract.

"I promise he is just fine," she says with a wink, and takes a sharp left into my new neighborhood.

I never thought I would live in a gated community. Madame Berenice doesn't have to stop at the security gate to talk to the guard because there's a huge eye painted on each of the car doors that lets the world know who's driving it. It's the same eye that tells cops not to pull her over if she speeds. The same eye that makes other cars slow down and let her cut. The same eye that makes other drivers avoid her at all costs.

The security guard smiles and presses a button to open the gate, and I hide my face from him because I'm embarrassed to be seen in this car.

I've said hi to this man every afternoon all week because the bus stop is right in front, and it feels like now he'll think I'm in trouble or something. And the worst part is, I truly don't know if I am.

We drive up windy hills with sharp curves to get to my street, which is the one good thing about getting a ride. The bus doesn't go up the hill, and hiking up this steep slope every single day under the hot sun is the most miserable existence. You might think the views are nice—to the left is the Pacific Ocean, to the right, giant slumbering mountains. But then you remember what had to be sacrificed in order to get you this view in the first place.

We pull around the cul-de-sac and stop in front of my house. Madame Berenice puts the car in park, lets out a large breath. "So, what now?"

I think about opening the door and running inside, but that would be stupid. So, I relent.

"What do you mean?"

"Well, the contract is not binding since you were, shall we say, unable to sign. I would like to draw up a new one, if you would oblige."

"What about my dad? How would he sign it?"

She narrows her eyes for a moment then smiles. "Easy. Will you both be home tomorrow if we stop by?"

If they *stop by*, as in they're not going to station a Watcher at our front door to make sure I don't leave the state or something? Maybe deep down, she knows I wouldn't dare. Knows my every courageous vision of fleeing would be dampened by my spineless urges to not rock the boat.

So will I still be home tomorrow if they come by? Of course I will be. I would never leave.

When I open my mouth to answer, I remember I agreed to switch shifts with Norah tomorrow and say, "Make it Sunday."

Judith will get to watch me sign the contract, and maybe that's serendipitous. Maybe all the shit with our dad happened for a reason. I want her to watch me sign it. I want her to know that I'm doing this for her—that I'm a piece of shit who couldn't stand up for her, and this is the price I pay.

As I think about it, I rub the top of my thigh and silently bask in the small jolt that runs up my back. It's a shame I won't be awake for the surgery—I'd love to feel them slicing into me—but I know from watching Judith that at least there will be plenty of pain afterwards.

A breeze blows in through the open roof of the car. Madame Berenice smiles and taps the steering wheel, the studded eyeballs in her bun glittering in the sunlight.

"Gladly," she says. "Sunday will do. Please give your sister my best, Monsieur. I trust she is under great care with a ferocious protector such as yourself."

Ferocious? Is that her idea of a joke? Clearly, the Drill Day scanners don't analyze our personalities, because if they saw through to the heart of me, there's no way they would want anything to do with me.

Chapter Eight

THE ENGINE TRAILS away into the afternoon sun, and I have no idea what just happened. All I want to do is go upstairs and hide in bed for the rest of my life. And I'll do it just as soon as I convince myself to go inside. For now, though, I'm fine standing like a lump on the sidewalk, getting burned to death by the sun.

Our new house has three levels including a basement, which is rare in California. Axiom wanted to make it as unique as possible, I think. When you look straight on, a wooden fence stretches out from both sides and wraps around the backyard but leaves the front, with its perfectly manicured grass, wide open to the street. Behind the fence, you can see a large dog-wood tree in the far corner, all the way in the back, its mammoth silver-petaled limbs reaching up to the sky.

On either side of the front door are huge bay windows framed by burgundy shutters on the outside and dark curtains on the inside. The curtains are usually drawn because my father doesn't like much sunlight inside—either for his hangovers or because he's paranoid that people are watching, it really depends on the day. Right now, the curtains are open. The glare of the sun's reflection makes it impossible to see inside, though.

I know I can't stay out here forever, so I make some sort of noise between a sigh and a grumble as I trudge up the driveway toward our three-car garage. Before we moved, I'd never seen one so massive, but here it is. Just for us. Yay. It's unnecessarily huge. We only have one car, a piece of shit my dad doesn't even bother to keep in the garage. He doesn't like to use the retina scanner on the post outside that lets only us open it. Which is strange because it's the same system for the front door—a scanner instead of a key—so I don't know why he won't use it. I think he's just lazy.

In the garden around the front porch is a sea of stones and pebbles in place of soil. There's a whole maze of succulents and cacti, some taller than me, and a miniature palm tree at the corner with bright-green palms. There's also the squashed remains of a blue agave plant with teeth sharp enough to slice through flesh, literally. The night we moved in, my graceful dream of a father fell into it and came out with these huge slashes on both his legs. He bled a crimson river leading up to the front door, which nobody has scrubbed or cleaned since it happened. An entire week of sunlight has baked it into a thick stream of tar like a trail.

I step into the shade of the porch, exhausted, every bone in me sinking toward the ground, when piano keys trill into my ears. I almost smile at the thought that they're just for me, like I'm actively dying and this is the soundtrack to my death. That's ridiculous, though, and I want to scream at the relentlessness of having to live.

No, it's coming from inside. Judith is playing. She's playing again!

Even after everything that's happened today—even with how dead I feel inside—tears prick at the back of my eyes. If she's playing, that means she's not drugged up and passed out, and damn, that's worth celebrating.

The piano was my grandmother's, who passed it on to my mother. It took up so much room in our apartment, and our neighbors hated us for the noise, but it's stayed with us. I wonder if Judith has been playing all week while I've been at school. She used to play for hours and hours at a time. She started lessons when we were kids, but I never got into it. I was more into things like eating grass and plucking the limbs off daddy longlegs, one by one, and watching them squirm.

How am I going to tell her about everything—Drill Day? This Third Eye bullshit? What happened with Dad?

An explosion of notes all at once. Judith smashing her hands on the keys. It's her thing when she doesn't get a perfect note. It's nice to know that after all these years, she hasn't changed. So, do I stay out here and avoid her bad mood, or go in and see if she needs help?

Something like my conscience tells me that even after today, I'm not the one who's had the worst week here, so I groan, plaster on my prettiest smile, and go to the door.

The scanner above the doorbell is different from the one at school. It scans only one eye and doesn't wrap around your head. I blink once, and as soon as the laser comes to life, the piano starts again. Different keys merge and blend like the sound of water gushing over a bed of rocks, while the laser shifts and dances around. The music gets louder, the laser swells. Then, almost as if it's planned, they both shut off simultaneously.

The door unlocks on its own. I nudge it open and step in. The staircase is right in front of me, the dining room to my right, and the living room with the piano and Judith to the left. I don't think I've been spotted yet, so if I wanted to, I could sneak through the dining room, into the kitchen, and down to the basement. That's where the new computer is, and I've been meaning to go figure out how to log into it.

But a sound that I think is a sniffle makes me reconsider.

The piano starts up again, louder and crisper now that I'm inside. Within a few seconds, though, there's an off-key note and it stops. Judith sighs, then it's completely silent.

Not completely silent. The slow *tick…tick…tick…* of the metronome in front of her.

I kick off my shoes and walk in, slipping just a little with every step, my sweaty socks slick against the white marble floor. The piano is right against the window. A strip of sunlight races across the top of it, illuminating the specks of dust floating in the air like the entire cosmos above it.

And there she is. There's Judith, looking down at the keys with a furrowed brow as though inspecting them for damage. Her patch is sky blue, and the mound of white gauze below it makes it look like a bullseye.

"Look at you," I say, mustering as much positivity as my voice will let me. She gasps, her eye wide as she looks at me, then whips her head to look out the window. I don't let it derail me. "I didn't think you'd start playing again so soon."

Tick…tick…tick…

She tucks her long, greasy brown hair behind her ear and turns to look out the window. The sliver of her freckled jaw that I can see is clenched so hard it looks like her entire skull might break off. The corner of her eye squints as if searching for something outside.

Tick…tick…

"I didn't mean to interrupt."

Tick…

I curl my fingers into a fist and dig my nails as hard as I can into the flesh of my palm, sawing and scraping fingers back and forth in time with the metronome.

"I heard you outside. I'm sorry, I should have stayed out there till you were done."

God, why are you saying all this, Henry? She obviously doesn't want you. Just go. Grab a knife from the kitchen and run up to your room and lock the door and saw your entire fucking leg off.

Except I can't. At the very least, I don't want her to be able to say I abandoned her in her time of need or whatever. So, I toss my backpack onto our giant leather couch and walk over to the bench. She's slouched like an apostrophe, and I make the same shape as though it will win me sympathy points.

"What's wrong, sis?" I'm so awkward. I scrape harder.

She turns to me. Her left cheek is glossy with tears. Her right one doesn't match, parched like a forgotten, unwatered flower under the patch.

She whispers something, but I can't hear it.

Another step until I'm practically leaning on the piano. "Hm?"

"You're home," she says blankly, and the lack of emotion tells me what I need to know. She's already realized I was selected at Drill Day. It's this early in the day and I'm already home. She must have seen me get out of Madame Berenice's car. Is now the right time to tell her what happened? That Axiom is coming back on Sunday to sign the contract for real?

"Good observation, genius. And you're playing."

She sighs. Groans. "Yeah, but I keep messing up."

I don't say anything, mostly because I don't know what *to* say. *I'm sorry* sounds cheap. *Whatever* sounds cruel. So, I just stand here deliberating, watching her dart her gaze anywhere but at me. She looks out the window again. Examines the curtains. Squints at the piano keys. Picks up the ticking metronome and wipes dust away from underneath it. All this, clearly waiting for me to say something.

So I do. "That's not possible, you never mess up."

She rolls her eye over to where her other used to be, as if searching for its old friend, then points to her patch like that's supposed to clear everything up.

Tick…tick…

"What are you talking about? I heard you outside. You sounded great."

She turns off the metronome but doesn't say anything, which is weird because won't she need that to keep playing? Or is she quitting now that I'm home?

I sigh and bend down to sit next to her, but she slides all the way to the end of the bench to block me. As if I don't know this game. So instead, I plop right down onto her lap, my full weight on top of her, barely more than her own. I thought it would amuse her, but I was wrong.

She only sighs. Doesn't even fight back. "I'm not in the mood," she groans.

But now I'm committed, so I can't just stop. I've lived with her for seventeen years. I shared a uterus with her. I can tell when she really wants me to go, and this isn't it.

I lift to a squat so she can scoot over, and when I sit back down, I reach out and pretend to play, dancing my fingers back and forth in the air above them like I know the first thing about the piano. Perhaps I thought this would be the thing to get her to smile, or at least shove my hands away and start playing on her own, but all she does is crack her knuckles, one by one, slowly and methodically.

I stop and turn to her. She drifts her gaze over to me, her eye lazily bouncing between both of mine like a slow-mo pinball.

This close up, I see how tired she is. She's paler than usual, and a grayish inkblot stains the skin beneath her eye—an eye that used to be as bright and wild as juniper. An eye that's all withered and dull now.

"Listen to me," I say softly to the keys instead of her. "You don't have to be perfect literally one week after your surgery. It was *eye* surgery, remember? Didn't the doctor say your depth perception or whatever would be all stupid for a while?" I turn to see the stoniest face she's ever given me. "I'm serious! Besides, you're probably overthinking it, perfectionist. What, did you mess up one tiny note?"

She gnaws at a hangnail and wipes the spit on her sweatpants. Her nails are raw and bright pink from biting. She catches me looking and folds her hands together.

"Number one," she says, "I can read the music, thank you. I can see the keys. It's not that. But *depth perception* isn't the point anyway."

"Okay, then what?"

"Can I just school you a little bit, twin brother?"

"Please do," I say, bowing gracefully.

"Playing isn't about seeing. It's trusting myself—well, no. Trusting the music. Feeling it course through me, you know? No matter what the song is, I always used to know what was coming next. It's a gut thing, not a sight thing."

"Mm-hm," I mutter, because none of that makes sense to me. I guess the closest I can relate is my poetry—at least the one I wrote for Sam. I was almost in a daze, like I had no clue what was coming out of me until I looked down and read it. That's sort of an exaggeration but it's the best way I can describe it. That's only happened once, though. Judith's been playing piano since we were five, so I'm sure her *gut thing* works a lot better than mine.

"You've never heard of Stevie Wonder or George Shearing?" she asks. Of course I've heard of Stevie Wonder, but I want to see where she's going with this so I shake my head. She takes a sharp breath. "*Ray Charles?*"

"Judith Marie Youngwell," I mock-gasp. "Do not tell me you're comparing yourself to Ray Charles?"

She flips me off. "My point is, it's possible to play music completely sightless—even the piano—because you're not relying on vision to play. Your fingers have muscle memory. Your bones *know* the music."

"Yeah, but I'm sure even they made mistakes while they were learning to play while blind."

"You're not listening to me," she grunts. "It's *inside of me*. Or it's supposed to be."

I can tell how frustrated she is. But I am too. Why can't she understand she doesn't have to be perfect right after getting her eye taken out? I rub my hands up and down my thighs to collect myself, centered by the pain splintering my leg. I might imagine it, but I think Judith glances down at me as I do, as if she knows what I'm doing.

I'm starting to sound as paranoid as my father when he's shitfaced.

"Jude, you have to know that—"

She cuts me off by pounding on the keys, a huge cacophony of notes exploding like a bomb. I'm offended she interrupted me, but then she starts playing for real, and the explosion starts piecing together into something more cohesive. It's a little jumbled, but I'm no expert. As far as I can tell, there's nothing obviously wrong with it. It's not her best, but it's still good. When she stops, I shrug. "That sounded great."

Her sourness in this moment is so similar to how mine usually is, I've never been more sure in our lives that we're twins. "Hen-Hen, don't lie to me."

I cringe, thinking of the way Dad called me that at school. "I hate that name."

"Maybe I wouldn't say it if you weren't such a liar."

"I'm not!"

"First of all," she counters, "I can always tell when you're lying because your right eyebrow twitches."

"Does not." I feel it jump, and she stares right at it. "Shut up."

She whips her long hair into my face. It smells stale, musty. "Second, I played the wrong keys on purpose because I knew you'd tell me it sounded great and I wanted to see if you'd lie."

"Okay, my turn," I say, crossing my legs away from her. "First of all, that's the most manipulative thing I've ever heard in my life, and I'm very proud of you. Also, I would never, under absolutely any circumstance, do that." I try to control my eyebrow.

"You are fascinating," she says blankly.

"Thank you. So why don't you play for real then?"

"Sorry, can't," she yawns. "All dried up."

"Fine, I will."

I hover my hands over some keys, my fingers bent into claws with no idea if I'm supposed to do the white ones or the black ones, or when to press the foot pedal.

"The hell you will," Judith says, shoving my hands away. I try not to smile, though I'm pleased with my own cunning. She pauses. Closes her eye. Inhales through her nose to the count of four. She's always done this.

The moment it starts, it transcends. It's gorgeous. Her fingers move across the keys like a shiver running down your spine. It reminds me of her very first recital. We were eleven. *Eleven,* and she was already a prodigy.

I watch her in complete awe. Her fingers are magical, each moving independently as if they have minds of their own. She's in her zone, eye closed, jaw clenching and releasing with the melody.

I don't know how she's doing it with her only eye shut. I can't remember if she kept them closed all that time ago or not. Maybe she wasn't bullshitting me about relying on sounds and feel.

As the music swells and swirls around me, I close my own eyes. I feel the music on my skin. It seeps inside me and sticks to my bones. I want to sway. I want to lose myself in this, completely and irrevocably, until I'm gone. Until I fade away like dust into the ephemera.

It's so beautiful, I want to hurt myself. Maybe while she's not looking, I can reach down and…

My eyes jolt open before I know what's happened. It's silent. She's not playing anymore. It takes me a few seconds to register, sort of like the aftershock of an earthquake, how sometimes the real damage doesn't happen until after the initial thing.

I realize after the fact that a couple of the notes sounded wrong. Even I can tell that. It sounded, I don't know, shaky? Lopsided almost. Her fingers must have slipped and fumbled. It lasted only a second, but it was long enough.

"Try again," I say before the silence has a chance to build and break over her like a raincloud. She does, but this time she starts immediately, without breathing to the count of four. I sit on my hands as I watch so I'm not tempted.

The music is gorgeous, but of course it is. She executes it as easy as breathing. Easy as a leaf floating through the air. Easy as blood flowing down my leg—

This time it happens quicker, only about ten seconds in. I'm watching her eye when it happens. It's already closed, but she clamps it even tighter.

"Again." I don't know why I'm so insistent. Do I want her to get this right for herself or do I just want the music again so I can slip into my fantasies?

She begins without opening her eye. I keep track of the time with my fingers, still trapped under my legs.

Six seconds until a slip.

"Again."

Three.

"You're close. Push through it."

Two.

Her eyelids flutter open, and she winces like a newborn seeing the world for the first time. She takes a breath. There's a fraction of a second where I think she's about to play again, but then she jerks and bites her lip, slamming her fists on the keyboard as hard as she possibly can. A detonation of keys, an atomic bomb of noise, like she wants to break the entire damn piano.

Reverberations of both high notes and low hum in the air around us.

And when I look at my sister, she's calm as can be, staring at the sheet music in front of her.

"Jude—"

"Don't."

"Maybe if you turn the metronome on—"

She sighs and rubs her temples. "It's not the metronome."

"Try opening your eye, maybe." It's an awful suggestion. Do I really think she hasn't thought of that? The moment it's out of my mouth, I want to die.

She turns her head my way so slowly that I'm sure if you listened close enough, her neck would be creaking like a door hinge. Her gaze doesn't quite meet mine, though. I follow her eye across the living room, across the marble floor and past the couch, to the stairs.

"I'm tired," she mumbles.

"I'm sorry. I shouldn't have said that."

"I'm just really tired, okay?"

I freeze, unsure if—if what? Rest might be good, but I'm worried *rest* is code for giving up entirely. Is it any of my business if she does? Well, if she plans to abandon the one thing in the world that's always made her happy, maybe I'd be a shitty brother if I *didn't* stop her.

But I err on the side of silence and stand so she can get up. When she glides by me, I get a whiff of stale BO, like she hasn't showered in…

Damn. The realization sits heavy in my stomach. Did I expect her to be freshly washed and pampered? It's weird I haven't noticed it these last few days, but I guess I haven't been close enough to smell her. It reminds me of how our classmates used to laugh at us growing up because there were weeks at a time when we couldn't bathe since our water got shut off so often.

"Hey, did you eat lunch?" I ask, trailing behind her. I glance at our new clock on the wall above the mantel place. It's in the shape of a giant cartoon eye, complete with lids and lashes. The iris glows, electrified, and changes color. Depending on the hour, one of the twelve eyelashes lights up. Bright numbers appear on the active one to tell you the precise minute and second. If that wasn't bad enough, the eye *blinks* when a new hour passes. When it opens again, the next lash lights up and the numbers start back at zero.

Axiom did all the decorating before we moved in, and I guess they wanted to remind us of why we got the house in the first place. I'd take it down, but it's too high up on the wall and we don't have a ladder. I bet it's bolted into place anyway. It's creepy, but it tells me it's just past one o'clock.

Judith sighs as she places a foot on the first step. The way her too-big shirt falls on her makes her shoulders look like they've been whittled to sharp points.

"What's it to you if I've eaten, Hen-Hen?" She's turned away from me, but I can imagine the scowl across her face.

"Just…making sure," I say carefully. "I can make you something if you haven't."

"And what exactly do we have to eat? Moldy bread?"

I control my face so that if she looks at me, she won't see the sting. I haven't been able to afford groceries since we moved, so we've been surviving on all the expired stuff we've accumulated over the years and never went through. I'm kind of used to going hungry, but mostly I hate not being able to provide for Judith.

Since she got fired, I'm now solely responsible for not only paying the back rent we owed our last apartment, but I've given Dad liquor money so he wouldn't lose it on us during the move. By the time I remembered about groceries, my paycheck had run dry. And even though Axiom provided all these decorations and luxurious furniture sets, they didn't bother stocking our pantry, so it kind of leaves us out of options.

"I think we have a can of beans," I offer.

"Yum."

"So, you didn't eat then?"

She takes two steps up. "Wasn't hungry."

"But are you now?"

Another step. "I'm fine."

I reach out and grab the back of her shirt before I lose her. She gasps. Shouts. "I don't *want* your beans, Henry!"

I let go of her shirt and grip the railing instead. My immediate reaction is to force out a laugh to make me seem less panicked, but I realize it would have the opposite effect.

"It doesn't have to be beans. We have sugar packets!"

That doesn't have the effect I want it to either.

"You're so pathetic," she says, turning around to grimace at me. She's not wrong, so I shrug very casually.

I expect her to book it to her room, but she doesn't. She's resigned to let me feed her, more for my sake, I think, than hers.

We walk through the brightly lit dining room, past the pristine white and gold marble table that seats eight—eight for a family of three. The bouquet of two dozen roses Axiom left us has already withered, but we haven't thrown them out.

"Have a seat, m'lady," I say, pulling out a chair.

She looks me up and down. "Mm-hm."

After she sits, I weave through the kitchen, past the giant island and ten-burner stove, the touch-screen fridge and triple sink. I eye the sharp, gleaming knives hanging by a magnetic stripe on the wall before I open the pantry.

The shelves here are empty except for a few cans of beans, a case of tuna, the moldy bread, a plastic baggie full of tea bags, some salt and pepper packets, a little sugar, and two boxes of mac and cheese that were on sale last month. I pick one of those. Our milk went sour so I'll have to use water, but that's okay.

"Aw, shit." The voice is muffled, but I hear the words.

"Jude?"

I step out of the pantry and look around the corner. She's still at the table, but her hands are over her mouth as she stares into the living room. I walk hesitantly back through the kitchen to see what's happening.

Before I can make it, there's a noise like the clatter of loose change dropping and scattering everywhere.

"Fuck's sake."

Dad.

Chapter Nine

HE'S SWAYING ON both feet like he's about to break into dance. My father looks as small and gaunt and gray as ever next to the front door that seems twice his size. His eyes are glossed over, but they're pointed in the direction of the floor at a shiny clump of keys at his feet. That must have been the noise I heard.

Not only are his eyes glossy, but when he blinks, his eyelids take several seconds to open, almost like he's taking tiny catnaps in quick succession. His pencil-thin legs are barely holding him up. He babbles to himself as if someone were in the room with him, and he hasn't noticed me or Judith even though we're in clear view.

He's wasted, and I have absolutely no idea how it happened so quickly. I left school an hour ago. The school nurse must have let him go shortly after. I bet he went straight to a bar and downed as many shots as he could. I also think he stashes bottles in the trunk of his car, so he probably drank from that too. I *want* to believe he wasn't driving like this, but I know better. He's had two DUIs in the last five years, but he never learns.

A flash bolts in front of my eyes. Did *I* cause this? My hitting him? Did it, like, do something to him, and now he's all funky?

He belches, and that thought jolts away as quickly as it came.

To my left, Judith sniffs. I look over, but she turns away so I can't see her.

"Are you crying?" I whisper.

She flips me off from behind and wipes her cheek. She stands very slowly, and I watch my father to see if he notices. He doesn't. I wonder if he even knows where he is. Judith tiptoes to join me at the edge of the island. She taps her fingers and thumb on its flat surface like it's a piano.

"Chriiist! Come onnn." His voice is the sound of tires squealing.

He bends at the hips. I watch in amazement as he attempts to retrieve his keys. It might be wiser to go from the knees, but no. His spine curves into a hook, the knobs of his vertebrae digging through the polo shirt that's accumulated more stains since I saw him last.

All of this, and the bruises up and down his arms from a body incapable of healing properly, he looks so incredibly weak, like if you coughed on him, he'd blow away. I'm embarrassed for him. *Of* him. I want to look away, but I can't.

Miraculously, he makes contact with the floor without falling, but he misses the keys by about six inches. Grunting like an animal, he walks his fingers inch by inch over to them, his back stretching into new shapes as he does. Next to me, the rate of Judith's breathing increases.

If he were to fall, he'd faceplant and probably knock out the rest of his teeth. Maybe break his neck. I allow myself the fantasy of making a sudden, house-shaking noise, like knocking over the fridge or tossing a dining room chair through the window, and him losing his balance.

He finally reaches the keys. They clink as he threads a finger into the keyring. He sighs, and his whole body shifts forward until he's a perfect upside-down U.

Then, nothing. I wait for him to stand. To fall. Something. He does neither, just stays bent over like this is the most comfortable position in the world or like he's doing some drunk downward dog shit. Maybe he fell asleep. Or died. I can't count how many dreams of him dying I've had.

They always wake me up. There's been car crashes, cancer, heart attacks, bear attacks, wild zebra stampedes, drowning, falling off cliffs, meteorites. I've even dreamed of killing him myself. Those seem to happen just as often as the other ones. They're the worst, though, because I wake up with my heart racing and my mouth dry, and I'm never able to fall back asleep.

From the corner of my eye, I notice Judith's hands stop, her nails still for once. Nails that are usually bright pastel colors but were stripped clean for surgery and are now bitten raw. I resist the urge to look up at her face and instead reach over to place my hand over hers. She flinches like she wants to yank her arm away. She doesn't, though. Her hand is ice and a little sweaty.

My father lifts his hand to his face, the keys dangling from his finger as though trying to plunge back down to the floor. He begins to cry and shake, his knees practically about to give out. He's making noises that are so inhuman, so awful, they're like a mix of a police siren with a dying pig squealing its heart out. I've never heard anything like it.

I don't mean to, but I feel myself squeezing Judith's hand. She turns hers around so that we can hold each other.

The keys thud as they hit the floor when his hand drops. Now exposed, his tears are free to fly. In the bright light pouring in from the windows, they shimmer all over his face from where his hand smeared them around, from his chin up to his forehead and around his temples. Even his eyebrows have tears beaded through them.

I kind of thought this would be satisfying because seeing him in pain makes me happy, but instead I've got this queasy feeling in the bottom of my stomach like I have to go to the bathroom. I don't think I've ever seen him cry like *this*. Normally, he's just mean and spiteful and angry when he drinks. Not depressed.

He sniffs. And sniffs. Then coughs. And coughs. I think it's because, upside-down, his snot has nowhere to go but back up his nose. His entire body is shaking like it's in full seizure mode. I'm surprised he hasn't collapsed.

"Unreal," Judith says.

"What the hell is happening?"

A beat.

"We should help him," she says.

At this, something leaps up into my throat—panic, I think. Or confusion. Panic because I absolutely do not want to touch him or talk to him or smell the liquor on his breath, and I think I'd die if I had to. Confusion because why does she? I take a second to compose my face before I turn.

"Help him how? Jude, come on, he's a bit past help."

She's so still in this moment it's as though she's afraid that if she moves, she'll break.

And after a few moments, she slips her hand out from underneath mine, the absence of it like a visceral thing I could squeeze. A pocket of air. A ghost. I don't know how to take it as anything but an act of rejection, a gesture that screams she's disgusted by my lack of empathy. A gesture that screams she wants nothing to do with me.

As she walks away, I curl my fingers into a fist again, right here on top of the marble, and dig my nails into my palm. It doesn't do a thing to relieve me. I dig harder, hoping for blood I can smear across this sterile bed of white, so maybe she will see how fucking serious I am.

It doesn't come. Tears rise behind my eyes, a full sob about to burst out of me. Somehow, I hold it in. I go to speak and I can't, the sob choking me. I force out a scream and finally gasp out some words. "What do you think you're gonna do for him?"

What I really mean is, *Judith don't leave, please, god, don't leave me.*

She doesn't say a word. At least I don't think she does. I'm lost at sea, swimming through the chaos in my own head. Between fits, I see her blob of a head leave the room, and I collapse to the floor, propping myself on my elbow. I'm so embarrassed but I can't help myself. Why is this such a big deal? Why can't I just go help my dad? A decent person would—a good son would. A good brother would help his sister.

I start to breathe normally, and I think I'm safe from tears now. A little snot pours from my nose. I'm sober. Emptied. I breathe in and out, my ribcage expanding against the floor, the hum of the refrigerator vibrating my skin. Down here, everything is still. This entire house. Everything. It's so quiet that I'm worried I've gone deaf somehow.

That wouldn't be the end of the world, though, would it? Judith has an eye missing. I'd have no hearing. We'd sort of match in a way. It's what

I'd get for not offering Axiom my eye instead. Then I remember Sunday. The new contract. It'll happen. And I feel a little bit of relief.

"Dad!"

A crash. The cabinet doors beside me rattle. My father's fallen to the floor, I'm sure. All that quiet was just the calm before the storm.

"Dad, no!" Judith sounds like she's a mile away even as she shouts.

I know I should get up to see if they need me, but I don't. I maneuver my arm so that I can lie face-down, the tile floor like a sheet of ice against my cheek. I've never been good at that stuff. She's always the one helping him to bed, taking off his shoes, making sure he has a blanket. I'd much rather leave him to waste away.

Judith's voice carries, so clear even from two rooms away and through the thick island. "Dad, Dad, look at me. Are you okay? Can you move your legs?"

I hear him mutter something back to her. I can't believe how much of a relief it is to hear, as muffled as it is from here—a relief mostly because I don't know how Judith would respond to him dying.

"That's right," she says, a chasm in her voice. "Your one-eyed girl."

There's some sort of half-whimper-half-cough from him in response.

The ensuing silence is long and awful. I see those kitchen knives on the wall, all lined up in a pretty little row from big to small.

"Such a beautiful eye," I think I hear my dad say, though I could be wrong. But if I'm right, I know exactly where he's going. He starts with backhanded compliments. *Beautiful eye,* of course, points out the obvious: there's only one of them. No matter how beautiful, how sparkly in the light or how rich the green, it will only ever be single. Alone. Grieving for its partner. Even if it remarries, in the form of a Third Eye, it will still be alone.

Not only that, he's reminding her he won. He got what he wanted. The nice house, the fancy furniture, the free utilities, and zero mortgage. And best of all, he got his ratty children out of his hair and out of his personal space. All for the measly price of his daughter's eye.

After the compliments come the insults. He will hurl them as quick and sharp as I could flick those knives across my flesh. That's precisely why I need to stop this childish bullshit and just go in there. That way, he can slice me instead of her, the way it should be anyway.

I get to my knees, about to jump in. But I can't. After a few deep breaths, the realization dawns. As much as I was committed to jumping in to rescue Judith, I am destined to do what I always do. Cower in the shadows. Literally. I don't go any further now in case the light catches my oily hair, glinting like the ocean in the sun, a light bright enough to catch my father's jaundiced eye.

I swear to myself, though, that if he gets any worse, I will. I have to.

"You used to be so pretty," he rasps.

"Let's get you upstairs."

A thud against the floor, maybe a limb dropping. A grunt. I angle my head but I can only see a sliver, so I crawl further out. Judith is kneeling over my dad, who's flat on his back, his arms limp.

"Come on," she says, a gentle hand rubbing his upper arm as though to keep him awake.

"No can do." His voice is clearer now that I'm closer, but his words slur together.

"Dad, it's okay, I'll help you." She ties her hair into a bun at the back of her head with the band she keeps around her wrist, all while scanning his body head to toe for injury.

He lifts his arm and moves his hand up to her face. She flinches but stills herself, as if paralyzed mid-flinch. Whether my dad notices, I'm not sure, but he slowly makes contact, caressing her cheek with his thumb. Her mouth curls into a frown. I want to run over there and kick his hand away and take Judith by the arm and run out of this house with her and never come back.

"I know it hurts, baby, hurts me too," he coos.

Judith whimpers. "Dad, don't."

"We should've kept your pretty face the way it was."

"Dad—"

His hand moves to her patch, tracing its surface delicately with his thumb. "Now you're just a no-eye-nothing."

The tears in her eye are thick, like a bubble about to burst.

His whisper comes clear and direct. "I'm so sorry."

I fall to a lying position and bite my lip as hard as I can. I clutch my thigh and squeeze, squeeze, like my life depends on it, like it's a window ledge and I'm hanging from it a hundred stories up and if I let go, I'll plummet to my death. The pain sears white behind my eyes, and the rush is incredible. I wonder if this is what drugs feel like.

"Should've been your brother. They cut the wrong twin. We coulda bargained, dontcha think? Coulda happened today, but—"

"Don't say that, Dad. Aren't you tired? Let's go to bed."

A long pause. I wonder what's happening. Did she leave? I'm too spent to look, but the suspense is even worse. I lift my head just an inch when my dad clears his throat.

"My ugly little cyclops. You look like a monster."

My head spins. I can't see straight. I'm falling into a vortex, one that has ripped through the floor underneath me. I want to jump into it, knowing full well it might kill me, but at least there's power in choosing to succumb.

Instead, I get up to my knees.

"Your mother would be so ashamed to see you right now, baby."

"Shut up." It's me. I'm baring my teeth. Growling.

Neither of them hears me, so I grip the edge of the island and pull myself to my feet. I say it again.

"I can't believe how ugly they made you."

I storm over there, screaming as loud as I fucking can. "Shut up shut up shut *up!*"

I can barely hear myself because my ears are ringing like I've been in an explosion. Everything's blurry, a swarm of lights and colors. I'm dizzy. I think I'm swaying side to side, my stomach inside out, my arms heavy as boulders.

The shape of Judith barrels out of the way, her patch a trail of blue lights lingering like floaters in the air. There are sounds I don't recognize, smells that are new to me.

I steady myself. Things start to shift into focus. I'm standing and somehow haven't toppled over.

The creature below me looks like an old, shriveled-up pile of dog shit someone didn't pick up, patches of uneven stubble on his cheeks like dead grass smushed around it.

And he's…smiling. His eyes are squinted, deep creases at their corners, as he grins like he's watching something hilarious.

That's what does it, his stupid fucking smile. It pushes me over the edge. Whatever reservations I had are gone. Did he not learn his fucking lesson at school? You do not attack my sister.

I drop to the floor and start blasting my fist at him, over and over again. His face, his neck, his chest. Anything that can break, I want to smash it to pieces.

Somewhere, someone is screaming—Judith, I'm sure—but I don't care. I'm gone. It's not even me. I slip in and out of my body, watching myself like I'm dreaming. But I know I'm not because I can feel the impact of bone on bone, the weight of my fist on his pathetic excuse for a body.

With each punch, I yell louder. "You—will—not—call—her—that. *Do—you—fuck—ing—hear—me?*"

I direct my knuckles into his eye so that he'll become a cyclops and know how it feels.

I'm vaguely aware of my own hand starting to hurt, but that's nothing. This is exhilarating. I've unleashed a kind of power I never in a million years thought I'd have. And now that I do, I think I could fly off a mountaintop or something, a freedom humans could only dream of. I think I'm smiling. Or laughing maybe. I can't help it.

"Henry!"

Judith wants me to stop. Of course she wants me to stop. But how can I, when I've finally found my purpose in life? It's a bigger rush than cutting, even as the stench of his disgusting breath, like rotting fruit, hits me. This makes me angrier, so I use both fists to hit multiple spots at once. I don't control them; I just watch in amazement wherever they go. I'm using my knee to pin his tiny waist to the floor so he can't squirm away.

"You had fun at school, huh?" I say, somehow very calmly. "Did you have fun *humiliating me?*" The calm is gone, only a moment's delirium.

My eyes start to sting from the sweat pouring down my face. I stop to wipe it away, completely out of breath, and my hands tingle like they've fallen asleep. The rotten breath I smelled is replaced by a metallic whiff of blood. I look down and see his face is shiny and bright red. My hands too. My shirt. My jeans. The floor.

"I'm glad your mother can't see you now," a voice snarls. Dad's? But he's so bloody and out of it, he can't have spoken so clearly. Maybe it was god. Maybe it was me.

Judith wails at the top of her lungs, jumping over to shove me off him. "Henry, you *psycho!*" I fly two feet backward and land on the ground curled and crumpled.

I was protecting you. I want to scream it at the top of my lungs, but I can't even catch my breath.

My hands are no longer tingling. They are *rushing* with all the pain I must have been numb to until now. The throbbing is exquisite. You'd think that all the cutting would have built up my tolerance, but this is like nothing else in the world. It's a thousand times worse. I can't move my fingers without wanting to scream. I think I broke them.

My dad is coughing. It's the only thing I can hear over the sound of my rabid breaths, shallow, fast, crazy. He coughs for what feels like ten minutes until he gives out and he's too weak, like a car engine wheezing and sputtering out its last few puffs.

What have I done? What if he dies?

I never actually wanted him to, even if I've dreamed of it for years. They'll throw me in jail like Mom. They'll take my eye and they won't need permission. That's what they do to prisoners. Some deal Axiom made with the government, even signed it into law. If that happens, Judith won't have anyone left.

Judith.

I arch my neck to look over to her. She's fluttering around the bloody heap of our father like a moth around a flame, her bun half-unraveled, hair flying everywhere. I've never seen her so panicked. She sinks to her knees and rips the blue patch off her head, the strap snagging the remainder of her bun so her hair avalanches down her back. Why take it off? Is she hot? Does it matter?

Her shoulders heaving, she scans my dad up and down, left and right, trying to figure out what to do. I wish I had an answer for her. I wish lots of things right now.

She turns on her knees to face me, and how can I not get lost in the relief of her coming to help me? I have no idea how she plans to, but Judith can do anything.

Except she doesn't. She doesn't even look at me. She gets to her feet and leaps over me, bound for the kitchen. I hear cabinets open and drawers slam, and all I can do is watch my dad writhe around like a seizing worm. He grunts and groans now, so at least he's not dead.

He's unrecognizable, a mere fraction of the half-man he used to be. His eyes twitch open and closed, open and closed. When they're open, the jaundice is almost neon yellow against the streaks and splatters of red across his face. When they're closed, his entire face is a solid sheet of rust, shiniest around his nose.

Despite my fears of him dying, part of me almost admires what I've made. All that blood, like a work of art. It's kind of beautiful in a way, isn't it? I imagine this is how a surgeon must feel after cutting out an eye: a battle of guilt over his destruction versus a sense of pride for a job well done.

It's not until I hear Judith slam another drawer that I feel the shame for what I'm thinking, as visceral as the bile at the back of my throat that I swallow down with a grunt.

From my periphery, I notice something appear below my father's belt. I glance down to his crotch, where a dark spot has formed. It gets larger, seeping down the thighs of his jeans and up toward his hip. I can't tell if he notices. He's only still groaning.

The throbbing in my hands is now in my wrists, steadily climbing into my forearms. The pain squeezes my bones like pliers.

Judith jumps over me again, now with fistfuls of napkins. We've collected them over the years, taking extras from school and from fast food places. Cuts down on the cost of paper towels. She drops a pile beside her, thirty or forty of them, all different sizes and colors, and takes the entirety of the other pile to his face. He hisses at her touch.

"I'm sorry, Daddy," she says, her movements gentle and slow. Daddy? I can't remember the last time she called him that.

I scoff loud enough for her to hear. "Don't you know I'm the one who saved you from him? You should be helping me first, Jude."

I say it calmly. Evenly. Judith turns to look at me and finally understands. She glides over as if on a moving cloud and wraps me in her sweet embrace, tender and healing. She smells of floral perfume and calming lavender.

That's only a dream, though. Hallucination, maybe.

Do I really think I was protecting her? Maybe I did when I started, but when I got going, all rapid-fire style, it was like some feral beast deep inside me took control. I could try to argue in a court of law that I had to protect her, but no judge would believe it. He wasn't hitting her or anything—no, he was only manipulating her, demeaning her. Is that illegal?

Does that warrant a full beatdown? Even if it did, it seems like Judith is on his side, so whatever. Not that I can blame her.

"I'm sorry," she says again. "It's bleeding so much. Can you hold it if it doesn't hurt too bad?" I only see the shadow of Dad's hand move because Judith's body blocks his torso. But then his hand reappears on the other side of her. It doesn't go to hold the napkin to his face. Instead, it cradles the side of his head, like he has a headache or something. I'll bet he does.

Judith coughs. She must have gotten a whiff of his piss, or his breath, or maybe just the heavy stench of copper in the air. She grabs the napkins and extends her arm toward his crotch but stops. It'll embarrass him if she does. It'll embarrass him if she doesn't. Not that my father is above any level of shame at this stage in his life.

But she doesn't have time to deliberate because he's saying something now. I can't hear it because it's so garbled, and Judith can't either because she asks him to repeat himself.

He lifts his head off the floor an inch, as if to make himself clearer, but drops it back down with a thud. A breath through his teeth. When he finally does talk, he shouts, annoyed that he has to speak twice.

"Ambulance…you stupid?"

"Shut up, old man," I bark, shocking myself. Apparently, I'm someone who just says what he wants and goes on violent rampages now.

And how does he propose we call them? With all the phones we have lying around the house? Axiom gave us a computer but no phones. I guess Judith could run to a neighbor's house. I mean, I could maybe crawl there if I forced myself, but I'm in so much pain.

Still bunching the napkins on his nose, Judith turns to me. Our first eye contact since before…this. Her face is even paler than it was, the mound of white gauze left on her eye since she yanked off her patch almost blending into her skin. She's emotionless. Blank. She's either completely numb or she's so done with me that she won't even do me the courtesy of being pissed.

It stings more than my hands do. I hold her eye with mine, almost as if for dear life, like it's keeping me from drowning. It sort of is.

"He does not need an ambulance, Judith. He's *fine*."

Okay, so he's not *fine* right at this moment, but I'm sure he will be once his nose stops bleeding. Let him take some Tylenol, drink some water, maybe sleep for a couple days, and he'll be back to his old shitty self in no time.

The real reason I don't want her to call is because if he goes to the hospital, I'll be the one getting in trouble. I mean, I beat up my incapacitated, drunk, weak, old father? They'll probably call the police, right? They'll send me straight to jail. Up until now, I thought I was ready to get my eye out. Thought it would save my relationship with Judith. But now I think I'm realizing how stupid that was.

To the sound of Dad's large, ragged breaths, Judith gives me no response before she turns away—not a look, not a word, not even a disapproving shake of her head.

"You have to hold it, okay?" she says to Dad. "I'm gonna go get help."

"Judith, I can *help*," I cry, though I'm aware she has no reason to trust me.

Dad doesn't take the napkins. I think he tries to—he raises his arm a few inches off the ground, but it drops with a loud thud.

I realize I actually *do* want to help. I wasn't just saying it. I mean, I'd rather not help *him,* but I need to be there for Judith.

It's hard to get up because every inch of me screams in pain, every nerve ending on fire, not just my hands. I feel like I fell off a building.

With a lot of grunting and cursing, and a point where I come *this* close to tears, I get to my butt and scoot over with my legs.

The napkins Judith's holding to Dad's nose are soaked through with rust, her fingers shiny and crimson, her sweatpants splattered. I'm not sure if she even realizes any of it. Her gaze darts all over the room as if searching for something. Her whole body trembles.

She closes her eye and breathes in deeply through her nose. "I've gotta go next door, don't I?" It comes out in a series of squeaks.

"Yes," I say, grabbing a bunch of fresh napkins. I can't believe I'm about to be all up in his swamp of blood without gloves or anything.

I touch her arm to tell her she can let go of Dad. With a shaky breath, she opens her eye again, her gaze full of a desperation so utterly unlike her that I think for a second I've dreamed this entire day. She lets go and I quickly press the napkins to my dad's nose, a warm and wet slab of silly putty. I don't know if I should squeeze or if that would make him bleed more. I go for a half-squeeze, my hand and wrist burning with each slight movement. Dad, lost in the wilderness of his own groans, his eyes clenched shut, doesn't seem to notice I'm even here.

Judith looks away. "I—I don't—" She closes her eye again. "Henry—"

I'm getting more anxious with each second. I don't know what's wrong with her, and I'm worried that she'll ask me to do it. I can't even stand, so how am I supposed to make it all the way next door?

One hand still clutching the bloodied napkins, she lifts the other to where her patch should be, like she wants to adjust it but seems to only just realize she took it off. That's when I realize why she doesn't want to leave.

"Don't tell me you're worried what they'll think, Jude. There's no *time*."

Her eye slices into mine like a scalpel. "You don't get to judge me, asshole."

"I'm not!" My hand slips off Dad's nose, the napkins like a sopping wet mop in my hand. "But listen, I know it sucks, and I'm sorry. I'm really, really sorry, but *please*. I would do it, but I can't. Look at me."

Maybe I hoped she'd pity me, that when she looked at me, really looked at me, she might see anything besides a monster. I was wrong.

"I can't believe you did this," she whispers, her voice as quiet as ashes scattering through the air.

"I was protecting you!"

"Like I need you." There's a sudden hollowness inside me, like someone's taken a spoon to my insides, scooped out my organs and my bones.

I take as deep a breath as I can manage. "He called y—"

"I know what he—" With a struggle, a shakiness that she tries to hide, she gets to her feet. "You think I don't know what—that doesn't warrant what you—" She gestures down to my creation, my destruction, and hobbles to the door. She hesitates before putting her hand to the knob. I think for a second she's about to turn to me. Forgive me.

She doesn't. With the ferocity of a starved animal attacking its prey, she twists the knob, nearly ripping it off its screws, swings the door open, and gasps.

Someone's there on our porch. An old woman. Her fist is raised to the level of her head, as if she was knocking on the door or just about to.

She's wearing black scrubs and blue sunglasses and has a shock of spiky white hair on her head. A man, also in black scrubs and blue sunglasses, though with no hair at all, stands slightly behind her. In the man's hand is a giant bag with a huge cartoonish eye on the front.

"Paramedics," says the woman, lifting her shades on top of her head. She smiles with one side of her mouth. "Someone in trouble?"

Judith says nothing. I say nothing. My dad has stopped groaning.

The woman looks over Judith's shoulder into the house and makes eye contact with me. My stomach turns to ice. I have absolutely no clue how they knew. Who called them? Maybe a neighbor heard us…but how? They're so far away.

Judith must have the same questions in her head, but she doesn't ask. Doesn't move.

The woman's cold blue eyes rake over my dad, then me again, and finally land on my hands.

She turns back to Judith, nodding.

"Wanna let us in, sweetheart?"

Chapter Ten

SIRENS SCREECH AND wail as we fly down the road. They're sort of muffled in here through the thick metal frame of the ambulance, but I swear they're practically right in my ears. I'm surprised paramedics can focus enough to save people's lives when they're bombarded by this noise all the time.

Judith turns around in the front seat. I will her to look at me, to see how sorry I am, but she's trying to see what's happening with Dad. From her angle, I don't think she can see much. Even I don't know what's going on, and I'm right here across from him, strapped in a tiny child-sized seat.

I do know they got his bleeding to stop. But his face still looks like a finger-painting—messy and chaotic, paint smeared to every corner.

Before we left the house, one paramedic worked on him while the other helped me. He cleaned up my hands in the kitchen sink, wrapped them in bandages. Gave me an ice pack, which isn't doing a thing for the pain. Not that I need or want it to, but what's the point of it?

"I don't think I need to go to the hospital," I said as resolutely as I could manage as he wrapped the bandages. I was hoping I could barricade myself in the house for the rest of my life, and if they ever came to arrest me, I could hide in a vent or something.

But without skipping a beat, he said, almost jovially, "Of course you do. You could have serious damage. They'll examine you more thoroughly there." What else could I do? If I refused, it would be so suspicious.

I watch the other paramedic now, the one who's back here with my dad and me. She's an old woman with wild, winter-white hair and steady hands despite how fast we're going and how much the car is rocking.

She kneels between the two of us, her wide back to me, hooking my dad's IV to a bag of water—or some liquid medicine that *looks* like water. She hangs it up on a hook above him—a hook right next to a monitor that's connected to him by wires and has all these numbers and graphs I can't make out. I know absolutely shit about shit.

My dad opens his eyes and mumbles something I can't hear. The woman leans down to put her ear by his mouth, but he just as quickly dozes off again. It's the fourth or fifth time he's done this. She shakes his shoulder to keep him awake when he drifts off.

"What's wrong with him?" I shout over the sirens. The first thing I've said since I sat down.

"You almost killed him is what's wrong with him," she says evenly, matter-of-factly, as though I hadn't gathered that already.

I look over to the shelves they have stacked in here. I bet I could find something sharp enough to rip my flesh open with. Surely, they've got scissors or a scalpel or something. But…obviously. The last thing I need is for

Axiom to know what I do to myself. That my violent streak isn't only directed at my dad.

I take a few breaths and say, "No, I mean like, physically? What's his diagnosis?"

The paramedic laughs sharply, like a cleaver thwacking through meat. She looks up to my dad's monitor. "I can't diagnose him. I ain't no doctor. I just get people from point A to point B without croaking, you know what I mean?"

No, I don't. "Is he gonna die?"

The seconds roll by. Perhaps she thinks her silence is an answer. While I wait, I look down at my clothes, splattered with dark-red stains like I ran through a sprinkler of blood. If you saw me, you might think I was dying too.

"Hope not," she says finally, while checking the gauze on his nose. She points to the liquid medicine on the hook. "He lost a lot of blood, you know? His blood pressure's down, that's why I'm giving him this saline, to help bring it back up."

Low blood pressure? That sounds bad. I glance up at the fluid dangling above my dad like a liquid chandelier, as though it contains all the answers I'm looking for. "But you stopped the bleeding, didn't you? Like, he'll be fine?"

Again, she takes a long time to answer. Few things irritate me more than being ignored.

Then again, who am I to deserve a response in the first place? So I try another question.

"Why were you at our house so fast?"

A smile. "Well, you needed help, did you not?"

"Yeah, but—how?"

"What do you—"

She's cut off by my father's groans. His eyes are open just a slit. Under the wail of the siren, he mutters something just as inaudible as the last time. The paramedic leans to put her ear in front of him. I bend forward too like I'd be able to hear it.

"What'd he say?" I shout.

Before she can answer, the ambulance takes a sharp turn, and everyone jerks and slides wherever gravity takes them. My father's head ricochets from side to side before the paramedic puts her hand out to keep it from snapping off his neck.

It only takes a few seconds to get steady again, but his eyes are already closed. I wonder if he's dead *now*, if this is what's killed him finally. I think the monitor would alarm or the paramedic would freak out if he did, though, so I force myself not to worry about it.

Through the back window, I can see the ocean, waves rocking under a clear blue sky. I remember seeing a view of it outside of Judith's recovery room last weekend, but there were no waves at all. It was eerily still, like the entire ocean was frozen or something.

The paramedic messes with something on my dad's monitor. He slips away again, but she shakes his shoulder, and he opens his eyes like he's just woken from a nightmare. It doesn't escape me how she didn't answer my question.

I think maybe I don't want to know what he said, so I won't ask. Instead, I just sit under the screeching noise for a minute that rolls into maybe an hour. Maybe a week. I'm so unbelievably tired. My hands are on fire but I'm grateful; the pain is keeping me awake.

The ambulance makes another turn and slows to a snail's pace. I don't recognize where we are. This isn't the entrance we came into for Judith's surgery, but the building looks the same, a massive tower of sheet glass.

Above the door is a sign with giant, white letters: EMERGENCY.

And above that is a neon eye, colossal and bright blue and in the outline of an eyeball, its pupil wide enough to take in the entire sky. It doesn't blink—just glows and glows and glows into eternity.

There was a smaller version of it in the waiting room when Judith was being butchered. It hung right above the door leading to the surgical suite.

I lower my eyes. A wave of nausea hits me when I see a line of forty, fifty, sixty people snaking out the sliding glass door and around the building. We could be waiting for fucking days. My dad could literally die before someone sees him. How can there be so many sick people in this city at this exact moment?

But the car keeps going until the people grow smaller and the neon eye is no longer visible. At first, I don't know why we're leaving, but then I realize that maybe there's a separate entrance for people arriving by ambulance.

In about thirty more seconds, there's another sliding glass door. This one has no people. There's another EMERGENCY sign too, and above it, the same blue eye.

Except this one has a bright red, diagonal line through it.

I crane my neck to double check the other eye to see if I missed a line through that one—but no.

That one was *Eye*. This one is *No Eye*.

And I know why we've been taken to this second one. Judith. Which doesn't make sense: my dad and I are the patients now, not her, and we clearly haven't had *our* eyes removed. So why are we over here? Is it only because Judith is here with us? Maybe this is where the ambulances always park, but they'll take us over to the other side to wait in that line.

But then the obvious answer rushes to me. Of course. *We're getting surgery too.* The contract doesn't matter anymore because I almost killed him, so I'm basically a convict anyway.

Panic shoots through me, every nerve ending riled and ready to bolt. Before I can think better of it, I drop the ice pack and start to fly out of my seat, ready to kick out this damn door if I have to and run all the fucking way to Mexico—but the seatbelt holds me down. I grunt in response and in my hysteria, I can't find the buckle. It's not on my left, not on my right, not on my stomach. I even feel for it under my thighs, ignoring the pain ripping through my hands and wrists, but it's not there. It doesn't make any sense. What am I missing?

"Excuse me, what are you doing?" The paramedic is looking straight at me for the first time. Her jaw hangs open, her hazel eyes wide and alarmed.

I realize I'm panting, so I hold my breath. "Nothing," I squeak. She peers down to my hands, which are still trying to find the buckle.

"You ain't getting up, Mr. Youngwell. Not till we come to a stop." Something about her addressing me by name makes this a thousand times worse. I don't know why. Then I realize she's using a regular voice, she's not shouting. The sirens have stopped. I can think.

I don't know what to do. If I try to get up again, she'll be onto me and probably restrain me herself. But if I don't, I'm basically surrendering. What's the point of trying to escape and rousing her suspicion, though, if there's no buckle and I wouldn't be able to get out anyway?

Then she does shout. "Mr. Youngwell?"

I look up, but it's not directed at me. My dad's head is slumped to one side. She's pushing his shoulder, but he doesn't react. She pushes harder and harder, simultaneously checking the gauze on his nose. No blood spurts out as far as I can tell. "Mr. Youngwell? Alister! Hey, Alister, wake up, we're at the hospital, okay?"

She even slaps his face a little, but no luck.

"What's going on?" It's Judith. Her head is turned, her terrified eye on me. I shrug because what else can I do?

The ambulance lurches to a stop. Both the driver and Judith jump out of their doors.

When I turn back, my hands are trembling. The paramedic is on her feet now, bending over him like a mother over her sleeping infant. Now is my opportunity to run if I'm going to, maybe drag Judith with me.

But when I look at my father, I can't.

I watch, as if through blinders, as she extends her arm toward him and pummels her fist into the middle of his chest. When she makes contact, she twists her wrist, grinding her knuckles into the bone. My dad gasps for air like a man on the verge of drowning who's just broken the surface.

The paramedic smiles at him. "Alister," she shouts. "You're at the hospital, okay? Need you to stay awake for me, can you do that?"

He doesn't say anything, but his eyes bulge like he's just seen what happens after we die.

The back doors fling open, a rush of sound and light flooding in, and standing right outside are the driver and five or six doctors and nurses. The Pacific Ocean is right there, maybe a hundred feet away. I can smell the salt, practically taste it on my tongue. I look for Judith but don't see her.

The paramedic starts yanking cords off my dad's chest, and he says something I can't hear. She leans down and asks him to repeat himself. Again, I can't hear.

She shouts behind her to the doctors and nurses outside.

"Losing consciousness. Pressure dropping below eighty. Weak, thready pulse elevated to one-fifteen."

She uses her feet to unlock the wheels of his gurney, then she and the driver pull him out. All that's left is the empty cavity where he was.

"Hey!" I shout to the paramedic. "Hey, what did he tell you?"

She glances up at me, her tufts of white hair flying back and forth. She yells something but it's lost to the loud, raucous wind. The last words he might ever speak, and I'll never know what they are.

The ambulance is hollow. I might be exaggerating, but I think I can hear my breath echo in here.

With a resolve I didn't know I had—or maybe it's a drive to be away from this emptiness—I start to get up again, only to forget about the damn buckle, so I scream. It lasts a second, so quick that maybe I was imagining it too. But the echoes are definitely there, resounding and singing their own grief when I'm done, so I know it was real.

I turn to see somebody in a stiff, white lab coat looking at me from outside, her head leaned to one side as though examining a specimen. I raise my hands to wave, to gesture that I'm fine.

Only then do I see that I've begun to bleed through the bandages.

*

IMAGINE YOU'RE A patient in the hospital. The building is right on the ocean. *Right* on the ocean. Twenty feet, give or take. There's no beach, no sand; just rocks and boulders. After that: the great green-blue abyss, motionless, still as death—no waves crashing up the boulders; no whales blowing water way far out; no mermaids coming to rescue you.

Now imagine that your room is on the first floor and faces the water. But instead of a small window, you get an entire wall made of glass from corner to corner. You feel like if you blink too hard or speak too loudly, you'd create a gust of wind powerful enough to crack the glass, that it would carry you a thousand feet from the room and toss you headfirst into the ocean. And since your parents never taught you to swim, you'd drown.

The thing you have to remember is that you're not drowning. You take a few breaths. You're in this room, in a place where there are people whose job it is to help you. To fix you. Yes, you. Your father too—the man who, you vaguely recall, you might have killed.

It's okay. All will be well.

Soon the sun will start to go down, but right now, in the beautiful pastel orange and pink sky, it's right in your face, that sun, bald and bright, not covered by a single cloud. It's right in your eyes but somehow it doesn't blind you. You're staring right at it but you're not even squinting because it's so majestic. You would draw the blinds, but when you look, there are none. Are you dreaming?

And then you smell it. Saltwater. It's drifting into your nose, settling somewhere deep in your body. You think it has to be fake, that the salt must be coming from a scent diffuser somewhere because, come on, this window—this glass wall—doesn't open.

That's when you spot the two vents at either top corner of the glass, letting in the smell of the sea. Your muscles begin to relax. You feel calm. It's nice. You can't remember the last time you felt so nice. Something about this is…perfect. If only there were an ocean breeze, this could be a spa treatment.

A nurse comes. She's so nice and so beautiful. She talks funny, but she soothes any lingering worries you might have. She has you lie down in the bed that's on the other side of the room. You're so tired, and the mattress feels like the sea. A warmth so unfamiliar yet so certain spreads through you. This is where you belong.

You're weightless. Free.

Chapter Eleven

SOMETHING, SOMEWHERE, PULLS me out from a heavy blackness, and the first thing that hits me is the smell of saltwater thick in the air. Was I dreaming? That felt so real. I want more than anything to slip back into it, to feel the weight of nothingness consume me. The sun is a little lower in the sky. I look down at my hand. There's a new ice pack. Everything still hurts. My whole body aches.

I notice now that the walls in this room are blank. Like, completely white. I don't know why I'd expect paintings to be hung. Or if not art, at least the eye symbol. But no art. No eyes. Not even a clock anywhere.

A knock on the door, and an immediate flash of myself with an eye patch. I blink my left eye then my right, and left, and right, just to make sure they're both still there.

"Hello?" A bald man in dark-blue scrubs, with a patchy beard and his own eye patch comes in. Behind him, he pulls a huge machine on wheels.

It has all different buttons and levers on it. I wonder if it's some super huge, advanced retina scanner, but it has to serve some other function too.

The stench of body odor and sweaty armpits assaults my nostrils as the man drapes a heavy vest over me. It's a weird mix with the saltwater smell. I look up into his eyes, and he lifts the corner of the vest. "I gotta put this on you so the machine don't kill you," he says with a smirk before he turns back toward the door.

Memories from the ambulance rush back, like diving headfirst into the ocean. I remember the flood of panic. Trying to get out of my seat. The medic's stern face telling me to sit back down. I remember not knowing what my dad said.

I know they haven't taken my eye yet, but they're going to, that's obvious. Is that what this guy's about to do? Right here? I don't know why, but I assumed the room would be a lot different—maybe bigger and with more things in it?

But no, I can't just let them do it. I know I wanted them to take it before, but now I *really* want to keep them both.

I look around for something to use as a weapon. There's only the bedside table. But unless I can lift it and break it over this guy's head, which I definitely can't, I'm out of luck.

Also…why does someone from Axiom have a patch? Do they operate on their own kind?

"Pulling your leg, pal." He nods to the machine. "This thing's harmless."

He flips a switch over by the door. Instantly, the entire room is pitch black, the ocean and sky completely gone. The glass wall's no longer glass—or maybe it is, but it's opaque now. I can't see a thing.

Another switch. Several recessed lights in the ceiling glow with a very dim twinkle like stars. I can make out the soft curves and short arm of the machine, the top of the guy's bald head.

Why the hell is he operating with no light? Doesn't he kind of need that to, I don't know, *cut out my eye?* What kind of Axiom bullshit is this, and why is there no one else here? This machine's got to be some sort of robot that's gonna hold me down or something. Or maybe *it's* the surgeon and the guy is its assistant.

"You ready for your pictures or what?"

He walks over to me again, moving the machine a little closer. I hold my breath so I don't get another whiff of his pits, even though I've smelled worse at our old apartment: the food in the fridge turning bad from the power being shut off, the toilet overflowing because we never owned a plunger, my dad pissing himself in the night.

I swallow. "What pictures?"

"X-rays," he says. "Your hands, right? Doctor wants to see if they're broken."

I don't say a word. I've heard of X-rays, I guess. That's a thing they do at hospitals, right? He comes over and takes the ice pack from under my hand—my hand that's so stiff and so sore. He has me sit up and swing my legs over the side of the bed.

"Attaboy."

"You don't know where my sister is, do you?"

She's probably with our dad, but I didn't see her at all when I got out of the ambulance. Someone put me in a wheelchair, even though I could walk just fine, and wheeled me to this room. They didn't say a word about what was going on or what they planned to do with me. And when I got into bed, I was mesmerized by the ocean view, and everything sort of melted away. It was like a dream. I vaguely remember a nurse. What was her name? I think something about her sounded funny, the way she talked or something. She took my blood pressure. I think she said it was high. Then she left, and I fell asleep.

"Sorry, kid, no clue," the man says as he presses buttons on the machine. He swings an arm out from the side of it and comes back over to me.

"How can I find out where she is?" What I mean but don't say is, *How can I find out if they're putting that Third Eye shit in her right now?*

"I'm just a tech, kid. Maybe your nurse'll know more, you know what I'm saying?" I wince when he takes my arm in his cold fingers and places it on this tray on the side of the machine. "That hurt when I do that?"

"Yeah, but I'm used to it." Wait, what just came out of my mouth?

He nods but doesn't address it. "Gonna assume you've never had an X-ray before?"

"Never."

"Just try not to move, and it won't bite ya." He presses a button, and I hear a few clicks. I expect a flash like on a camera, but it doesn't come. He tells me to remove my hand and put the other one in its place. A few clicks later, he's done.

Behind the machine, a square of light appears on the floor. It slowly gets wider and wider, then smaller and smaller, as the door opens and closes. I'm aware of the breath in my throat.

"Henry Youngwell, is it?" It's a low voice. The machine blocks my line of sight and the room's still dark, so I don't know who it is.

I hesitate, as though I could leave if I said no. But that's stupid, so I say yes.

"Perfect."

The X-ray guy bolts over to me and leans down until his scruffy chin itches my ear.

"Don't trust 'em," he whispers, taking off the heavy vest. "Not a word."

I hear the flip of the light switch, and the room is bathed in light again. The ocean view is back, and the sun's a little lower still than where it was, but not quite dropped to the water yet. The sky is more orange than pink, with a few electric-blue clouds that weren't there before. One thing that's stayed the same is the water remains flat and motionless, reflecting a wide stripe of sun that's seemingly pointed right at me.

The person who came in clears their throat, and I turn my head to see a short man in light-blue scrubs and a white lab coat. But I'm not interested in him, which is fine because he seems to care more about the tablet in his hands than me anyway.

No, I'm more interested in the X-ray guy and what he said. The problem is he won't meet my gaze as he packs up his machine, folding in the arm and the tray. I lean my head to try to get in his line of sight, but all he does is press a button. Then, with a kick, he unlocks the wheels and begins pulling it away without a glance.

"Lester, a word?" says the short man.

The machine halts with a slight jerk. "Yes, doctor?"

Normally when someone wants a word, they go off to the corner or to another room entirely so that when they whisper, nobody else can hear. But that's not the case here—either because the room is small or because the doctor wants me to hear. He doesn't even move or lower his voice at all.

"How are things in your bunk, Lester?"

Bunk?

I can't see Lester behind his machine, but I hear him clear his throat a few times more than he probably needs to.

"My bunk, sir?" His voice sounds weak, almost like it's not there at all.

The doctor lowers the tablet and folds his arms in front of himself. "I'm just curious how you find the amenities."

"The amenities? They're wonderful, sir," he says carefully. "Is something wrong?"

"Well, I was only wondering if you found the shower acceptable. You must not be using it. I could smell you from the hall. So I only wondered if they weren't up to your standards."

"Oh." I hear Lester swallow a lump in his throat. Then a quiet gulp of air. "No, the showers are great. I'm so sorry. I won't let it happen again."

I lean over to get a look at Lester behind the machine. I can't see much, but I do watch him pick a hair from his beard with his fingers, adjust the strap of his patch.

"Good," the doctor says with a smug sort of air. "What do you think, Mr. Youngwell?"

I jump a little, shocked to hear my name. His eyes are blue. Dark blue. Impossibly dark with just a flash of light, like the ultramarine of the ocean in a lightning storm.

But the longer I look, I realize only one of them is dark. The other is light blue, pale like early-morning sky. I don't think I've ever seen anyone with vastly different eye colors before.

I've been staring into them like a deer in headlights, I realize. I blink and look away, hoping he hasn't noticed.

"Wait, what?" I ask.

A smile flickers across his mouth and vanishes just as fast. He takes a small step toward me, and it feels like he's grown a foot taller. His white coat is crisp and ironed, the veins of his hands are as thick as garter snakes, and his sneakers are blue to match his scrubs.

And when I look closer at his feet, I'm pretty sure something seems off. But I can't tell what. Something's not where it should be, or maybe there's something…extra? I don't know.

"Surely your nose has been unfortunate enough to make contact with this *technician*," he sneers, visibly cringing like the word is bitter in his mouth. "So, what do you think of us now that an agent of Axiom, whom you have trusted to provide quality care for you and your family, smells as foul as he? I can assure you this is not the norm. The rest of our staff do believe in hygiene."

What I wish I could say but obviously can't is that a) I haven't "trusted" my care to Axiom, I was literally forced to, b) how does he know *I'm* not the one who smells bad? and c) I couldn't give two shits if this guy's never showered a day in his life. Why would I? It doesn't make him any less qualified to do his job, does it?

But I already know this man—this *doctor*—is reaching for exactly one answer. And if I don't make him happy, who knows what he'll do? Not fix my dad? Let Judith literally die from grief?

"Yeah, it's, um—he could shower, I guess?" I say, shifting my eyes the other way from Lester. I feel bad for him. And what's worse is I can't believe I feel bad for someone from *Axiom*.

"Well, well. This is awkward." The doctor pauses like he's waiting for Lester to respond, which he doesn't.

I see only Lester's hand gripping the machine—or trying to. He misses twice, and when he finally gets it, he rolls it away. Around the corner of the machine, I watch a laser scan his eye at a post on the wall like the one above our doorbell at home—which must mean they lock their patients in the room, since I'm assuming only Axiom employees are programmed in their system.

After he leaves, the doctor inches to the foot of the bed, heel to toe, heel to toe, and turns his gaze back to his tablet. He's smiling to himself and puffing his chest, and I really wish I could go back in time and beat *him* up instead of my dad.

"Hey, do you know where my—" I'm trying to ask where Judith is when he interrupts me.

"Your results are in," he says.

"Results?"

"Looks like you've got a fairly clean cut in the fifth metacarpal." As if I'm supposed to know what that means.

Before I can ask, I glance at his feet again and realize what was bothering me before: his shadow. It's not where it should be. The sunset is *right there* behind the glass, like smack dab in our faces, beaming like a spotlight. This means his shadow should stretch, long and black, all the way over to the door. So should mine, and the shadow of the bed. They should be oblong in weird shapes that little kids would think were monsters.

But they're not. Weirdly not. The lighting is all weird. There are shadows, sure, but they're just regular and vague like any random shadow that you get so used to seeing you don't even think about. I glance up at the recessed lights that are still on, just white bulbs placed randomly in the ceiling.

I don't know if this is actually strange or if I'm losing my mind. I know for a fact the hospital is right on the ocean. But I guess I'm not sure if this particular room is. If it's not, then all of this—the sunset, the ocean, the glass, the vents diffusing the scent of salt—has to be some weird Axiom technology.

"So, a broken…what was it?"

"Your pinky finger, Mr. Youngwell. Right hand. What they're teaching children in school these days, I'll never know. I digress. Are you right-handed?" I nod, and he inhales sharply through his nose. "Perhaps you should have thought of that before you committed battery against your father."

Is that just common knowledge now? I don't remember confessing to anyone here, but maybe Judith did. Or they probably pieced it together themselves. With all my dad's blood and the state of my hand, I guess that wouldn't be hard to do. I take the ice pack from the bedside table again and squeeze it even though the pain surges up my arm, into my elbow, when I do it.

"What's happening to him? My dad?"

The doctor taps his foot a few times, his shadow barely moving. "Let's worry about *you*," he says.

"Is he okay?"

He narrows his eyes and takes a few breaths to consider. "Let me tell you something, Mr. Youngwell. When a criminal comes in for treatment, it is very hard to feel sympathetic toward him, especially knowing his very own actions are the sole cause of his injuries. If it were up to me, I might let him see how he heals up on his own."

What the fuck kind of doctor talks like this to their patient?

"Unfortunately," he sighs, "given your sister's donation, and the fact that you are the apparent *chosen one* to receive this Third Eye thingamajig, I'm afraid it's not up to me."

"Judith? Do you know where she is?"

He smiles. "You will not be able to use that hand properly for at least two months until you are healed, Mr. Youngwell. People either learn to write with their other hand or just hold their pens differently, whichever is simpler for you."

I give exactly zero shits about that. What the hell is going on with my family?

"I will put the order in," he says, "and your nurse will be right in to set you up."

He turns away. I open my mouth to speak, but he turns back with the widest grin, raising his tablet like it's a glass of champagne or something. Something about the gesture—the way he's dismissing me—replaces my question with rage. I squeeze the ice pack and practically feel the break in my finger get even bigger as it screams in pain.

The doctor turns again and walks away, pulling the door shut behind him.

"Wait! What's going on with my dad?"

He stops the door with the heel of his foot, pauses, and pushes it back open with his hip, chuckling.

"I almost forgot. I'll also be ordering up a round of antibiotics. You would be wise to take them."

Chapter Twelve

I'M STARING OUT into the calm water, hoping for some sort of osmosis that will calm my nerves, when a light tapping comes to my door. Before I can answer, it opens, and I see her.

Madame Berenice.

"Monsieur!" She beams like we're old friends. I swallow a lump and hold up my broken hand in a pathetic attempt to wave.

She's holding several things in her hands, and she's also changed into scrubs. Her poofy eyeball-studded bun is now a long braid down the front of her shoulder, also studded with eyes. It makes me wonder if they are somehow implanted into the strands of her hair. They look like they're watching me.

"I am sorry to see you again under these circumstances. I am not sure if you recall me in your room earlier to get you settled and assess your vital signs. You seemed…not all here."

Yes, I remember now. Something about the adrenaline and the crazy shift of calming energy when I got here made me, like, crash or something. Or did they inject me with something?

"What are you doing here?" I ask.

She holds up the things in her hands. "I'm going to change your bandages, apply your splint, and give you your antibiotic, of course."

"My nurse was supposed to be doing it."

She throws her head back and laughs. "I can see why you are confused. Let me explain." She carefully places the items into different pockets of her scrubs, even the large cast thing that I'm guessing is for my hand. "You see, long before I became Seer of donations, I was but a humble nurse. When I came to this country and raised my family, I started to— what is the phrase?—grow in the ranks, up the proverbial ladder, yes? Now, although I am in my current position, I still have quite the passion for patient care. I will be truly pleased if you would allow me to be your nurse."

She makes it sound like I have a choice, but I doubt anything good would come out of my saying no. I nod, and she removes the things from her pockets and places them on a small table, which she then wheels over to me.

"Let's see the damage, shall we?"

When she takes off my bandages and cleans the wounds—several cuts and lots of blood—she's surprisingly gentle. I thought she would be bitter about me destroying the contract and her tablet, and she would take it out on me. Maybe the gentleness is a tactic in its own right, a way to manipulate me into getting the surgery.

She hums to herself as she applies ointment and wraps me up in fresh gauze, and I notice that her blue gloves match some of the plastic eyes in her braid. I also notice she too doesn't have a shadow.

The splint is a black sleeve around my wrist and hand with an opening for my thumb and first two fingers. My other two are completely useless now, the supposedly broken pinky and the ring finger it's now conjoined with.

"There we are," she says softly, and throws the packaging and bloody bandages into the trash, along with her gloves.

I wiggle my fingers, trying not to wince in front of her.

From the pocket of her scrubs, she pulls out two tiny packets.

"I thought you might be in pain. I brought you something for it, along with your antibiotic."

What she doesn't know is that I like the pain. That I want to experience it. I shake my head, and she puts one of the packets back in her scrubs.

"So, just the antibiotic. Got it."

She opens the packet and shakes a pill into her other hand. I have a vague feeling in my gut that it's *not* an antibiotic. But I can't say that.

"Uh, what's it for?" I ask.

She doesn't bat an eye. Because she's trying to get me to agree with her, she says, still smiling, "Every fracture receives an antibiotic, I'm afraid. Just to be safe. This is especially important when there is a wound involved, yes? So you will not develop any kind of nasty infection."

I have no idea if that makes sense, but I don't trust her. Judith would know. Maybe I'm paranoid and blowing this out of proportion, and I'm passing up on real medicine that might save my life. The trouble is, I can't afford to make a mistake right now.

Don't trust 'em. Not a word. Even one of their own employees said not to. But I've already been through a spiral trying to decide if I can trust *him* or not, and I still can't decide.

I just need time to think it over. And I need to find Judith.

"But they're just scrapes," I say, raising my hand as if she could see through the splint and bandages. "I don't really need medicine, do I?"

"Hmm. Well, let us think about this." She closes her fingers around the pill. "You have said no to the pain medication already, which is, how you teenagers say, totally fine, dude." She giggles at what turned out to be a joke, then clears her throat when I don't laugh back. "But I would say this is the more important one. You are a smart young man, are you not?"

Would a smart person refuse everything she has to offer even if it would truly help me? Normally, I would think this level of caution is appropriate, but part of me knows that even if I keep refusing, she will get my eye another way—a more violent way, one where they wouldn't even put me under sedation at all. They'll just force it out of me.

"Now, Monsieur, if you do not wish to ingest the pill by mouth, perhaps you might be more comfortable taking it intravenously."

"What does that mean?"

"My apologies. This means through the vein. I would quickly insert a needle into your arm and—"

"No!" Agreeing to that is a straight shot to getting knocked out, isn't it?

Slowly, she places the pill inside a pouch, which she slips into her pocket. She looks up and smiles a thin-lipped, patient smile that doesn't quite reach her eyes. I think she's mad. A certain electricity in the smile feels foreboding, like a tiny rumble of thunder before a storm sets in.

I fumble for words because I don't want to seem like I'm *refusing-refusing* and say, "I just don't like needles." Fear of needles—that's a thing, right? Clever, Hen, clever.

Finally, she nods, the smile replaced with a blank face I can't read. "If you truly do not wish to, of course I will not force you."

I feel relieved. Then I feel scared. She's so straight-backed, so tight-jawed, so sharp in her enunciation that her simple act of speaking is terrifying.

"I'll—I mean…can I think about it?"

Squinting, she searches my eyes for something—for the truth? For a vulnerability she can pounce on? She nods again, only very slightly, and backs away from me. My heart throbs in my neck as I envision myself on a surgical table.

She scans her eye and reaches for the door handle. And right when I think she's about to leave to go call a Watcher or a doctor to hold me down, she sighs. Lifts her chin. Changes her mind about something.

I follow her with my eyes as she glides over to the glass and peers out to the sunset, to the furious orange sky striped with now-lavender clouds, to the bald, fat sun that's barely kissing the lip of the ocean—a sun I still don't have to squint to look straight at.

The water remains so incredibly flat, it almost looks like a painting, that's how motionless and picturesque. I don't think there have been any waves at all since I've been here.

Then just like that, to prove me wrong, a ripple. Small waves, way out there at the horizon, right in front of the sun.

More movement. They're not waves, they're…fish or something—another and another—these little shapes bobbing out of the water and sinking under the surface like ice cubes.

A flash.

I'm on the beach again, buried in the sand. I can't move a muscle or else I'll risk cracking it. I'm a sand monster with all my armor. Judith's at my feet, piling more and more on top. She's stopped blowing it into my eyes because I think she got bored with my not fighting her.

Mom's sitting on her chair, munching on the trail mix.

I close my eyes because the sun is bright and listen to birds caw. I wonder what they're saying. Probably warning one another to fly away because they know I'm a terrifying monster.

"Kids, look!"

I open one eye, squinting. Mom's not in her chair. She's standing and pointing out to the ocean, her dark-purple fingernails straight in front of her. Her sun hat almost flies off her head, but she catches it with her other hand. "Henry, sweetie, look out there!"

I sit up, and sand flies everywhere. I'm like a sand Godzilla. All the tiny cities and people below me get crushed and buried like an avalanche.

"Jude, Hen, do you see?"

I don't know what I'm supposed to be looking at—all I see are waves. I look left and right and left and right, but nothing.

"What is it?" I ask. I wonder if there's a shark or a mermaid. My heart races.

"So cool!" Judith shouts. Her hair is in pigtails, and I wonder what it would be like to have long hair like her and Mom. I look to where I think Judith is looking. So far out, there's…ice cubes? Like the ocean is one big bowl of water, and all the ice has come to be in this one spot. I have no idea what they are. I know they're not *real* ice cubes because that's dumb.

The longer I can't tell, the madder I get. I can't ask Judith to tell me because she always knows everything, and it's so annoying, and I hate looking stupid in front of her.

I run over to Mom, and she lifts me into her arms so I can see better. Her body is so hot and sweaty from the sun. She puts her hat on my head and laughs, so I laugh too, but it's fake because I'm mad at her—for lots of reasons. First, for taking me away from Dad. Second, for *hurting* Dad. And third, because she knows I'm dumber than Judith, but she pointed out these *things* and won't tell me what they are even though she knew that Judith would know right away, and now I just look like an idiot, and I hate hate hate looking dumb, and Judith is so much smarter than me.

"Do you see 'em, sweetie?" Her voice is scratchy and soft, and I wish I could never hear it again. I wish she would eat sand. This is the same voice that reads me stories at night and sings to me when I'm sick, but I never want her to sing again.

As she points out to the ice cubes, I look at the black edges of the band-aid around her finger from when Dad burned her with a cigarette last week. Judith and I heard them screaming and fighting about it. They called each other bad words.

One of the ice cubes pops out of the water, and that's when I finally see more. It's not ice, duh. It's dark. It's black. Some kind of fish, but bigger? It's like a sea monster from a movie—like me! Except I came from the sand.

I watch as it sinks into the water again. Before it disappears, it slaps its tail on top and makes a gigantic splash. Water spraying so far up into the sky like a blaze of blue fire. It's the coolest thing I've ever seen.

"They're so beautiful," Mom says. I'm still really mad, though. I wish I could punish her. Then it hits me.

"*So* beautiful," I say, finally knowing exactly how I'll get her back.

"So beautiful, no?" It's the nurse now.

I'm in the hospital bed, my eyes squeezed tight. I don't want to open them because I don't want to lose sight of Mom again.

As hard as I try, it only takes seconds for her to fade. And when my hand starts to ache, reminding me of everything from the last few hours, she vanishes completely. I wonder when the next time she'll come is. And Judith—I wonder when the next time I'll see her is.

I turn to Madame Berenice, rubbing my forearm just below the splint with my other hand like it'll make the pain go away, because what kind of freak am I to want this pain? I'm about to ask her if I can see my dad, but before I can open my mouth, she opens hers.

"This is one of the perks of working here." She smiles as she says it, gazing out at the ice cubes that are sinking and not resurfacing.

"What perk?" I ask.

"Whale watching, yes? Right from the comfort of inside."

"But they're not real," I almost laugh.

Only when she bunches her eyebrows together do I realize what came out of my mouth. It makes me gasp, and I realize that gasping is even more suspicious, so I bump my hand against my leg to make it seem like an accident—and *fuck,* it hurts. Hello, my name is Henry, and I'm a nightmare human.

But is that what I really think—that the glass, the sunset, the whales are an illusion? Is that the conclusion my brain came to? It makes sense with there being no waves, with not having to squint to look at the sun. With the lack of shadows.

"Aww," says the nurse. Her face doesn't change or move a muscle. She sees right through me. "That looked like it really hurt."

"It's totally fine." I try to smile, to will away the tears. My free fingers and thumb are bent into claws. It takes me several seconds to straighten them out and relax.

"You don't need to pretend, do you know?" I look up and she's turned back to the window, except she's not looking out to the water. It seems like she's looking straight at the material of the glass, like she's examining it or something.

"Pretend what?" I ask, squinting at the glass too, trying really hard to focus on it. All I see is water.

She raises a hand and moves it half an inch, an inch, two inches, to the window, and strokes her chin.

"You are in the hospital, are you not? You have every right to ask for help."

I don't mean to, but I chuckle because of course I can't ask for help. She sweeps her eyes up to the vents and peers at them like she's looking for something. Then she turns and walks over to me, smelling of cheap floral perfume.

"Well, just in case you think of something, you can always ring this bell." She points to a blue button on the wall behind my bed with a big, swirly eye painted on it. "I will be right here in a blink. Consider the antibiotic, yes? An infection, I'm afraid to say, could be quite sinister."

"Okay," I say before I realize what she means. Think about it? As in I don't have to take it if I don't want to?

And exactly like she's reading my mind, she leans her head to one side, her hands clasped together in front of her, her long braid now dangling by her waist. "Remember, Monsieur. You always have a choice."

I don't know what she means, but a tear falls down my cheek, instantly cooling as it leaves a trail. I wipe it away as secretly, as nonchalantly, as I can. Which doesn't work, of course. Madame Berenice smiles like I'm the most precious thing in the world, which is embarrassing.

Something dawns on me. "How long am I staying here?"

"We would love to keep you overnight just to make sure everything is fine," she says, which seems excessive for a broken finger. It sounds a little like they want me to fall asleep so they can sedate me and I'll wake up with a Third Eye.

"Are you sure?" I say, as if I could change her mind. "You guys seem really busy. There was that huge line of people waiting outside to get in and be seen." I remember the nausea and dread I felt when the ambulance pulled up to the building and I saw all of them in a single file line, snaking around the hospital.

"Oh, do not waste your worry over that bunch," she says, waving a hand in the air to dismiss them…which is kind of weird because shouldn't she, a nurse, *be* worried about patients? I don't know. "Let us say it's a good thing your sister is here. We are…loyal to those who help us."

My heart thrums in my chest.

"Judith? You know where she is?"

The nurse flips her braid behind her back. "Of course I do. I am afraid, however, you cannot see her just yet."

"Why?"

"I believe she is busy with the surgeon at the moment."

My heart turns into a hammer trying to crush my ribs. "What surgeon? She's—is she having surgery?"

Madame Berenice's brown eyes flicker for just a moment. She opens her mouth to answer but closes it. "What on Earth would she need an operation for? She was not injured in the incident, was she?"

"*Incident* is a nice way to put it," I say without meaning to. What I should say is, *You literally said the word surgeon, so what else am I supposed to think?* I tap my finger against my thigh. The nurse doesn't seem to notice or care. I obviously can't tell her that I thought Judith was getting her other eye taken out.

"No, um, I guess she wasn't," I say. "Why is she seeing a surgeon then?"

She pulls out a tablet from the back pocket of her scrubs. I didn't even know she had one. These pockets are turning out to be quite cavernous. She turns it on and swipes through a few screens. It's damage-free and completely functional, so I guess it's a new one. "Yes, just as I thought," she says. "To update her on your father, for *he* is the one undergoing an operation."

I gasp so loud it makes her look up at me in shock. "What? He is?"

"Oh, yes, but there is no need to worry, Monsieur. He is receiving utmost care, please rest assured."

"Tell me why you want my dad's eye," I demand, as though I'm in a situation to demand things from Axiom.

She closes her eyes and breathes deeply into her nose. When she opens them again, she smiles gently and sits on the end of the bed, turning off her tablet.

"You misunderstand me. I am sorry to be the one to tell you, but it is better you know. Your father suffered a stroke when he underwent the physical trauma. His brain began to bleed and, unfortunately, because of his chronic alcoholism, his liver is sick. This means that his blood could not develop a clot, do you understand? He endured a massive hemorrhage, and therefore must have an operation to vacuum out the brain, for want of a better term. I do not believe they wish for a donation at this time."

She blinks, and her eyelids move in slow motion. My deep, heavy breathing is going in slow motion too. I'm a murderer—or could be.

After who knows how long, I return. To my left, the sky is now a mix of ruby red and violet.

My mouth is dry. "He could…die?"

"It is possible, yes. I would be surprised, however. We have the very best surgeons working on him. And we must get him back so that he can sign your consent form once again! Otherwise, we will have to wait until your birthday, which is—" She consults her tablet. "—not for six more months."

So, she wasn't lying? About the antibiotic or anything? They're not going to force me down and operate against my will? Sounds nice, but I don't know if I believe it.

"How do you know all this? Can you see him on your—" I nod to the tablet.

"Let's just say nurses have eyes all over the hospital, yes?" I think she means it to be a sort of joke, but the irony is thick, even for me.

Except something doesn't add up.

"So, my sister is getting the same update that you just gave me?" I ask. "Right this very second? It says that on your tablet?"

She smiles a little but furrows her brows ever so slightly. Nods.

"Can I see?"

"What? You mean my…" She gestures to the tablet.

I nod a little too eagerly and hope I don't come off as indignant as I feel.

She stands and snaps her back straight. "I don't know what you are getting at, Monsieur."

"I mean, really, though," I say, "does it say *doctor giving update to Judith Youngwell* or something? It has to. That's why you checked, right?"

"I am so sorry, I do not understand what you mean."

She knows exactly what I mean. She's acting more and more confused, trying to pretend like she doesn't understand English when she's been very fluent up till now.

"Where's my sister? What are they doing to her?" Because I'm positive what it really says is *Judith Youngwell undergoing Third Eye transplant.*

The nurse is backing up now, inching backward toward the door, the tablet clutched in her fist. "I will be back in a bit to check on your hand," she says.

A barrage of knocking and pounding on the door.

Madame Berenice gasps and turns to look, but there's nothing to see. Just the door. Just the voice screaming on the other side of it.

"Is my brother in there? Henry? Henry!"

Chapter Thirteen

THE POUNDING ON the door is so loud and so forceful that the glass sunset shakes each time it's struck. I imagine it shattering into a million tiny shards, the ocean rising to a tidal wave and flooding the room, taking me far away out to sea.

"You need to calm down, Miss," a man's voice calls, as crystal clear as if it were on this side of the door.

"*Maybe if you weren't taking so fucking long,*" Judith shrieks.

Here's the thing. Obviously, Judith is pissed, but I have no idea with whom. Me for giving our dad a stroke, Axiom for god knows what's been happening for the past hour, or is she finally unleashing all the pent-up fury she's had over her eye?

"Henry? Henry, are you in there?"

The nurse whips her eyes over to me. She widens them as huge as saucers, her nostrils flared, mouth a straight line. Both her hands clutch the tablet to her chest. She shakes her head so subtly it could be that her neck is so tense, she's trembling with fear. And why exactly is she freaking out, a woman who is so confident and put together? What is she trying to hide?

"Yeah, I'm here," I call, because fuck Axiom. If Judith wants to kill me, that's fine, but I would love to help her to destroy these assholes in the process.

"See? What did I tell you?" she shouts.

"Miss, please don't speak to me in that tone," says the man.

"Maybe if you did your job, huh?"

"The machine is malfunctioning. There's nothing I can do."

"What machine?" I ask the nurse. Her eyes and mouth clamp shut, and she doesn't answer. "What machine?" I shout so Judith can hear me.

"He's trying to do the stupid retina scanner," she calls, "but it's not freaking working because—"

"Shh," the man seethes.

"Who is that?" I shout.

"A Watcher!" Judith shouts.

"Why isn't it working?"

She pauses a moment too long. "Because he's incompetent."

She's lying, I know she is. And instead of telling me what she knows, she's…insulting him? Which is mind-boggling on its own, but even weirder is that he's letting her do it.

"Can you open the door from your side?" she asks.

"There's a scanner on this side too."

I look at the nurse, who closes her eyes and makes the sign of the cross, muttering to herself. She turns on her tablet and swipes to another screen.

"What are you doing?" I ask her, but no response. She starts typing with one finger. My heart gallops. I repeat myself, louder, but she still doesn't answer. What do I do, what do I do?

Judith calls. "Is someone in there with you?"

"My nurse, but she won't open the door."

Judith groans. Maybe I should get up and take the tablet from her hands. I swing my legs over the side of the bed, but the movement makes my head rush. I feel like I'm about to fall, so I stay in bed.

"Ma'am? Ma'am, this is Judith Youngwell," she says calmly. "Could you please open the door so I can see my brother? I want to talk to him about our dad. Please. My dad's in surgery. He might not make it. Please." She's trying for sympathy.

But Madame Berenice doesn't look up from the tablet. She continues typing, biting the side of her cheek.

"You took my eye," Judith calls, her voice shrill like she's on the verge of tears. "Please, I just want to see him. You took my eye, that's the least you can do."

"Yes, and for your donation, you received a *home*," spits the nurse. "A very nice and *expensive* home. You should be grateful. Instead, with your insolent behavior, you force a Watcher from his post, march down to this room, and bang on the door like you own the hospital. Who do you think you are, hm? Oh, I will show you who you are, little girl."

The nurse presses the screen one final time like an astronaut pressing the red panic button. I expect alarms to sound. I expect the hospital to burn.

Instead, there's only silence. Sheer, utter silence. Even Judith is quiet. She's not pounding on the door. She's not speaking or crying.

"Jude?"

"I hate it here," she whines.

The nurse smiles to herself, smug and satisfied with whatever she's done.

Outside the glass, the moon has somehow appeared while I haven't been looking. It's a perfect crescent hanging low to the water. Thousands of stars fill the sky, soft ocean waves shimmering with fractals of light underneath. I still feel like it's not real, but I stare at it anyway, hoping for whales to appear in the distance, hoping that Mom will come back to me.

"Didn't you say I had a choice?" I say quietly to the nurse.

"Hm? I'm sorry, I did not hear you."

"Earlier, you told me I always had a choice. Remember? I didn't want to take the antibiotic, and you said, 'Remember, Monsieur, you always have a choice.'"

"Ah," she says, chuckling as though nostalgic for the memory. "So I did. So I did."

I get to my feet, steady and no longer dizzy. I thought I could tower over her but we're the same height. I point my finger in her face. "Well, what I choose is to open this door and talk to my sister. We're going to leave. Do you understand?"

"I believe that is a wonderful idea," she says.

"Do you now?"

She smiles. "Yes. I do."

A scream erupts on the other side of the door. I know the scream. Judith? No. It's not close enough, I don't think.

I run to the door and pull on the handle, but it doesn't budge. I try again. Another scream, low-pitched and horrible.

"Judith? *Judith?*"

"Henry!"

I bang on the door, trying to break it down, but it's too thick.

The scream gets louder. It's guttural, like someone's being tortured to death. It pierces my chest and splits me wide open. I swear I've heard it before. I know who it is, but I can't think. I can't think.

"Henry, don't come out," Judith squeals through a sob.

I try the handle again. I try with all my strength to rip it off. "*Judith! Are you okay?*"

"It's not me!"

"Who? Dad?"

More sobs. "Henry—"

"Judith, who?"

"Would you like to see, Monsieur?" the nurse asks casually. She's a blur as she moves around me and taps on the door. "Excuse me, this is Seer Madame Berenice coming out. Please guard the doorway and do not allow the Youngwells to interfere, if you would be so kind."

"Yes, Madame," says the Watcher outside.

The nurse moves her face to the scanner mounted into the wall. The yellow laser lights up and begins its dance. I can see its reflection in her eye as it gets bigger, wider, and scans her.

Even through the sound of the screams, I hear the door's lock un-latch. She pulls the handle, turns to look at me, and opens it, the screams erupting like lava.

Judith sprints past her and wraps her arms around me, her tears wet and cold against my neck. "Henry, don't look," she pants. "Don't look. It's awful."

I ignore her. As she cries into my neck, I look up to see a baton-wielding Watcher in one half of the doorframe, making sure I don't run out, but leaving enough space for me to see. Past him, the nurse is off to the side, her back straight as an arrow, a triumphant air about her.

And beyond her is exactly what Judith warned me of. Exactly what I don't want to see. Exactly what breaks what little was left inside me.

Sam.

He's writhing on the floor in a hospital gown, screaming as loud as he can, the veins in his neck thick and stretching away from his body like the roots of an uprooted tree.

Three Watchers surround him, each pointing tasers or guns at him or both. Blood pours down his face. But tasers don't leave wounds, do they? They don't make you bleed.

That's when I see it. His eye.

It's been ripped from its socket, and they haven't even sewn it up yet. It's an empty cavity pouring dark-crimson tears down his face, into his mouth. Splattered across his gown. Pooled on the floor around him. It reminds me of my father. Reminds me of what I'm capable of.

Sam opens his jaw and screams more. "*Where is he?* I saw you fuckers pull out of his driveway in your little ambulance. Did you give him that Third Eye bullshit at his *house?*"

A cold consumes me. He came looking for me? He was at our house and saw the ambulance there, then came *here* to console me? And now they're torturing him—all because, what? Judith and I were disobeying the almighty Axiom?

"Shut the fuck up!" A Watcher kicks Sam in the back.

Only he keeps yelling. The blood spilling into his mouth sashays and sprays through the air all around him as he screams.

"You won't get away with this, assholes. This Third Eye fuckery. I know what it really is!"

What it really is? What? And how is he screaming so fresh out of his surgery? Did they even put him under anesthesia, or did they do it just minutes ago?

Another Watcher stomps on his neck. This stops him. He doesn't say another word, only curls into a ball and whimpers when the Watcher lifts his foot.

Judith squeezes me tighter, and I realize I've let go of her completely, my arms limp at my sides.

"Why is he here?" she sobs. "I didn't even know he was having surgery, did you?" Judith isn't as close with Sam as I am, but she's had classes and eaten lunch and hung out with him and Norah and me on several occasions. She loves Sam because it's hard not to, and I'm pretty sure that, just like Norah does, she knows I fell for Sam a long time ago.

"He—he wasn't," I choke. "It was supposed to be me. Drill Day. It was me. I—"

I break free of Judith's grip and charge toward the door so I can help. I'll attack all three Watchers at once and make them pay. I'll—

The Watcher steps fully into the doorframe, huge and overpowering, and lifts the baton above his head. I cower away. But what if I didn't? What if I just tried to get around him anyway? I could kick away his baton and slide through his legs, couldn't I?

No, of course I couldn't. I'm weak. Slow. I could beat up my dad, but only because he's frail and only because he was drunk. I stand next to Judith, who's breathing like she's running a marathon.

Sam hasn't screamed again, but he's grunting and coughing.

I catch Madame Berenice's eye. Maybe I expect her to wink or to smile maniacally. She does neither. She says something so softly I can barely hear her voice. The Watchers replace their tasers in their belts, and when one leaves and comes back with a gurney, they lift Sam, who's hardly struggling anymore, and roll him away.

"Now, doctor, be a darling and see to it that Mr. Oakes is treated with the utmost care, hmm?" The nurse smiles.

"Sure thing, Madame," comes a voice. A shape comes into view and trails after them. It's the same doctor who was in my room, the short one with two different blues in his eyes.

"And you, dear," says the nurse. The one Watcher remaining, the one watching over Judith and me, turns to meet her, his posture matching hers. "I do not believe the Youngwells will have a lift back to their place of residence. See to it that they do within the hour, yes?" Her eyes flick over to me, then away again. "That is, only if they wish. After all, our patients always have a choice. We are not barbarians."

"Of course, Madame." The Watcher nods.

"You won't get away with this!" Judith shouts through her sobs. "How can you just—we'll tell everyone!"

Madame Berenice smirks and inches her way over until she's just an inch away. The smell of chemicals. I see every single groove around her mouth and eyes.

"You poor girl," she whispers. "Do you think they will believe you?"

"His name wasn't called on Drill Day," I say, my breath ragged. "When he walks out of here without an eye, of course they'll believe us, you psycho."

"Ah, but that is where you are mistaken. Your friend will be walking out of here with two of them, and we have a way of making them identical in every way. That is, if he walks out of here at all. Ta-ta, Mademoiselle. Monsieur. Do take care of that hand now."

At this, she glides away, the eyes in her braid swaying side to side with each step.

It feels so final. So, she wants me to leave? Now that they have Sam, do they not even want me for the Third Eye anymore? I guess not. And that must mean they won't try to save my dad now.

The Watcher turns back to us and reaches for the door handle. As he pulls it shut, I want to scream and lunge at him, tear his throat open. Demand answers, or else I'll kill him. But all of that's just a silly fantasy.

The door closes. The lock clicks. The laser in the scanner lights up and resets. It's me and Judith alone in this room. Me and Judith and the moon. And the ghost of Sam's scream.

Chapter Fourteen

TIME OOZES AND bleeds. It doesn't feel real anymore. I feel frozen.

We both stand completely still. I'm exhausted, and all I can see is a bloody black hole of an eye. For a while, I try to blink it away, but I give up. It's here. Present. The smell of rust is still thick in the air.

"I'm so sorry," Judith whispers. "I know he's your—"

"Did that just happen? Am I tripping?"

"If you are, then so am I."

My legs are weak, but I don't sit. Don't lean against the wall. I think about going to chase after Sam, even though I'd have no idea where to look. But that would be stupid. Impossible. Instead, I dare myself to not fall over. Make a game of it. A little part of me hopes I'll pass out, hit my head, and never wake up.

Judith takes a deep breath. Holds it. "That was the most horrific—"

"Yeah, well, leave it to Axiom."

She exhales in a long, steady stream. "Are they really just calmly driving us home after that?"

"Supposedly."

"I can't," she says, still in a whisper. "I can't leave Dad. He's having *brain surgery.*"

Is he? Or are they letting him bleed out and die now that they're giving Sam the Third Eye and not me?

Every time I try to close my eyes, the image of the boy I love writhing in pain haunts every cell in my body. It was my fault. His eyelessness, his torture…that was all me. What kind of future is there for him? Because there's certainly no future at all for me. For *us.*

How will Norah react when she learns about this? Will she never talk to me again? Oh god, and it's her birthday. She will always associate this day with what happened. The tragedies keep compounding, and everything is my fucking fault.

"You don't have to leave," I say. "But I do. I can't be here right now."

Judith clears her throat, speaks louder. "Yeah, why don't you go get some sleep?"

I open one eye, then the other. I catch her wringing her hands.

"Are you trying to get me to leave?" I ask, then throw my hands up, resolved to let everything go. "Actually, you know what? I don't care."

"I just mean that if something happens," she says, "I'd rather be here to deal with it, all right? Also, he needs one of us here so he can recover faster."

I sigh and grumble, then begin walking in circles. There's no stopping her. "Go ahead, lecture me. I know you want to."

"Listen, there's so much data to support the theory that patients recover more quickly and more fully when they have support from people around them, especially support from people they love."

I start to cackle and put my hand over my mouth. "You're not serious," I say. And when she looks up at me with her sad little doe-eyed look, I pounce. I attack. I want to hurt her because why does she not seem to care about what just happened to Sam? Who cares about Dad when we saw somebody we *actually* love get tortured in front of us?

"Dad doesn't love us," I hiss. "You don't believe that, do you?"

She raises her eyebrow and doesn't respond right away. With one hand on the pristine white wall, she begins inching the perimeter of the room, all the while tapping her fingers.

"It's funny that you think just because he's an alcoholic, he doesn't love us, Hen. It's a medical condition, you know."

"That's obviously not what I meant. It's not that he's an alcoholic, it's how he treats us. He refuses to get help."

She doesn't respond, and her silence infuriates me. With my good hand, I grab a fistful of my hair and pull it as hard as I can. She sees me but ignores it.

"I cannot do this with you right now," I whine.

She scoffs. "Do what?"

"Listen to you lecture me about the science of addiction when all I'm saying is that if he loved us, he wouldn't treat us like shit. Lots of people get happy and carefree when they're drunk! He's just an asshole. And why do you think that is? Because he loves us? Don't tell me you're forgetting what he called you."

Her fingers stop just short of the glass wall, and she gazes out with tears in her eye.

"You mean right before you beat the living shit out of him for no other reason than you could?"

"That's not fair," I say, even though it's maybe the most accurate thing in the world. Maybe I did it just because I could—just because I knew that it would feel good.

"Whatever," she grumbles. "Well, despite his faults, I care enough to stay. And you know what? At least he loves one of us."

"Yeah, right. He loved you enough to sign your eye away." As soon as it comes out, I feel an inch tall. I want to die. Not just die. I want her to kill me, to take me in her hands and pulverize me.

"Very nice," she says instead, mindlessly reaching for the glass wall.

"I'm sorry," I whisper. "I'm sorry, Jude."

She's silent. Remains silent. She stays like that for the longest time, and her cold shoulder makes me feel a thousand times smaller.

"Judith, I didn't mean it, I swear. I'm so sorry."

Still, nothing. Not even a tap of her finger against the glass, an imaginary piano key.

My jaw quivers. "Don't hate me. Please don't hate me," I breathe. Then quieter: "You're all I have."

Her silence fills the room. It cleaves through all the noise in my head.

"Jude…"

Cautiously, I walk over to her and place my hand on her shoulder. Maybe I expect her to freak out. Maybe I expect her to scream. To recoil from my touch. To go limp. To cry.

What I don't expect is this frozen shell of a person in my hand. Her skin is as stiff as a sheet of ice, her muscles hardened, her entire body locked in place.

"Jude?" I shake her, but nothing. "Jude, come on. Judith? Judith!"

My eyes trace her arm all the way to the glass. I grab her forearm and tug a little, but she still doesn't give. Her eye is totally fixed. Her lips are slightly parted. I wrap my hand around her wrist and pull like it's a cord in the wall. Nothing.

"Judith, what the fuck? What the *fuck*?"

I reach for a finger to pry it away. My skin makes contact with the glass.

A surge of cold. A surge of happiness. Electricity.

Is this what it feels like to get struck by lightning?

When I open my eyes, I'm in a dark auditorium like the one at school, except it's ten times bigger. Each seat is filled, everyone breathless, silent, as they stare intently at a man on stage who's lit by a dozen spotlights. Beside him is a large red sheet covering something much taller than he is.

"Thank you all for your attention," he says, his voice booming as if through a microphone. "Today, I would like to share my new invention. It has been in development for more than a decade, and I'm so pleased it's finally ready to show the world."

The audience stares in wide-eyed anticipation.

"May I please present to you today, the Mirror of Memoria!"

He pulls the sheet with a *whoosh!* It's a huge plate of glass that climbs halfway up the ceiling. The audience is transfixed.

"Now, allow me to demonstrate. I will need a member of the audience for this part. Ma'am, how about you?"

Without hesitation, a woman in the front row makes her way onstage, and the spotlights move to her.

"Please close your eyes and think of a memory," the man instructs. "It can be any memory you wish, though please be certain it's appropriate for the audience."

The woman chuckles, turning red, and closes her eyes. After a few moments, she nods.

"Open," he whispers, the word echoing around the room.

In a blink, the glass plate is no longer transparent but a photograph of sorts, or an amazing work of art. It's a mountaintop covered in snow, bright white everywhere you look, except for the clearest blue sky above and the most vibrant pine trees in the world.

"Is this your memory?"

The woman, tears in her eyes, nods vigorously. She tells a story about how she fell in love with a stranger on this mountain, how they were married on this same mountain just a year later, and how they now have four beautiful kids, and they're a big happy skiing family.

"Incredible." The man turns back to the audience and smiles. He lifts an arm to gesture toward the top of the mountain. "Note the two plaques up in the corners. These are the true power. They can see a person's deepest, most intimate memory and configure the glass to display it. That, my friends, is the power of the Mirror of Memoria."

He lifts his arm toward the glass and bows deeply to his knees.

Every single member of the audience, just a second ago breathless and still as a corpse, now stands. They clap slowly at first, and soon they're cheering and hollering like their lives depend on it.

But it only lasts a moment before each of them freezes mid-cheer, some with hands in the air, some with their faces contorted into a scream.

Silence.

The man is stuck mid-bow, his head at his shins.

A bell rings from nowhere and everywhere at once, almost like the bike Judith and I used to share as kids, then a woman's voice. "Surgical Revolution, by Axiom."

I feel something press into my arm and turn to see a hand there. A singular juniper eye meets mine. Judith's. White light surrounds her, almost like she's glowing.

The hospital room shifts into focus, the walls white, pristine, vacant.

"What happened?"

"I'm not…exactly sure," she whispers.

I peel my hand from the glass and look at it. It doesn't look any different, but it feels alive. I know that sounds ridiculous, but little pops of energy crackle in my palm and fingertips like miniature fireworks or even bursts of static.

"I think I had a bad dream," I say, backing away.

Judith looks out to the moon. "Were you in an auditorium?"

I nod, but my brain's going fuzzy. "I think so."

"I had the same dream."

I follow her stare outside to the barely moving waves and the perfect crescent moon. It's so close to the water that a fish could jump out and leap over the pointed hook of it.

"So, this isn't real?" Judith asks, gesturing to the ocean.

I remember how I realized that earlier all on my own. It was like the first smart observation I've ever made. "I'm pretty sure it's not."

"But how did they…"

I don't know what to say, so I shrug. They took this man's invention? But that doesn't explain…

If Judith and I were both in that auditorium, either it was some weird psychic twin thing or it was actually real. But, like, it can't be, can it?

"Were we there at the same time," I ask, "or in separate auditoriums?"

"You mean two different time continuums?"

I squeeze my eyes shut, a headache forming at the base of my skull. "I have no idea what I mean."

"The good news is I don't think it has anything to do with time travel or astral projection, so we can cross that off our list of theoretical physics."

I lie down on the bed and cover my face with a pillow. I'm dead tired, but I don't think I could fall asleep if I tried. What the hell just happened to us?

"Hey," Judith calls.

"Be quiet," I cry. I don't want to be here. I can't—not with Dad in surgery because of me, Sam getting mutilated wherever he is, and me not being able to do anything for either of them. They better come get me soon or I swear I'll have a meltdown.

Judith's weight shifts the bed. "That thing with Sam was a threat, right?"

I don't say anything because I want this conversation to be over.

"No, seriously, it seemed like they were all, 'If you don't do what we say, this is what'll happen to you,' right? 'If you try and get out of this, we'll make sure to torture your friends.' And we are nowhere near the surgery wing. We're still in the emergency department. So it doesn't even make sense that Sam was over here unless it was done intentionally to scare me—us, I mean. Scare us, right?"

I turn over and throw my pillow across the room. She looks over at the pillow, then at me.

"Listen, Jude. I know you're onto something right now, and I fully support you, but can we at least have like five minutes of silence after *every-thing* that just happened? Sam? That freaking *glass thing?*"

She nods and doesn't say anything. I turn back around and realize there's not another pillow, so I put the crook of my elbow over my eyes.

All I can hear for a while is the sound of my breathing. I force myself to be still, but then what I hear is Judith. I'm sure she thinks she's being silent, but she makes the quietest little noises when she gets lost in her thoughts. She always has. For seventeen years I've been able to ignore it, but right now I want to kick her off the bed.

I sigh and sit up. "Okay, I'll bite. Why would they threaten us? We have nothing more they want. They already took your eye, and I really don't give a shit if they want mine."

"Well, we know they want your eye," she says.

"Yeah, and then put in the Third Eye thing."

"Wait, they want to put it in *you?*" she asks.

I narrow my eyes. "Yeah, they presented it at Drill Day. Wait, how do you know about the Third Eye? I haven't told you about it."

I flash back to the auditorium. My friends were acting weird. Way weirder than usual when the Third Eye was announced. Then Sam screamed what he did—*I know what it really is!*

"Judith, what aren't you telling me?"

I watch her face twitch as she tries to calculate a lie. When she can't think of one, she sighs and says, "They want me to have it."

"*What?*"

She stands up and lowers her voice. "Upstairs, when the doctor was explaining what was happening to Dad, he told me about the Third Eye and said that I was a perfect candidate for it because I just had my eye out. Something about capillaries and sewing together blood vessels? I don't know—even I didn't fully understand it. That was when I kind of just *ran* like an idiot. I ran down here to find you, even though I didn't really know where you were exactly. It was stupid, I know. That Watcher chased me, and I convinced him to bring me down to you."

For a while, I don't know what to say. I open my mouth several times, but no words come out. At last, I muster something.

"Yeah, that was pretty fucking stupid, Jude. But also kind of impressive."

"Thank you."

"You were talking to that Watcher like you owned the place, like you were his boss or something. You have never in your life *dared* to talk to someone like that—let alone a Watcher."

Silence. More things click into place.

"Wait," I say. "Were you trying to convince me to go home so you could stay here with Dad by yourself and have the surgery in secret? All that shit about him needing a person he loves so he can recover faster?"

"What? No, Henry, I'm not gonna do that. I just know you need to sleep. Look at you. Besides, they can't *do* the surgery unless Dad wakes up anyway."

"That's not true," I say. I really don't want to explain, but when she furrows her brow, I have to. "Sam. We just saw that they don't need any contract or permission. They can do whatever the hell they want."

"They wouldn't—" Judith starts, but she's interrupted by a hard knock on the door.

I shoot to my feet. The lock unlatches. But I thought the scanner was broken on the outside? The door shoots open, and there he stands, dressed for a night out on the town. Kent Cross.

Chapter Fifteen

I THINK I blacked out. Is Kent Cross here in my hospital room?

His smile is mischievous, his suit is two sizes too big, and his shiny blue sunglasses look ridiculous. He removes a stick of gum from his jacket, unwraps it, and holds it in front of his lips. He would almost look suave if he weren't so gross.

Kent sighs, but it feels unnatural, like he's rehearsed it. "You freaks ready to go or what?" It's not a question, more a statement of fact. He lifts the shades to the top of his head, then bites down on the gum.

Judith gawks as he wads up the foil wrapper and flicks it across the room. It hits the glass behind us and falls silently to the floor. I wish it had frozen still once it made contact with the glass, like Judith and presumably I did, just so I could know for sure I wasn't hallucinating.

"What the hell are you doing here?" I ask Kent.

"Now, Youngwell, is that any way to speak to someone doing you a favor?"

"I…I don't understand," says Judith.

Kent looks her up and down with a curled lip, pausing at the bloodstains on her sweatpants. Her patch next, and he scoffs. "Don't tell me the surgeon chipped off a bit of your brain when he was in there," he laughs.

I bolt over to him so quickly I don't know what I'm doing until he lunges backward and I run into the wall.

"Ooh, rough going. Gotta be faster than that."

I kick my leg at him, thinking I'm close enough to make contact, but I'm not. Even I know it's pathetic.

"Henry, stop." I can hear how embarrassed Judith is for me, but I'm too tired to care.

"That was fascinating," says Kent. "Now could we please go? I have other things to do, you know."

"What are you even doing here, Kent?" I ask.

He retrieves a set of keys from his pocket and dangles them in front of me. "Giving you a ride, duh."

"But how are you here at the hospital? I thought a Watcher was gonna drive us."

He scoffs. "Those lemmings? Believe me, you shouldn't trust any one of them behind the wheel. Please. That's why they called me. I have a much sharper eye, if you know what I mean." He winks, and it sends knives down my spine.

"Do you work, like, for Axiom, or…?"

"Junior agent," he says proudly. "My mother got me the job, thank you very much."

"So, you wouldn't have gotten it on your own?" I laugh, and it feels good to be on the other end. His nostrils flare briefly, and when they do, I also notice his upper lip. It's split from when I punched him this morning. It looks like he tried to cake some makeup onto it, but it looks bad, and I'm pleased with my work.

"And who would your lucky mother be?" Judith asks.

He doesn't have to say it before I realize. The way he stood for her in the auditorium and clapped. The way he shouted at me this morning, *"You have no idea who my mother is, do you?"*

He looks at me and grins. "I believe she was your nurse? Madame Berenice? And if I'm not mistaken, Youngwell—" He trails his eyes down my body. I cringe and recoil. "—she put that splint on your hand."

"Oh my god, Henry!" Judith gasps, apparently not noticing it until now. I just thought she wasn't saying anything because it reminded her of our dad.

"It's not a big deal," I say, putting it behind my back.

She circles me so she can look at it. "Um, it kind of is. Did you break it when—"

"He almost killed your drunk of a father, that's right."

I bite my tongue so I don't spit on Kent or try to lunge again. I'm pissed he knows about that because he will one hundred percent be blabbing it around school. Aren't there privacy laws or something for patients?

"Did your mother tell you that?"

He ignores me and looks at his watch, yawning. "I'd love to rock and roll, if you dweebs would follow me."

"I'd like to request another driver, actually," I say.

Kent erupts into laughter. It comes from deep in his gut, maniacal. He doubles over. "You—you want to—"

Normally this might anger me, but right now it fills me with shame more than anything. There are few things worse than being laughed at.

"You want to—request—"

My heart rate skyrockets. Judith cracks her knuckles beside me, like she's getting ready to fight him for me. But finally, he stands straight and wipes tears from his eyes.

"Oh my goodness, thank you for that." He sighs and leans his elbow against the wall. "I mean, you're welcome to take the bus. Walk home, for all I care. We offer rides to patients who have donated their…you know, services, blah blah. It's out of the kindness of our hearts, but you are under no obligation to accept. If you do, however, I am the only driver tonight. Believe me, it disappoints me just as much as it does you."

I think about spitting on him, but I don't. "Absolutely no way in hell I'm going with—"

"Psst."

I turn, and Judith nudges me over to the corner. Kent raises his hands and turns to walk out of the room, acting like he's not about to eavesdrop. I step over to her, very conscious not to lean on or even brush up against the glass.

"Just go," she says. "I know you're worried, but I really doubt they're going to touch me. They wouldn't risk forcing two people in a row to have surgery. Especially two minors. They can make an excuse for one, but two?"

As I look into her eye, all I can hear is Sam's scream. All I can see is them kicking him. "I really don't have a good feeling about it, Jude. At least come with me."

"I have to stay with Dad. I wasn't lying about the recovery thing. You need sleep, though, I know you have work tomorrow. I'll try and make it back home at some point to grab some new clothes." She looks down at her sweatpants and grimaces.

"Don't you worry about that, Miss Judith, they have pajama pants for you," Kent calls from around the door. "A toothbrush too. You'll have all you need."

I flip off the door. There's no version of reality where I would have ever thought I'd get in a car with this asshole.

I look into the glass—glass that's not a window, glass that's somehow a…what? Memory projection? Nothing's changed, not the moon dipping its toes into the water, nor the soft rippling waves reflecting the stars.

"Hey," I say, hesitating. "About what I said earlier—"

"I know," she finishes. "It's okay."

It's not, but I'm not about to argue. It's hard to accept that I'm the kind of person who, on top of almost murdering his father, says shitty things to the person he loves most in this world.

I follow her into the hall, where a ghost-white housekeeper is mopping up Sam's bloodstains. She has a wide, strong back that's turned to us and brown and gray-streaked hair tied into a bun at the back of her head, the two different colors making it look like some twisted, giant peppermint candy. I can also see the edges of a pale-blue eye patch on her left side. Her huge housekeeping cart is next to the wall, stacked with towels and bedsheets, with what I think is a trash can on one side.

Don't clean that up. Leave it. Remind everybody of what they did here.

I want to scream it at the top of my lungs. She'd understand. She probably feels the same way. She knows what it's like to be mangled and cut to pieces for no reason. But I do wonder why somebody who got their eye cut out would return to the very place it happened and come work for them.

It seems illogical. Same with Lester. Why stay somewhere the people you work with treat you like shit?

Kent claps to get our attention. He makes no acknowledgment of this woman or the blood she's cleaning up. Instead, he signals to a Watcher standing nearby and turns to Judith.

"This gentleman has graciously agreed to escort you back to your father's room while you wait for the surgeons to close him up."

Judith scowls at Kent and pulls me aside. "Don't kill him. Please don't kill him. It'll be bad for everyone."

I promise not to and awkwardly hug her. I watch as she follows the Watcher toward a set of doors down the hallway, her tail tucked between her legs.

"And you," Kent grins, "come with me."

Before I go, I watch as Sam's blood turns into streaks and swirls of pink before my eyes. The housekeeper's strong, muscled back bends and twists, moving the mop with a slow determination to erase the stain from existence. I feel smaller and smaller the more it disappears, as if I too am being erased from existence.

Kent clears his throat, and I follow him. As we walk out, someone shouts, "Hey!" and it makes me jump.

I turn and see a man in a white coat pointing at the woman mopping the blood. Her back is still to me.

"You are not to be in this wing tonight," the man spits. "Your manager should have made it very clear."

"Sorry, sir. We're short-staffed in housekeeping today. The charge told me to come here for a priority clean." The housekeeper's high-pitched babydoll voice comes out with an accent I can't place.

"I don't care what your charge told you. You shouldn't—"

The man in the lab coat looks up and meets my eye. He softens his face as though he wasn't just shouting and smiles when he turns back to the woman. She begins to turn, and he pulls her back, whispering something I can't hear because Kent tugs at my arm.

"Hurry up, Youngwell, I don't have all night."

*

WITH THE PRESS of a button, Kent pops open the top of his mother's convertible, instantly bathing us in moonlight.

Funny enough, the real moon isn't even a crescent like the glass had me believe. I guess I should have known the other was a fake, but I can never keep track of things like what the moon looks like from one night to the next. Tonight, it's high in the sky and round as an empty eye socket. There are a bunch of stars, though, one thing the glass got right. Some are big, some are tiny, and all are bright against the night sky.

"You like my ride?" Kent looks over to me and smirks. He's still wearing his blue sunglasses, which look so stupid at this time of night.

What I should tell him is that I was in this car earlier today and I know plenty well it's not *his* ride. I don't say it. I'm determined to not say a word this entire trip, just like I was earlier. I actually think I'll take a nap to avoid any interaction at all. But as soon as I close my eyes, he takes a turn way too fast, and I'm suddenly too afraid of dying to sleep. I should have just stayed with Judith.

Kent laughs like he can sense my fear. "I knew you'd love it. I picked it just for you. We could have taken the van, but I said to myself, 'You know, Cross, it's just the two of us gents, let's drive in style.'"

At my silence, he laughs again, and it has this way of squirming into my ear canal. Another turn onto the highway before he shifts gears and slams on the pedal. We fly into oblivion, and the wind roars in my ears. I'm freezing cold. He must be too, but he doesn't close the top. He just turns up the music, switches lanes without looking, and has the time of his life about to kill me.

After a long twenty minutes, we get to the security gate, and the guard—a new one I haven't seen before—waves us through. Second Axiom escort in one day. Must be all the rage in the gated community.

As we ascend the hill, I glance in the side mirror and don't even recognize myself. My hair's flying in every direction. My earlobes are pink and windburned. My eyes are bloodshot.

Finally, we reach the end of the cul-de-sac, and Kent puts the car in park.

"Aw, how nice," he says. "What a cute house they gave you."

I don't answer. If he thinks this is *cute*, I can't imagine what his house is like. He and Madame Berenice probably have separate wings of a mansion and three swimming pools.

I see Judith's piano through the window, the metronome perched on top like a little statue. The lights are on because no one thought to turn them off before we got in the ambulance.

The ambulance. I remember how they showed up without us even calling for them. I remember the paramedic grinding her fist into my dad's chest to wake him up. I remember how she tried to tell me what his possible last words ever were. How they got lost in the wind.

Kent sighs loudly and leans his elbow on the center console between us. His hand almost disappears into the too-long sleeve of his suit jacket. I feel him looking at me, but I refuse to look back. Am I imagining it or is his hand creeping closer to my leg?

I reach for the door handle but can't find it. It must be blended into the door and hidden in shadow. "Um, thanks for the—"

He cuts me off. "No thanks required, my good man."

Good man? My heart skips a beat. His fingers are doing this little dancing thing, swirling around in loops around the cupholder.

I glance at the clock—eleven—and without even thinking, I look up into his eyes. They're dark walnuts, with rings of white moonlight around the pupils. He's biting his lip.

"I think I'd better—"

He winks. *Winks.* "What's the rush? It's so early."

I know I have a tendency to misinterpret things, but is he… No, he can't be. Is he? I don't like this one bit.

I still can't find the door handle, which is ridiculous because I just used it earlier today. I know there *is* one, so it must be my nerves. My hand is trembling. I try to take a deep breath but I can't seem to breathe any deeper than into my throat. I try again and again, and now I think I'm hyperventilating. Which makes me freak out.

"Relax, man," Kent says in a slow voice. He leans back in his seat and puts his hand on my leg—*definitively* puts his hand on my leg, as in, I'm not making it up in my head. I feel the weight of it. I *see* it.

I'm getting lightheaded, and I can't breathe at all now, and I am positive I'm going to die…in Kent Cross's car. I'm going to die of asphyxiation in Kent Cross's car.

His hand squeezes my knee, and I flinch. He quickly leans away and laughs to himself.

"Whoa, whoa," he says, gripping the steering wheel. "Listen, Youngwell. I know I joke around with you, but you're hot, okay? I'm hot, you're hot. Hot people hook up, right? And, whatever, I'm not the bad guy you think I am. I'm sorry I called your sister that *word* this morning, but you punched me, so I think we're even."

"Even? *Even?*" It bursts out of me like a bomb, and suddenly I can breathe again—jagged, painful breaths, but I'm breathing. "You think we're fucking even? Are you out of your mind? You're the smartest kid in school, and you think we're *even?*"

I go to hit him, but now he's the one who flinches, and it feels incredible.

He laughs. "Please, Youngwell. I know you have a thing for Sam Oakes or whatever, it's so obvious how you *dote* over him. I don't know if you think it's a secret, but you're very bad at hiding it if you do. Perhaps it would do you well to go out with a real man. Someone in power. Someone—"

I ball my fist again, but then think of Judith asking me not to kill him. She said it with such sincerity. But I would love nothing more than to split his lip again, on the other side. Give him a little symmetry.

Kent must read my mind. He chuckles and waves his finger like I'm a dog and says, "Ah, ah." He points to the dashboard, to the display with the little clock. "Careful, careful. There's always someone watching, you know. I wouldn't hit an Axiom agent if I were you."

"*Junior* agent," I say. "You think an itty-bitty job your mommy gave you gives you power?"

He begins shaking his knee, and I squint at the display to see what he was talking about. At the top of it is a little notch that blends into the blackness. I can barely see it in the moonlight, so I lean my head closer.

That's when it flashes yellow. It's identified me—or taken a picture or something.

"Forget this," I say. I give up trying to find the handle and unbuckle my seatbelt.

"What is the big deal?" Kent says. "I do you a favor, and now you're freaking out for no reason? Youngwell, chill."

I lift myself onto the top of the door and pivot my way out. I expect him to grab my leg, but he doesn't, and I end up falling into the street on my knees, ripping even bigger holes in my jeans. I stand and glance back.

"Are you—you're serious right now, aren't you?" he says, and he somehow looks so big in this convertible, like he's doubled in size. It's bizarre.

I don't respond. I refuse to give him any more of my time. I sprint toward my house because fuck walking. He shouts after me, but I don't stop—not until I reach the door.

I put my eye up against the retina scanner, practically *scraping* it with my eyeball, and it's the longest scan of my life. My breath bounces off the doorframe, hot and pungent in my nose, as the yellow light—the same one as in Kent's clock—swirls around and around.

What if he's chasing after me? I can't even look back to check because the scanner will stop, and I'll have to do it all over again.

Finally, the laser flashes and shuts off, and I turn the knob. I glance behind my shoulder, and I think the car is gone but I jump inside and slam the door, unsure. The house is freezing cold because the air's been running all day.

The giant bloodstain is in front of me. Dad's blood, practically in the outline of his body. A tiny part of me wishes I had a camera so I could admire it forever.

But I jump around it and book it up the stairs, two steps at a time, the automatic night-lights in the shape of eyes lighting up the staircase as I pass them. They're ugly things my dad has tried but has been unable to pry off the drywall.

My room's at the end of the hall. I lock the door and dive into bed, my breaths heavy and loud—so loud that I realize I wouldn't hear it if Kent came inside. He works for Axiom, so he could probably get in through the scanner. I close my mouth and try my hardest to breathe quietly, but my nose whistles.

Maybe I should get a weapon. I have more razor blades, but they're too thin and flimsy. I could go downstairs and get a knife, but what if he's already in the house? I take a quick survey of my room bathed in moonlight. It's bare bones because I haven't unpacked a single box. Not like I have a lot, just however many Axiom could stuff my clothes and poetry books into when they packed up our last place.

The closet is empty. There's a shelf above my head that I try to grab, but it doesn't budge. I turn around again, desperate. My desk. There's a small metal lamp on it. Both were here when we moved in. I yank the cord from the wall and clutch the lamp close to me.

I put my ear against the door to listen for sounds of Kent walking around. Nothing. But would he really attack me? His mom is Seer of the hospital, so that means he can probably get away with whatever he wants.

Better safe than sorry. Before today, I never would have thought he'd be a threat. Annoying, yeah, but not actually dangerous. But I also never thought I'd witness something like what happened to Sam, so I guess I'm wrong about a lot of things.

I have to go into Dad's room because his window faces the street. With the lamp slipping in my sweaty fist, I crack open my door to look and listen. Still nothing.

My heart is in my throat as I tiptoe into the hallway. One of those night-lights clicks on. Fuck. I raise the lamp above my head, ready to attack in case Kent sees the light and races upstairs.

I sneak past Judith's room and the bathroom and the two guest rooms, all the while listening for signs of him. The house is dead quiet, the only sound the hum of the air conditioning.

Dad's door is closed. I got one quick view of the room the night we moved in, but otherwise, he made it very clear to Judith and me that neither of us can go in there under any circumstance, saying we'd regret it if we did. Logically, I know he's not inside, but I can't help this weird feeling that maybe, somehow, he is—or maybe he set up cameras.

Nah. I turn the door handle and push. It's pitch black. He's got the shades drawn, so there's not even moonlight to guide me. I'm definitely not turning on the light, so I put one arm out in front of me. While keeping the lamp above my head with the other, I inch myself toward the opposite wall, my hands shaking the whole time.

I was expecting a certain odor or mustiness like a wet cellar—maybe even some spilled vodka or the stench of throw-up—but it smells normal in here. I bump my knee against something and almost scream. When I realize it's the bed frame, I half-laugh, half-groan. I know the bed is situated underneath the window.

The sheets are cool to the touch. I climb on top with my knees and slowly pull one side of the shades away. Out in the distance, palm trees lit by moonlight are everywhere, green against the dark velvet sky. Mountains stretch as far as I can see. I pull the shade a little more, angling my head to see the street.

There are no streetlights, but my neighbors have their porch lights on, and the moon helps. It's empty. I get a bit higher so I can see my driveway, and all that's there is Dad's car, crooked.

Relieved, I sigh and drop to the bed. I lean over to put the lamp on the floor, laughing now that I can breathe again. Dad's bed is huge. I roll over three times until I reach the other side. The mattress is both firm and soft, and the pillows are made of straight-up clouds or something. They're definitely softer than the ones in my room. I don't know how he lucked out with such a nice bed.

Even with the adrenaline, I feel drained. I'm already in here, and it's so comfortable—what if I just slept in here?

I've left the shade partway open, allowing a slice of white moonlight to spill down the bed and across the floor. The corner of his otherwise empty nightstand has a blinking clock on it. The drawer is open. I go to shut it, and when I lean over, I see something inside.

I prop myself up on my elbow. It's a picture frame reflected in the moonlight. We have exactly zero family photos, so I wonder what it is and pull it out.

Mom. Maybe I should have expected that. More specifically, it's of the two of them together—a much younger version, before Judith and me. Mom's big, juniper eyes are unmistakable, just like Judith's. Her hair's not the long, flowing sea of brown I knew when I was little. Here, it's in a short bob that frames her face. Freckles sweep across her nose and cheeks.

She and Dad are lounging on a lawn chair—side by side, my dad's arms wrapped around her. They're looking straight at the camera, and even though they're not smiling with their mouths, they look incredibly content, incredibly in love.

My dad is beautiful too. He has strong hands, inquisitive eyes, and a sharp jawline—none of which are true today. I wonder if he's an alcoholic yet in this picture. I'd guess they're maybe eighteen or nineteen, but I have no idea. I wonder if, the very first time he put a drink to his lips, he was already destined to be devastated by it.

I bring the frame to my face and sniff, as if I could smell Mom. I can't remember what she used to smell like. I place it on the nightstand, facedown, and pull Dad's blanket up to my neck. It's heavy. I think it's weighted.

All the pain of this awful day starts to melt away. I know it'll be there when I wake up, but for now, it sort of slides off my body like water. It's funny—the weight of the blanket almost creates a weightlessness inside me.

I close my eyes, and exhaustion grips my ankles and pulls me under.

*

"HELLO? HELLO? MY name is Alister Youngwell. Come quick. My wife— she tried—she poisoned me!"

"For crying out loud, I did no such thing. You tell them I did no such thing!"

"My cocktail. It tasted funny and now my stomach's in knots. I puked twice already. All over the couch. There's some weird powder all over the kitchen."

"Those are crumbs from dinner, moron. And you puked because you're a drunk. You tell them you're a drunk, then hang up that phone. We only use it for emergencies. You're eating up all the goddamn money we don't have, Alister."

"This *is* an emergency, you crazy bitch!"

"How many times do I have to tell you to keep it down? If you don't shut your fat mouth, you will wake the children."

We're already awake, though, and huddled together under the blankets in our room. Judith woke me up a few minutes ago when she heard them fighting, and she's crying, holding my stuffed penguin to her chest. They fight all the time now. I used to cry too, but now I don't really care. I'm keeping as still as possible so I can hear every word. I like to write down the bad ones so I can remember them for later.

"Kids, come see what your mother did to me!"

"Well, you can't be that bad if you're running around the apartment, talking your damn mouth off in complete *sentences*, huh?"

"You shut your ugly face."

"Hang up the *phone*, Alister!"

"Would you quit hollering? I am trying to hear this poor girl. Yes, hello? Hello? They'll be here soon? Thank you very much. There, I hung up. Happy?"

"Alister, I swear to Jesus on the cross, if you rack up another goddamn medical bill, that'll ruin us. End. Finito. You know very well we can't afford no such thing."

"Maybe you shoulda thought of that before you put *rat poison* in my drink, woman! Did ya think of that? Huh?"

"You're an idiot. You never finished school, you got sacked from every job you had, and now you're a certified moron."

"Yeah, and you married this moron, so what does that make you?"

"Don't you dare—"

"You crazy bitch, you slapped me! Oh, I'm gonna get you for this."

"Ha! I'd like to see you try, you miserable—"

Chapter Sixteen

THE SUN IS high in the sky when I walk into work the next day, your friendly neighborhood convenience store. Before I even clock in, Boss laughs at me from behind the register.

"Holy smokes, kid. Don't tell me you jogged here."

It's always great when your superiors make you feel like trash.

I could explain to him for the third time this week that I moved, so I don't live down the street anymore, and since I don't drive, I have to transfer buses *twice* and wait anywhere from ten to thirty minutes between them, so yeah, I know I look and smell like crap, thank you very much.

I could also explain what a nightmare of a day I had yesterday. I could raise my arm and show him my splint, which he apparently hasn't noticed even though he's looking right at me. I could tell him how I slept in till eleven thirty, exactly an hour and a half ago, because of the nightmares I kept having about my mom, because of the screams I kept waking up to—

Sam's screams—or how I haven't had anything to eat yet because I had to run to catch the bus.

But I don't feel like pouring my heart out to someone who'll just ignore me anyway, so I grumble some bullshit under my breath, log into the register that's not being used, and start clocking in.

A customer in green sunglasses comes up to the counter and tosses three candy bars and a Mountain Dew in front of me. I know I shouldn't be too mad; he couldn't really know I'm not on the register right now. I mean, he could've guessed by the way I'm refusing eye contact, but maybe he's just not paying attention.

"So, y'all are planning to clean up that mess in the back or what?"

I lift my head. "Wait, wh—"

Before I can finish, Boss leans on the counter with his elbows and scowls. "Man, what are you on about?"

"Came by for a slushie and a cigar, maybe some munchies, you know how it is. Then I walk over and find y'all are *out* of slushies because they're all over your freaking floor. Hence the Dew."

I watch the veins in Boss's neck rise up like zombies from the ground. "You for real didn't say nothing till right now, man? How long ago was that? Not one person has said a *word?* How long's it been like that?"

He looks to me as if I would know, as if I didn't just get here. There are other customers and at least one other employee, so it can't have been too long. It was probably some kid who thought it was fun to watch the bright colors drip, and their dick parent didn't notice. It's happened before.

Boss speedwalks to the other end of the store. He deflates when he sees it, his shoulders sagging forward. I watch his mouth start to move and know that he's muttering to himself in Spanish, which he always does when he's pissed. It's kind of amusing, if I'm honest. He's always a dick to me, so anytime he struggles, I quietly celebrate.

The customer cracks a wide grin. "My bad, man. Guess I should've spoken up. Don't know what came over me."

We quietly laugh, which is a mistake because Boss comes storming over. He glares at me, and I already know I'll have to clean it up. But that's not surprising, I'm always on grunt duty. If it's not scraping up burnt taquitos from the warmer or restocking the coolers and freezers without gloves or a coat because the owner is too cheap to provide them, it's mopping up other people's messes.

But maybe I can get out of it. I'd love to be on front end today—the cash register and serving pizza slices and taquitos and hot dogs. It sucks in its own way, mainly dealing with rude customers, but at least it's not manual labor.

"I got injured," I say, holding up my arm. "I went to the hospital yesterday. It really hurts. I can't move it too much."

Boss makes a production out of frowning. "Aw, boo-hoo. Looks painful, kid. How will you ever survive?"

"That's messed up," says the customer. "You know what? I think I lost my appetite." He walks out of the store, leaving the drink and candy bars on the counter. As he walks away, Boss flips off his back. Then he looks at me.

"Now," he mouths.

*

THE SLUSHIE PUDDLE is bubblegum pink. *Puddle* isn't exactly the right word. It's more like a river—a thick, sugary, sweet-smelling river that's seeped under the counter where the slushie machine sits, as well as the shelves across from it. I don't really know if Boss expects me to lift the shelves to clean underneath, but I will not be doing that.

Mopping it up takes a calculated effort. Not only do I already know I'll need to change the mop water at least once, I keep having to go around the neighboring aisle because it's too wide to step over. Also, I can only use my good hand because every time I twist the splinted one, a burning pain tears through me to the point where I'd rather amputate my entire arm.

I can't be too slow, though, or else I'll get yelled at. Which means I have to work faster than I want to, which in turn means I'm working up a sweat while also yawning every few minutes because I'm still tired from yesterday.

Dreams of Mom and Dad kept pulling me awake—dreams of them fighting, dreams of us leaving, of Mom being taken by the cops. They were more like memories, not dreams—memories come back to haunt me.

After the ambulance came for Dad that time when we were eight, Mom packed a few bags—clothes, toys, blankets, some money she'd saved that she was keeping from him. We got in the car and left.

By that age, I had stopped crying when she and Dad fought, but right then, in the backseat of the car, looking up at the moon, I couldn't stop. Everything felt so final. What got me was the absence of fighting, the realization that they would never fight again, as though their screaming had comforted me all that time on some level. It felt like I was quite literally dying. It compounded in my chest until I couldn't breathe.

"Shh, shh, little one," Mom kept saying from the driver's seat. She was wearing a sweatshirt even though it was unbelievably hot and there was no air conditioning in the car.

She reached back to stroke my leg, but I smacked her hand away. "I want Dad!"

"It's okay, Hen, I promise. Both of you, listen to me. You're not going to see your father again, okay? He's a bad man. A bad, bad man."

"I love him!" I wailed as hard as I could, to which she was silent. The truth was, I didn't know if I loved him. I didn't know if I loved *her* even, or Judith. I didn't know what love was. I saw how parents smiled at their children at the supermarket and things, put them up on their shoulders, or played ball with them outside, but mine were always too preoccupied with making one another miserable to notice Judith and me. And Judith was always playing her piano or doing homework, so she never had time for me either. I only had myself to rely on.

We drove and drove. The first night, we stayed in a motel with roaches that ran up the wall. Then we slept in the car the rest of the way, my mom surviving on cat naps and coffee, till finally we reached the other side of the world. That's what she called it when I asked her where we were going. It was only South Carolina, though.

We stayed with one of Mom's old friends from school or something, and the next morning, she took us shopping for bathing suits. I picked a pair of trunks with dinosaurs on it because I knew that all the dinosaurs were dead just like Dad was to us now.

I told that to Judith, who had on a bright-yellow one-piece, and on our way to the beach, she asked Mom point blank.

"Is Daddy dead now?"

Mom didn't answer for the longest time. I thought maybe she didn't hear, so I asked too.

"Yes," she said quietly. "Your father is dead. That's why he went to the hospital, remember?"

I was old enough to know that people went to hospitals to get better, not to die. I also remembered Dad telling the 9-1-1 people on the phone that Mom poisoned him. So I knew she was lying. He went to the hospital to get un-poisoned.

After Mom slathered us in sunscreen, Judith and I sprinted to the sand. I wanted to play in the water even though we couldn't swim—which was the idea, because it felt risky—but she wanted to build sandcastles. When that got boring, she had a new idea. She wanted to bury me in the sand and play sand monster.

Something pulls me away. The bell chiming above the door at work.

I'm surprised to find I'm almost done with the first round of cleanup. I'll just have to change the water and rinse. My back's killing me. So is my entire left arm because I've been using it exclusively. It burns, but there's no alternative.

I hear Boss's deep voice say hello to whoever has come in, then there's some muffled conversation I can't make out. I tune it out and dip the mop in the water to soak, thinking about my dad and his bloody, broken face. I wonder if he made it out of surgery okay. Maybe he's paralyzed. I wonder if Sam has the Third Eye now. I wonder if Judith slept at all.

I haven't been able to contact her to get an update, obviously, but I think I'll try to call the hospital from the work phone later. I don't know if I'm allowed to just *call* and ask for her, but it's worth a try.

"I hope that's not blood," someone snickers.

The mop flies out of the bucket, and the wooden handle smacks into an entire section of chips, sending them soaring off the shelf. The mop head seems to do a backflip out of the dirty water, splashing everything in sight—the floor, the chips, the shelves, my jeans.

I try not to groan as I pray to whatever god will listen that whoever said that is not who I think it is.

But of course it is. Kent grins at me like this is all a joke to him, like seeing Sam's blood on the hospital floor last night was all fun and games. I will end him if it's the last thing I do.

"Get away from me," I seethe, trying my best at intimidation. But I do it quietly, so Boss doesn't overhear.

He wipes off his smile and looks down to the puddle of water I'm backing into. I'm conscious not to slip and break my neck. I'm showing him as best I can that I don't care; that I'm just as psychotic and cavalier as he is. I wonder how obvious it is that it couldn't be further from the truth.

His dark-walnut eyes seem to lighten. "I just wanted to say that I'm really sorry about last night," he says. "I know I crossed a boundary, but—"

I don't hear what else he says because I think of him squeezing my knee again, and I physically cringe. I think of having to climb out of his car since I couldn't unlock the door, and I nearly do slip, grasping the edge of the shelf closest to me as though it could really keep me from falling.

"—so how about it?" he asks. I have no idea what he means.

"Huh?"

He squints at me. "Are you—you look like you're gonna be sick. Good thing there's a bucket right here, I guess." He smirks at his joke.

It's true. I could vomit all over him. I'm not actually going to—he's just that revolting. I bend down and grab the mop with my splinted hand. It sends a crunching, gnawing pain through my arm, but I ignore it and make sure it doesn't show on my face.

"Anyhoo," Kent says and scratches his cheek. "Like I said, I would love to take you out tonight. I know we've had our differences, but I think we could have some fun. It would be my honor. I promise, no funny business, if you don't want."

The store goes quiet. Even the music seems to shut off, replaced by a low ringing in my ears. Did I hear him right?

When he doesn't say anything and just keeps looking at me with that stupid face of his, but with a strange doe-eyed expression I've never seen him make before, I realize I did hear him right. But, like, he can't be for real. Obviously, it's a joke. I stand frozen, squeezing the mop like it's going to save my life, and wait for him to laugh.

Except all I see is a nervous, self-conscious child flattening a crease in his shirt and trying to stand as straight as he can.

What do I do? I've never been asked out before. And the first time is by Kent effing Cross? Exactly my luck. I would love to laugh in his face, but that would only enrage him. And I can't say yes because, much to my surprise, I might actually have at least a tiny bit of self-worth.

"No thanks," I say. There. Clear and simple.

After a moment of what seems to be him processing it, he nods his head, looking at the floor as he does it. A faint smile reaches his lips, then he puckers them.

"Are you still mad at me for last night? Because if you are—"

I stop him by raising my hand. He makes it sound like it's a temporary thing, like the disdain and resentment I've been holding in my chest is only a childish temper tantrum or something.

"I'm not interested in you," I say, with a small step toward him. It's tiny, but it's the biggest step of my life. I take another. "I don't want anything to do with you. If I could help it, I would never have to look at your spoiled little face again." I don't know what comes over me, but I can't stop. "You are the worst kind of person, and you wanna know why? Because you know you're a sleaze, you delight in it, and you never change."

By the time I'm done, I'm standing above him as though he's getting on his knees to beg for my forgiveness, and that's just what I want. The truth is he's several inches shorter than me, but I like the thought of him cowering before me.

He smirks. Clears his throat. Lifts his chin to meet my gaze. "That's where you're wrong, Youngwell. I'm not the worst kind of person. You are."

"Please, enlighten me."

"Because you're insignificant. You'll never amount to anything, and I think you're fine with that. How pathetic. You're so small and mediocre that Axiom doesn't even want your eye anymore. My mother gave up on you last night, you know, now they have Sam Oakes's. You're nothing."

I could react. I could knee him in the groin, punch his face, throw him into the shelves. But he's right—I am mediocre. I'm nothing. He's right about the other thing too: I'm fine with all of it, with being ordinary. But that doesn't make me the worst, it just makes me a realist. What's wrong with knowing your limits?

"Shame too," he says. "I was going to tell you what they're planning to do to your little cyclops at the hospital tomorrow."

*

HE'S BLUFFING. HE has to be, right?

That wasn't my first thought. My first reaction was terror, an immediate vision of Judith screaming like Sam after having her second eye ripped out, bleeding profusely from the socket, while being paraded around the hospital like an effigy. My face must have gone white as bone because Kent cackled before walking out of the store, the bell dinging as he went. I knew they *wanted* to give her the Third Eye—Judith said so last night before Kent drove me home. But the way he worded it made it seem like it was definitely in the works.

Now it's an hour and a half later. I'm on my lunch in the break room, staring at the phone on the wall. I'm alone in here, thankfully, because I'm sure I look like a mess. I know I smell atrocious. The store sells deodorant, which I can buy at a discount, but I don't have any cash on me. For lunch, employees get one free hot item and fountain drink of choice, so in front of me, I have a slice of pizza and a Coke. But I can't eat. I can't even look at the food without gagging.

I'm terrified to call the hospital. Realistically, the worst they would do is tell me, no, I can't speak to Judith. But if they tell me no, I won't know why. They might tell me one thing, something innocuous like she's in the bathroom, but I'd have no way of knowing if it was the truth.

And even worse, what if my calling upsets them for some reason? I know that's stupid, but I remember how irrationally angry the ER doctor got at Lester for smelling bad and how, at the click of a button, Madame Berenice had Sam tortured because Judith and I were banging on doors or whatever she was mad about.

I think she was also mad at me for calling her out on lying about what they were doing with Judith. Yes, I remember. She was looking at her tablet and said the doctor was talking to Judith about my dad, but that seemed shady because why would it just say "Doctor talking to patient's daughter about patient"? Maybe it did, though. Maybe it did and I called the nurse a liar for no reason other than I'm an idiot, then she did what she did to Sam because…

Because of me? I already know he came looking for me after he saw the ambulance pull out of our driveway. But if he showed up at the front desk asking for me, they wouldn't just gouge out his eye for that, would they? No, they had to have a reason. And the reason was because I pissed off the woman in charge.

I look around the break room and double check that no one's in here. There's a box cutter on one of the shelves near the door. Before I can change my mind, I push back my chair and lunge for it.

I've never done it at work before, which surprises me when I realize it. So I don't really know where the best place is. There's only one bathroom, and employees have to share it with the public, so it's not exactly private. I could risk it, but the panic is roiling through my veins. My whole body is shaking with rage, and I feel the sob starting to rise. I have to do it now.

I go to lock the door so I won't be interrupted but then I see there's not a lock at all. How did I not know that? Fuck fuck fuck.

Do I just go for it anyway? Yes. I lean up against the closed door; that way I can block someone from coming in. It's only Boss and one other employee, so maybe the chances are low anyway. It's not like a customer would come back here.

I undo my belt and lower my jeans to my knees, then lift the leg of my boxers to expose my thigh. Just seeing it is a relief, the web of cuts, my beautiful creations.

Before I can think too much, I press the button on the side of the box cutter to reveal the blade. It's dull from all the tape and cardboard it's cut through, which means I'll have to really carve to break skin, but that's no problem. I shouldn't be making myself bleed anyway since I have to be quick about it. I have fifteen minutes left on break, and I still have to call the hospital. God, how messed up is this? I'm doing it at *work* now? It horrifies me. I wonder if I'll be doing this for the rest of my life.

But I'll figure that out later. I lower the blade to my skin and lay it flush with my thigh for a second. It's cold like an ice cube. Like the ocean. Just the feeling alone, the anticipation, relaxes me, dampens the noise firing through my head. I almost wish that were enough.

Holding my breath, I twist my wrist and drag it slowly across an empty patch of skin. It produces nothing but an indentation. Doesn't even hurt; tickles more than anything. I do it again and again, pushing harder each time, but still, nothing. The blade is duller than I thought.

I lift it high in the air, above my head, and tell myself to go for it. With my eyes squeezed shut, I swing it down, exhilarated and terrified—

The door bumps me from behind just before I make contact, and the box cutter flies out of my hand. My eyes pop open, and I slam my back into the door to make sure whoever it is doesn't come in. It would be very, very bad if someone caught me in here with my pants down. The blade has landed under the table.

"What the—?" Boss.

"Uh, just a second," I say, frantically pulling up and buckling my jeans.

"Who the fuck is that? Henry?"

"Yeah," I call, trying to sound calm. I open the door when I'm all situated, trying to contort my face into a relaxed smile.

He squints at me. "What do you think you're doing in here?"

"Sorry, I just dropped…something."

Silently, he steps in and scans the room. His gaze lands on the table where my untouched food is, the box cutter in clear sight below it. I try to think of an excuse in case he sees it.

He turns to me, his eyes full of suspicion. "Dropped what?"

"My wallet." It's the first thing I can think of. "Let me know if you see it." Then I scurry back to my seat to hide the box cutter with my foot.

"Are you doing drugs in here?"

"What? No!"

"You sure about that? I have to say, you stink real bad. And I know you didn't clean up the slushie as good as you could have, and besides, you're acting kind of…squirrely."

He lowers his eyes in the direction of my feet, and I realize that while I've been hiding the box cutter with my right foot, I've been tapping my left because obviously, I'm really fucking nervous. I force it still, but it's too late.

"Sorry," I say, and take a sip of my Coke to seem natural. A little bit dribbles down my chin, and I turn my head so I can discreetly wipe it away. I'm pretty sure he notices, though.

"Uh-huh. And what about your hand?"

I look down at my splint. "What about it?"

"Looks bad. I'm sure you got some painkillers for it, huh?"

"Actually, funny story," I laugh. "I refused the painkillers."

"Why is that funny?"

Shit. It's not. It's not believable either because who in their right mind would refuse painkillers if they broke a bone? He wouldn't believe my theory about the surgery.

He looks at me sideways. "You're high as a kite, ain't you? I bet that's why you're not eating."

I could tell him I'm not eating because I'm anxious about literally everything happening in my life. But at this point, what's the use? So, I pick up the pizza and take the most miserable bite of my life.

"Nope," Boss cries, raising his voice. "Uh-uh. I don't like it. I don't need no drug addict working for me, do you understand? I know you're only sixteen—"

"Seventeen."

"You think I give a shit? I seen a ten-year-old shooting up the other day, man. I don't fuck with that shit."

It takes me a few seconds to register what he says, but the second I do, tears spring to my eyes. "*What?* No. No, please. Please, sir. I swear I don't do drugs."

"I'm supposed to believe you? Look at yourself. You're a mess."

"I swear. The nurse asked me if I wanted painkillers, but I said no. I swear. Please, I need this job, sir. You don't understand. My sister was fired because Axiom took her eye, and my dad's in the hospital because he had a stroke, and I'm the only one working. Please. Please!"

Snot pours out of my nose. My tears soak the table. My throat is tight from the effort of talking and trying not to scream.

"Sorry, kid," he sighs. "Tell you what. You can finish out your shift because I feel sorry for you, but I've got to let you go. I can't be having an addict in my store. Shame too. I saw potential in you, kid."

"Please! I've never been late to work. Not once. I've never called in sick either. You can trust me. I need this! Please."

But he's already out the door.

I drop my head, and it thwacks the table. The pain dulls something inside me. So, I do it again, and it's even duller. Again.

Again.

Chapter Seventeen

"HI, UM, CAN you connect me to Alister Youngwell's room, please?"

"And with whom, please, do I have the pleasure of speaking today?"

"Henry Youngwell. I'm his son. I don't actually—I know he's probably not up for talking right now, but my sister, Judith, should be in the room."

"Certainly. One moment, please."

I feel drained, like someone's cut me open and emptied all my blood. Plus, my head hurts. It feels like…well, it feels like I've been smashing it into a table repeatedly. I wonder if I have two fractured bones now, my skull and my finger.

Surprisingly, no one came to stop me. I'm sure I was making a lot of noise, maybe scaring away customers, but I was alone through it all. Maybe Boss came in to check, but once he saw how absolutely wild I was getting, he let me be. I'm sure it didn't help my whole "you shouldn't fire me" case.

At some point—I'm not sure how much later—I stopped. The first thing I felt was shame.

Well, that's not totally accurate. First, I was dizzy—like really, scarily, maybe almost fatally dizzy. You hear about the room spinning or whatever, and it did, but that wasn't all. Something happened to the light. It was flickering in and out, like someone was flipping a switch on and off as fast as they could. And the sound—*the sound*—my ears were popping like fireworks or gunshots or something. I thought: did you just give yourself a stroke like your dad, you fucking idiot?

After a few minutes, the sound dulled to a low-pitched buzz. The light turned to a muted sort of grayish sepia tone.

Then I felt embarrassed.

I mean, I'm probably dying. But I had to find out what Kent was talking about. I had to warn Judith. Even if he was bluffing, I still have to tell her.

So I got up, fell back into my chair because my legs did not anticipate how heavy my head was, got up again, and inched myself over to the phone. I dialed the operator and asked them to connect me to the hospital.

Now, as I wait for Judith to answer, I'm only slightly dizzy again. Thankfully, no strange light or sound effects with it.

"Ah, if it isn't my favorite patient," says a French woman on the other end.

I spoke too soon. Now there's a buzzing in my other ear. I go to speak, but my mouth is dry. I glance over at the Coke I've barely drunk and wonder if the cord is long enough to reach the table. Might as well try.

"Hello," I say with a raspy throat, my feet dragging. Doesn't this nurse have other patients to tend to besides the Youngwells?

"And how are we feeling today?"

Besides the beating I gave myself and being fired from my job? "Fine, thanks. Is Judith there? My sister?" As if she doesn't know my sister.

"Oh, yes, of course, of course."

A pause. I wait for Judith, but then the nurse clears her throat.

"Before I put her on the line, I would like to ask a favor from you, Monsieur. And my wish is for you to give it your full consideration."

I reach the table and sit with a grunt. If only I'd known before that it could reach this far, maybe I could have saved myself all this trouble. Wait…she said she's asking me for a favor?

"Okay," I say with a small voice. I sip through the straw, and it's better than anything I've tasted in my life. It's cold and sweet and perfect. It makes me able to hold my head up instead of slumped down to my chest.

"Perfect. It is not a light request. What I need from you is a certain amount of willingness to be as loyal to us here at Axiom as we have been to you."

I take a long drink and almost finish it. "What?"

"I hope you will recall my telling you last evening how we will always hold in strong favor those persons and families who have donated their services to us."

"I remember," I say.

"So, you remember too that incredibly long line outside of the second emergency room."

Of course I do. The *Eye* ER and the *No Eye* ER. It clicks into place. The *Less Than* and *Better Than. Unworthy* and *Worthy.* Only those who give up their eyes receive medical care—or at least *good* medical care? Does that mean any care for the rest of their lives, like if someone were to get cancer or almost die in a car crash? I'm trying to think of what other things someone would need care for.

A stroke.

I clear my throat. "You want my *loyalty* in exchange for…for what now?"

"No exchange, Monsieur. I only wish for you to remember how wonderful we have been to you Youngwells." *Like rip out my friend's eye in front of us?* "We would hate for anything to jeopardize that. If ever there comes a time, relatively soon, when you doubt how much you mean to us here at Axiom, please remember that we do care very much and will always hold your wellbeing in our hands."

My heart skips a beat. Relatively soon? Tomorrow, like Kent said?

Before I can ask what she means, she says, "Here is your beautiful sister. Too-da-loo, Monsieur."

My brain goes blank, like I'm frozen in time or I've slipped into a vortex. There's a voice talking to me but I can't hear it until they say whatever it is they're saying again and again.

"Hello? Henry? Henry?" Judith.

I sigh, but I'm not quite relieved at hearing her voice. The room trickles back into place.

I take another sip until my drink's completely empty and I'm just slurping. "Did you hear any of what that nurse said?"

A pause. "Yes, Hen, I did. And I hope you'll consider it."

"You hope I…what?"

"That you'll consider what she said."

I can't believe this. "I have *no idea* what she said, Jude. She was talking nonsense about, like, loyalty? About something happening soon?"

"I just mean they're not as bad as we thought. Take what they did for Dad, for instance."

Oh, yeah. I guess that's sort of why I was calling too. To see if they actually saved him. I thought maybe since they took Sam's eye, they were done with him. I guess not. I want to point out that they should have done everything they could to save him regardless of whether they had taken one of our eyes or not. Regardless of our so-called loyalty. That kind of proves they *are* as bad as we thought.

Instead, I ask, "How is he?"

"He's great," she sighs. "He made it through surgery, and now he's…well, he hasn't woken up yet, but you should see him. He looks so peaceful. This might not mean much to you, but he has an IV that's hydrating him, and he's making urine through his catheter. Madame Berenice says that's a really good sign."

"That's great, Jude," I say slowly, but she's right. It doesn't mean much to me. "So, the surgery was good?"

"According to the neurosurgeon, yeah. She said it all went as planned. She removed all the blood from his brain and repaired the broken blood vessels."

"So what now?"

"We wait." I expect her to say something else, like to finish the sentence, but she doesn't.

"For what?" I ask.

In the silence, I can almost hear the tears form in her eye and drip down her cheek. I wonder if Madame Berenice is in the room with her still and that's why she's not sobbing like I imagine she wants to.

"We wait for him to wake up," she says, "and see if he's paralyzed."

"But you said they fixed him. He can't be paralyzed if they, like, did everything, right?"

"That's the thing with strokes, brother." Did she just call me brother? The venom in her voice stings. "You can catch it early and do everything right, but sometimes the damage is already done. And when there's head trauma, especially when it's severe, like when your own son beats you senseless, the effects can be devastating."

The phone nearly slips from my hand. I want to be resentful that she's bringing it up, but what right do I have to be upset? I deserve the shame. I deserve the headache traveling around my brain and seeping down into my neck. I deserve it all.

"So yes," she says, "we will have to wait and see."

The darkness grabs hold of my ankles, and I start to spiral. I think of Sam and feel like I'm being dragged down through the floor into hell. The image of Kent, of all things, stops me.

"Jude," I croak. "You know Kent Cross, right?" She doesn't say a word, like she's waiting for what I'll say next. Of course she knows him. Get to the point. "And you remember him saying his mother is the nurse?"

Silence. "Yes, you could have killed Dad, that's right," she finally says with a misplaced smile in her tone, like she's trying to explain something to a toddler.

I peel a pepperoni off the pizza and study it. "Wait, what?"

"I said I'm *positive* he might not be able to talk."

"Judith, I—I know. I'm asking about Kent."

"Well, of course I'm in his room, brother. So is Madame. She's just making sure everything looks good with him. They're turning him every two hours to prevent bed sores."

She's speaking in code. She's saying *yes, I could have killed Dad. Positive* he might not talk. I put the pepperoni to my mouth and lick off the grease, enjoying the saltiness.

"So, you do remember that she's his mom?" He told us both at the same time last night in my room, but maybe she wasn't paying attention.

"You're right," she says. "He might not be able to eat again either. His swallowing could be impaired."

"Kent came into work today," I say, planning to avoid telling her how I got fired and also about Kent hitting on me because she doesn't need any more stress right now. "He said that the hospital was planning to do something to you tomorrow, but he wouldn't tell me what."

A brief pause, like a hiccup. "Yes," she says.

I drop the pepperoni back onto the paper plate. A stain forms underneath it when a corner of it curls under itself.

I don't know if that's a code. I feel like if it were, she'd give more than a one-word answer. Does that mean she's affirming they're planning to give her the Third Eye? That she *agreed* to it?

"Do you know what he—"

"Don't worry, Hen, I'll be fine," she says all at once, in half a breath. "I don't need my toothbrush. They gave me one."

Now I'm changing my mind. Was that code for no, she doesn't know what Kent meant? No, she's not getting the surgery?

I wrap the phone cord around my finger. "Judith, I—what do you mean? Oh my god. Jude, they didn't give you the Third Eye already, did they?"

"I'll be okay sleeping here another night or two. Dad needs me. But don't worry, I have everything I need. You don't need to come. I know you're busy."

"I don't need to come?" Is that another code?

"No," she says flatly. "Don't come."

So she *does* want me to come? Or is the buzzing in my ears making me insane? "What are you saying?"

Silence.

"Jude? What are they doing—"

"Nothing! Thanks for calling. I'll see you Monday at school, okay?"

"Jude? Jude?"

But her name is only a whisper because I know she's already gone.

The dial tone sounds. I drop the phone and watch as the cord retracts and yanks it back toward the wall, and when it hits, the thud is as loud as a head cracking.

Chapter Eighteen

AT SOME POINT, my back starts to hurt from sitting for so long. I push back my chair, but it takes another while to muster the energy to even think about standing. When it seems inevitable that I have to, no matter how bad I just want to fall asleep on this table, I drop my chin to my chest. And there I see it.

The box cutter winks at me and sings a slow, seductive song. I dream about the fun we could have, fantasizing about walking back into the store with blood pouring down my legs, leaving a trail as I glide down the aisles and tell Boss (non-Boss?) he can't fire me because I quit.

That kind of makes me laugh because I don't even have the strength to lean down and pick it up, let alone the balls to say something like that.

The buzzing in my ears is gone, so I take that as a good sign and push myself up from the chair. I make sure I'm balanced on my feet and trudge my way to the door. The phone is still on the floor, lying faceup, the busy tone audible from here. I think about picking it up and hanging it back on the line. I think about picking up the box cutter and slicing through the cord. I don't do either.

Remnants of slushie are all over the floor, streaks of pink like dried, diluted bloodstains. I can't believe how terrible a job I did. I also can't believe someone else didn't clean up the rest. How long was I in there? Maybe they were waiting for me to come back to finish up. I don't have plans for that, though.

My shoes crackle as I walk through it. I turn the corner, and Boss looks up from a magazine he's reading behind the counter.

"You good, bro?"

I don't respond. Don't make eye contact. All I do is unbutton my vest and drop it on the floor. I push open the door, the bell signaling my exit, and step out into the cool air.

The sun's lower than I'd expect. I study the long shadows of the trash can, the buildings, the street signs. Even the bus all the way down at the corner waiting at the stop light has a huge shadow.

Shit, that's *my* bus.

My heart picks up as I run toward it. I need to get to the hospital even though Judith told me not to come. It hurts to run—not my feet or legs, but my head. It pounds and throbs with each step.

The light turns before I'm anywhere near it, and I'm not fast enough to chase after it, so I let it go. Defeated, tired, I walk over to the bench and plop down, head in my hands.

I let myself spiral into the pain until I'm pulled out by a voice.

"Henry?"

I look up. Norah's walking toward me.

"Dude, are you okay?" she says when she's close.

The automatic urge to smile, to ignore everything. "Yeah, why wouldn't I be?"

"Because the last time I saw you, you were about to get your eye taken out? Also, you're, like, sobbing on a bus bench. And you have a huge bruise on your forehead. What is going on?"

"I'm not sobbing," I say. "I just look like I am."

She takes a seat next to me. "Oh, I guess that's…better. What happened to your head? Oh my god, and your *arm*? Is that a cast? You have both your eyes! Is one of them fake? Henry, explain everything to me. This very instant."

"No, a splint. Long story. I'm so tired. What are you doing here?"

She sighs and looks across the street. "Okay, so you're ignoring me. That's fine. Well, if you must know, Boss texted me and said I could come in early if I wanted because somebody wasn't feeling well. My niece's recital has been over for a while, so I figured why not? I'm guessing the somebody who isn't feeling well is you?"

I lean over and put my head on her shoulder. Making contact doesn't hurt my brain as much as I thought it would. She smells like soap. This is the first time I've seen her since she tried so desperately to keep me from going up on stage. How do I even start to tell her about everything that's happened since then? It's not something you just chat about on a bus bench.

My forehead throbs. I want to start with that—I want to tell somebody about the things I do to myself—but I can't. If she were a rational person, which she is, she would stand up and leave me forever, saying my violent tendencies have gone too far. She saw what I did to Kent, to my dad the first time. She knows what I did to that kid in class last year. But if I tell her I gave my dad a stroke, if I tell her what I've done to myself, how can you come back from that?

"How was the recital?" I ask instead.

"It was good. I was sobbing and shit because she was so beautiful in her little tutu. My mom, aka my niece's *grandmother*, kept shushing me and I was like oh my god, how are you *not* crying, you heartless wench? Here, I took photos."

I love Norah so much. I can't ever lose her. But how can I go around lying to her?

She pulls her phone from her pocket and scrolls through so many pictures. Her niece is gorgeous and has Norah's perfect button nose. Her long black hair is pulled back into a perfect braided bun. In every single picture, she's smiling so bright.

"They weren't supposed to smile, but she kept on grinning," Norah says. "She *loves* it."

"Why couldn't they smile?"

"I don't know. Something about…professionalism or whatever? Like these six-year-olds are supposed to be professional dancers and not experience joy or some crap."

"I hate every grownup on Earth," I say.

"Hard agree, my dude."

"Speaking of grown assholes, your boss in there fired me," I say.

"He *what?*"

I sit up straight and rub my neck. "He thought I was on drugs or something."

I don't tell her the full story because I couldn't explain it without telling her about my cutting, about how my pants were around my knees, about slamming my head into the table, about everything. I want to tell her. I want to tell her so bad. How can I just…keep this in?

"Oh, hell no," she shouts, jumping to her feet.

"What are you doing?"

She punches a fist into her open palm and jumps twice. "I've been *waiting* for a reason to quit, are you kidding me? Fuck this place. Fuck him. Watch this place crumble without us." She's grinning ear to ear. Something about her smile looks just like Sam. Maybe it's the way the light is hitting her.

Fuck. How do I tell her about that too?

"You are not allowed to quit," I say, standing to join her. "Not because of me."

Her smile grows even wider. I just now realize she has two French braids on either side of her head, the right side threaded with emerald.

"It's not you," she says. "I mean, this is the last straw, yeah, but I've been wanting to leave for a while. I cannot stand that man in there. Can't stand the *customers*. Oh my god! Besides, we can find other jobs like *that*. Freaking everywhere is hiring, I swear. You and I are solid, dude."

I don't know how solid I feel at the moment. If I wanted to, I think I could collapse into a pile of dust. I definitely know what she's saying, but I just don't want her to leave on my account. What if she can't find another job and she ends up resenting me?

And look how happy she is right now. If I tell her about my head, my thigh, my bullshit, then follow it up with a side of Sam-getting-tortured-right-in-front-of-me, she will break. And I don't know if I have it in me to break my best friend. Not when she's so happy.

"Are you sure?" I ask.

"Never been more sure in my *life*."

*

NORAH AND I take the elevator from the parking garage to the first floor, and the doors open to a Watcher, who…smiles at us? He bows and lets us pass. A Watcher who acknowledges us? We cannot be in the right place.

But we are. The elevator button said Lobby, and behind the Watcher is just that. It's as vast as an open field and lit only by the skylight above. The entire ceiling is made of glass to show a pink and orange sunsetting sky. I wonder if it's as fake as the glass wall in my room yesterday. I wonder what would happen if I climbed a ladder and touched it.

A long gate splits the front section—the entrance, the foyer of sorts—from the rest of the lobby. Out here, the front of the building that exits to the street, with the elevator we came in off to the side, is a giant sheet of plate glass extending down from the skylight.

I catch Norah's eye in warning. "Do. Not. Touch. That." Because who knows where it would take you?

The receptionist's desk is in front too, as well as a pianist playing light music in the far corner. Their face is concealed by the large sheet music in front of them. I don't remember there being a piano when I was here last week, but it's an interesting touch.

Behind the gate, plants are everywhere, like a jungle. Huge potted plants, even potted lemon trees and cherry blossoms, plus several long garden beds with everything from bushy hydrangeas to giant sunflowers to rose bushes of all different colors. Three humongous palm trees are situated in the middle of the space, reaching up to scratch the skylight. On the very far wall is a waterfall that seems to pour *from* the skylight, as if the sky itself is raining tidal waves of water into the fountain below.

I have no idea where Dad's room is. I vaguely recall where-ish Judith's room was last week, but they might keep donation patients in a different place than regular-surgery patients. Also, this building is ginormous. There's no way we wouldn't get lost if we went walking around on our own. Not like we'll be able to get past the gate to go explore anyway.

With all my nerves on fire, Norah and I walk up to the receptionist, someone in plain clothes and a buzz cut, and who looks like they might be our age.

Before I can speak, their eyes travel up to my forehead, squinting as though trying to diagnose my bruise. I wonder if they can literally see the pain lightly thrumming through my mind to the back of my head, where it feels like it's slowly hammering away at my skull.

They finally look into my eyes and smile, revealing a gold-capped canine.

"How may I be of help?"

"Hi. My father had surgery last night. I was hoping we could go see him."

They look to Norah and back to me, amber eyes seeming to flicker with gold, like they're catching reflections of their tooth as they smile. Or maybe it's a Third Eye.

"May I have the last name?"

"Youngwell."

Their smile falters for just the tiniest second before saying, "Perfect. And you are…"

"Henry Youngwell." Beside me, Norah clears her throat. "And this is my friend, Norah Jeong. But she's practically my sister."

"Perfect," says the receptionist. I watch them resist the urge to look us up and down. Instead, they turn their attention to a screen inlaid in their desk.

As they type, I lock eyes with Norah, who widens hers in response. I move away, taking several steps to my right. I hope this person is just looking up my dad's room number so they can tell us where to go, but that feels unlikely. Last week, a Watcher came down here to guide us.

She led Judith, my dad, and me up a massive elevator and into a large room, where a nurse was waiting already. He asked Judith a whole bunch of questions about her medical history—there wasn't much to tell. He drew her blood, inserted it into a machine, and instantly said that she was "clear to go." He attached wires to her chest to look at her heart. He inserted an IV into the crook of her elbow and gave her medicine through it.

"Take one last look," she yawned. She looked at me, but I wasn't sure if she saw me.

"If we had a camera, I could take a picture of those pretty juniper eyes," I said. "At least you'll still have one of them."

She smiled and closed her eyes. They stayed closed, and the smile remained for a few seconds before it drifted away right along with her. The nurse wheeled her bed out of the room, and Dad and I were left in silence for the next few hours until she came back.

Now I look up and see her again, striding toward me. Wait, but I'm...am I hallucinating?

I look up at a palm tree and back down again. It's definitely Judith. She's walking toward us with long steps and a stern look on her face. She's changed out of her bloodstained clothes into a pair of blue pajama pants and a stark white T-shirt, her hair freshly washed and flowing as she walks.

Madame Berenice trails behind her, back perfectly straight, chin tilted up, her impractical but gorgeous cerulean high heels clicking and echoing around the lobby. The plants seem to cower as she struts past them.

Judith approaches the gate but doesn't open it. Madame Berenice lingers several yards away, pretending to examine the bark of a palm tree.

"See? Nothing is happening." It's the greeting I get instead of a smile or a hello. Then she turns to Norah. "Hey, girl."

"Hello," Norah says quietly.

"Wait, what the frick happened to your head?" she whispers.

The receptionist looks over at me, and I keep my voice down, even though I'm sure they could hear regardless. "I tripped at work. And I was really worried, Jude. You were a total freak on the phone."

Judith rolls her eye. "You're exaggerating."

"Am I?"

"Didn't I tell you not to come? You're wasting your time. You should be doing homework so you don't fail *every* class this semester."

Fuck. School's been the last thing on my mind, obviously. Will I be expected to go on Monday? When do I get to say, "I'm sorry, but literally everybody in my family has had some life-changing surgery in the past week, so I'm unable to come to school right now, thank you"?

"Jude, I thought—" I glance at Madame Berenice, who averts her eyes as if she's just caught a whiff of the nearby rosebush, and I lower my voice even more. "I thought that meant you *did* want me to come."

My own sister scowls at me. I don't know what response I expected, but it's not this. Her jaw is clenched, her brow knitted into the bridge of her nose. She's angry, and I don't really get why. Is she annoyed that I'm trying to help her?

But then I realize it's not me she's scowling at. She's looking over my shoulder at something that's maybe happening outside the window.

I turn to look too. It's the piano she's scowling at, the juniper in her eye darkened several shades. I still can't see the pianist's face from this angle save the curve of their jaw, but I do see their arms gliding back and forth, their shoulders rocking with the chords, their foot pressing the pedals. *Was this here last week?* I truly can't remember.

When I look back at Judith, she relaxes, her jaw unclenching.

"You really shouldn't have wasted your time," she says. "I'm fine."

"You're fine now," I say, "but Kent said they were doing something *tomorrow.* Do you have any idea what he means?"

"Listen—" she starts, then glances over her shoulder at Madame Berenice. She slowly takes a few steps forward so she's practically touching the gate. She lowers her voice. "Kent Cross doesn't know what he's talking about. When have you ever believed a word he said?"

I don't know what to say to that, so I let it go. "And what about Dad? Has he woken up yet?"

"I am afraid you are unable to visit with your father, Monsieur," Madame Berenice calls. Her heels click as she approaches and stands beside Judith. Her lips are a taut slash of red, and her hair is pulled into a tight bun on the top of her head.

"Um, why not?" I ask.

"Because patients are allowed only one visitor at a time, and it appears your father has reached his quota." She smirks at Judith, who nods sheepishly in return. Then her eyes shift down to my splint. "And how is your hand, might I ask? I am still your nurse, as it were."

I lift it to show her that it looks completely normal. No swelling or discoloration. It's fine. It's not even painful right now, the one part of me that isn't. That's not something I would say to her, though. Or anybody else. I do find it ironic that she's saying she's still my nurse, yet she hasn't said a thing about my forehead.

"Very good." She nods, and without a second glance or another word, she walks several paces over to admire the pianist, her head swaying with the music.

"Sorry," Judith mouths.

"I shouldn't have left," I whisper.

"Yes, you should have. Nothing changed anyway."

Norah steps to be beside me. "Do we know where Sam is?"

Judith looks down, as if to examine the structure of the gate, then up to me. "You told her?"

"Yeah. On the way here. In the car."

There was no other time or place to talk about it, and it's not like I could keep it from her even if I wanted to. But maybe I should have waited until we weren't on a busy street, because when I got to the part about how I could see into his head, the black hole where his big blue eye had been, Norah swerved and almost crashed into another car. A minute later, she almost hit a guy on a bike. She switched lanes without looking. Cars honked, but she had no other choice than to pull over and park. She stumbled out of the car. Howled. Jumped up and down. Punched the roof of her car, over and over.

I look down at her hands now, but they're folded across her chest and out of sight. How could I possibly have told her about my cutting too? Not then. It was already so much more than one person should have to bear.

"I'm so sorry," Judith says to Norah, who nods. She looks over at me with tears in her eyes, and I don't know what to do. What to say.

"You know, Henry Youngwell," Madame Berenice calls over the music. Her voice sours an already unbearable moment. "There is a way you could see your father. We could lift our one-visitor policy, and you could even help him—or rather, help *us* to help him."

"Help you to…what? How?"

Her head continues to sway until the song is over. Once it's silent, except for the distant waterfall, she turns her head and pierces me with her stare. "You remember what I told you over the telephone, I presume."

What, the creepy commentary about how I should never doubt how much Axiom *cares* about my family once *something* happens, relatively soon? Vaguely. That was right after I bashed my head in, so it's a little fuzzy. "Sort of."

With a light chuckle, she takes her place beside Judith again. She turns toward her and gazes at my sister's profile, as though analyzing her or admiring the structure of her face.

"The music is beautiful, no?" she whispers. "Of course, you used to be quite the pianist yourself."

She reaches out and strokes Judith's cheek. Judith doesn't even flinch. Doesn't move a muscle or blink or anything. She stares blankly into some void in front of her, but not quite at me. The green of her eye again darkens, but now to a deep forest color, like she's lost inside an impenetrable thicket of trees.

"Well, I'm sure you will get your groove back." Madame Berenice turns to me. "Now, what I will ask from you, Monsieur, is your loyalty to Axiom. In return, I am prepared to offer you a one hundred percent guarantee that your father will wake from his sleep wholly and beautifully intact.

Good as new."

I'm silent. I search her eyes for something I can't even name. When I don't find it, I form words. "You mean not paralyzed? Able to walk and talk and everything? Like, totally back to normal."

"Totally."

"You can do that?"

"We have the…technologies, you might say, to guarantee as such."

Why wouldn't they just do that anyway, if it meant saving a patient? I look to Norah as if she could read my mind. She shrugs, and in that slight movement, I have my answer. They don't do it out of the kindness of their hearts because then they wouldn't get anything out of it.

"What do you mean by loyalty?"

A new song starts, and wild, uproarious laughter bursts out of her mouth. Norah gawks in disbelief, tapping her foot anxiously. I look back at the receptionist, who frowns at me. I can't tell if it's an empathetic frown or one of disgust, like they can't believe how stupid a person could be.

After a few seconds, the laughter sputters out to a series of soft chuckles before it stops completely.

"I do apologize," she sighs. "I thought you knew! Can you believe that, Judith, dear?"

"*Dear?*" I growl, and Judith shoots me a shut-the-fuck-up look before turning to Madame Berenice and giving a very convincing laugh herself.

"Sorry, Madame. My brother has always been a bit of a dunce, you know. There's one in every family."

A chill blows across my body, like a snowstorm, soundtracked by chaotic piano chords.

"Oh, you do not have to tell me. If you could meet my cousin back in Arles, you would see a true simpleton."

I catch Norah's eye. "Do you wanna go?" she asks quietly.

I don't answer. I don't know how to. I have no clue what's happening or why Judith is laughing at my expense with this woman.

"Now, Henry Youngwell, allow me to be crystal clear. By loyalty, I mean the original agreement we made onstage before you so viciously attacked your father." I ignore Judith's questioning eye. She doesn't know about the first attack. "If you swear to give us your donation, and to also insert the Third Eye, we will cure your father of his current state of disrepair." Disrepair, she says, like a car.

"But you already helped him," I try to argue. "You gave him surgery, right? They fixed his stroke."

She smiles condescendingly and shakes her head. "Oh, of course we did, but there is more! Science has evolved. We now have a cutting-edge medicine that will guarantee a complete reversal of the damage, something that, in the olden days, could only be slowly and tediously achieved through months or years of grueling physical therapy, speech therapy, and so forth. And even all that was no guarantee for a higher quality of life, do you see? Now, thanks to our brilliant scientists, we can promise you almost instantaneous benefits with zero—that is correct, *zero*—adverse effects. It is totally risk-free."

Except for me having an Axiom eye, I think, and who knows what *those* risks are yet? "Then why do the surgery at all and not just give him the treatment?"

She looks up as if to ponder the question, but I think it's for show. I think she's already practiced her answer.

"A logical query," she says. "You see, the drug we will give him reverses the devastating aftereffects of the stroke. It does not treat the damage itself, the damage you caused—the brain bleed, the burst blood vessels. He required an operation in order to live, and so we gave him one. He does not *require* this drug to ensure his *quality* of life, however. That, Monsieur, is up to you."

"And you'll only give it to him if I let you give me surgery," I clarify.

Her eyes flash peach and purple, the colors of the sky in front of her, before she smiles again. "If you agree to that which you have already agreed, yes. As you know, the contract was voided, but we are comfortable in assuming that your father would give his consent again if he were able. We will only need your signature."

"Why ask me instead of forcing me down and cutting it out? Shoving the Third Eye in me?"

Norah and Judith both gasp quietly, but I think it's a very appropriate, if not warranted, question.

"Oh, *do* be serious," Madame Berenice scoffs, uncharacteristically. I've seen her be harsh, but this makes me feel two feet tall. "We are not in the business of forcing people to do anything. You will recall yesterday when I said to you that you always will have a choice. You do. Please refrain from thinking of this in that ugly, nefarious way. We are simply giving you a choice to help your father after you, yourself, nearly killed him."

She must have conveniently forgotten. "But Sam Oakes—" I start, but a voice interrupts me.

"Excuse me, ma'am?"

I look over. Norah has stepped to the other side of me so that she's face-to-face with Madame Berenice, the gate separating them seeming much taller than chest level.

Madame Berenice lifts her chin, her nose practically pointed to the skylight. "Yes?"

"Instead of Henry, I'd like to receive the Third Eye to help his father."

I practically scream. "*What?* Norah, what the hell? No. Absolutely not."

"I can't let you do this, dude. And I also don't want your dad to, like, suffer. My grandpa had a stroke, and he was never the same, so I know what kind of hell it is."

"Out of the question," I say.

"Um, no disrespect, but I don't think it's up to you," she says, standing tall to match the nurse. I don't think it's up to her either, I want to say.

Madame Berenice lifts her hand the same way my mother used to, to get me and Judith to stop bickering.

"I must say, this is very noble of you. Norah Jeong is your name, correct?"

"Uh, how'd you know that?" Norah asks.

"Easy. You scanned your eye in the parking garage, did you not?"

It's true, we had to scan both of our eyes for entry into the garage. I wonder if, immediately when we did so, she was alerted to our presence on her tablet or something, or if our names were announced over some loudspeaker. Does that happen when we scan at our house to get in, so Axiom can track who's inside? This whole time, I thought it was just a fancy, high-tech security lock, but maybe not. How am I such a fucking idiot?

"So, Norah Jeong. The email savant. You want to help your friend."

The email savant? Norah's eyes are wide, but I can't tell the emotion. Fear? Shock? Then I notice Judith's eye is just as wide.

"Well, I am sorry, my dear," Madame Berenice continues, "but based upon the scans you have provided at your school, you are not an ideal candidate for Surgical Revolution. I do apologize."

I sigh. She's…on my side? That's the wrong way to put it, but I am grateful. They already took Judith's eye because I wasn't strong enough to volunteer. They took Sam's because of me too. If they ended up taking Norah's, I don't think I would survive. And I need to survive long enough to figure out who Norah's been emailing. Must be a lot of people to be dubbed *email savant*.

Norah clasps her hands together behind her back. "Don't you need, like, as many donations as possible?" she asks, clearing away a catch in her throat.

Madame Berenice copies by placing her hands behind her back as well, but when she speaks, her voice is firm. "I will let you in on a little secret. Axiom's retina scanners do a lot of different things. They are extraordinary machines. Here at the hospital, they provide security by identifying who is in the building at a given time, yes? We also have them outside the patient rooms so that only those qualified may enter. Then we have the machines at your school and many others around the country. These are the most advanced machines in the world. In a matter of a few measly seconds, they also allow us to detect a particular material in your eye."

"What kind of material?" I ask.

Madame Berenice glances at my sister, who still hasn't moved an inch, before turning to me. She stretches her neck to the side and cracks it.

"A very special kind that you younger Youngwells—that is to say, not your father—are in possession of, and one which I'm afraid Ms. Jeong is not." She smiles at Norah and says, "Although I appreciate your allegiance."

When she turns to me again, she sneers, likely because I have not shown this apparent *allegiance*—which is an interesting word inferring a battle or war of some kind.

"Monsieur, might I remind you that to insert a Third Eye will not only help your father, but it will *advance* the very state of humanity. It will help us to better understand and therefore cure previously incurable ailments, such as—"

"A stroke," I interrupt, and Judith snaps out of her trance to glare at me. I know she doesn't want me to be *difficult*, but this is just information the nurse herself has already provided. "You found a cure for a stroke, didn't you? *Because* of people's donations. One that immediately reverses the damage and apparently has no side effects? But you won't give it to my dad unless I let you take my eye and replace it with one of Axiom's."

Madame Berenice traces her eyes up to the wall and smiles softly. "I am sure it helps you to sleep at night to think of us as the villains. But we are nothing of the sort, Monsieur. We have already saved your father. We didn't have to, yet we did. Now we are offering *you* the choice to bring him into the light. All for the cost of once more agreeing to that which you have already."

The end of her speech is punctuated by a swell of music, and she begins to bob and sway again like she's at a concert or something. My blood boils as I watch her. *This is a hospital*, I want to scream. *Of course you fucking saved him, that's your job!* But to say it would be futile. To point out that real doctors and nurses don't bribe and threaten people by withholding health care would be just as pointless as saying her son is a creep who won't stop hitting on me. Just as pointless as telling her that ripping people's eyes out right in front of their best friend, in some atrocious act of retaliation, doesn't make me want to get the Third Eye.

This is all so fucked. I can't lose my head right now, though. I remind myself to breathe.

"A true ethical dilemma," Madame Berenice whispers, a new kind of light in her eyes. "Do you save the man who raised you, even though it will mean losing your natural-born eye—or do you let him suffer because he is a miserable drunk who burns through your hard-earned income and spews hateful words at your sister here, the so-called victim in all of this?"

"H—how do you know that?" I ask. I'm sure I'm turning red. I try not to look at Norah because I'm fucking embarrassed.

A tear forms at the corner of Judith's eye. Madame Berenice sees it and smirks. "Perhaps it is time for brother and sister to have a heart to heart. What do we say, hmm?"

For the second time, she reaches out to stroke Judith's cheek. This time, Judith pulls away—not flinching. Refusing.

"Ah, there is the fire. Much like your brother. We knew both of you would make great Third Eye candidates. But we've already spoken of that, sweet Judith. Now imagine both Youngwells doing this act of service for the world. Your names will go down in history. It is time for you to decide."

Judith tucks her hair behind her ear and straightens out the front of her shirt. She avoids looking at me.

"I will leave you to it," says Madame Berenice, her eyes narrowed as she studies her wristwatch. "As I told your sister, Monsieur, the offer is only good for forty-eight hours post-injury, and I am afraid she has already wasted a large chunk of them trying to decide the value of your father's life. It seems she herself is not ready to make the commitment to save him. This is why I am offering you a chance now."

Judith opens her mouth just a little as if to say something, but radio silence.

I was right. Kent was right. She was planning to have the surgery tomorrow, without telling me.

"This means you have until, *ehh*, tomorrow at about this time. I hope you will choose correctly. I hope *both* of you do, but know that we will accept just the one if we must. If either of you agrees to your conditions, we will give him the drug. You know where to find me."

She starts to walk away, then stops.

"Oh, and you are not to eat or drink past midnight tonight if you plan to have the operation. Just a word of advice. But we will do what we must regardless. It just won't be as pretty."

With puckered lips, she struts over to the front desk but doesn't acknowledge the receptionist. She leans close to the scanner perched near the desk, and when it clicks for her, she pushes open the gate door and nods to Judith, who straightens her spine and inhales so deeply through her nose, it's like she's trying to fill herself up with enough air to float away.

"You—you don't want me to…?" she stammers. "I thought I would stay with my dad."

"He does not need you at this time, dear," says Madame Berenice, already walking away. "Do let me know what you decide."

Judith crosses through the gate door like a ghost and stands still, staring at the large plate glass in front of her, her shoulders deflated.

"Wait," I shout, and Madame Berenice turns, surprised. And before I can stop myself: "I'll do it."

On either side of me, both Norah and Judith gasp. One of them—I'm not sure which—says, "Henry, no," but I ignore them and stride to the gate.

"On one condition," I hear myself saying. "You return Sam Oakes. No Third Eye. None of that. Give him his old eye back and let him go." I'm not sure if they're even able to give someone their old eye back, but if they can put in one of their own eyes that apparently works just like a natural one, why not? I know it won't erase what happened to him, but at least it's something.

The slash of Madame Berenice's mouth disappears as she tucks in her lips, thinking of a response. I hold her eyes and refuse to break first. Finally, she does.

"Monsieur, this is not possible. Sam Oakes is already the recipient of a Third Eye."

The anger in me swells, but I keep my composure.

"Oh, yeah? Did he sign his consent form before you gave it to him? Before you ripped his real one out and had those Watchers beat him?" My voice is low, but my tone is sharp. "I thought you weren't a villain. When I asked you earlier why you weren't just holding me down to cut it out of me, you know what I meant."

"*Henry*," Judith hisses, but I shrug it off.

"Of course I did," Madame Berenice says with a tiny shrug, and I'm surprised she doesn't just lie. "But we will not do that to you, Monsieur, or your sister, unless we have reason to believe you mean us harm."

I scoff. "How did Sam mean you harm?"

"He physically threatened several of our Watchers. He came barging in here, ready to attack. I believe he was looking for you, if I'm not mistaken. But whatever the motive, we do not tolerate that, as I'm sure you can understand."

I don't believe it for a second. Sam wouldn't be stupid enough to try something like attacking a Watcher. Only I would. But this conversation is pointless now, and I have the brief thought that I might as well get the Third Eye now too, to match him.

I turn and listen to her high heels click as Madame Berenice saunters away.

Judith glares at me, cutting right through my skull, the flame in her eye fiercely unrecognizable. I don't know what to say to her. I open my mouth to attempt something, until I'm interrupted by the tactile silence of high heels no longer clicking.

"Doctor? Oh, Doctor?"

The piano stops mid-note, a high key tinkling for half a second.

"I do believe your break is over. Certainly you have patients to treat. Come."

The pianist clears their throat. "Yes, Berenice, of course." It's a low voice. Familiar.

The shuffling of papers as he closes the music book. Shadows shifting on the floor as he stands. A yawn as he stretches his arms. As recognition floods in, my stomach drops.

"Woooo! I have *always* wanted to learn the piano since I was a boy!" the surgeon sings. Judith's surgeon.

There's something misplaced about him. Off.

He smacks the top of the piano like it's someone's ass and not an expensive, delicate instrument. Then he smiles and nods at me and Norah. My mouth has dropped open, but I don't care to close it.

As he salutes Judith next, both of his eyes beam with the same giddiness she used to have when she played.

That's when I realize what's off.

"Are his eyes different colors?" Norah mutters beside me, thinking the same.

"Uh-huh. Sure are."

"The left one's, like, blue, right?" she asks. It is—it's baby blue, bright and bubbly and icy. "And the right one's…green?"

I nod, but it's not just any green.

Judith comes up behind me.

"Juniper."

Chapter Nineteen

FOR THE FIRST time in a long time, my stomach is beautifully, uncomfortably full. I wolfed down a cheeseburger and fries, which were amazing and greasy and perfect, but I think it was chugging the strawberry shake that's doing it: making me sit back as slowly as possible in the backseat and moan like I'm dying.

"That was epic," I whisper-groan. I'm torn whether to remain completely still or lie down and curl into a ball in Norah's backseat. The second time in two days my stomach is betraying me.

"I know, right?" says Norah through a fry.

We're in the parking lot of a fast-food place, under a tall yellow streetlamp. It's already night out. The clock on the dashboard blinks 8:31. I'm not sure that's accurate, but I have no reason to trust myself. Time means nothing to me anymore, hours and days slipping out from underneath me. When I think of the week before last, when we were still in the apartment, when we all had our eyes and never thought to worry about a thing like a stroke, it seems like it was last year.

Norah insisted she take Judith and me through the drive-thru, and when I tried to refuse because she literally just quit her job, she insisted even more. I don't feel *too* bad, knowing she doesn't have to pay for things like groceries and school shit because both her parents work, but I do still plan on paying her back when I can. *If* I can.

And that's a strong if, because if I go through with the surgery, chances are I wouldn't be able to find work anywhere. And then what? We'll just starve to death? It's not like Axiom's going to give us that small fortune they were willing to give us yesterday. No, the exchange is my dad's quality of life. Not that he deserves it—it's not like he would sober up and straighten out his life and get a job after he wakes up. So why do this for him at all?

All of this hurts my head. Hurts my already hurting stomach. I have no idea what to do. I wish I knew what Judith was thinking, but she hasn't said a word since we left the hospital.

Norah clears her throat. "This is definitely better than the bulgogi my dad would have made for dinner anyway. And I am not about to tell *him* I quit. Or my mom. You know, I'm not sure who I'd be more scared of in this situation. But I do know they would have simultaneous aneurysms or something. If you think about it, us getting greasy burgers saved their lives, and I'm actually a hero."

I think maybe she was hoping for a chuckle out of Judith, but she doesn't get one. Maybe the aneurysm crack hit too close to home. Or maybe seeing your own eye in somebody else's face has a way of blocking everything else out. Maybe she didn't hear Norah at all.

It's too uncomfortable to bring up, so I go the safe route instead. Through a stomach cramp, I say, "Norah, honest to god, you save the entire world on a daily basis, and I don't think you get enough credit for it."

"You're right." She yawns and takes a bite of her food. "I don't."

"Yeah, apparently you're, like, some email savant or something," I say. Or at least I think I say it. I expect Norah to explain what the hell Madame Berenice meant, but I get nothing in return, so maybe I was just thinking it. I would say it again, but if she's ignoring me on purpose, there's a reason.

Silence grows. The windows are down, and the parking lot is full, but there's still no noise.

"You bummed about going back to school on Monday?" Norah asks Judith, who doesn't answer but takes a bite of her burger. Chews. Crinkles her wrapper. Takes another bite. Swallows.

"Not really," she finally says. "But it's almost the end of the year, so I don't know why I have to go back at all, to be honest."

"Yeah, I feel like everybody's checked out anyway," Norah says. "It's not like we're getting anything done in our classes."

More crinkling of paper. The smell of grease is thick even with the windows down.

"Did you have to do any homework over your break?" Norah asks, and as soon as it comes out of her mouth, I hear her minute gasp that would have been totally inaudible if the car were on and music were playing. She made the same careless mistake Sam made yesterday morning of assuming Judith's been on some vacation away from school. The fleeting memory of Sam makes all the other memories flood back. The screams. The blood. The housekeeper mopping it up.

"Oh my god, I'm so sorry," Norah says quickly. She glances at Judith's patch, then at her food. "Of course it wasn't a *break* break. Shit. I'm really sorry. I'm such a—"

"It's whatever," Judith sighs. She reaches into her bag, takes out a handful of fries, and shoves them all into her mouth at once.

Silence. The pain in my stomach ebbs and flows. I wish I could control myself; whenever I have a lot of food in front of me, I just tend to inhale it all at once. I've never learned to take my time. Dad's kind of the same way.

"Wait," I say. "How is *Dad* eating?"

Judith freezes, her hand halfway between the bag and her mouth, more fries in her fingers. "He's not," she says, then devours them.

"So, they're just letting him starve?"

She swallows and wipes her mouth with the back of her hand, then looks back and bats her eye. "I think they're waiting to see if we take them up on their offer," she says in the flattest, most monotonous tone of her life. "If not, they might give him a feeding tube. It'll depend on when he wakes up and if he can even swallow properly."

If anything will perk up my sister, it's an opportunity to lecture me, so I keep going in hopes that she won't sink back to where she's been.

"But he *could* swallow…properly…on his own?" I ask.

"I don't know the statistics of hemorrhagic stroke and traumatic brain injury and alcoholism, but it's pretty unlikely he'll be able to do anything on his own again. He could need years of physical therapy, but even then, he'll probably need a walker."

Okay. A walker. That doesn't seem *too* bad, I try to tell myself. I'm fully aware that I'm just reaching for straws, though, that of course it's bad.

"Some people lose function in their arms and legs forever," she says through another bite of her burger. "Some can't ever talk again. Can't eat or drink or go to the bathroom on their own. Can't change their clothes. Can't do anything but lie in bed and stare at the ceiling until they become a burden on their families and just—"

"All right, I get it," I whisper through a wave of nausea.

"Are you okay back there?" asks Norah.

"Yeah," I lie through my teeth. "Totally fine."

"What an interesting choice of words. Fine."

"Jude, don't be a dick," I say.

She scoffs. "If I wanted to be a dick, Hen, I'd just punch you so hard your brain starts to bleed and you become incapacitated."

The edges of my stomach throb like they're about to rip at the seams. I close my eyes and try to breathe as little as possible so as not to provoke them. I can't decide if this nausea is worse than yesterday's. Why does this happen to me?

"Please just stop," I whisper.

I feel Judith's eye on me, but I won't open mine to look at her. I need to be as still and quiet as humanly possible.

"What are you doing?" she asks.

"Stop talking, or I'm gonna puke."

She does stop, which is a miracle, but I hear both of them chewing some more, and suddenly it's the most annoying thing in the world. The crinkling of paper, the smacking of saliva, the gnashing of meat and bread. The smell of fried food. All of it's revolting.

I go to open the window, but I forgot it's already down. I slowly lean my body toward it for fresh air, and the breeze flits by me. It cools me down and makes me aware of the sweat beaded on my forehead.

A bell dings. It sounds like the bell at work, but I realize it's the restaurant.

A man walks out the door with his young child, who's taking huge bites from a tall vanilla-and-chocolate-striped ice cream cone, white and brown smears all over her cheeks and chin. They walk behind our car and around the other side toward their own.

The little girl waves at our car and smiles to show two missing front teeth. Judith waves and says, "Oh, that looks yummy!" She's always had a thing for kids, and before last Drill Day, she was planning to someday have a whole boatload of them. But now…

The girl juts her ice cream cone high in the air, and her father looks up from his phone. He looks like he just got off work, his button-up shirt wrinkled and untucked, his tie loose around his collar. He glances at our car, smiling for a split second, and back to his phone. Then he double takes.

At the sight of Judith, he drops his phone to the ground. He picks it up and grabs the girl, who drops the ice cream and begins to scream at the top of her lungs. But the man doesn't say a word. He looks back in open-mouthed disgust at Judith and drags his daughter away. He opens the backseat door and sets her inside. There's a car seat, but he doesn't bother to buckle her into it before he slams the door, opens and shuts his own, and drives off as quickly as possible, tires squealing as he turns out onto the road.

The silence that follows is deafening. Judith doesn't turn her head, just stares out the window. This is the first time she's been out in the world since her surgery. The first time someone besides Dad and doctors and nurses has reacted to how she looks. And based on how it went, I'm pretty sure she'll never leave the house again.

"You okay?" Norah asks.

"Yeah," Judith says, a scratch in her throat.

I meet Norah's eyes in the rearview mirror. "What about you?"

I nod, though I'm not sure what to think. I'm hurt, obviously, and wish the world were a better place.

"Listen, Jude, I—"

"Don't," she says.

"Okay, but—"

"Hen, I can't. I can't."

"Then let's talk about Dad," I say. She looks forward and clenches her jaw. "I wish I could take it back. What I did." I don't know where it comes from, but we can't not talk about what happened and what the plan is. We don't have a lot of time to just sit on our asses.

She turns back. "I know."

I look down at my thigh and picture my hand reaching for it. Even without doing it, I almost feel the shock it would send through me, the ache that would stay in my thigh for a time afterward. How nice it would be.

"I think I'm gonna go through with surgery," I say. It feels right. Even though I can't leverage Sam with it, maybe saving Dad is the right thing to do. Even if he is a nightmare human, does that really mean I should just let him rot? Then I would be just as bad as him.

Norah unbuckles her seatbelt and turns around to look at me. "What are you talking about?"

"I owe it to him," I say. "How else are we gonna get him out? Stage a coup or some shit?"

Judith turns. Shrugs. "Why not?"

I cackle, and my stomach immediately cramps.

"Maybe it'd be fun, I don't know," she goes on. "But anyway, was what you did shitty, Hen? Sure, but I know that in your own twisted way, you were trying to shield me…to a degree. I mean, obviously, some of it was your rage issues—which you're gonna need therapy for at some point, by the way, which I'm pretty sure I've been telling you since middle school. But whatever. Even still, you're not the bad guy here." Little does she know. "Besides, it's me going through with this Third Eye thing, and I won't let you steal my thunder."

Norah chokes on her drink. She coughs and coughs, and when she's done, she's bright red and out of breath.

"Are you dying?" I ask.

She and Judith exchange a look. I can't get a read on it.

"Yeah, fine," Norah says.

Judith clears her throat. "After you left the ER last night, Henry, that French lady came to me with the same offer. I kept saying I had to think about it, and she was getting impatient with me, saying I was wasting time. I wanted to tell you when you called, but she was right there and she told me I was not, under any circumstance, to tell you about it in case you tried to change my mind. She literally followed me everywhere I went, even to the bathroom, like she thought I had a cell phone or something. I'm like, don't you have patients you have to take care of or something, psycho-path?"

"Well, you can't go under the knife twice in a week," I say. "That's insanity. Absolutely not."

"Apparently, I can. They seem to think it's safe."

I scoff. "Of course they do."

"Look, I know you're worried, but I'll be fine," she says. "Besides, one of us has to do it, and it might as well be me. I need two eyes if I want a job again."

"You'll *find* work without getting this risky fucking surgery that we know nothing about, Judith. In your own time. It doesn't have to be right away! Let me worry about job stuff. Besides, better me than you, anyway. I should have been the one to make a donation in the first place."

She purses her lips and takes a quick breath. "I—" She stops herself. "You are—" Frustrated, she squeezes her eye tight and shouts, "First of all, I never needed you to save me, asshole, so stop thinking that."

I don't say anything to that, even though she might be right. "What else?"

She opens her eye. "Huh?"

"You said 'first of all.' Is there a second of all?"

Her jaw tightens. "Yeah, Henry. How are you gonna take care of job stuff if you get your eye out too? Do you think *you'll* find work if you're a cyclops?"

The word vacuums the air out of my chest, and I watch as the color of her eye softens. She shrugs and turns to face forward. Norah stares wide-eyed into the center console, biting her top lip. I know she's wishing more than anything in the world she weren't here right now. *I* wish I weren't here right now.

Then, while still facing forward, Judith shrugs. Shrugs like it's no big deal. Shrugs like I haven't been punching people left and right over that word.

"I can say it now that I am one, you know."

"Okay," I say. She's probably right. I have no idea what the rule is, but she can say whatever she wants. *She's* the one it happened to, not me, so why should I place my discomfort over what she wants to call herself? I think she's free to call herself whatever name she can think of. I wonder if other people call themselves that word too.

"It's all about reclaiming the word for yourself so other people can't hurt you with it," she says flatly. "So that I don't want to fucking kill myself every time I think of what happened." A small quiver of her chin before she clenches her jaw as tight as she can.

Silence hangs in the air, thick and heavy. I find myself wiping away tears, then sniff deeply and look out the window, at the other cars parked in the lot. It was packed when we started eating, but the cars have weeded out.

The space next to us is empty, but there's a black car in the next one, its windows tinted. I can't tell if anyone's inside.

It dawns on me that our windows have been down the whole time and anyone could have heard. I don't think we said anything incriminating…just sad stuff about Dad? But you can't be too careful. A very slight pang of nausea, so slight that I wonder if I'm actually hungry again.

"Norah, close our windows," I whisper, as if those four words are a secret themselves.

"Okaaay?" She turns the key in the ignition, and music blares from the speakers for just a second before she turns it down. As she closes all four windows at once, Judith squints at me, the light from the streetlamp silhouetting her eye patch.

"Did I…did we say anything bad?" I ask. "About Axiom?"

"Just now?"

"Yeah," I say. "I mean, we implied that they're, like, shitheads, right?"

"That's not exactly news," Norah scoffs.

"And I think we joked for a second about doing some sort of coup," Judith says, "but that wasn't serious."

"Okay, but…pretend they followed us here." I think of the Watcher who was planted outside our apartment 24/7 before Judith's surgery. "Do you think they could have misinterpreted that?"

"Why would they follow us?" Norah asks, digging in her bag for rogue fries.

"Because, as I keep saying, they're *shitheads* who might have an interest in keeping tabs on us to see if we, I don't know, have something to say about a certain something?"

"I mean, I guess you could say that."

Judith looks around the parking lot and lands on the car by us. She looks at me and squints again. When I nod in agreement, she shrugs. It's not exactly the reaction I was hoping for.

"Could be," she says and swallows the last bite of her burger.

"Is anyone as concerned about this as I am, or am I just completely paranoid?" I ask.

"You may be paranoid, but that doesn't mean you're wrong. That reminds me. So, you know how yesterday, those paramedics came before we could call them? I think I figured it out this morning."

"Wait, what happened?" Norah asks.

Judith explains it to her, then says, "I think they have cameras in our house. That's how they showed up without us calling them."

Norah gasps. "Nuh-uh."

"No, think about it. They just randomly showed up and were like, oh, we were wandering around the neighborhood just in case anybody needed help, so just let us know, don't want to be a bother, oh, someone's bleeding, we can help!"

I narrow my eyes and gesture for her to go on.

"I wasn't really thinking about it until this morning, when the French woman came into Dad's room to check his blood sugar—you know, because he obviously hasn't eaten anything, and if it gets too low—" She sees the boredom in my face and stops. "Anyway, so she opens her tablet to scan the barcode on his wrist, and the first thing that's on her screen, before she switched to the barcode reader, was *our living room.*"

"Get. The fuck. Out of here," whispers Norah.

"Like, our couch, our coffee table, our rug, the *piano.* Dad's blood smeared everywhere on the floor."

"Jude, what are you—" I start, closing my eyes and massaging my temples.

"Think about it. They have a hidden camera in that ugly clock on our wall. The view I saw was from up above, like bird's eye. It has to be that clock."

I squeeze my eyes next and think of what Kent said last night in his car. "There's always someone watching." He was pointing to a clock too—the little clock on his dashboard, where there was a camera hidden inside.

"And must not be the only thing they're watching," Judith adds.

I slowly open my eyes and let the world come back into focus. Judith and Norah are staring at each other, Judith with her hand over her mouth.

"Wait, what?" I ask.

"The emails," Norah whispers. "Fuck."

"Email savant?" I ask.

Norah looks at me in the rearview mirror, her eyes wide. Desperate. "Henry, we have to tell you something."

Judith glances at Norah. "Maybe we should go to your place."

*

NORAH LIVES NEAR my old apartment complex, just a few streets over. I used to walk to her house two or three times a week to get away from my dad. But now that we've moved, I'll have nowhere to go to escape for a night if I end up having surgery and he keeps on drinking. Absolutely nowhere.

As soon as I walk through Norah's front door, I'm greeted by the familiar sound of jazz and smell of home-cooked Korean food, salty and tangy. It perfumes the house even hours after the Jeongs have eaten. I can't remember the last time my mac n' cheese or rice and beans hung in the air and made the whole house smell like love.

"Hello, dears. Come, come, sit," says Norah's mother with a big smile. She's a straitlaced, no-nonsense but very bright and friendly attorney. She's dressed in pajama pants and a sweatshirt, and her long, silver-flecked hair is tied back in a bun. Her mascara is smudged, and I wonder if she's been crying, if she and Mr. Jeong were fighting before we got here.

Before we left the parking lot, Norah texted her parents to ask if Judith and I could stay the night.

"Are you sure?" I asked. "Norah, you don't have to do this."

"Don't be stupid. I want to," she said. "It's not like you can go back home with them watching and listening."

"Thank you," Judith mutters now as she takes a seat on the far end of their couch.

I watch as Norah leaves the room, excusing herself to the bathroom. Before I sit next to Judith, I nod at Norah's dad. He's sitting in his recliner with his legs crossed, reading something on his phone. He barely looks up, which isn't surprising. I don't think he's said three words to me in all the years I've been coming here. Are all veterans this quiet? I think back to the auditorium yesterday and wonder what his new job is that Norah swore she's told me three times.

Her mom sits next to me and squeezes my knee.

"So how *are* you, my darling?" Before I can answer, she looks up to my forehead and gasps. "My, Henry! How did this happen? It looks awful, just awful." Then she notices my splint and puts her hand over her mouth. "Oh, my poor baby! What on earth? Are you all right?"

"It's…nothing." My neck grows hot from all her concern and attention. Even Mr. Jeong has looked up.

I reach up to the bruise with my good hand to hide it, and while I'm there, I decide I might as well see how it feels to…softly, not too obviously, I press down. It's like splashing in a puddle. I didn't realize how swollen it was, but my fingers sort of dig into it. I wouldn't say it's better than squeezing or clawing a fresh cut, but it's definitely a new kind of hurt. Where bothering a fresh cut is a sharp jab or a bolt of electricity, pressing into this bruise is a slow, dull sort of twinge. The pain percolates through my head like a paper towel absorbing water. I think of how resolved I was to tell Norah about hurting myself, and now here I am, doing it in plain sight in front of her parents.

"I slipped at work, that's all," I say, my facial muscles stiffened to hide the pain.

"Slipped?"

"Um, a slushie. Some kid spilled a slushie, and I was cleaning it up, and—*bam*. Right into the counter."

She winces, dramatically scooting away, one hand to her chest.

"Oh, no, no. I'm so sorry, Henry. Here, I'll fetch you some ice."

"No, Mrs. Jeong, it's fine."

But she's already on her feet, rushing out the room. I watch her go, and my eyes land on Norah's dad. He's not looking at me or my bruise, though, he's looking at Judith. From this angle, it looks like he's paying careful attention to her patch, though his face doesn't betray what he's thinking. I'm sure he's seen a ton of bloodshed, but I wonder if he's seen anybody with a patch up close and personal. When he notices me noticing, he looks back down to his phone.

I look over and try to smile at Judith like everything's fine, like I couldn't be happier. She's hunched over like a question mark, her elbows on her knees, staring at me.

"What?" I whisper.

She's quiet for the longest time, looking back and forth between my eyes and my leg and the bruise, my eyes and my leg and the bruise. It's not until Norah's mom yells from the other room—"*Coming!*"—that she gives me a response: "Nothing."

It seems that where I spent so much energy trying to find a way to tell Norah about what I do to myself, Judith really does already know, just like I suspected. I remember squeezing my leg at the piano yesterday, and she looked at me like she wanted to say something. Or maybe I'm making it up. Either way, I'm uncomfortable. This is the wrong place, wrong time.

Mrs. Jeong comes back in, a glass of water in one hand and the ice pack in the other. She hands me the ice pack, wrapped in a dish towel, and says, "Here you are, sweetie. I also grabbed you some medicine, just in case you need it for the pain." She digs into the pocket of her pajama pants and pulls out two pills.

A flash to the pill in Madame Berenice's gloved hand. Refusing because I was so sure they were going to knock me out. Whether it was true or not, they've figured out a whole new way of getting me to have surgery.

I grab the pills and swallow them with a big chug of water.

Norah comes in while I'm drinking and says, "What's with the ruckus?"

Her mom ignores her and pats my back. "There, there. You'll be okay. Now, did you and your *beautiful* sister eat already?"

I note the way she says "beautiful," with a special lift in her voice. Did she say it because of Judith's patch? Maybe she's trying to let Judith know in her own way that it doesn't matter if her eye is gone, that Axiom didn't take away the person just because they took away the eye.

From the corner of my eye, I see Judith place her elbow on the arm of the couch and cup her chin with her hand. She pivots her head away from us, her fingers hiding her patch like she's trying to be nonchalant about it.

"Yes, we're fine, Mrs. Jeong," I say. The thought of having any kind of food again makes me cringe. Norah sits on the floor in the middle of the room, even though there's a whole other couch. Maybe she doesn't want to be that far away. She begins taking out one of her French braids.

"Well, there's popcorn if you get hungry." Mrs. Jeong bursts into applause, her dark-brown eyes wide and beaming. "Yes! I made a big batch of my famous cinnamon popcorn for you kids. Norah's favorite for her special day."

"Please not now, Mom."

Mrs. Jeong rolls her eyes and laughs. "Always so modest."

"…special day?" I ask. "Oh, you mean the ballet? Yeah, Norah showed me pictures. Your granddaughter is so, *so* cute."

She leans over and bumps my shoulder with hers. "Indeed, and she knows it too. What a happy accident the recital fell on today of all days." She looks over to Norah and frowns. "Oh, but then you had to go to work, my poor baby. On your birthday! How was the store, darling?"

Time stops—like actually, literally, not figuratively, comes to a screeching halt.

Fuck fuck fuck. I thought it was yesterday! I was scolding myself in the auditorium for forgetting, then it turned out I was wrong, and so I had an entire day to realize it was actually today—and I forgot again? I didn't think of it once after work or when we were in the car for all that time. What is *wrong* with me?

While reaching for the second braid, Norah glances at me for only a second, but I can see the fear wild and ravenous in her eyes as if we were staring at each other. It's like a raging fire. Is it fear I'll spill to her parents about her quitting? No, she must know I wouldn't do that.

If anything, I should be the one who's afraid. I can't believe she didn't tell me. Was she testing me to see how good of a friend I am? Clearly I've failed on many fronts. I didn't even realize it was coming up. I was too busy worrying about Judith. Too busy drafting the perfect poem for the reading I didn't get to do. Too busy cutting myself. Moving house. Committing battery.

How many times have I proven to be the world's shittiest friend and brother and son?

I stare at Norah until she looks back at me. "I'm so sorry," I mouth.

She waves a hand to dismiss it, and I can't believe I made her quit her job, then buy me food on her birthday. Tears come to my eyes for the fiftieth time today, and Mrs. Jeong puts a hand on my shoulder.

"I love her too. I'm so proud of her. *Everyone* loves little Norah. Hard to believe she's already the big one-eight, eh?"

"Yeah," I sniff, trying so hard not to sob in front of Norah's parents. At some point, I turn my gaze to her dad, who is now looking up from his phone and gawking at me, his mouth hung open enough to give him a double chin. He has huge bags under his eyes like he hasn't slept in weeks. It takes him several long, horrible seconds to correct himself and go back to his phone, clearing his throat, uncrossing and recrossing his legs.

"So, is it just you three tonight, or did you invite any of your other buddies over, Nor?"

Yeah, right. Norah knows how fragile I am right now. How fragile *Judith* is right now. I really just want to go up and sleep. I've got possibly the biggest decision of my life to make, and I know that after a good night's sleep, I'll know what to do. That'll only happen with some peace and quiet.

"Actually, I think I will invite some friends over," Norah says. She raises her brows at me as if to say, *Why not?*

Why not? Because I'm dead tired. Because I literally might get my eye taken out. Because of everything that's happened to me and Judith?

But there I go again, putting myself first like classic Henry, world's worst homo sapiens.

"Oh, wonderful!" says Mrs. Jeong, clapping. "I'll make more popcorn."

"The more, the merrier," Judith sighs.

"Indeed, my girl, indeed," says Mrs. Jeong with a wink—at who, though, I'm not sure.

Chapter Twenty

EVERYTHING IS STILL. The entire world has stopped.

Tears fall from Sam's eyes. He grabs the poem from me and stands, rereading the words I wrote for him over and over like he needs to confirm they're real. When he does, and he finally looks up at me, the entire sky is in his eyes, and the ground collapses beneath us.

"Oh, Henry," he breathes, pulling me into him. That we're midair doesn't matter. We are here, together. Forever.

When we kiss, his lips are softer than I ever imagined. Around us, orange and yellow flames erupt, as if to cheer us on.

Slowly, wretchedly, the earth reassembles. And those flames? Not for me and Sam. He's not here, of course. The fire's in Norah's backyard—a bonfire for her birthday. And in the place where Sam should be, there's only an empty chair.

Wrapped in a quilt Norah's mom lent me, I stare into the flames dancing malevolently in front of me. They roar and howl, belting some powerful ballad, as crickets play light orchestra music behind them. I'm shivering now that the heat of the day has dissipated, and wondering how extreme, how irrevocable, the pain of self-immolation would be. How bitterly cold you'd have to be to light yourself on fire. Cold, or desperate for a way out—desperate because I can't think of a more extreme way to go. In history class, I've read about people doing it in protests as a demonstration of sacrifice for a greater cause. I don't think I would ever have the balls.

Almost all the members of Ink Stain are here, the only people in the world I call friends, and everyone but me is in some stage of s'more assembly. I'd make one, but after almost getting sick in the car, I'd rather not risk it.

I don't know if it was conscious or not, but we've all arranged ourselves as if we're in group. Norah's to my left, lying back in a white plastic pool lounger and licking melted chocolate off her hand. Patrick's on a tree stump next to her and simultaneously playing some racing game on his phone while holding his marshmallow in the fire. He's too wrapped up in his game to notice when it incinerates.

To my right, Greta is perfectly content in a chair like me, eating popcorn instead of a s'more because Norah's mom provided us with as many snacks as humanly possible, and next to her, Sari and Mel rock back and forth on the porch swing they carried down from the deck, Sari with both of their marshmallows on one stick.

Finally, on the other side of them, the empty chair. We're saving it for Judith, who wanted to shower before coming out. But if we were in Ink Stain, it's where Sam would be if he had never come looking for me yesterday. His absence is a palpable thing I can feel in my body, like a tumor or something. Nobody out here but Norah knows the truth of what happened, and they haven't asked where he is or if he plans to come. They probably assume he's on his way. I want to bring it up, to tell them the truth—but not on Norah's birthday. What's the protocol for something that needs to be discussed but it's weird because we should be celebrating, but maybe we also *shouldn't* be celebrating?

"So, I don't want to state the obvious here," Sari says, and she pulls the marshmallows from the flames and blows on them. "But what happened yesterday, Henry? What happened to your head and your hand? You didn't have the surgery yet, did you? Like, I'm staring into both of your real eyes? Or did you decide against it?"

I hold the quilt to my chin even tighter. It's Norah's great-grandmother's, who quilted it when Norah was a baby, and I feel like an infant myself as I use it. I just need to be swaddled, and everything will be okay.

"Oh, please say you said no," says Greta quietly.

I look into the fire for advice or insight into how to start, and Mel must take my hesitation for something else. "Dude, I told you not to bring it up," she says to Sari, finagling a scalding marshmallow off the stick with two graham crackers. "He'll talk about it when he wants to."

Sari's marshmallow oozes when she squeezes it between her own crackers. "Sorry, Hen."

"No, you're fine," I say, "but—"

Mel quickly changes the subject. She holds up her s'more as if showing off her creation and says, "Norah, these are so magic. I can't believe your parents gave up their fancy, good chocolate for us."

"Ooh, what kind of chocolate is it?" Greta asks through a bite of popcorn.

Shit, I lost my chance. Do I bring it up out of the blue? Stop all conversation in its track and just scream like I want to?

"It's orange flavored," Norah says. "It's the only chocolate my mother eats. It's so weird."

"Orange and chocolate, really?"

"Yeah, it actually tastes beautiful in s'mores. Want me to make you one, Greta?"

"No, I'm content with the popcorn, thank you," she says, and pops a piece into her mouth. "Do I detect maple syrup in this?"

How did the conversation veer so wildly from Drill Day to this?

"And cinnamon," Norah mock-whispers. "Don't tell my mom I told you. She thinks it's a family secret."

"Safe with me," Sari says and zips her mouth.

"Sure thing, but I'm definitely making some at home, like, every day of my life now," says Patrick, without looking up from his phone. He's devoured his s'more and now has a bowl of popcorn on his lap. Something like a grudge simmers under the surface as I remember that Patrick's not the only guy in Ink Stain to vow to eat something every day for the rest of his life. Sam and his blueberry muffins. What if this morning was the last time I'll have ever smelled it on him?

"I will also keep quiet," Greta says. She lifts a single kernel to her mouth, like she's been doing for the past half-hour, as if plucking flowers from a garden one by one. It's almost hypnotic to watch her. With her nystagmus, the flames reflected in her eyes twist and turn wildly, erratically, as her eyes move round and round.

I decide to bring up Sam later, after we've celebrated Norah for a while, and I turn my head to smirk at her, to slice through the pain with a smile, no matter how fake.

"I, on the other hand, promise no such thing. I might have to tell your poor mother you're spilling all her secrets."

She tips her sunglasses and scowls. "I dare you, Youngwell." When I roll my eyes, she lounges back again and yawns.

Patrick straightens his back, glancing up from his phone, and smiles. "What's up, Judith?"

I turn around to find her closing the sliding glass door. At the railing of the deck, she peers down like a queen gazing upon her subjects, crickets announcing her entrance. Her wet hair drips beads of moonlight onto the wood. She hasn't put her eye patch on, so there's just a big, white mound of gauze where it should be. It matches the white T-shirt she must have put back on. We're used to putting dirty clothes back on after a shower. I wave, but maybe she doesn't see me.

As she approaches, I watch as her pupil adjusts to the firelight, the dark-green iris slowly twisting with it. I'm reminded of the video at Drill Day. Why does Axiom want both of us to have this Third Eye?

"Aren't you freezing, you crazy person?" I ask. "I'm sure Norah has a coat you can wear."

"Yeah, a hundred percent," Norah says and starts to get up, but Judith puts her hand out to stop her.

"I'm fine," she mutters, but surely every inch of her is cold, from her wet hair down to her bare feet as they glide through the grass, around the fire, to her seat. Norah tips her sunglasses toward me, but I shake my head, unsure. The others don't seem to notice—Mel and Sari wrapped up in a cuddle, Patrick absorbed in his game again, and Greta too busy licking her sticky fingers to say anything.

Judith crosses her legs at her knobby knees and seems to stare into the space just below the firepit, as though the flames themselves are too bright to look at. I think about what she said in the car—how she's reclaiming the cyclops slur so she doesn't want to kill herself when she thinks about her surgery. Like the very act of saying it has the power to save her. Like when the other Kent Crosses of the world use it to tear her down, it won't be able to touch her.

Maybe she was being dramatic about wanting to hurt herself. Or maybe she's like me. Maybe the very moment she enters a space, she finds a way she could do it, should the need arise. A box cutter. A roaring fire. A body of water. Maybe that's why she was so acutely watching me press my forehead inside the house.

"You know what this party needs?" Mel calls, swiping and scrolling through her phone. "How about we get some jams up in here to loosen things up. It's the weekend and almost summer, baby, we can't just be moping around! Norah, it's your birthday, what are you in the mood for?"

Norah smirks and lifts the sunglasses to the top of her head. The smirk could be chiseled out of stone, immobile, implacable, as she stares into the flames. Embers pop and crackle. One side of the fire is slowly starting to fade, so she leans forward and uses the poker to shift around the logs until it bellows back to life. I wonder what she's looking for in there, but I have a feeling I already know.

"Nah, I'm not really in the mood for—"

Her voice carries off, and right before she lowers her glasses again, her eyes begin to water. Instead of finishing her thought, she clears her throat and sits back in the lounger.

"Everything all right, Nor?" Greta asks.

Through the silence that follows, everybody tenses. Everybody except Judith, who softens at the shoulders, closes her eye, and leans forward, elbows on knees, like she's readying herself for what's to come.

The whisper coming from Norah's lips is so quiet, it might not be real. "Sam."

But Patrick hears it. "What about him?"

Mel too. A beat, then she laughs. "Yeah, where's that clown at?"

Norah's head drops to her shoulder. She doesn't want to be the one. Neither do I, but maybe this is the one thing I can do for her on her birthday.

I clear my throat, once, twice. "I, um…" I fumble for words.

Patrick drops a popcorn kernel onto the ground, picks it up, and flicks it into the flames. It hisses and spits and gives rise to a black curl of smoke.

"I, uh…" I look up to the sky, like maybe the words are up there.

"Has something happened?" asks Greta, pulling me back down.

I remind myself to breathe and start at the beginning, with Dad, because I can't explain what happened to Sam without getting into what led up to it. I don't leave anything out—not the fury that overtook me, not the blood that was like a pheromone and made me go even harder, not the way he slipped in and out of consciousness. I tell them about how the paramedics showed up to our house without us calling them and how Judith figured out about the cameras. The stroke. The brain surgery. His chances of recovering with physical therapy. The chances he might not recover at all. I also tell them about what Axiom offered Judith and me in exchange for a guaranteed cure.

But I don't know how to go on. I don't know how to tell them about

Sam.

Sari must think I'm at the end of the story. "That is messed up," she says, a manicured hand to her mouth.

"They have a cure?" Patrick asks.

I don't answer. I have to get it all out.

A few words roll out, then a few more. It's awful. After a while, I lose focus and can't continue a thought, so Judith fills in. Then me again, then her. We tell it exactly how it happened. The blood like a torrential downpour. The empty socket. The beating. The impossible screams. How he got there, how he was looking for me. How it was my fault. Judith protests that, but I stop her. I even tell them about the slow, dreamy way that housekeeper cleaned it up later. And finally, about how Sam knew what the Third Eye "really was," but add that I have no idea what he meant.

By the time I'm done, there's not a single dry eye in the circle. For a long time, there's only the crackle of flames, the slow lament of the insects, until I remember the rest. I quickly tell them about the glass sunset and what happened when Judith and I touched it. The Mirror of Memoria. Expressions turn from grief to shock. They're all speechless, except Judith.

"You forgot something," she says.

"I didn't know if you'd want me to tell them."

"There's more?" asks Greta.

"They're not curing diseases," I explain. "They're stealing ideas. Talents. Inventions. I don't think they found a cure for stroke; I think they stole it from somebody whose eye they took and claimed it as their own discovery, one they can use to get what they want out of people."

"When we touched the glass, it didn't really make sense," says Judith, the firelight a soft glow on her face as she leans forward and talks to the flames. "I thought I was having visions, like they'd slipped me drugs somehow. But then today, that doctor—*my* doctor, my surgeon, the same one who cut out my eye—put it in himself, and now he can play the piano like I used to."

Sari's brows furrow. "Does that mean—"

"I can't play anymore." Judith starts rubbing her hands, as if heat is all she needs to play again.

"Oh my god," says Sari, grasping for Mel's hand. "I saw that concert you gave in…what was it? Seventh grade? You were brilliant."

"I don't really get it, though," says Mel. "They…took your talent, found a cure for a stroke, and figured out how to magically display memories in a pane of glass, all by taking people's eyes? How does that make sense?"

"Makes perfect sense if you ask me," Patrick growls. He shoots to his feet, and it's as if he's absorbed the flames. He's never looked so colossal, so strong. As he paces back and forth, the reflected fire is wild in his eyes— or maybe the flames are *behind* his eyes, somewhere deep inside. "If you think about what we know about this Third Eye shit, it all clicks."

I cross my legs and squint at him. "So you *and* Sam know about that?"

When I look around the fire, not a single other person seems as confused. Mel and Sari glance at each other, then away. Then Mel and Norah. Norah, Judith. Judith, Patrick. Even Greta is shoving popcorn into her mouth to avoid saying something.

"Okay, you *all* know? What the fuck is going on? You were all acting so weird at Drill Day, I thought you were all about to have a collective nervous breakdown. Norah, you were eating your *hair.*" I look away, tears pricking the back of my eyes. "Miss email savant. You and Judith are hiding something from me too. What is happening?"

Norah strokes the green streak of hair with her fingers and raises her sunglasses to her head, sighing. "We were scared to tell you, okay?"

The rage gets hotter, but I can't let it show. I breathe. Actively, purposefully, breathe.

"I don't—why would you be scared to tell me about this?"

"It's just, you kind of have a tendency to—"

I widen my eyes, daring her to go on. But she doesn't. She lets her silence answer. This is exactly what she's referring to, my penchant for— what did Judith call it earlier? Rage issues? But I still don't get how that relates.

"Okay, I'm sorry," I say calmly, breathing again. "You're right. What were you scared to tell me?"

But she still doesn't answer. Instead, she's staring up at a motionless Patrick with her mouth hanging open. Moments ago, a wildly dancing flame, zipping back and forth as if across a trail of gasoline, Patrick is now a stone.

His limbs have gone still. His face is chiseled somber as his eyes peer up at the house. It's like he's seen a ghost. Judith is staring too, but I can't read her expression. Mel looks, then Sari, both of their faces curious.

Norah doesn't look at all. Her eyes fall to the grass, like she's afraid of what she might find if she turns. Maybe I can carry this weight for her. It's the least I can do. I turn for the both of us, prepared for the worst, but it's nothing of the sort.

Norah's mom is waving at us through the kitchen window, her smile wide. She holds up a big bowl and points to it to ask if we need more.

"We're good, Mrs. J," Mel shouts, but she doesn't hear, cupping her hand around her ear. I stand and make two thumbs-down, then she makes a thumbs-up like she understands. She waves once more and walks away, smiling. Why was Norah afraid to look? And why was Patrick just standing there like he forgot how to move, looking all scared?

Then I see a flicker. There's movement in the window above the kitchen, curtains fluttering. I think that's Norah's parents' bedroom, but I'm not sure. Was her dad looking down at us too at the same time her mom was? He's not exactly for the faint of heart, so if that's what Patrick saw, I can understand why he looked like he'd seen a ghost.

Norah bites her lip, still hesitating. It can't be that bad, can it, whatever they were afraid to tell me? I look around, and everybody except for Judith avoids my eyes. I wish she would too, though, because what I find in her face doesn't make me feel good. Pity. Relentless, all-consuming pity. It's almost like she's looking right through my skin.

"Okay," I say, trying to ignore her. "How about this? Before you tell me what's happening, would you care to explain *how* you knew about it?"

"My dad," Norah whispers.

I make a hand motion like, you have to continue with your statement because you can't just drop something like that and expect me to understand, please. But she doesn't. Instead, she slowly surveys the backyard, looking for intruders or spies or something. Her yard is big, with tall wooden fencing on all sides. Plus, it's been really quiet out here, save for us, the fire, and the crickets, so I think we're safe from peering eyes and ears.

"Okay," she sighs. She sits up and straddles the lounger, the yellow rubber ducks on her socks bright against the grass. "You know how he was in the—" She slowly marches in place in her seated position, pantomiming a soldier, I think.

"Obviously," I say. It's hard not to remember whenever I look at Mr. Jeong. Given how quiet and stern he always is, he seems like the quintessential soldier.

"Yeah, well, he kind of still is."

I squint. "Still is…still is what? In the—"

She nods once, tersely.

"Your dad is—"

"Shh!"

"No, you *shh!*" That part was accidentally too loud, so I lower my voice. "I thought you said he had another job! You said you told me three times! I thought I was losing my fucking mind."

"I lied, okay? God."

"That's such a weird thing to fib about," I whisper.

All I feel about it is confusion. Why would she lie about that? Like, okay, he's not retired? I don't know what that means exactly or how it's relevant to our current discussion anyway.

"Wait, what does that have to do with—" I stop and point to my eyes.

She hesitates, but Patrick jumps in for her. "They have some intel, her dad's…employer."

The military? The government? I'm more confused than ever.

"Yeah, except he wouldn't dish everything," says Norah. "He just told me to refuse the Third Eye no matter what Axiom said or what they were gonna offer in exchange. Like, he knew Drill Day would fall on the day before my eighteenth birthday, and that it would be possible they'd pick me and bribe me into waiting a day to sign the contract and not tell my parents. So he made me swear on my life I'd refuse. And my dad *knows* when people are lying. He was, like, trained for that shit."

I sigh once, and because it didn't make me feel any better, I sigh again.

That still doesn't answer my question about what the Third Eye *is* and why everybody was freaking out. "And he didn't tell you what the big deal was? Like, why is this so much worse than a regular donation?"

She turns around toward the house like she's scared he's listening. And maybe he is. Maybe he has been. Whatever Patrick saw is still giving him the creeps, as he looks into the fire with a blank face.

"I asked him, and he got all quiet," Norah says. "You know how he is." I do. He's never said more than two words at a time to me, basically. "And then he also told me not to tell a soul."

"So, naturally, you told Sam," I say.

She nods. "That's correct. I couldn't just not tell *someone*."

I know she doesn't mean it to hurt me, but it does. I've been friends with her longer than anybody else here, *and* longer than Sam. That's probably selfish, but whatever. Not telling me because I occasionally have anger issues doesn't seem like a good reason for everybody besides me to find out something so huge.

Under the quilt, I squeeze my thigh, ensuring my face stays completely still when I feel the sting. It jolts lightning through me. The pain of not being told doesn't go away or anything, but it's nice to have some physical pain to go alongside it—to split the difference. I look around to see if anybody's noticed, even though I was discreet, and sure enough, Judith is staring at me, leaning back in her chair with her hands folded across her chest. I give her a face like, what are you looking at, freak? Then I notice she's shivering.

"Will you take this quilt, please? You look like you're about to convulse."

"I'm *fine*," she scowls, and that's the last time I'll do something nice for her, I think. So, I shake out the quilt around my feet if not just to brag about having something warm to cozy up with.

"Okay, so you told Sam, and he—"

"Figured it out in two seconds," Norah says. "Or at least, like, theo-rized."

"Which was…"

"Dude, you don't even wanna know," Mel says as she stretches her arms and yawns.

"Everyone else does!" I yell on accident, and she shrinks back into herself, frowning. Sari looks away, embarrassed. Blood rushes into my face.

Greta turns her head toward me with a faint smile. "It's okay, Henry, please. We were going to tell you, but we just didn't have a good oppor-tunity. I am so sorry we hurt you."

"I *tried* telling you, just for the record," says Judith. "Yesterday, before school. Remember?" A flash of me ignoring her as she was trying to be sincere. The slow creep of guilt starts in the bottom of my stomach. "I was trying to say that if you were picked, you couldn't sign your name, even if Dad came and signed his." But she couldn't tell me because I was too busy worrying about my poem. That stupid fucking poem. I literally ignored her and maybe laughed in her face. The guilt makes me look away from her.

"I'm sorry I never listen," I say quietly.

"Yeah, well, you've always sucked at that."

"But okay," I start to reason, "*how* are you in on it, Jude? You've been out of school for an entire month!"

"You might have noticed we have a computer at home now," she says plainly. "Get with the times, Hen."

"Yeah, but—"

"Hey, hey, hey, who would've thought? Little Henry keeping up with the times," Mel jokes, trying to ease the tension. I ignore her.

"I haven't had time to get on it," I grumble.

Judith smirks. "Lucky for me, I have."

"I thought you've been holed up in your room all week."

"Well, when you're at school, I get bored," she says. "It's not like Dad's any fun. I have to occupy myself somehow, don't I?"

"It was my fault, Henry," Norah interrupts. "I emailed her the other day telling her everything. You had said at some point that your house came with the computer, and I thought there might be a chance Judith might read an email if I sent it? I just wanted her advice. Like, I didn't know if maybe we should tell you after all, and I was like, oh, Judith will know what to do, she's his twin freaking sister."

"Wait," I say. "Email savant?"

Norah nods. "I think so."

"Which *means*," Judith says, "they're spying through the computer too, not just the clock."

"Oh my god. Wait. Nor, what did you put in the email?"

She rubs her hands together. "Oh, not a lot. Just, like, everything."

"Such as…"

Patrick answers. "This Third Eye. Sam figured out what it is. It's a weapon…but like an intelligence weapon."

For a second, the fire stills, then roars back to life, like a hiccup.

"Weapon?"

"Axiom's building an army, Henry."

He's telling a joke, obviously, but I fail to see the humor. I look around to see if anybody is laughing, but they are all either nodding their heads or staring wide-eyed at the flames, and I realize he's being serious. I'm not sure what my face is doing, but it must flash all my questions because Sari jumps in.

"This Third Eye shit isn't just a cure for blind people, it's—"

"Not that all of us want a cure, by the way," Greta interjects. "Some of us live free and happy just the way we are. I can't speak for all blind people, but I am just stating a fact. My blindness is part of who I am, for example, and I wouldn't change it for the world."

"Thank you, Greta," says Sari. "See, that's part of it. It's not for the good of humanity or whatever they're claiming. Everything those fuckers do is for themselves."

"Yeah, Henry," says Norah. "So, when I told Sam that my dad said they were rolling out new Axiom eyes or whatever, he immediately knew what was up."

I look up at Judith. She nods, knowing exactly what's happening. *That's* why they took out his eye when he came looking for me, not because he "threatened" some Watcher, or whatever bullshit Madame Berenice was spewing.

"But wait, I'm still confused," I say, "because how does this thing help them build an army?"

"It's some freak intelligence device," Norah says.

"Yeah, we think it has GPS tracking and camera capabilities. For spying and things like that," Patrick says.

I have to refrain from laughing again. GPS and a camera in an eyeball? That makes the least amount of sense out of anything.

"At least that's what our pal Sam said, and I have to agree with him,"

Greta says.

If all this is true, and Madame Berenice was telling the truth about him having the Third Eye already, does that mean Sam isn't Sam anymore? That he's on Axiom's side?

Flashes of Madame Berenice telling me she liked my *spark*, my *fire*, after I punched Dad onstage. She said the same thing to Judith at the hospital this evening when she showed sass and some bite. Is that why I was chosen for the Third Eye? Because of my anger issues? Because that would make me a perfect soldier?

"But it doesn't, like, turn you into a soldier," I offer. "You're still *you*, right? Your personality isn't changed."

Judith shrugs. The pity's returned to her eye. She again knows exactly what I'm thinking, and I fucking hate it.

"Presumably not," she says, "but there's no way to know, Hen. They could theoretically use nerve pathways from the eye to the brain to send whatever signals they want, but I'm not for sure."

I stare right into her eye, trying to dig into it as deep as I can for an answer. "You've known this whole time, and you wanted to get the surgery anyway?"

I watch Mel's and Sari's eyes shift over to her, and her own eye narrows.

"No, I don't *want* it," she says, her face hardening, "but I do want to save Dad."

Fuck. I came so close to forgetting. It confuses me to no end that Judith wants to save him after everything he's done. After the hell he gives us and all the torture over the years. But maybe I don't need to understand. Maybe all I need to know is that it's complicated and that, despite everything, she doesn't want to see him suffer, because she's a much better person than me.

But that still doesn't mean I'll let her go through with it.

I cross my legs and sigh, letting the blanket fall to my lap. "So…an Axiom army." I turn to Norah. "That's what your dad thinks too?"

"I'm not sure, but probably. He said it was really bad."

"Why wouldn't he just tell you outright what it was, though?"

"Some secret military thing, maybe." She shrugs. "I don't know, he probably knew I would blab."

"It's one of your strengths," I say. "You blabbed to Sam, who blabbed to everyone else. Except for me, by the way." She rolls her eyes, but I don't stop. "But then you also blabbed in an email, and now Axiom knows the military knows because you specifically mentioned your dad in it. Am I up to speed?"

Norah frowns. "Jeez, Youngwell, you don't have to be salty. But yes, you are accurate on all things. To be fair, though, they probably knew the military was aware of what they were doing before I stepped in. But maybe I'm an extra-special informant, who knows?"

"Henry, can I just say something?" Mel says. "We really wanted to tell you, I swear. We just had to take every precaution because we thought, you know, that you might freak out on one of the Watchers." She gives an awkward chuckle as if that wasn't a horrible thing to suggest.

"Do you really think I would do that?"

She shrugs, and I don't have to look around to know that, in fact, everybody does think I would. But I'm not *that* stupid, and it hurts to know they think I am. Do I have a tendency to get emotional? Sure, I'll be the first to admit it. Should I have attacked that kid last year in geometry? No, of course not. Kent? My dad? Well, the lines are blurred in those cases, but seriously, a Watcher? You'd have to be the world's biggest idiot. And I may be in the top ten, but I'm not number one.

"No, we don't think you're dumb enough to physically assault one," says Mel, apparently a mind-reader. "But do you really think you could hold your tongue?"

"I don't know. Maybe."

Greta smiles. "We love you, Henry, but we think not. You are one of the most sarcastic people I have the pleasure to know. Besides Norah, of course."

"That's really sweet," says Norah, her hand to her chest.

It's true. Where Norah is just as sarcastic—which is why I enjoy her company so much—she knows how to hold her tongue and keep her emotions in check. I have this weird thing where I am on either end of the spectrum and nowhere in between: I over-the-top react to something in an instant, or I bottle up emotions and resentments for months or years, only to blow up when the pressure builds to an extreme. Balance is something I am just becoming aware of.

I remove the quilt because it's making me hot and throw it over the fire to Judith. She catches it, and her jaw quivers. Is she cold or…touched?

"Well, it's not like I would go up to a Watcher and tell them I know all their secrets."

"Yeah, that's why you leave it to me to blab the secret and *really* make sure that Axiom knows we're onto them!" Norah sighs deeply. "I'm sorry, Hen. I'm truly no better than you."

"I guess we're both huge dumbasses," I say, and she flips her hair. "But wait a second! None of this can be true, though, because if Axiom knew that you and your dad were onto them, they would have kept you at the hospital tonight and not let you leave."

"I don't know about that," says Patrick, leaning forward. "They know who her dad is. If she went missing, they must know the military would swarm the hospital. Shut them down."

"They *should*, though," Mel calls angrily into the fire. "Swarm that place. Why the fuck don't they?"

"Couldn't agree more," Patrick says. He pokes his empty s'mores stick into the fire. "Might be waiting for the right time, though."

"No time like the present," says Mel. "Especially now they got our boy."

"I tend to agree with you, Mel, but I think it's probably not that simple," Greta says. She's done with her popcorn and places the bowl on the ground. "I think Axiom has a lot of power over your government and also military, and so that is why they have not been stopped yet. Money equates power, you know."

"Who gives a shit about *money*?" Mel yells, rubbing her eyes. "They're domestic fucking terrorists, and now they're building an *army*? I mean, fuck it!"

She has a point. Lives are worth a lot more than money. But Mel didn't grow up in poverty. She has no idea what it's like to go to bed hungry every night for weeks or to wake up and not be able to flush your toilet because your water's been shut off again. I know that's a lot different than greedy corporations exploiting people, but to say that money doesn't mean anything is crazy.

Greta smiles. "Yes, exactly. Fuck it."

Fuck it. A flash to Dr. Maas's class yesterday, when she wrote that on the board and had us split into groups and brainstorm how to—

"Is Dr. Maas in on this too?" I ask, and Norah's face twists.

"*What?*" she asks, horrified.

"Then what was up with yesterday? *Fuck it?*"

Mel cackles. "Maybe she is. Who fucking knows with that lady?"

"Can we get back to the topic at hand?" Sari asks.

"We're all ears. You got any ideas?" Patrick asks.

Sari claps, her eyes widened. "We should go to the news. Tell them everything."

"Axiom would just deny it," says Judith. "And that's *if* the news even runs our story. If I were a journalist, I would be too scared to speak out against them. It's a good idea, but I don't think anyone in their right mind would risk that."

"Yeah, plus my dad would freak out," Norah says. "He told me to keep this a secret, and I'm pretty sure he would murder me if he found out I told."

Sari frowns. "Whatever. What do you guys suggest then?"

"Are we above arson?" I ask, and Mel laughs.

"You're stupid," she jokes.

Patrick smirks. "If you feel like going to prison, sure."

I think of my mom. I don't remember the last thing I said to her before I got her taken away. Something about whales? I wonder where she is now, if she's even in California or if they moved her somewhere else. Axiom has surely taken her eye by now, like most other felons, and I wonder if they were the first lab rats for the Third Eye.

"Well, whatever we do, it has to be tomorrow because they're expecting Henry and me to come back," Judith says. She rubs her temple right next to the mound of gauze, massaging it like her brain hurts. I watch her start to shiver then abruptly stop, like she's trying not to give in to it. Trying to force herself to be warm.

I take a deep breath, inhaling the smell of the fire as far into my lungs as I can, as if it will give me strength. But it gives me more than that. As she rubs her temple, her pinky finger grazes the white gauze, and it gives me an idea.

"Wait, before we decided *what* to do," I say, "should we, like, give ourselves a name or whatever? To be official?"

"Ink Stain Bosses," Mel says, and everyone chuckles—everyone but Judith, who's lost in her own world.

She lowers her hand from her head and smirks, the light from the fire wild in her eyes.

"I've given this some thought, actually," she says. "How about The Cyclopes?"

Chapter Twenty-One

"UM, YES. HI."

"Hello again."

"I'm…"

"You're…"

"Sorry, I didn't sleep much. We're ready for surgery, if you could, um, let Madame Berenice know we're here."

"Perfect," the receptionist says. Their gold canine disappears as they close their mouth to swallow, looking down to the screen inlaid in their desk. As they type, they seem drained, like they could close their eyes and fall asleep standing up. I wonder if they worked overnight or how long their shifts are. And what about Madame Berenice? My stomach sinks as I realize she might not even *be* here in the mornings. But maybe that would be better for our plan.

The receptionist scratches the back of their buzzed head. "Done.

You will be collected shortly."

Collected? Interesting word. I glance out at the vast garden of the lobby, from the sunflowers to the rose bushes to the palm trees—one last look at something beautiful—then turn around and give a cynically large but hopefully persuasive grin.

"Don't do that," Norah says.

"Yeah, it's not a good look on you," Patrick agrees.

"Thanks, guys. I love how sweet you both are."

My eyes travel to Judith for an opinion, but she's busy looking out at the gray morning sky through the huge window and skylight. She wouldn't give me one anyway; she's barely said a word all morning.

I'm kind of worried about her—she's a little pale and just the tiniest bit sweaty. Before we left Norah's house, I asked if she was okay. I thought maybe she was coming down with a cold or something from sitting outside for hours after her shower last night. She only grimaced at me, so I backed off.

Behind her, a Watcher stands by the front entrance we came in, not the elevator down to the garage this time. Mel and Sari dropped us off, and they'll wait for us in a parking lot a few blocks away. Who knows how long this will take? Hopefully not hours and hours, but they brought snacks just in case.

The Watcher's not wearing sunglasses, and one of his eyes is a little darker than the other. Third Eye, maybe? One of Axiom's loyal soldiers? He'll need to be dealt with somehow. So will the receptionist.

Patrick looks around the lobby with a kind of wonder I'm familiar with. The empty and closed piano and the long gate dividing this front section from the giant garden. The palm trees scratching the skylight. The waterfall way in the back, beyond all the plants.

"It's like the Garden of Eden," he says. I don't know much about that story, but I know it's religious, and it does seem very on brand for Axiom to think of themselves as a religion. Almost like they themselves are gods.

Norah rubs her eyes, while Patrick yawns and scratches between two of his twists at the back of his head. I don't think they slept much either last night. Patrick ended up on Norah's couch, while Mel and Sari claimed Mrs. Jeong's home office that had a pull-out bed. Judith and I took the guest room. I let Judith sleep in bed while I took the floor. It wasn't too uncomfortable, but my mind was racing, so I didn't get a lot of sleep. When I did, it was fitful and gray and hazy. I kept hearing these noises coming from somewhere, like another room, but they were so muffled I thought I was dreaming. It was like that for what simultaneously felt like hours and just a few minutes. I'd be asleep, then sort of wake up, then hear something and wonder if I was dreaming, then fall asleep again. It was dizzying. The third or fourth time it happened, I realized it was real. And I realized who the voices belonged to. Norah and her parents. I sank back into sleep, and when I woke up for good, it was through Norah shaking me. "You ready to go fuck shit up?" she whispered.

"Ah, who do we have here?" comes a voice behind me. *Her* voice. My heart leaps into my throat, but I let myself close my eyes and take two breaths before I turn.

I take in the sight of Madame Berenice. The wrinkled blue scrubs, which I suppose means she'll be acting as nurse again today. The bare face without a trace of makeup. The puffy, sleep-deprived eyes. If I had to guess, I'd say she was woken up the moment the receptionist alerted someone. But that would have to mean she slept here somewhere.

"These are my friends," I say, cementing contact with her grayish-brown eyes, cold like morning frost on soil. "You know Norah. This is Patrick. They'll be waiting for us until we're done. That's okay, isn't it?"

"Of course it's okay!" If her voice goes one octave higher, it would be a dog whistle. "The more, the merrier, yes? We will have staff escort them to the visitors' area."

"Oh." I pause. "We thought we would all go up together to discuss the plan."

She narrows her eyes, and a chill ripples down my back. "Is the plan for them to have surgery, Monsieur, or you and your sister?"

I swallow. "Me and Judith."

"Then I must insist your friends wait here while I take you two upstairs. They will be here for you when you wake up, do not fret."

How can I not, though? There's every chance in the world that Judith and I will both be having surgery today. Or worse. We've planned everything down to the T, with backup plans to our backup plans. Three alternatives for everything that could go wrong. But even still, what if something completely unexpected happens and I wake up not myself anymore?

I meet Norah's eyes, full of trepidation as her brows raise to her hairline. Not because she's not going upstairs—we planned for that—but because it's getting real. Because, even with all our plans and logistics, realistically, there's no guarantee this won't be the last time we'll ever see each other. And how do you say goodbye to your best friend?

I reach out and stroke the emerald streak of her hair. "Have I told you this is my favorite color you've ever dyed it?"

Tears come to her eyes, and she hits me on the shoulder. "Shut the fuck up, idiot."

"I love you."

"I love you," she says, then holds out her arms for a hug from Judith.

Patrick grabs my shoulder and pulls me into one too. His combination of fading deodorant and morning breath is such a strangely endearing smell.

"We'll be fine, man. Go," he says. And so I do.

I turn to find Madame Berenice staring with a smile that doesn't reach her eyes. "Such a sweet display of affection. I can tell you are deeply cared for, Monsieur."

"I'm lucky," I say, to which she doesn't respond.

She strides to the reception desk in two steps, and as she leans over and scans, the receptionist looks over and stares at me with vacant eyes. Yesterday, they were amber—almost golden to match their tooth. Now they're like ash. Third Eye? But no, they're both the same dark shade. I want to look away, but I can't. I keep thinking *they'll* look away, but they don't. Not until the gate clicks to unlatch. When their eyes finally release me, goose bumps run up my arms.

Madame Berenice opens the gate and smiles. A breath falls out of my chest. I turn to look back, like I could just leave. Like it's an option. But Norah gestures with her hands to *go, go, go,* and I do.

There's the smell of something sweet and spoiled as I pass the nurse. It brings me back to the time my dad made me pick up a single raw pork chop for him after work last year, then when I got home at eleven at night, he was shitfaced and ready to grill it on the stovetop, but as he waited for the pan to heat up, he laid down on the kitchen floor for a nap, and the pork chop was sitting out on the countertop in our hundred-degree, un-air-conditioned kitchen, leaking out its raw pork juices, so when I woke up for school in the morning, the entire apartment smelled like rotting, sickly-sweet meat, and he was still on the floor, snoring like a chainsaw, fat black flies everywhere—on him, the pork chop, the dirty dishes in the sink. Everywhere.

She smells like that. And when she nods at me encouragingly, I can't believe what I'm about to attempt just to save him.

"Is Sam Oakes still a patient here?" I hear Patrick ask the receptionist as I drift away into the garden.

"I'm not sure. Let me look it up."

*

"*EIGHTH FLOOR*," SAYS the elevator.

"Perfect." Madame Berenice grins as she holds the door for us. She leads us around a far corner and down a long windowless skybridge with a single door at the end: my execution chamber. Okay, not really. I hope. But that's what it feels like.

Dangling from the arched ceiling of the skybridge are a thousand eyeballs so real-looking, I think for a moment they are. They have red, squiggly blood vessels running through them, and they're all dangling from little strings. Optic nerves. No eyelids, so they don't blink, but some do trail us as we walk, different colored irises following me. It's like a poster, where the person on it follows you no matter where you go, except a hell of a lot creepier.

If our plan doesn't work out and my eye ends up getting taken, I wonder if this is where it'll end up. Maybe this is where Judith's would be if her surgeon hadn't taken it. Maybe this is where all of them go to wait before they're given to new owners. Do I know any of them—seen them at school or something?

"Is this where they brought you last week?" I whisper to Judith because she never mentioned a thousand eyes dangling from a ceiling.

She doesn't answer, and it only further punctuates the silence. Besides the swishing of pants legs and my shaky, loud breathing, there's nothing. There's no click of the nurse's high heels because she's wearing gym shoes today. Something about this small change adds to my anxiety, and I'm not sure why. It's like she's preparing to run or something. I try to tell myself I'm being dumb because I already decided she's just woken up. Which means she and Kent *do* have a bunk here, like Lester. I like the fact Kent lives in a hospital and not a home.

Finally, Judith says something, but it's not to me. "Madame?" A scratch in her throat.

The nurse slows but doesn't stop or turn. "Oui?"

"I just wanted to go over the plan."

"There will be plenty of time for details, my dear. I am just glad you both decided to come. You must really love your father."

"Yeah, about that—"

"Here we are!" Madame Berenice suddenly stops, and we almost run into her.

The door is tall, arched, and painted bright blue. A retina scanner is posted on the frame. She leans forward, scans, and pulls open the door.

Inside, a waiting room—at least I think that's what it is, except not a single person is here. There's an empty reception desk beside a sliding glass door that looks like it goes to another short hallway. Empty metal chairs line the walls, with small tables between that have brochures boasting SUR-GICAL REVOLUTION across them. A single potted plant droops morosely in the corner by the door, like it hasn't been watered in too long. Nothing like the thriving, bountiful plants downstairs.

If this is indeed a waiting area, why isn't this where Dad and I waited for Judith to come out of surgery? Why couldn't Norah and Patrick come up to wait here?

"Why is it so—" I want to say dead. Bleak. "—empty?"

Madame Berenice smiles and clasps her hands together. "We do not normally take patients on Sunday. It is the one day of the week our Donation staff takes off to rest. But for the Youngwells, we are happy to do it!"

We follow her through the sliding glass door, down another hallway, and into a small room. It has large cabinets, a sink, a tablet docked in a charger, lots of medical equipment, two chairs, and one of those big leather exam tables you're supposed to sit in while the doctor listens to your heart. Or at least that's how I remember them when my mom used to take us for checkups. I don't know the last time I went. Definitely not since she left.

A cabinet slams. I gasp, and something flies past me. I recognize the scent of bleach before I realize Madame Berenice has tossed two hospital gowns onto the table.

"Change into these. Your surgeon will be with you shortly to examine you. You may leave on your underpants."

"Wait, what about the plan?" Judith asks.

She groans, and I'm surprised. What happened to the excited, bouncy nurse? I guess she can switch off and on in a second. "What is it?"

I suddenly don't feel confident making demands. It was different when we were discussing it among ourselves, but now that we're here, everything feels shakier.

"You said only one of us needs to have the surgery to save our dad,"

Judith says.

Madame Berenice narrows her eyes, almost imperceptibly.

I take a huge breath. "But we'll both get it if you agree to release Sam Oakes—if you take out his Third Eye and let him go."

I couldn't figure out how to word it without implying that we know the Third Eye is dangerous. Because why would we bargain this if it were truly some harmless, innocuous thing? Some actual clinical trial? But now it's out in the open, and Madame Berenice doesn't seem happy.

"This is impossible," she says sharply.

Judith tries to stifle a cough. "No, it's not."

After a moment, she looks Judith up and down and says, "You are too smart for your own good, dear. Let me see what I can do."

Before either of us can respond, she scans her eye next to the door and walks out. The lock clicks as it latches, and I exhale for what feels like the first time in my life.

"I am *freaking out*," I say, jumping up and down to get the blood back into my legs.

"You're fine. You're doing fine. You'll *be* fine," Judith says. She puts her hands on my shoulders—the first time she's really spoken directly to me all morning. It feels weird.

"But are you? What was that cough?"

"Who knows? Who *cares*? It was nothing." She leans right into my ear and says, "Cameras."

A flash to last night, before Judith and I fell asleep. The moonlight poured in as stripes through the half-open blinds.

"What if this works?" I asked.

It took a long time for her to answer. I thought she was asleep, and I sat up on the floor, grunting through the pain of resting on my splinted hand and wrist. Her eye was wide open in the moonlight. Maybe she saw me, maybe she didn't.

"If it works," she said, "then it works." As if that answered everything. The problem was it didn't. The more time passed, the more reality settled in, the more it no longer felt like an out-of-reach fantasy. If we went through with it—if we somehow got Sam *and* Dad out of there safely, who's to say Axiom wouldn't retaliate?

"Yeah, but…do we go on the run? All of us? How does that work?"

She coughed and said, "Maybe. I don't know, Henry. We keep on fighting. This is the whole point of the Cyclopes. They mutilate us, mutilate people we care about, and so we fight back. It's called a resistance. If that means we run, then I guess we run."

A thought ran through my mind. I tried to ignore it because it sounded ridiculous, but I couldn't help thinking it over and over: She *wants* to go on the run. *Wants* a new life.

And didn't I owe her a chance to live out at least one of her dreams?

The click of the door lock unlatching pulls me out of the memory. My heart pounds in my ears. Tears prick the back of my eyes.

A man comes in, but I don't look at him because I turn around to face the wall, embarrassed.

"Hi, doctor," Judith says.

"How have you been, Ms. Youngwell?"

"Fine, thanks."

"Healing up nicely, I hope. Any pain?"

"Sort of, but it's been getting better."

"Very good," he says. "I trust you've been following our aftercare instructions for cleaning it and changing the gauze. Do you mind if I take a look?"

Judith never mentioned aftercare instructions. I never thought to ask because I'm the world's dumbest person. I don't know how I made it seventeen years alive. Of course it needs care, it's a wound. But no doctor or nurse last week ever mentioned it to me, so it never crossed my mind.

She hesitates. "Yeah, I guess so, if you need to."

He laughs. "Well, I'll need to assess it at some point if we're going to operate!"

She chuckles politely in return. She can't very well say, "Sorry, no, I don't plan to have that today."

"And you, Mr. Youngwell, we'll also need to give you a thorough assessment to make sure you're up for the procedure."

It's the strangest thing, but I can feel two of Judith's eyes on the back of my head. I don't know how to describe it. When I turn, that's exactly what I see. Only they're in two different people.

He smiles at me, one eye blue, one eye Judith's.

"Good to see you again, Mr. Young—whoa there, what happened to your head?"

"I slipped," I say, looking at the floor. "At work."

"Oh, I'm sorry to hear that."

"No, he didn't," Judith sighs. The doctor scratches his chin with one hand and gestures for her to elaborate with the other. She doesn't.

He smiles at me congenially, like he's mildly inconveniencing me at the grocery store to get to a can of tomato soup or something. "Well, that's a shame, but it should be fine. And I did hear that you broke your finger, so I'm glad to see you using the splint. That also won't interfere with the procedure, don't you worry."

I'm in the corner, now absolutely fuming. Not only at Judith for, I don't know, calling me out on something I need to be called out on? But also that this surgeon—this man who carves out people's eyes for a living—is trying to be friendly. Cut the charade, asswipe.

"Shall we?" the doctor asks Judith. "It should only take a minute."

"Um…" She looks at me, and I shrug because what else am I gonna do? I don't exactly want to piss this guy off. "Sure," she says and sits on the table.

The surgeon gathers supplies from a drawer, more gauze and ointment of some kind. He washes his hands and snaps on a pair of gloves.

"I'll need you to remove that," he says softly, smiling.

Without a word, she takes off her eyepatch and balls it into her fist. She taps her foot and doesn't stop until the surgeon's hands make contact with her face. I expect her to flinch, but she doesn't. I do.

The surgeon glances at me, and I cross my arms against my chest. When he refocuses on Judith, I lift my hand and press into my bruise as hard as I can, over and over, and contain the moan, the warmth, washing over me. It crashes through my head, down my neck, and into my chest. There's no greater feeling in the world.

With my mind a little more dampened, I look back. Judith's gauze is peeled off except for the tape at the bottom, from which it dangles upside-down on her cheek like a child hanging by the legs from a monkey bar. The exposed part—the side that was touching her wound—is a chaotic swirl of colors: black, brown, yellow, green. It might almost be beautiful in another context, like if it were an artist mixing paints.

I try to will myself not to look at the actual wound. The wreckage.

But I have to.

It's puffy and bruised—black and blue and yellow and purple all at once—from nearly her eyebrow down to her cheek. It's been covered by the gauze all week, so I haven't been able to tell. A row of *Xs* marches across the middle: her stitches, her eyelids that were sewn together like fabric, like ripped jeans, like something meant to be attached. Some of them are green with pus oozing from the sides.

"Oh, not too bad!" exclaims the surgeon, but I think I must have heard wrong.

"Oh, good." Judith smiles, her eye still closed. She sighs.

Then I get a whiff. It's foul like rotting garbage, and I gag. Cough.

"Henry!" she snaps.

The doctor glances at me again and almost imperceptibly shakes his head, fuel in his eye—Judith's eye—as though warning me not to…not to what? Say anything? Does he just want to pretend like everything's fine? That's unfathomable. Well, maybe for a real doctor it would be. But I'm sure Jude can smell it too, she's right there. It would be stupid to cover it up.

She bites her lip and clamps down as hard as she can. And then I start to understand: she intentionally never mentioned aftercare. She hasn't been taking care of it on purpose. She was hoping for an infection.

Why? For the same reason I cut myself. The same reason I gave myself this welt on my head. It's why she so keenly notices me do things like squeeze my thigh and press my head. She knows because she's the same. And I wonder when it started for her.

But an infection is so much worse, so much more dire, isn't it? She could get sick—she *has been sick*. She was shivering almost all night around the bonfire. She's been coughing and sweaty. Tears come to my eyes. Could she die?

"It looks bad," I say, and the doctor's jaw clenches twice. And now I'm pretty sure we have to change our plan.

I was going to fake chest pain so they would have to delay surgery, because Judith was absolutely certain they wouldn't risk operating if there was any chance I might be having a heart attack. I told her I was too young to have a heart attack and it would be so obvious I was faking, but she was adamant. But now, when the doctor seems more than annoyed, I'm pretty sure he would love to make sure I *do* have a heart attack. Now what?

But then he chuckles, and he's going to pretend none of that just happened. "What, this? This looks perfectly normal after an enucleation, believe me."

I would wonder why he's lying, but it's obvious. He doesn't care if it's infected. He wants the Third Eye in her as soon as possible.

"Don't mind him," says Judith, "he doesn't know anything."

"No, Jude, I swear—"

The surgeon puts his hands on his thighs and turns in his chair. "I have been doing this for a long time, kid. I promise you, this is just a part of the healing process. Once I get in there later this morning, I'll cut the stitches and scrape all of this away anyway, to make room for the new eye." He gestures to the pus oozing around her stitches and smiles.

Judith opens her eye and glares at me, but I don't care if she's angry.

"Are you sure?" I ask.

He gives me a tight smile. "I'll tell you what. I'll go fetch one of my colleagues and have her take a look at it. That way, you can get a totally unbiased second opinion. How's that sound?" I know he means Madame

Berenice. She'll say the same thing he did, and there won't be anything un-biased about it. But what can I do? So, I nod and act like I'm relieved for this option.

One good thing he does do, though, is he peels off the dirty gauze and replaces it with a fresh one, carefully placing it just under her eyebrow and at the corner of her nose before he tapes it. He stands with a grunt and peels off his gloves to throw them in the trash. One of them misses and lands on the floor next to it. If he notices, he doesn't care.

"Don't you two go anywhere." He grins. I give him a thumbs-up, not sure how to form words.

He scans his eye and leaves. I don't know what takes over me, but as the door swings shut, I leap over and pick up the glove from the floor. I pound on the door, shouting for the surgeon. I try the handle, but it doesn't budge. In a few seconds, he pops his head in.

"Something wrong?" he asks.

I grin. "I was just wondering, um, what time it is."

"Oh, right." He looks at his watch and says, "Nine-oh-four. Anything else?"

"Not a thing," I say and push the door shut for him.

"What was that?" Judith asks.

"Just being a lunatic." I step aside to show her the blue latex fingers dangling out of the doorframe next to the handle. I tried to bunch the glove up a little as I stuck it in to prevent the lock from latching.

"What is wrong with you?" she whispers, hopping off the table.

I test the handle to see if it worked, and there's no resistance.

"Henry, tell me what is happening."

"We have to get out of here," I whisper. I turn and look her straight in the eye, which she promptly rolls. "No, listen! Your eye is *bad*. Like, bad-bad. I don't know shit about medicine, and even I can tell it looks horrible. I think you're really sick, and they're not gonna help you."

She scoffs but doesn't say anything.

"Please, just trust me," I beg, and reach for the door handle.

"Wait wait wait!" She's frantic. "What about Dad?"

"I don't know. We'll figure it out."

"What about *Sam?*"

"I don't know, okay? I don't know, I don't know. But you're going to *die* if we stay, okay?"

Her jaw quivers. She shrugs. "And?"

My heart crumbles into pieces. I wouldn't have to worry about faking chest pain now, because it is legitimately aching.

"Jude. Please."

"I hate you so much," she says, and I know she doesn't mean it, but it stings regardless. I can't believe I have to argue about this.

"That's fine, I hate you too. Come *on*."

She taps her foot. I count six until she says, "Okay, well…what now?"

"Tentatively?" I ask, opening the door. The blue glove falls silently to the floor. "Run."

Chapter Twenty-Two

MANEUVERING THIS FIRST hallway is easy. We pass door after door, but the way back to the waiting area is easy to spot because of the sliding glass door. These other ones are probably more patient rooms, and if what Madame Berenice said is true about no donations on Sundays, they should all be vacant.

The waiting area is empty too. Still no receptionist, still nobody in the chairs. Just the sad plant in the corner.

A shadow shifts behind us, and I pull Judith to the side, where we duck behind the reception desk. I didn't get a good look, but it was probably the surgeon with Madame Berenice going back to the room. In about three seconds, they're about to find out we've escaped and call for help.

"Follow me," Judith says as she starts to move around the desk. I hold my breath and zip over to her. She's examining the scanner on the doorframe. Fuck. What are we supposed to do now?

She leans forward like a little kid at a candy shop looking at all the treats.

"What the hell are you doing?" I ask, tugging on her arm. Maybe she doesn't realize she's about to give away our location or tell Axiom we've escaped, because I know these scanners are tied to some internal monitoring system. And now that they know we've left, what about Sam? What about Norah and Patrick?

She doesn't budge or answer me. The yellow laser swells and brightens and begins to swirl around as it scans her.

"Jude, stop, they're gonna—"

It dawns on me. The surgeon has her eye now, which means the scanners could be programmed to recognize her retina as an employee's. They wouldn't have, though. Axiom can't be that careless.

But they are. I hear the click, watch the laser disappear. Judith pushes the door and smiles at me. Maybe after her surgery, they thought she would never come back.

"You're so genius," I whisper.

As we run down the long skybridge, I try not to look up at the eyes moving back and forth. I wonder if they're literally watching us and telling Axiom where we are. They have to be. If our house has a camera in a clock, this hospital has to have cameras too—maybe in the form of real eyeballs. What if they detach and swarm us like bees?

"Hey," I shout between breaths. "Your room—was on the—eighth floor last week, right?"

"Yeah, why?"

"That's where—we are now—maybe Sam's—up here too somewhere?"

"Maybe, but do you wanna—run around looking for him?"

"What else would we do? Leave him?"

We're about two-thirds of the way through, and she stops and puts her hand out to block me. "You know that's not what I meant."

"I know, but we can't just abandon them."

"Okay, yeah," she wheezes.

"Hey!" The voice echoes from a mile away until it's right in my ears, deep and angry.

The surgeon. He stops for a second, shading his eyes with his hands as though we're in bright sunlight, then breaks into a full sprint. The door behind him slams.

When we start running again, I can't help but look up. The eyes are totally following us.

"There's a stairwell by the elevator," Judith says.

"Got it."

"I think not," says a voice that's not Judith's, and I see his stupid face before I register what he said. Kent. Fucking. Cross.

But then someone who's not Kent Cross grabs me by the shoulders. A Watcher. Judith screams as another one grabs her.

For the first time in my pathetic little life, I'm determined to not be afraid—especially not of a Watcher.

I writhe and squirm and kick him hard in the shins. He doesn't let me go and yells for me to be still. I don't. I kick again, and he shouts, shoving me to the ground. He sits on my stomach, bearing down his full weight.

"Get the fuck off me!" I scream. I try to punch his front and drive my knees into his back. He leans back and wraps his hands around my shins, pins them to the ground, and smashes his boots into my arms, paying particular attention to my splint, all while forcing his ass as hard as he can into my stomach.

It's excruciating. I howl and can't move at all except for my head. It takes everything inside me to not repeat what I did at work and smash my skull into the floor until my ears ring.

"Stop it!" Judith screams. I tilt and angle my head to look back, and a Watcher has her pinned to the wall with one arm. His other hand is clenched around the handle of his taser.

"Oh, boo-hoo, you little cyclops," Kent sneers. He's looking at me as he says it.

I start screaming and spitting. "I will murder you, asshole, do you hear me? I'm gonna fucking kill you."

"Enough," whips another voice. "Enough, enough, enough."

From upside-down, Madame Berenice comes into view. Her high heels click as she draws nearer. I see a braid too. I guess she's had time to dress up.

"My two favorite troublemakers. You have not disappointed me."

She slowly walks over to Judith, and I watch helplessly as she lifts her hand to stroke Judith's cheek.

"Don't touch me," Judith spits. She thrusts her jaw out to bite her, but Madame Berenice snaps away just in time.

"Ah, very good. I knew you had it in you, dear."

"You evil bitch," Judith mutters.

"Do you know what I thought to myself as I brought you two up the elevator? I thought, 'I will bet these two ungrateful children will change their minds about the donation today, and they will not want to help their poor, miserable father. In fact, I will bet they don't even believe we have a cure for his condition. I better prove it to them.' Because, as you know, Axiom holds true to their promises." She leaves Judith and stands over me. "I don't know why you would not believe us. We always keep our word, do we not? We have given you the most extravagant house you could have dreamed for, and yet you are distrusting. Well, I am here to prove you otherwise."

"Where are our friends?"

"Shut up," Kent sneers.

"Not to fret. You shall see them soon enough," Madame Berenice says. "But first, I will show you once more that we do not let our patients down." She stops to smile at me, then takes a deep breath and sings, "Please bring him out!"

A door nearby creaks open. A Watcher comes into view, walking backward, slowly pulling something large. I arch my neck but still can't see.

"Oh my god," says Judith, staring right at whatever it is. She has a better angle.

It slides into view. There's a wheel. Bedsheets? Another wheel. An entire bed. Another Watcher at the other end, pushing.

What in the—oh. Oh, no.

"Merci beaucoup, darlings," Madame Berenice says, nodding at the Watchers, who lock the bed into place and stand aside wordlessly.

Tears blur my sight, and I can't even wipe them because I'm being pinned down.

I haven't seen my dad, actually seen him, since they put him in the ambulance. He has bandages around his head. His eyes are closed and sunken deep into his skull, lost somewhere in a deep sleep. He's covered up to his neck by a thick white blanket. Hooked on to the side of the bed frame by his feet is a bag full of dark-amber liquid. I think it's his piss.

"Perhaps now you will behave," says Madame Berenice, looking at my father as if she's talking to him instead of Judith and me. Maybe she is. Maybe he can hear her evil voice in his subconscious.

I don't say a word, and breathing is becoming more uncomfortable with this Watcher on top of me. I try to squirm, but he doesn't relent.

"What do you want?" Judith whispers.

"I wish only to show you that I stay true to my word—and that Axiom is not the villain you think we are."

She struts over to my dad and softly folds down the blanket and sheets, exposing his elbow. The IV still juts out from it. She positions his arm so the IV faces up. From her pocket, she pulls out a dark vial of liquid and a needle and syringe. She holds the vial up to the ceiling and shakes it back and forth.

"Is that the cure?" Judith asks.

"We call it Golden Tonic, yes."

"Get—off," I growl to the Watcher, but he only tightens his grip on my legs and pushes his foot harder into my splint. I scream like I never have in my life.

Madame Berenice clears her throat, as though to redirect my attention back to her.

When she has it, she begins to hum to herself, then plunges the needle upside-down into the vial and draws liquid into the syringe until it's half-full of bright-golden liquid.

Why do I get the feeling this isn't a cure at all but will make his heart stop beating?

"Perfect," she whispers, then removes the needle, covers it with a sheath, and places it in her pocket.

At the foot of the bed is a box. She retrieves a pair of gloves from it and slowly peels them on, finger by finger, left hand then right. Sighing, she turns and smiles at me. I think about smashing my head into the floor again because maybe it will divert attention away from my dad and back to me. If it knocks me unconscious and they take my eye while I'm out, so be it. But I don't. Even in this moment, I realize it would be futile. They'll still do whatever they want.

"Don't you see we are good?" she says. "I am about to do the impossible. I can understand how, on a primitive level, you believe we are evil. But you must understand that donations and the Third Eye are used for good."

She looks up, and I follow her gaze, whipping my head in the other direction. The surgeon, who's been hiding around the corner of the skybridge, comes out and nods at me.

"Good? Is that why *he* took Judith's eye, so he could play the piano like her? Is that helping the *greater good,* you psychos?"

The surgeon cracks his neck one way and the other but doesn't say a word.

"We have found a cure for your father thanks to what we do," says Madame Berenice. "Is that not enough for you, selfish boy?" She smiles at Judith next, her brown eyes wide and crinkled at the corners. "Are you ready to say hello to him again?"

"Don't do it," Judith says, choking on tears under the Watcher's hold. She must think Dad's about to be killed too.

Kent, standing with his chest puffed and hands behind his back, has a wicked grin on his face. I wasn't lying about killing him the next chance I have. I envision squeezing his skull between my hands until it pops and little bits of brain fly everywhere.

The nurse inspects her gloves for rips and tears, as though making absolutely certain none of the Golden Tonic will get on her skin. Which makes me even more sure that it will kill him.

"I hope you are ready to see your lovely children again, Alister," she says, leaning down to remove a cap from his IV. "They've been waiting."

"No!" I shout, and Kent laughs.

Madame Berenice connects the syringe to the IV by their tips and looks at Judith, then me, grinning. "Here we go."

I hold my breath as if time will stop. It doesn't; Judith is still crying.

"I beg of you," she sobs. "*Please!*"

"You do not know what you are asking, child, for if you did, you would be pleading for me to do it *more quickly!*"

With her thumb, she barely pushes on the plunger, and I watch the golden liquid disappear slowly, drop by drop, into my dad's arm. It's excruciating how slowly she goes, as if she wants this moment, when our pain is so huge, to last.

When it's empty, she smiles so genuinely for once that it reaches her eyes, deep grooves forming at the corners of them. She twists off the syringe, caps it, and places it in her pocket. She replaces the cap on Dad's IV and moves his arm back to where it was, then places the blanket at his neck again, as though tucking in her child for bed.

I almost wait for him to rise and start walking, just like she promised. But she lied, of course. He doesn't move. I can't even tell if he's breathing. She killed my father right in front of me, the very thing I came close to doing myself on Friday. I just watched her finish the job for me.

Judith's sobs are frantic and wild now, her face and neck and chest drenched with a mix of tears and snot and slobber. "Why would you—how—*reprehensi*—" A horrendous cough interrupts her. It takes an eternity for it to stop.

Madame Berenice has embraced Kent. She hugs him to her side, kisses him on the forehead. "I love you, my sweet boy," she says.

"You too, Mommy."

He winks at me while she squeezes him tighter, and something inside me, like I wasn't broken enough, snaps. Shatters. It's a sucking sensation, as though a collapsed star somewhere inside me is igniting a supernova, forming a black hole, sucking in and devastating everything around it, a massive galactic surge of energy unlike anything I have ever felt.

I scream and rip my splinted arm out from under the Watcher's boot, my hand screaming in pain along with me. For just a fraction of a second, his balance shifts off his center of gravity, and I take the opportunity to knock him off me with my hips. I inhale a breath like I've been starved of air and turn onto my stomach so I can stand.

The sound of Judith howling is so distant in the background, it feels worlds away.

He's still got his arms around my legs, and he digs his claws into my flesh. Hot liquid pours down my calves, and I'm pretty sure it's blood. He cut through my thin, papery jeans.

I kick free of one claw and use that leg to drive my foot into his stomach. It doesn't seem to affect him. My knees crunch into the tile, but I get myself to a kneel and reach for his face to punch him. His reflexes are too quick, or maybe he was expecting it, and he moves his head to avoid me at just the right time.

He stands and pulls me up by the skin of my neck like a cat with her kitten. In the reflection of his sunglasses, I look dead already.

I could resist. I could fight. But what's the point?

He turns me around and pins my arms to my body with one arm. The other's a noose around my neck, and if he were to squeeze any tighter, I would leave this world in a second.

Everything moves in and out of slow motion. I meet Judith's eye and barely register that it's her. But I do. I *do* realize it's her. She's crying, so at least she doesn't hate me for everything. For letting them do what they did to her. Or maybe she does. Maybe she's just crying for Dad.

The surgeon steps in front of me. "Hi, Henry. Thank you for helping us with the Third Eye. You're going to help a lot of people."

"No problem," I say, struggling for breath. "Anything to help."

He pulls out a needle and syringe like the nurse had, and I watch as the shape of him pulls up my shirt sleeve. Jaw clenched, he sinks the needle into my arm.

The pain is exquisite, but it lasts for only a second. It's been the most beautiful second of my life. Warmth spreads up my arm and through my chest, and I hope this is the same thing that killed my dad. I hope this warmth is nothing less than sweet death filling me from the inside out.

I look around, and everyone is staring at me. Past the surgeon with two different eyes, there's Judith and the Watcher holding her to the wall. There's the evil nurse, and there's her evil son. And there's—wait, who's that?

Oh.

"Hey, Dad," I think I say. He looks funny sitting up in bed like that.

I wonder if he remembers me.

Chapter Twenty-Three

MY EYES HURT. My head hurts. My whole body just…hurts. Every muscle *aches* like I've been swimming for hours through a sea of thick honey.

The lights are so bright I can barely even squint one eye open, my left. It feels…dry and crusty almost, like I've either been crying really hard or I have pink eye or something.

Where am I? Why does it feel like my arm's been ripped off my body?

I hear some faint beeping somewhere, and I'm pretty sure it's my heartbeat. Am I dead? Would I have a heartbeat if I was dead? That seems like the opposite.

I open my eye wider even though the light burns. It's so blurry, all I can see is white. Fuck, is this real? My right eye doesn't want to open. I can't even move my eyeball or squeeze it shut. Why won't it—why can't I—

Oh no. Oh god. I remember.

The beeping gets louder and quicker, more urgent. I can't move. I can't *move!* I kick my legs, but nothing. They work, but I think they're strapped down. And they're cold. I think someone changed me into a gown. My back and ass are sweaty against this thing underneath me—a big metal table?

Even through the pain, I try to move my arms, my hips, my head. Nothing. I am rattling the table or whatever it is.

"Ooh, sounds like he's awake!" The voice is near. It's jubilant. Bubbly.

Someone pops into view, three inches above me. At first, I can't tell who because they have on a mask and a cap covering their head, but then it's obvious. Two eyes—one green, one blue, both dazzling in this light.

"Welcome back, Mr. Youngwell," says the surgeon, grinning. I can tell he's grinning because the corners of his eyes crinkle.

I try to talk, to ask what the fuck he's done to me, but my mouth is bone dry. Too dry to utter a word. Nothing's working the way it's supposed to. It seems the only things that are, are my eyes—wait, not plural. Tears prick me at the realization. I try to open the right one again, but it just won't. It feels crusty like the left one.

I start to cry, and because I'm lying flat, the tears collect and pool on top of my eyeball until they build up like a rising flood and leak out by the corner of my nose. This man has cut my eye out and sewn me up.

One of my first thoughts is that it'll get infected like Judith's.

Judith. When I think of her, the machine starts to beep even wilder— a shrill, nonstop, hysterical cry like an angry baby. Where the hell is my sister? Is she okay? What *exactly* have they done with her?

I try to shout her name because it's all I can think to do, but all that comes out are coughs and mumbles.

"Don't worry," says the surgeon, still grinning, a ring of white light inset in the blue of his left eye. "You're okay. You know what? You'll be asleep again in no time, but I wanted to give you a little show first."

Show? I don't have time for whatever game he's playing. But then I realize: actually, I have all the time in the world.

He slides away, and left in his place are the lights above, bright and sterile and hypnotizing as in a dream. I have to tell myself not to look right into them so I can save what vision I have left. I want to turn my head to see what else is around me, but the pressure squeezing into my forehead tells me my head is strapped in place.

I hear other people in the room. "She's going to look fabulous when she's back to normal," one of them says. I think it's Madame Berenice.

"Such a beautiful young woman," says another. "Pity it had to be this way."

Then I hear a click somewhere behind me, and almost immediately, I begin to move. No—I begin to *be* moved. The table is turning somehow, and I'm just along for the ride. Slowly, I swivel around one way and come to a jerking stop. Then I'm lifted to a standing position but still suspended in the air, my feet not touching the ground. Straps everywhere on my body, from my head to my ankles, keep me from falling over.

And what I see breaks me. Judith. Also strapped to a table.

She looks so much like me—the hollow cheeks, the sharp chin, the pale-gray undertones of her skin. She's connected to a monitor just like I am, and she's not moving. Covered with thin blue paper, she looks like a corpse. Her eye is closed. The gauze over the other eye is off, the almost technicolored and swollen mass of a bruise in its place.

The show he wants me to see is them putting in the Third Eye.

I start shaking in my straps, but it does nothing. If anything, they seem to tighten even more, and the table underneath me—no, behind me—doesn't even budge.

Someone looks up, their eyes the deepest shade of brown I've ever seen. They complement the pale-blue mask over her mouth. "You may as well stop that, Monsieur, for it is not going to help."

So it is her after all. How is she everywhere? The emergency room *and* operating room, not to mention everywhere in between. Does this hospital not have any other nurses?

Maybe. On the other side of the room, somebody else turns around.

"Take a breath, Mr. Youngwell. Calm down." It's not the surgeon or Madame Berenice, but the other voice I heard. They're in a mask, cap, and blue plastic gown too.

I shake some more, but nothing. My arms are completely useless, my splinted hand and wrist on fire, and my other shoulder in searing pain like a thousand giant needles are piercing it. I try to thrust my hips to loosen that strap, but I'm weak and sore from the Watcher sitting on me.

"Please relax," the surgeon says, taking a few steps toward me. "It will be okay. Your sister will be restored of her full sight. Then you will make your donation and *also* be receiving a brand-new eye, so it will be like nothing has changed. You'll have a new, better, even *stronger* eye. And then you'll get to go home and sleep. How does that sound, huh?"

Wait, I *do* have my eye? Why can't I open it? It feels like when I had pink eye once and I could hardly open my eyes after I woke up in the morning—like I was stuck in the blackness. I try to pry it open, but it doesn't budge. Is he lying?

"Fuck you," I say. Wait, did I say that? Did my mouth make words?

His eyes crinkle again, smiling. "Perhaps this isn't the best time to be difficult."

"You'll pay." My voice is scratchy. My throat is parched. I don't know if I'm making any sense.

He chuckles. "Hey, I'm only holding you to your word. This was our deal, no? We heal your father, and you all do as we ask."

Oh shit, so that was real? I thought I was hallucinating. The way my dad sat up in the bed like he'd been risen from the dead, it was…at the time, it was kind of funny. I was so out of it. Where is he now? Just because they cured him doesn't really mean he's free to go or anything. They could be holding him hostage.

"Only one of us," I say, my throat starting to burn. "Do me. Let Judith go."

The surgeon sucks in a breath. "No can do, I'm afraid. What with the hassle of you two trying to run away, and the damage you inflicted on one of our staff. Well, we figured we'd go ahead and fit ya both in. And at the same time too! Sort of like a family discount, how's that sound? Now, if you have no further questions, I really need to—"

"Why me?"

He steps closer, cautiously, as if I'll get him. "One more time? Didn't quite catch that."

That's not true. He's making me talk because he knows it hurts. I try to swallow as if I actually have saliva, and it feels like razor blades dragging down my throat.

"*Why—me?*"

"It's a fair question," he says quietly. "The short answer is that you possess a great passion in you, the likes of which we rarely see in the world. We think you would be perfect for our new…reign."

"Reign?" So it's true. What Mr. Jeong said, what Sam theorized.

The surgeon stops to make sure I'm looking at him. I am. I stare right into Judith's eye as if I could tie a lasso around it with just my gaze and yank it out of him.

"I can see it right now as you look at me, Mr. Youngwell. It's incredible. Once you have the Third Eye, you will be unstoppable. And, if I can say, quite malleable to our direction. There will be no stopping you after that."

I start to laugh, but my throat makes weird choking noises.

He must think I'm trying to talk because he says, "Oh, your sister! Your poor, poor sister. You might be wondering about *her* donation. You see, I was the sole claimant for that one. After all, I was the one who labored over it, carefully removing the beauty from its orbit, scraping away the muscles, severing the optic nerve, what have you. We almost sent it to auction, but why shouldn't I get first dibs? Oh, I always wanted to play the piano so badly, but my parents were never interested in letting me take lessons. They wanted me to study, study, study for *school*. I remember my father saying the only reason I should take my nose out of a book was to *eat* and *sleep*. Well, when I became a surgeon, they were very happy all their pestering paid off, but I suppose I always felt something…missing."

He stops to pat the corner of his eye, as if a tear has formed. It's melodramatic and annoying.

"That's stupid," I say.

He examines his fingertip like he's studying his reflection in the moisture of his tears he's dabbed away—wait, his tears or Judith's? Do they take the tear ducts when they take the eye? I guess I don't know.

"Don't underestimate the lengths someone will go to for that of which they are deprived, Mr. Youngwell. Surely you've wanted something so badly that you would do anything for it."

Why is the very first thing I think about cutting? Slicing my leg open? I'd do anything to be able to do that right now. It wouldn't take away my memories of this place, but it would surely dampen them. For a while.

But that's not what he's talking about.

"Now! We have wasted a lot of precious time, have we not? What do you say we get this show on the road?" He turns and struts away. "Nurse, if you could please get the anesthesia dripping, and Berenice, if you could glove me, we'll get started in just a few minutes."

"Yes, doctor," say the other two simultaneously.

I try to shout, but it falls flat, so I keep shaking and shaking in my straps despite knowing it won't work, despite all the pain I'm in, because I have to. I have to try, don't I? There's nothing else I can do.

In minutes, I'm drenched in sweat, out of breath, and physically unable to keep going. And it was all for nothing, I'm no looser in any of the straps, no closer to getting out of here.

"Her pulse and respirations are elevated, doctor. BP and temp decreased, as well as her oxygen," Madame Berenice says, eyes glued to the monitor.

"Eh, no worries." The surgeon shrugs. "I was made aware of a possible infection this morning. This too shall pass, yes?"

The other nurse, who's sitting by a large machine at Judith's head, looks up. "Are you sure you want to continue, doctor? The patient is visibly perspiring."

"I'm positive. That's nothing a little antibiotic won't fix. Why don't we start another IV and infuse the Golden Tonic? That should fix her right up to where we need her to be. I just hope the pharmacy has some in stock and doesn't have to mix it from scratch. They are so damn slow down there, it's like another world, I swear."

Golden Tonic? To cure her infection? That was the same thing Madame Berenice said before she gave it to Dad. So, it does more than just cure a stroke? I wonder if it's another invention they stole from somebody when they took their eye.

"Yes, sir," says the second nurse, and she runs to the door, pulling off her mask and gown before she exits.

Madame Berenice clears her throat. I can tell she wants to say something, but she's weighing her words. Her eyes flutter as she converses in her head.

"You know, doctor," she says slowly, hesitating, "as much as it pains me to say, if she is unwell, perhaps she is not the ideal candidate for this. Do you wish to examine the infected sutures closer? Perhaps we could, I don't know, run a culture?"

"A culture? We don't have time for that, are you stupid?"

She tilts her head to the side. "What did you say to me?"

The surgeon clears his throat. "I only mean that I've just ordered the Golden Tonic. Why would we run a culture?"

"We have limited supplies of the tonic. You know this, do you not? We mustn't waste precious resources when we could simply hold off on giving her the Third Eye while we let her heal with traditional antibiotics."

"That could take *weeks,* Berenice." He sighs heavily and paces. "I've made up my mind. I know you are Seer of donations, but in this room, I'm in charge. You are blessed in many ways, but you are not trained as a surgeon. We'll wait to see if the pharmacy has the tonic. In the meantime, make yourself useful and start a line."

She closes her eyes. "Of course."

I would have thought seeing her bossed around would make me happy, but all I want to do is cry. I have no idea what I'm supposed to do. I thought maybe with how sweaty I am, I'd be able to slip out of the straps and just, I don't know, karate-chop these people and carry Judith out of the hospital on my back, all heroic like?

But that doesn't appear to be possible. Shaking and rocking my body hasn't done anything. I am literally out of options, and I'm in so much pain it'd be useless to even try.

Wait…I am in pain. I'm literally in pain—everywhere.

"I have chest pain," I whisper, but they don't hear me. I say it louder, making sure not to sound too exhilarated by it. Nothing. Again.

Madame Berenice looks up from Judith's forearm, where she's placing an IV, and squints at me.

"What are you saying, boy?"

"My chest hurts." The fire in my throat grows hotter with each word, but I say it one more time for good measure. "My chest hurts." And when they're both silent, I go on. "I think I—"

"You have *got* to be kidding me," the surgeon shouts. "You do not have chest pain!"

"Yes, I do." My muscles and my ribs are sore, so technically, isn't that chest pain?

"You are seventeen years old," the surgeon shouts. "You could not possibly be having a cardiac event."

Either he's lying about that, or for once in our lives, I was right and Judith was wrong. I knew chest pain was a stupid plan.

"I don't know what to tell you," I manage to say, mustering, I hope, a really solid poker face.

"Then shut up," he spits.

A small squeak and a whooshing sound to my right. It must be the nurse returning with the tonic. I can't turn my head, but I can sort of see her if I whip my eyes as far as they'll go.

"Uh, Madame Berenice, may I have a word?" she asks. It's not the same nurse—or at least I don't think so. It's not the same voice. But I do feel delusional and tired, so there's that.

"Almost finished." Madame Berenice rips off a piece of tape and adheres the IV to Judith's arm. "There. How may I help you, dear?"

"Um…" She takes a few steps, and I can see her better. She's short, but she's decked out in surgical gear so I can't tell much else about her. Except one thing. She has an eye patch. It's green, though, not blue.

"Yes, what is it?" Madame Berenice asks impatiently.

"Could you…"

"Out with it, girl."

"There's something wrong with your son. He's asking to see you."

"What? Kent? What is wrong with him?"

"He said something about how he wants to quit working for Axiom?"

Madame Berenice throws up her hands. "Oh, that boy is so theatrical. Every other day, it is something new." She hesitates, then says, "Well, since we are apparently waiting for this Golden Tonic, you are to be scrub nurse in my absence. The nurse anesthetist is out grabbing the tonic from the pharmacy currently, and when she is back, you will infuse it into the patient so that she can monitor the anesthesia, of course."

The nurse nods silently. I watch as her eye darts to me and just as quickly darts back. Madame Berenice notices too.

"Do not worry about him, he will not bother you. I promise to be back long before we are ready for his procedure."

Her saying so reminds me of my eye. I try to pry it open again, but it doesn't budge. If they haven't taken it yet, it doesn't make sense for it to be sealed shut, so I don't understand why I can't open it.

"Great," the other nurse says, her eye glued to the floor. I keep thinking there's something familiar about her. I'm probably making it up, but I *swear* I know her voice.

I count the clicks of Madame Berenice's heels as she struts toward the door. She removes her mask and sighs. "Page if you need me. I am off to deal with the daily frustration and disappointment I call my son." She chuckles at herself. I think it's the first time I've seen her amused, and I'm a little pleased to know it's about how much she seems to despise Kent.

When she's gone, the surgeon turns toward the new nurse. "What's your name?" he asks.

"Ida." Ida… Does that sound familiar?

"Beautiful name. Have you ever scrubbed in on one of my surgeries?"

"I don't believe so, sir. I was just transferred recently. I've traveled all around the country working at local Axiom chapters. I love being part of a donation—in my own little way, sir."

"Good, good. Well, you'll learn a thing or two watching me. I have a very exact, tried-and-true method." He plops down on a small, rolling stool on one side of the room by some of the cabinets. He has his hands raised in the air because I think he's not supposed to touch anything with his gloves until he starts the surgery.

"Is this your first Third Eye procedure?" he asks.

"Oh, yeah," says the nurse softly, now walking casually toward Judith. Her voice seems to drift and carry. "I mean, yes, it is. I'm very…honored to be here."

"It's still in the experimental phase," the surgeon says. "I'm one of the few in the entire country trusted enough to perform it. My name was on the scientific paper, you know."

"Ah," she says. With her back to me, she stands at Judith's head and, I think, stares down at her. Her head isn't angled up to look at the monitor like Madame Berenice's was but rather downward. Maybe she's just seen how awful Judith's oozy, bruised stitches look.

Her hand lifts and hovers above Judith's arm for just a second—for *just* a second—and lowers. It was only a second, but I saw it. Maybe she realized she wasn't gloved yet, so she wasn't allowed to touch her.

"Hey, green patch, huh?" says the surgeon, and she startles like she forgot where she was. "That's exciting."

"Yes," she says. "I'm blessed to be receiving a donation in just a few days."

Fuck. Just when I was starting to get my hopes up, like maybe she was a good one somehow.

"Ah, wonderful!" The surgeon's eyelids crease deeply. "And what specialty?"

Specialty?

"Spiritual," she says.

The surgeon's eyes go wide. "How rare! We almost never get a spiritual donation. How lucky you are."

Spiritual donation? Are they split into categories? If so, Judith's would have been musical or artistic, maybe. That man who invented the Mirror of Memoria would have been, what, magical or some shit? And whoever came up with Golden Tonic, scientific. Now there's spiritual?

The nurse nods. "Yes, very rare. He's a minister who lives in the region, which is why I wanted to transfer. His scans have shown direct communication with—"

"Fascinating," he interrupts her. "Best of luck to you, Ida."

I remember where I know that name from, but I haven't thought of Ida since I was a kid. I think I lost her in a move somewhere, or maybe my dad threw her away. But there's no way *this* is Ida. Ida was a stuffed penguin.

"Thank you," Ida, but not my Ida, says.

"Where in the hell is that nurse with the antibiotic? I swear—no offense, but nurses will be the death of me."

I glance over at Judith to see if maybe she's woken up yet. No luck.

A phone rings. The surgeon pops off the stool like he's been caught doing something. Ida strides over to the wall, where the phone should be. I can't turn my head to see it.

"Hel—uh, Donation Suite. Yes, it is. Yes, he is. That's right. Well, he's about to begin collecting a donation any minute now. Would you like to speak with him?" The surgeon's eyes pop, Judith's side going even further than the other, more pronounced. "What's the name now? Got it. No, not presently, but he'll begin any minute. We're just waiting on—okay, yes. Got it. Right away."

She hangs up the phone. I can't see, but I imagine she turns to look at the surgeon, because he's gesturing for her to hurry up and tell him.

"That was Detention Care. There's apparently been some sort of emergency with a Samwell Oakes?"

Everything inside me stops. There's no air moving in my chest. No blood pumping in my veins.

"The intraocular pressure in his original eye seems to have skyrocketed. They need you right away. They're afraid it may burst."

He scoffs. "How could that—wait, why do they need me?"

"To perform emergency surgery, I believe."

"I'm already about to perform *two* surgeries! Have one of them do it."

"That's what I told them! They said since you're already familiar with the patient—"

He's familiar with Sam? Is he the one who ripped out his eye on Friday?

"Oh, unbelievable. I swear it's a curse to be me. Well, what about these two?"

"They're sending in a replacement for you right away, sir."

"*Replacement?* Ha! I'd like to see them try. I will have a word once I'm finished, believe me. This is inexcusable. I had my whole day lined up!" He rips off his cap and mask and balls them into his fist. "Well, just keep an eye on them, I guess, until one of them gets here. Maybe she'll be back with the damn tonic soon. Not that this ugly bitch deserves our drugs. Let her die, see if the world would be worse off. *Fuck!*"

He storms off, the door slamming open and closed. His muffled yells get quieter and quieter until, finally, everything is silent.

I don't know why, but things feel more ominous now that it's just her. Like, somehow, the room is closing in.

She glides over to me. She looks at my feet for the longest time, and tears form in her eye. As it travels up my body, the tears fall down her cheek.

When her green eye meets mine—a green so bright, so wild, so fantastically dazzling—I hold my breath.

"My sweet boy," she says, and pulls the mask off her face—the face I've dreamed of for nine years. The face I sent to prison. The face I think about whenever I cut my leg open. Finally, she's here. Her eye is as bright and wild as juniper—as juniper as I remember Judith's to be.

I think I must be dreaming.

I exhale a breath in the shape of a single word. "Mom?"

Chapter Twenty-Four

BLACKNESS FADES TO a blue so bright I have to squint.

"Um, hello? Can you help me?"

The lady in line at the concession stand bends down and pats the top of my head. "I can sure try. You okay, sweetie?"

I can't see her eyes because she's wearing sunglasses. But that's okay because I'm afraid she'll look into my brain and see how stupid I am anyway. I look at her chest instead. Her freckles make it look like someone sneezed on her with a bloody nose.

"I'm scared," I whisper, trying not to cry.

"What's that?"

"I'm really scared." I bite my lip as hard as I can, until I'm sure I'll crack all my teeth on the other side. Mom just got done showing me the whales, and now I'm supposed to be using the bathroom. She let me go all by myself, even without Judith. I tried to pee, but I was too mad at her still for liking Judith more than me and also nervous because of what I was about to do.

The lady grabs my shoulder. Her fingers are sweaty and warm. "Oh no, are you lost? I'm sure your mommy and daddy are around here somewhere. You want me to help you look?"

"My mom…"

She squats down. "Huh? What's that? What'd you say, hon?"

It's now or never. Now or never, now or never, now or—

"I heard them on the phone. My mom killed my dad."

I know it's a lie. But it's not *my* lie. Mom's the one who said he was dead, and I know she was lying even though she doesn't know I know. He went in the ambulance to get un-poisoned. I'm just telling this lady *Mom's* lie. I also know it's going to get Mom in loads of trouble, and I'm still furious at her for the whale thing, and for hurting Dad. She's always yelling and stuff, and he's just trying his best. It's not his fault he's sad all the time.

The lady grabs her chest and laughs nervously. "My child, that ain't a joke. We don't joke around about things like that, do you understand?"

I sniff and go really quiet. I don't know how to tell her I'm not kidding. No one ever thought I was funny before, so why does this lady think I am when this is the most serious I've ever been?

"Oh, my word," she says after a while. She takes off her sunglasses, and her eyes are so wide I can see the white around the entire circle of brown. Normally you can only see white on the left and the right—sometimes the top too, if they're really excited. But I can actually see white around the whole thing. I wonder if it's bad. It's probably bad.

"Where do you live?" she asks.

And now I kind of wish I could take it back. This is starting to feel really, really real. I tell her anyway.

"California."

"Honey, this is South Carolina. What do you mean you live in California?"

"We drove here in our car after my dad went to the ambulance."

"Oh, sweet Jesus."

She stands up really quick and fans herself with her hands like she got really, really hot all of a sudden. After a minute of heavy breathing and sweating, she grabs my hand and pulls me with her to the front of the line. People complain and tell us we can't cut, but she ignores them and leans over the counter.

"Call the police immediately."

"Huh?"

"Right now. Do it!"

I try to get out of this woman's sweaty grip, but she just holds on to me tighter. I look back at where Judith and Mom are on the beach, way far away by the water. I can barely see that far, but it's definitely them. I think. Mom is holding Judith now, and it makes me sure I did the right thing.

Chapter Twenty-Five

SHE LOOKS SO much different than she does in my dreams, paler and more wrinkled. I know almost an entire decade has passed. I know she has an eye patch. But is this the same woman who tried to rescue us from an abusive father?

She takes her wrist to her cheek and wipes the tears that have crashed. I want to ask what the hell she's doing here, *how* she's here, but the words don't come.

A strange look creeps onto her face—a sinister sort of frown—and without warning, she lunges forward, no doubt about to attack me for what I did. I squeeze my eyes and go to kick my legs out of pure self-defense, even though I deserve whatever she wants to do to me, but of course I can't.

But the punches, the rage, and the screaming don't come. I open my eyes and look down. I can't bend my neck to look back, but all I can see is her back, now horizontal and bent over. I feel her at my feet, at the strap around my left ankle. The pressure gets tighter, then looser. I hear the clink of metal. Is it just like a belt buckle?

The weight of my body shifts against every other strap, digging deeper into my body, because they're the only thing keeping me from falling forward. I realize if she undoes every strap, I'm going to fall into her.

"Don't," I grunt, the single word clawing at my throat.

She doesn't respond, only shifts over to my right ankle. My left foot dangles in the air. Blood rushes into it, a swarm of pins and needles that is so uncomfortable I feel like the whole foot is going to snap off. Moving it hurts worse.

"Stop." It comes out as a whisper. Maybe she doesn't hear it.

My right foot hangs there. Pins and needles again surge into it, more painful than the first time.

The strap across my thighs digs right through some of my scars and into my bones. She undoes it and releases them. All my weight shifts to my waist, where the next strap is. I'm so skinny that I briefly think I might just slip on through, but no. The strap squeezes whatever organs are inside me.

"Mom," I say, breathing hard. "Mom, Mom."

"Not now," she says, laser-focused as she works on my waist.

"Mom, stop!" I scream it without meaning to. She snaps upright and looks at me with a raised brow, more sadness than anger. I shift my gaze away from her, up to the lights. "I'm sorry. I didn't mean—Mom—"

I don't recognize my own voice. I only know I'm the one talking because my throat hurts so bad. I want to tell her about how there's a button that moves the table somewhere.

But we're running out of time. That other nurse will be back any second with the tonic. It sounded bad, what Madame Berenice was saying about Judith's temperature and all that. Maybe my mom, who's apparently a nurse now, will know what to do. How did she have time to become a nurse when she's been in prison?

"Do my hands, do my hands," I say.

Without a word, she unbuckles my right wrist. I move it around in circles, lucky the pins and needles don't come surging in, and feel for the buckle of the strap across my shoulders. It's right in the middle, but it's too stiff and complicated to do with one hand. When she gets my left hand free, I can do it just fine. All that's left are my waist and head.

The skin of my forehead is scraped raw and bloody, the metallic smell thick as blood and sweat pour down my cheeks, next to my nose, and drip down my chin. I grunt in pain. I feel like I'm digging into my skull as I undo the buckle, but I do. My head slumps to one side without my meaning to, then forward, my neck weak and painful. At least I get a clear view of my mother working on my waist, though I can't see her face. Only the top of her surgical cap.

"I'm gonna fall when you're done," I say.

"I'll catch you," she says. And I believe her. Her hand is pressed hard into my stomach, as hard as the straps were, as she undoes the buckle. That hand then shoots up to press into my chest. She's using all her strength. I'm not heavy by any means, and I think she's taller than me anyway, but this still seems effortless on her part.

Slowly, she slides me down the table until my feet touch the floor. They're not screaming with pins and needles anymore, but they're weak. And when she lets me go, I fall into her. I barely have the wherewithal and strength to avoid smacking her head with mine, and instead let it crash into her shoulder.

"I got you. I got you."

I don't mean for it to, but my body goes limp. I let her hold me. She smells like bleach. It's the scrubs, I think.

"There's no time," I say, more to remind myself than her.

"We'll be okay," she pants.

I breathe heavily, grunting while I try to shake out my legs.

"You're a nurse," I sigh. I don't know where it comes from, but I've said it.

"No, I'm not. I'll explain when I get you two out of here." It's a different voice than the one she was using with the surgeon and Madame Berenice.

"But you're taking a minister's eye?" I'd sound angry, but I'm so exhausted.

"I'm not, sweetheart."

It feels so weird to hear her say that.

"Ida?"

She laughs a little. "Now, I wonder where I got that name from."

So, it was after my penguin? I was obsessed with it for years. My dad always told me to stop being a baby, but my mom came into bed and tucked me in with her every night.

But that's the only thing I could figure out. I don't get *anything* else. I don't get how she could have concocted that entire story. It was so detailed. Was she faking the story about Kent and Sam too, to get Madame Berenice and the surgeon out of the room? What's gonna happen when they figure out they were lied to?

Somehow, I gather strength in my legs by bending my knees. I back myself onto them, holding on to her for balance. The stretch in my lower back feels fantastic, but I don't let myself stay there because that other nurse is coming back, and we still have to figure out what to do with Judith. Or maybe my mother has a plan.

She helps me stand on my own. "Are you okay?"

I nod, and when she lets go, I'm able to keep my balance. I stand there and try to stretch some more. My arm where the surgeon stabbed me aches.

"Do I still have my eye?" I ask, afraid to reach up and feel it.

"I'm not sure, hon. It's taped up."

Why would they tape it? I don't understand.

"He said they haven't done mine yet. They were doing Jude first. But why would they—"

She softens. "They must've been taking your photos. They need some to put in your file. Before-and-after prototypes, or what have you. They have one in my file too."

"But I thought you said you weren't—"

My mother turns and runs over to Judith, who's still under the dead sleep of anesthesia. She presses a button on the machine, and the screen goes black. Just like that. I can't believe she did it so easily. But is that safe? Can you just…turn it off? She has to be a nurse if she knows that, doesn't she?

For the first time since learning who she is, I start to doubt her. I watch her back muscles move as she undoes Judith's straps, working from her head down to her feet. They're in the same placements as mine were, so the surgeon must have been planning to make her watch my surgery too.

How could this woman walk past Watchers if she didn't work here?

How could she have gotten into the surgical area if her eye wasn't programmed in the scanner? Fuck.

Fuck fuck fuck. This is some kind of trap. But why would my own mother go through this whole charade if she was on their side now? I feel like if she were one of them, she would just let them cut us open. Unless she's undercover or something.

I'm so confused. My head is spinning.

She frees Judith's feet, and I'm kind of disappointed Judith doesn't wake up. I was sort of hoping maybe she'd open her eyes, finally free, and be nice and rested and ready to go. But she just…remains. Her swollen, discolored eye is the only part of her that looks alive, its own sentient being. I'm probably imagining it, but it looks like it's pulsating, as though with Judith's heartbeat.

"Excuse me, what is going on here?"

That other nurse is by the door, now breathing hard and sweating buckets like she's been running. She holds a small dark vial in her fingers— the same vial Madame Berenice had when she resurrected my dad.

"Hello," my mother says calmly.

"Who are you, and what are you doing with these patients?"

My mother turns to her and smiles. "I'm the replacement, dear."

The nurse's eyes are darting between all three of us. "Where's Doctor—"

"He had other matters to tend to. But I suspect he'll be back soon, don't worry. I was asked to step in and keep the patients safe."

The nurse's eyes move to me. I take a step back and feel the stiffness in my legs and my back again. If she comes for me, I'm screwed.

"Why are they out of their belts?"

"Because I took them out. This poor boy was bleeding from his head. Look! And he's severely bruised."

"He was bruised before we strapped him in."

"Do you have photo documentation?" asks my mother.

The nurse takes a step backward. "Who did you say you were again?"

"My name is Ida."

"Right," says the nurse, taking another step back. She nods like she's considering. Then, with a grunt, she chucks the vial hard at my mother, maybe thinking it will distract her, and turns to run toward the door.

My mother holds out her hand so the vial doesn't hit her, and it falls to the floor. She already suspected this, I think, and she sprints out the door after her.

It takes me a minute to find the vial all the way in the corner, and by some miracle, it hasn't shattered. Maybe that was another invention Axiom stole: a type of glass that doesn't break no matter how hard it lands. I pick it up and stare at it, as if I have any idea how to give it to Judith. I carry it over to her other side, to the anesthesia.

My mother already turned off the machine, so maybe it's safe to disconnect her. But what if it messes things up? I have no idea what I'm doing, but I find the connection of the anesthesia tube and Judith's IV, a little plastic knobby thing that looks like it turns. With a deep breath and a glance to the ceiling, as if to the god I never thought I believed in, I twist it off.

Blood doesn't start pouring out of her IV, she doesn't blow into a seizure, and as far as I know, the sky doesn't crack open. So now what? Madame Berenice had a needle and syringe. Where do I find those?

I hear the muffled sound of shouting, then a thud. I freeze. If something happens to my mom, I am a thousand percent positive I'll die. I have to wake Judith so we can get out of here, even if it's without being cured.

She's breathing so fast and sweating, even in her unconsciousness. Lime-green pus crawls like a caterpillar across her eyelids, the stitches like its fuzzy black legs. I put my hand on her forehead to feel if she has a fever, and it's the opposite. She's freezing cold. I shake her and shake her and shake her.

"Wake up," I beg, my throat completely ravaged and scorched. "Wake up wake up wake up."

The door slams open. I see my mother's strong back, her wide neck, and the back of her cap. She's dragging something—someone. The nurse.

"Did you kill her?"

"Nope," she says simply.

"What happened?"

She doesn't answer. She just drags her slowly over to the stool where the surgeon was sitting and slumps her into the corner. In one of the cabinets, she finds a blanket and drapes it over her.

Then with a sigh, she walks back over to the door. She stops, reaches into her pocket, and pulls out a big syringe with a needle on one end. She must have knocked out the nurse with the same thing the surgeon used on me.

"Where did you get that?" I ask.

She drops it into a red bin on the wall that says SHARPS across the front and says, "When you're a housekeeper for as long as I've been, you tend to learn about where things are located and how to access them."

A housekeeper? For Axiom?

"Speaking of which—" She leaves again and returns, dragging something behind her. Not a person this time—her huge housekeeping cart. It's stacked with folded towels and has a trash can and mop on one side. I feel like my legs could give out. I remember.

Friday night, after I was splinted, after Sam's horrible assault.

His screams. His black hole of an eye. His blood, so much blood, everywhere.

As I left with Kent, the housekeeper mopping up the blood, swirls of red becoming pink.

The very edge of her jaw. A sliver of her blue patch. Her strong back. The brown and gray of her bun twisted into a giant peppermint candy.

The man in the white coat yelling at her, saying she wasn't supposed to be in that wing. Why? Because of me? Because they knew who she was and they wanted to keep her away from me and Judith?

"You do work here," I say.

"Yes," she says sternly.

"Have you been here since—"

She pulls her cart as she talks. "Listen, I would love to explain everything, but there's no time. Help me put your sister in here."

"Where?"

She steps aside and gestures to the cart. I'm so confused. This is our escape plan?

"Don't think, just do," she says, and lifts a little curtain on the side to expose a compartment, which I think normally holds extra towels or cleaning supplies or whatever. But now it's empty, so I guess it can hold people too. Maybe she doesn't realize Judith and I are tall and lanky? We won't both fit in there.

"Won't work," I croak.

Mom straightens her back and places a hand on Judith's leg. The juniper of her eye has paled. Dulled. "We have to try."

I know she's right, but all the anxiety and worry in my stomach is starting to feel more like sickness. I nod my head.

"Great. You get her feet. I'll carry her shoulders."

"Wait!" I almost scream it, but I contain myself. I hold up the vial and ask, "Do you know how to use it?"

She rips the blue papery drape off Judith and tosses it to the corner, exposing her entire body to the harsh lights. I don't know why I didn't expect her to be in a gown like I am, but she is. Her stomach is concave, as if someone's taken a giant stamp and flattened her into the table. Her legs are almost as hairy as mine because I don't think she's shaved since before her surgery. Her toenails are long and unclipped.

"I'm sorry, sweetie," she says, wiping a rogue tear that's fallen. "I'm just a maid."

"But you knew how to inject *her*," I say, gesturing to the nurse in the corner.

"I didn't prepare that syringe. Somebody else did for me before I came up here. I was just told to use it if I had to."

I search her eye for something I can't find. "Who prepared it?"

"There's no time, Hen-Hen. I'm sorry. Help me with your sister."

Judith feels like ice. I'm afraid she's freezing to death from the inside out. I ignore the tears behind my eyes and grab her frozen ankles.

When Mom tells me to lift, I do. She maneuvers Judith's body around the table, and soon we're carrying her over to the cart. She's lighter than I imagined, but I think that's because Mom's carrying most of the weight. Maybe that's why she told me to get her legs. I only have to walk a couple of steps in total, so it's not so strenuous that my body gives out. Still, I'm careful.

Somehow—and I have no idea how—we fit her into the little compartment in the cart by bending her knees and folding her like a pretzel or something. It feels so wrong to do, like we're stuffing a dead body into a trunk or something.

"What if she wakes up?" I ask, afraid she'll start making noises or fall out. I have no idea how long it takes for anesthesia to wear off.

"We have to be quick," Mom says, replacing the curtain. There are zippers on either side of it. She closes one but leaves the other so Judith can breathe, I guess, and ties together a strap that's around the whole cart, top to bottom. I don't know if the strap is supposed to be there or if she fashioned it herself before she came to rescue us, but it comes in handy.

"She's already breathing so fast," I say. "What if…"

"In about five minutes, you two will be out of here, and she'll be okay."

"*You two?*" My voice is high. Desperate. "Are you not coming?" Why did I assume she would just come with us? That she wouldn't leave us again? That was stupid.

Her eye widens. "I'm sorry, baby. I've got more work to do."

What does she mean? More fucking rooms to clean?

"It's fine," I lie. I *cannot* lose it in front of her. I just can't. Not only because we're running out of time but because maybe if I don't make a big deal out of it, she'll think I've grown up since the last time she saw me. Even though I've done no such thing.

"I really wish I could," she says, and a dark part of me wants to believe she doesn't care about leaving with us. She just wants to *leave*. She's still a prisoner, technically. After she's done with her housekeeping duties, they must keep her locked in a cell, like Madame Berenice and Kent, but worse. At least Kent has driving and school privileges. I think of Lester and wonder if he's a prisoner too.

Wait. Is there a resistance group here, *inside* the hospital? The prisoners? I wonder if they call themselves the Cyclopes too.

I could dwell, I could sulk, I could throw a fit—all of which I would love to do. But I'm here for a reason.

"Do you know what happened to my friends?" I ask, and I know it's a long shot. How could she know I came here with friends? But she does.

"Your friends? Norah and, uh—what was his name again?"

"There were two others. Patrick and Sam."

"Ah, right. Of course. They're fine." She doesn't sound convinced, which could only mean one thing: they are most definitely not fine. She's just trying to persuade me to move. Whatever it takes.

"Oh." It's all I have the capacity to say.

With a weak smile, she rips off the plastic gown and takes a gray shirt from off her cart, then puts it on over her scrub top. Same with a pair of gray pants that she puts on top of the blue ones. Must be her housekeeping garb.

Then she removes the patch from around her eye, the green one, and pulls a blue one from the cart. I catch a glimpse of her bare face before she puts it on. It's just a flat expanse of skin from her eyebrow to her cheek, with a faint scar where her eye should be. Nothing more, nothing less.

"I'm so sorry, my sweet boy," she says, turning to me. "We'll see each other again."

How many times can I be the reason people leave me?

Chapter Twenty-Six

I'M TREMBLING. WRITHING. I feel like I'm suffocating. Maybe it's my time to go, finally. To leave this hell. How fitting that it'll be inside a trash bin.

But it's only a fantasy. Real life is always so much more complicated.

I can barely breathe, but I actually *can* breathe. All I can think of is Judith. If I'm having difficulty, I can't even imagine how she's doing. She's already so broken. I think part of the reason I'm shaking is because I'm so scared for her. Also myself. Also Mom.

But mostly Judith. God, if she...

I try not to think of it. All I have to do is make it through the next five or so minutes without moving a muscle or making a sound. Which is already hard because my muscles are all contorted and they're *screaming* to be stretched. Only I can't let them.

I thought maybe my mother would dress me in a housekeeper's

uniform and pass me off as her trainee or something. But no, it's the cart for me too. I'm literally inside her trash can right now, my knees tucked into my chest, half-covered by a heap of towels on top of me. She claims to know where all the cameras in the hospital are, so she'll tap her finger on the cart twice when we're about to pass underneath one, and I'll cover myself completely with the towels.

Before we left the operating room, I asked, weren't there cameras in there watching everything? She said the surgeon had turned them off because he doesn't like to be watched. Which was convenient for us, sure, but just another example of the corruption running throughout Axiom. The evil. No one to hold him accountable when he performs a donation so badly the patient winds up with a life-threatening infection.

I hear a sliding glass door open. I think we're in the waiting room. We stop. Mom moves to the door. Silence for several seconds, then the latch of the door unlocking.

She taps the cart twice, so I move the towels on top of my head. Of course—the skybridge with all the eyes along the ceiling.

It's unbearably hot in here already. Soon I'll melt into the cotton fabric of the bin. When she opens the door, I hold my breath because I feel like my breathing has been so loud. I'm worried my heartbeat's audible too, as though the trash bin is an echo chamber or something. I'm squeezing the vial of Golden Tonic like it's the only thing keeping me alive. Maybe it is. The hope for Judith, I mean.

As we roll along, I get the sudden urge to puke. I don't know what it's been about these last few days, but if I make it out of here alive, I've got to figure out my stomach. It could just be the combination of not seeing where I'm going and the heat irritating everything else in my body, but still.

I gag and swallow it down, but that's no guarantee it won't happen again. I've never been motion sick in my life, but maybe it's the feeling of being trapped while in motion.

My mother strolls, taking her time. She goes slowly because she knows I need to keep my balance. She starts to hum. After a while, I recognize it as the song she used to sing to me when I was sick. I wonder if she's humming it on purpose now to ease me, or if she's been doing it all these years out of habit.

I want so badly to move the towels for some breathing room—it feels like it's been *at least* five minutes just going down the skybridge, and I've barely taken three breaths—but I know if the eyes capture an inkling of unusual movement, Watchers would swarm. Tears flood my eyes but I'm not able to let them fall like I want to.

We turn a corner, and Mom clears her throat, which is the signal I can move the towels. I do and take deep breaths. I also wipe all the sweat from my face.

Finally, we stop. I feel her move past me like a breeze almost. The loud click of a button. We must be at the elevator.

A soft noise I don't recognize. A quiet bang and kind of moan? I stop breathing so I can hear it. Mom doesn't seem to notice because she's humming still.

It comes again, but this time it's just a moan. Then a soft, quiet cough.

Judith. She's waking up. Fuck fuck fuck. At least she's not dead, but *fuck.*

What do we do, what do we do? If she starts talking or shouting, we're all dead. If Mom opens the curtain thing, someone could walk by and see, and we're dead then too. But Judith could be seriously sick. God, how much longer till we're outside?

Mom's still humming, and I am absolutely amazed she can't hear her. Or maybe she does and she's ignoring it.

The elevator dings. Mom taps the cart twice, and I cover myself with the towels, fully panicked and shaky. When the door opens, my mother gasps quietly and whispers, "Oh." Someone else must be in the elevator already.

A man clears his throat. His footsteps grow closer. Closer. My heartbeat is *wild*.

"Hello," my mother says in a new, much higher-pitched voice, almost like a babydoll.

We stay dead still. I want to tell her to knock him out so we can get on the elevator and *go*.

The man doesn't say anything. I can only sense where he is by his footsteps.

I know he's getting closer, but I misjudge exactly where because he bumps into my side and gasps as if he doesn't expect the trash to be so solid. Like a bag of bones. I bite my lip so I don't gasp too, but I do it so hard I taste blood.

"So sorry about that," says my mother in a strange accent, with that babydoll voice. I couldn't guess the accent if I tried. "So much trash. You know." Is this how she always talks as a housekeeper, or just for this moment?

"You should really empty that damn thing. Could've scratched me." It's the surgeon. My heart goes so hard, so fast, but I can't compensate by breathing deeply, and I think I'm on the verge of passing out.

"Yes, sir," my mother says.

"Seriously. Isn't the incinerator nearby?"

"Correct, sir. On my way right now."

He scoffs and begins walking away. As my mother pushes the cart into the elevator, Judith makes another noise. Her moaning becomes constant and loud.

"What was that?" the surgeon asks. He sounds like he hasn't quite turned the corner into the skybridge yet.

"Silly me," my mother says as she rolls us into the elevator, with a voice so different from the voice she was using before. She gasps softly, realizing her mistake. She clears her throat and says in the high voice, "Just humming to myself, doctor."

But as she says that, Judith moans some more.

"Excuse me. I don't know what games you're playing, but I will not be mocked in my own hospital. Especially not on my own wing."

His footsteps grow louder as he comes toward us, not quite walking, not quite charging.

I hear my mother clicking buttons—to close the doors faster, I'm hoping.

"Hey!" The surgeon is shouting now. "Wait one minute here. Weren't you in the—"

The doors close, dinging as they meet each other.

My mother lets out the largest sigh, and I join her. I want to be louder, I want to move the towels out of my way, but I know there's a camera in here.

My stomach drops as the elevator descends. I hear my mother move around the cart, toward the back where I am. She whispers, and her voice is low to the ground. She must be bent over pretending to tie her shoe or something. "He's going to call Watchers. When we get out of the elevator, if I see one, I'm making a run for our lives. Okay?"

"Okay," I whisper back. "Judith—"

She grunts and moves over, maybe tying the other shoe now. I can barely hear her muffled whisper, but I think it's something like: "Please stay quiet, Judith Marie. You're okay. Please be quiet. Soon you will be out of here. Please."

I have no way to know if Judith understands or even hears her. But she's not moaning anymore, which might be good. Or it might turn out to be completely devastating.

The elevator dings. Mom stands. Taps twice. Pushes.

We turn a corner, and we're in the main lobby. I recognize it by the crashing sound of the waterfall. It sounds like paradise. Through a gap in the towel, I can see the water spilling out from a space between the top of the wall and the skylight, and not from the actual skylight itself like I thought. I have no idea what time it is, but the sun's out—well, if the skylight's to be believed, it is. We could have spent all day and night in this place for all I know.

"Oh, no," Mom says, sort of to herself, as she keeps rolling.

"What?" I whisper in the darkness, the vomit in my stomach growing again.

"Watcher," she says under a cough. Another set of coughs as she says, "Your friends are by the front gate."

I'm not sure if the Watcher's immediately a problem because how do we know for sure if the surgeon warned anybody about her? They might not even be coming for us. But he almost certainly did, and they almost certainly are.

The problem is that I think there's only one way to go: through the lobby. If there's another, it might look suspicious if she suddenly turned around.

"Hello?" It's a very deep voice. The Watcher's, I'm guessing.

"Excuse me," Mom says in her high accented voice, apparently abandoning her run-like-hell plan. I might be less nervous if we were charging at full speed.

"Miss, please come with me."

"I'm sorry, I have to get to a patient room. They requested a priority clean, top to bottom."

She pushes the cart a few more feet, but it stops with a jerk. I shift onto my side, my entire body smashing into the fabric of the bin, my neck now bent ninety degrees. After it's too late, after I've already fallen, I let my shoulders and ribcage remain stretched into the fabric. I don't sit back up because it would be even more suspicious to the Watcher if garbage moved on its own.

A long, excruciating pause. All I can hear is my heart. All I can smell are the bleached towels.

The vomit rises as painfully slow as attempting to cut through my flesh with that dull box cutter. I try to take a few deep breaths as completely still as I can, but having my neck bent this way makes that really fucking hard.

I also realize I don't even have the awareness to guess how my body's contorted right now. I've gone completely numb *everywhere*. My spine could be twisted. My legs could be tied in a knot. The only way I know I'm not upside-down is because the stupid towels are still on top of my head, though they've shifted a bit in the push-and-pull of the cart.

"I really do have to be going," Mom says, and I lurch forward and almost immediately stop again.

"I can't allow that."

"Excuse me! Why not?"

The puke's almost at the back of my throat. I don't know if I can keep it down much longer. Actually, I know it would give me away, but nothing would feel better than blowing chunks everywhere right now, getting it out of my system.

"There she is! That lying woman!" It's Madame Berenice, who's screeching from what sounds like a mile away—across all the gardens of the lobby. A voice so normally measured is now raging. Her heels click and clomp as she runs toward us.

I'm crying now. I'm about to puke, and my body is full-on quaking. And this is when I come to the realization that I actually *am* going to die. Either by choking on my vomit or at the hands of a French nurse, I'm going to die. Who's to say which would be less pleasant?

"I don't know what she's talking about," Mom says frantically. She laughs, and *bam!* My body whips to the other side, then backward, the towels falling into new spaces around me. I hear a *thwack* that I'm pretty sure is Judith's head smashing into the shelf.

I get another whiff of bleach and immediately taste the bitter puke. Oh god, here it comes. I have no control anymore. My back straightens out on its own, my knees part, and I retch all over myself, making the worst noises of my life.

It lands in my lap and slides down my legs. Some goes down the hospital gown, uncomfortably warm against my chest. It smells like death and tastes even worse. The farther and faster my mother runs with the cart, the more my body rocks and the harder I spew. It's like it's releasing every demon inside my body.

People are shouting and screaming outside, but it's my own little vortex in here, and I have no idea what they're saying. I grab a towel and puke into it, then we turn a corner, so I shift to the side. All the towel's contents slosh back into my face, and that makes me puke again.

It's the last time, at least for now. I'm left shaking, bathed in my own vomit. The stench is unreal.

I think the cart is still barreling forward, but I almost can't tell. And I kind of don't care. I'm so done. Let them catch me. Let them pull me out of this hell, gouge out my eye if they still want it, and just fucking kill me afterward.

I'm pretty sure Judith is dead anyway, so what's the point? I couldn't stop them from taking her eye last week, then I couldn't just let her live in peace. I made her watch what I did to Dad. None of this would have happened if it hadn't been for me. I'm the reason for all of this. Everything.

Something bangs hard into my shoulder. It hurts, but it makes me smile. Then my head crashes into something, and it's like a huge wave of relief as I feel what I hope is my life draining from me.

I smell it first: a sweetness among all the putrid odor.

Then I see it: light flooding all around me. Heaven?

No: the towels shoot out above me like lava. How is that possible? Am I exploding?

The cart has toppled over. I don't realize it, can't recognize my freedom, until I hear a groan. It goes on and on.

I roll onto my stomach and crawl out of the bin. I don't look at what's around, but I think there's a tree in front of me—one of the stupid fucking palm trees in the lobby. It grounds me. The scent of flowers hits my nose again. In my periphery, I see the vial. It must have slipped out of my hands. I start to stand up, but my bare feet are wet with vomit. I grab hold of the cart for support and rub my feet on a towel nearby. My whole body is screaming in pain, but I can't think about it now.

I see the curtain that's holding Judith inside, the cart having luckily flipped the right way so it's facing the sky and not the floor. I go to rip it open, but the strap is holding it in place. I squeeze my fingers around the wide band of leather and pull as hard as I can, but it won't break. I pull harder and harder, but it's worthless. I don't see a buckle, and I can't even slide the strap to the side because it's too taut.

"On top!" someone shouts. I look up. So far away, there's my mom, her eye as wide as the patch on the other side of it. Her mouth twisted in pain. A Watcher has her in a vice grip, a huge, deadly bear hug from behind. He's practically twice her size. It's the same Watcher from the entrance, by the reception desk. He must have been the closest one available when the surgeon called for backup.

"There you are, you ungrateful—" From the corner of my eye, Madame Berenice appears. She must have been going toward the elevators once she knew the Watcher had my mom. She's far enough away that I have time to take action if I just stop thinking.

I look back to the cart, to the top of it, and spot the clasp holding the strap in place. I reach for it, grunting through the ripping pain in my ribs and shoulder and feet, and undo it. The strap loosens, and I tear the curtain away so hard it rips and soars out of my hand.

"Jude."

She's curled into herself like an armadillo, the knots of her spine digging through the hospital gown.

It takes several moments for her to look up. Her mouth is slack open. Her eye looks even worse than it did. Still black and purple, now it's ballooned to twice the size it was, and it's weeping with pus and some sort of clear fluid, as if tears.

I reach down and pull her out by the armpits, being so careful not to slip, not to drop her.

I let her rest against me while I look around for Mom. The Watcher is dragging her away, and I don't know what to do. Don't know how to help her.

"Henry!" I turn to the voice. At the gate, Norah's waving her arms. Patrick's beside her, looking the saddest I've ever seen him. Where's Sam? The receptionist watches me with a straight-backed, evil stoicism.

I try to push Judith onto her feet to see if she can stand on her own, but her knees give out. I try again, but nothing. Which means I'll have to carry her. One arm under her armpits, I bend down and put the other one behind her knees. I try to sweep her into my arms this way like I think I've seen people in movies do. But I'm so weak and she's so limp that I almost fall.

I'll have to drag her instead.

"Henry Youngwell, do not move an inch!" Madame Berenice's voice cuts through me, and I shiver at the sound of it. She breaks into a sprint, and I freeze. I freeze. I panic.

When she staggers, I snap out of it. Her heel must have bent, or her ankle, and she almost falls. She bends down to take the shoe off, undoing a complicated strap. Hopefully, it hurts.

"I'm so sorry," I say to Judith.

I lower her so her back is against my knee, and before I start pulling her by the wrists, I reach down with one hand and grab the vial. I bite the neck of it and carry it in my teeth as I pull Judith backward with me. My feet throb with every step. Judith's sweaty, grimy heels squeak like sneakers on a basketball court as they drag across the tile.

"You ingrate!"

I look up, and Madame Berenice is limping toward us, now barefoot, her mouth screwed up into her nose and unrecognizable. She's limping way faster than she should be. Her pain tolerance must be higher than mine.

The Watcher and Mom are even further back—over by the waterfall—about to turn the corner to the elevators, the way we came. Mom looks defeated in his grasp.

This is what Mom would want. Me rescuing Judith. I can't save her, but I can save her daughter. So I do. I go faster. Faster.

But so does Madame Berenice. Then she opens her jaw and shouts louder than I thought was possible. "You at reception, call for reinforcements!"

"Yes, Madame!"

More Watchers? Just when I had the littlest bit of hope.

Tears blur my sight. The stench of vomit is back in my nose.

"Jude, I'm so, so sorry for everything. Please forgive me."

"Let us in! Let us in!" Norah. She's screaming.

"Norah, no!" I scream back, my head turned to the side, though I can only halfway see from behind. If she and Patrick come in, the nurse is going to get them too.

But they don't seem to care. For some reason, the receptionist bends over to scan their eye, and the gate opens. Footsteps stampede toward me.

It sounds like more than just Norah and Patrick. Watchers?

Other shapes too. I glance above me, and it looks like storm clouds outside the skylight. Storm clouds so dark and so perfectly shaped, they're almost like people. Then there's rain. Actual rain coming through the glass! Or is the glass itself rain? Wasn't it sunny just a few minutes ago?

But I have no time to admire. Madame Berenice is gaining in on us. As she runs, she smoothly pulls a syringe and needle out of her pocket and lifts it high in the air, her mouth wide with a scream so ear-splitting I stop in my tracks.

Judith's wrists fall out of my grip, my hands drenched in sweat and tears and vomit.

I yell for her, and as I reach down to try to grab her again, I watch her rise as though she's floating in the air, ascending into heaven.

But it's Patrick. He sweeps her up into his arms in the same way I couldn't. He grabs the bottle of tonic from my mouth and runs back toward the front.

Norah clutches my hand and pulls. My arm feels like it's ripping straight off my shoulder as my body twists and turns around. I start to run despite it all, toward the gate. Toward sweet escape. Norah doesn't let go through all my screams of pain, her emerald strands ricocheting wild and free through the air.

Every cell inside of me is on fire.

I manage to look back as I continue on. My mother has gotten free of the Watcher and sprints toward us. The Watcher chases her with his baton raised. Madame Berenice grunts as she limps, so close I can see the plastic eyes in her braid bounce as she does. Her needle glints in the sun shining through the skylight. Wait, sun again? I thought it was raining.

My mother, only feet from her now, leaps. She grabs hold of Madame Berenice's braid and yanks her back. As they fall, the needle disappears. They both scream as they struggle and fight. The Watcher does a sort of slide and leans down over them, then something shoves him out of the way. Something, or someone?

I look around, and there are so many more bodies. Not Watchers. Not hospital staff. They're dressed in camouflage.

But I don't care, I have to go help my mom. That's all I know. Now that Judith is taken care of, I can rescue her.

I pull my splinted hand out of Norah's grasp, but I can't get free of the other.

"Let me go!" I roar, my voice barely even real anymore.

"No!" she yells. "Henry, stop!"

As more bodies surround me, I hear the crunch of glass underfoot. It's everywhere, I realize. I look up to see the skylight shattered, and the sun really is shining so bright above. What is happening? Who is here, the military?

I glance at Norah, her eyes wide with fear. Did she do this? Her father? I don't care. I go limp and try to fall so she'll let go of me, but she tightens her grip and grabs me by my bad shoulder, pulling me farther and farther against my will. I scream. I scream for the pain in my body. I scream for my mother. For Judith. For Sam. For everything.

Norah pulls me through the open gate, and the receptionist gets into my face and demands my attention.

"You have to go *now*," they say. I can see the gold canine through their parted lips. "I'm sorry, but it's what your mother would want."

"How would you know?" I shriek.

"You have to trust me."

"You're insane. Why would I—"

Because they're a Cyclopes too. They were the one who called the operating room to get the surgeon out of there.

The receptionist. My mother. Lester. All working from the inside. How many others are there?

Norah pulls me to my feet, and when I deliberately try to fall again, she catches me.

"Henry, get a grip. Please. They rescued me and Patrick from another Watcher. I'll explain later. We have to leave."

"Then fucking leave!"

"Not without you, asshole!" She sounds angry. Livid. I don't blame her.

A knock on the glass behind us makes me jump, but I don't look. I feel Norah turn.

"Judith needs you," she says after a second.

"What?" I turn my head and find Patrick outside in the sunlight, still holding her. She's ghost white. Her chest might be moving, or it might not be. I have no idea.

"Hurry!" he shouts, the word muffled through the glass.

Somebody else grabs her. A soldier. She's a sheet of white paper limp in his arms.

Wait, it's not just any soldier. It's Norah's dad. My head goes weak for a split second and falls forward, then it bounces back up, and I watch him turn and run across the sidewalk with Judith in his arms to a van with a big cross on the side. Patrick chases after them, waving the vial of tonic frantically in his arms.

"Henry, let's *go!*"

When I don't answer or move, Norah sighs. She's done, like she's one split second away from giving up on me. Maybe she should.

My mother's shrill scream rings in my ears. I turn back and see the syringe poking out of her chest, the needle plunged deep inside.

Something inside me clicks off. If only I could plunge it into my chest instead, or use the needle to saw off my leg.

"I'll take care of her," the receptionist says. "Don't worry. Please. The Cyclopes need you. Just go."

Norah lets go of me, and I fall to the ground, this time not meaning to. She kneels beside me, her hands on my stomach.

"Where's Sam?" I ask.

Her eyes flutter away. After a moment of searching, they find their way back to me. "I don't know," she squeaks, her jaw quivering. "They still have him, somewhere, I think. But the soldiers will find him, I promise."

The first thing that crosses my mind is I never got to read my poem to him. But nothing like that even matters anymore. I'll never write again.

Norah clears her throat and says, stronger now, "I told my dad, Henry. They weren't planning on moving in so quickly, but with you here, they had to. They'll get Sam. They'll get your dad. But for now, you're here and you need to come with us. They'll check you out, make sure you're okay. Come on, we're all here. Judith will be fine. We'll all be fine. *Please.*"

Not all of us. The enormous, visceral absence of my mother. The weight of what she did for me, only to let me fly.

How badly I want to reach for my thigh, just to squeeze. Just to replace the hurt inside me for only a second. But then I think of Judith's stitches. How she never cleaned her wound, and on purpose. How she got sick and didn't care. I need to make sure she'll *really* be okay before I can think about hurting myself again.

And if she's not okay? Then I can do whatever the hell I want.

"Henry, are you in?" Norah holds her breath like it's the end of the world.

I look to the receptionist, their amber eyes flecked with gold. I look up to the skylight, the shards of glass jagged around the edges. I look around to the dozens of soldiers storming this way and that, a flurry of bodies. Then, finally, I look back to Norah, strands of emerald glued to her sweaty face.

Maybe this is it. Maybe this is how I keep going—to just *go*.

"Yeah," I say. "Okay."

Acknowledgements

Thank you to my agent, Stephanie Hansen, whose patience with me and commitment to this book was way more than I deserve. Also a debt of gratitude to those at Metamorphosis Literary Agency who gave invaluable feedback during the (many) rewrite phases. This book would be dead in the water without you.

My editor, Elizabeth Coldwell, who seemingly effortlessly shaped this beast into what it is, and all at NineStar who took a chance on this haywire band of Cyclopes: thank you. This has been my #1 dream since I can remember. I couldn't imagine a better place for Henry than in your hands.

I owe so much to a very early champion and reader, and very dear friend, Ty Gardner, whose insight into the bones of this world helped me build the solid foundation to land an agent. More importantly, you helped me gain some faith in myself when it was all but lost. You da real deal.

To the person who first showed me that writing was a real thing that people could do—and that it matters. Kensey, if by some grace you read this paragraph, I will always be here when you decide to return. Please do.

The people I'm lucky enough to call my family—especially my parents, who have supported me in every way possible, always believed in me (especially when I didn't), and pulled me back into the light when I was close to death: where would I be without you? And to my eleven nieces and nephews, who each bring me more joy and perspective than I've ever had before: it is an absolute privilege to be in your lives.

Special note to my two goddaughters—I know you had no choice in who got to be your godfather but thank you for having me anyway. It's the honor of my life, and I love you both more than I ever thought possible. Thank you for always making me laugh and thank you for being the light in this sometimes dark world.

And finally, to my Goose, my first reader, and Benny, my even firster and better reader: no words are enough. I don't think any of this would exist without you, which is not hyperbole. (That's not lip service!) Thank you for letting me live out every dream I've ever had. You're everywhere to me, by Michelle Branch, our personal bff. I love you boys.

About the Author

Jeffrey Haskey-Valerius rarely knows what's happening. He works in healthcare by day and writes weird fiction and poetry by night. His shorter work has been featured in numerous literary journals and has been nominated for prizes, including Best of the Net. He currently lives in the Midwest with his unbelievably handsome and perfect dog, and also a human whom he loves. The Cyclopes' Eye is his debut novel.

Email

jeffreyhaskeyvalerius@gmail.com

Facebook

www.facebook.com/jeffreyhvwrites

Instagram

www.instagram.com/jeffreyhvwrites

Twitter

@jeffreyhvwrites

Website

www.jeffreyhaskey-valerius.com

www.ninestarpress.com

www.facebook.com/ninestarpress

www.facebook.com/groups/NineStarNiche

www.twitter.com/ninestarpress

www.instagram.com/ninestarpress

www.threads.net/@ninestarpress

www.ingramcontent.com/pod-product-compliance
Lightning Source LLC
Chambersburg PA
CBHW060617100726

47907CB00006B/1661